# Wicked Games

USA TODAY BESTSELLING AUTHOR

# T.K. LEIGH

WICKED GAMES

Published by Carpe Per Diem

Edited by: Kim Young, Kim's Editing Services

Cover Image Elements:

Vasyl © 2019

Used under license from Adobe

# Books by T.K. Leigh

## CONTEMPORARY ROMANCE

### *The Dating Games Series*
Dating Games
Wicked Games
Dangerous Games
Royal Games
Tangled Games

### *The Book Boyfriend Chronicles*
The Other Side of Someday
Writing Mr. Right

### *The Redemption Duet*
Commitment
Redemption

**ROMANTIC SUSPENSE**

*The Temptation Series*
Temptation
Persuasion
Provocation
Obsession

*The Broken Crown Trilogy*
Royal Creed
Fallen Knight
Broken Crown

*The Inferno Saga*
Part One: Spark
Part Two: Smoke
Part Three: Flame
Part Four: Burn

*The Possession Duet*
Possession
Atonement

*The Beautiful Mess Series*
A Beautiful Mess
A Tragic Wreck
Gorgeous Chaos

For more information on any of these titles and upcoming releases, please visit T.K.'s website:
www.tkleighauthor.com

# One

I've often wondered what hell would be like.

Not really out of fear. More like curiosity.

Is it full of fire and brimstone, as I heard them speak of the handful of times my parents dragged me to church as a child?

Or maybe everyone's hell is personal. Maybe Hitler's hell is filled with all the people he thought were inferior to him. Jack the Ripper is probably surrounded by prostitutes who emasculate him, cutting *his* throat and abdomen. And Ted Bundy is most likely alone, not a single person there to impress or feel self-important around.

Just like my hell would be a nightclub fifty stories above the Vegas strip, drunk people grinding up against each other. And the sentence Lucifer would give me when I arrive at the fiery gates? To serve eternal damnation at a bachelorette party that never ends.

Yup. I have arrived at my own personal hell.

"Blowjobs! That's what we need right now!"

I close my eyes, summoning the strength to feign excitement over the idea of drinking a disgustingly sweet mixture of Bailey's, Kahlúa, and half-and-half, all topped with whipped cream. If my cousin, Hannah, and I weren't like sisters when we were kids, I wouldn't be wearing a a necklace of penises and a tight black tank top, "Bride's Bitch" bedazzled on the front, enduring this bachelorette party that's filled with one cliché after another.

I sure hope this city's marketing slogan is correct. This entire experience needs to stay in Vegas.

"Yes!" Hannah slurs, agreeing with Bernadette, her older sister and maid of honor, who planned this excursion to the tenth circle of hell. She struggles to get up from the couch where she's sitting, tripping over several pairs of legs as she attempts to flag down our cocktail waitress. "Blow jobs all around!"

Whistles and cheers erupt as two guys with far too much hair product jump at the opportunity to join us. "I'll buy you those if you return the favor with the real thing," the tall, slender blond says, his suggestive gaze scanning our group in a way that reminds me of someone selecting produce at a farmer's market, looking for the ripest tomato, the juiciest peach.

I glance to my left, giving Izzy a knowing look. Hannah, Izzy, and I were inseparable growing up. For the longest time, I couldn't imagine my life without them at my side. We went through all of life's big changes together. Puberty. First boyfriends. First kisses. Then my parents divorced and my mom took me from Connecticut to New Jersey, where she unsuccessfully attempted to piece her life back together.

"I'm not sure you could handle the real thing," a petite brunette named Carmen says, suggestively licking her lips.

Desperate for a break from what's become a sex-charged day in the city of sin, I extract myself from our group.

"Bathroom?" Izzy asks. "Or did you change your mind on the scavenger hunt and decide to..." She picks up a printed piece of card stock and reads, "build a penis with objects found at the bar?" She rolls her eyes at the absurdity of it all.

"Tempting…" I give her a tight smile, "but I think I'll pass. I'm going to the bar to get a drink."

"But they ordered blow job shots," she retorts sarcastically, taking a sip of her vodka tonic.

"I refuse to do any shot made in such a way to make it appear I have cum on my face when I drink it."

Izzy coughs, liquid spraying out of her nose and mouth.

"Who the hell invented that shot? Probably someone who didn't give or receive blowjobs that often. If you do it right, you won't end up with cum on your face. Unless that's what you want. If that's the case, more power to you. To each their own."

She coughs a few more times, then clears her throat. "God, I've missed you, Chloe."

"Missed you, too. Want anything?"

She holds up her glass. "I'm good."

"Okay. I'm off to brave the elements." I spin on my heels.

"Good luck," she calls out.

At least now that night has fallen and we're in a darkened space, the stereotypical tank top that's been my bachelorette party uniform isn't as noticeable. Bernadette thought each of us wearing a shirt with "Bride's Bitch" on it was hysterical, and hers saying "Bitch of Honor" even more so. I bit my tongue so hard it almost bled in order to prevent myself from telling her how juvenile I think this entire weekend truly is. That it's not the kind of bachelorette party Hannah envisioned. She's too nice to say anything. She's always been that way.

Strobe lights pulse as I maneuver my way through crowds of people congregated around small tables and lush leather couches. The smell of perfume, combined with beer and fruity alcohol mixtures, fills the air. Scantily dressed wait-resses pass by carrying trays overflowing with drinks while the vibration of the driving club music seems to make the floor shake.

Despite the temperatures being on the chilly side, consid-ering night's fallen, the sheer number of people present increases the heat level, causing perspiration to form on my brow. All walks of life are represented here, everyone pretending to be someone they're not for one weekend of sin.

I don't need a weekend of sin. I sin on a regular basis.

I squeeze my way up to the bar and catch the bartender's attention immediately, my gray and lilac-colored ombre hair standing out in a sea of blondes and brunettes.

"What can I get you?"

"Martini. Dirty."

"You got it." He turns and grabs the vodka bottle, pouring a heaping amount into the cocktail shaker. "Having a good time?"

"Absolutely." I grit out a smile.

"Liar," he responds with a wink.

"That obvious?"

"Maybe I'm just observant. You don't seem to fit in with your friends over there." He nods toward the bachelorette party.

I look at him incredulously, wondering how he'd notice me when pouring drinks all night. Then I glance back at the girls, raising my five-foot, two-inch frame onto my tiptoes to peer over the ocean of people, grimacing when I see Bernadette's shoved a brightly colored shooter between her boobs and one of our new "friends" is taking the shot from her without the use of his hands. We're definitely hard to miss. Bernadette made sure of that.

"What makes you say that?" I muse when I return my attention to him.

"You don't exactly scream 'desperate housewife'." He grabs a long metal spoon and stirs my martini. If nothing else, he understands a great martini should be stirred, not shaken, as Mr. Bond would have you believe.

"At least I'm doing something right."

"You certainly are." He pours the liquid through the strainer and into a chilled glass, then pushes it toward me. "Enjoy."

With a smile, I place a bill on the counter and turn from him. If I were anywhere else, I might have given him my number with instructions to call when his shift was over. I'd rather not leave any piece of myself in this town.

As I emerge from the mosh of people, I look in the direction of the girls, only to find most of them grinding with complete strangers. Except for Hannah and Izzy. They're off to the side, distancing themselves from the debauchery currently underway amongst the rest of the women. All I can do is pray this kind of behavior doesn't rub off on Hannah. Then again, she's twenty-eight. She had her fun during her younger years, unlike her sister, Bernadette, who got married when she was twenty — a shotgun wedding because she was pregnant.

"How much?" I hear a voice say as I start toward them. It's so random and out of context I don't react at first. Then a hand grips my bicep, preventing me from taking another step.

I whirl around, my fierce eyes settling on a man of average height and build. His black shirt is tucked into a pair of dark jeans, a gray blazer finishing the ensemble. "Excuse me?"

"I said…" He loosens his grasp on my arm, licking his

lips as he leers at me, wavering slightly. I can smell the alcohol on his breath. Great. Another guy emboldened with the help of Jim Beam, Jack Daniels, or Jose Cuervo. Possibly a combination of all three. "How much?"

"For what?"

He chuckles in feigned amusement. Then his expression falls, his eyes heating as they rake over me.

"I get it. You're discreet. I can be discreet, too." Winking, he reaches into his pocket and retrieves his wallet, flashing what I estimate to be several thousand in hundreds. He either got lucky shooting craps or hit up a few ATMs earlier. I'm guessing the latter. "Like I said, how much?"

I shake my head, backing away from him. "I am *not* a prostitute." My tone is firm, leaving no room for argument.

He blows out a laugh. "Sure. You're not a prostitute, just like I'm the fucking Easter Bunny. I can pretend to be someone I'm not, too, sweetheart. Trust me. I have an eye for these things, and any woman who comes into a club wearing a ridiculously tight tank top, a skirt that rides up her ass, and has hair colored like yours just screams whore."

Fire flames on my face and I ball my free hand into a fist. Before I can reel back and land a blow, he grips my hip, yanking my body against his, causing my martini to splash between us.

"We can do this the easy way or the hard way, but every second you play hard to get, the amount I pay you will decrease. If I were you, I'd give careful consideration to the next words that come out of your mouth. Ya got me?"

My jaw clenches as my distaste for him grows with each heartbeat. "Like I said..." I place a hand on his chest, glowering, "I am *not* a prostitute. So I'd suggest taking your disgusting paws off me before I kick my apparent hooker heel into your balls and press so hard they'll hear them pop all the way in Los Angeles. Ya got me?" I finish, throwing his words back at him.

His composure cracks momentarily, but he's either too drunk or too dumb to get the hint. "You're a feisty one, aren't you? I dig it." He loops his arm around my waist, pulling me even harder against him. "Come on. Tell me your price."

My heart rate spikes and bile rises in my throat when his erection pushes against my stomach. What the hell is it about men these days who think they can treat women like property? Who think it's their God-given right to exert dominance over the opposite sex?

"Like I told you. I'm not—"

"Oh, there you are!" a deep voice bellows, cutting through.

I whip my eyes in its direction, disoriented when an arm wraps around me, prying me out of the creep's grasp. I'm startled at first, taken aback by the strong embrace currently holding me. But unlike before, I don't feel the overwhelming sense of dread and disgust.

"I can't leave you alone for a second, can I?"

When he pulls back, I meet brilliant green eyes that seem to penetrate deeper than they should, considering they belong to a stranger. Then again, there's something oddly familiar about him, making me think I should know him. But I'd remember someone like him. Wouldn't I?

He towers over me, making me estimate he's six-three or six-four, since I only come up to his pecs. He has a proud face, chiseled cheekbones, square jaw, masculine nose. His dark hair is a little messy, but in a sexy kind of way. Although he sports a beard and mustache, it's impeccably groomed. In fact, everything about him is impeccably groomed.

Granted, we're at a club in Vegas with a rather strict

dress code, at least for men. But something about the way he carries himself with a cool confidence makes him stand out amongst a sea of men just looking for a quick piece of ass. The dark jeans and tweed jacket make me think he'd be more comfortable at a cigar bar, sipping scotch, jazz standards playing in the background.

"Can I?" he repeats, giving me a knowing look, encouraging me to play along. So that's what I do.

"I guess not." I face the creep, a smug smile on my face as I burrow deeper into my mystery man's embrace. "Like I said. This…" I gesture down my body, "isn't for sale. Even if it were, you would never be able to afford it, baby. Not with that wallet you flashed me."

He opens his mouth to argue, but all my mystery man has to do is puff out his chest and he snaps his jaw shut, turning from me.

"And for future reference," my mystery man calls out, keeping his arm wrapped around me, despite the threat waning.

The creep looks back at him.

"When a lady says she's not interested, it's not an invitation to press the issue. If I find you've caused any more problems or offer any other woman money to sleep with you, there are two rather large gentlemen manning the front door who will have no problem helping you learn this lesson differently." He smiles a fake smile. "Ya got me?"

"Yeah. Sure. Whatever." He shuffles away.

"What a tool," my mystery man remarks as he drops his hold, turning to face me, his eyes filled with concern. "Are you all right? He didn't hurt you, did he?"

"I'm fine," I snap. "I can handle myself. But thank you for intervening on my behalf. It wasn't necessary."

I begin to retreat from him. If I didn't hate Vegas before,

I do now. With it being the stereotypical destination for a hormonally charged bachelor or bachelorette party, it's open season to hit on anything with a pulse. I wish people had to take a test before entering the proverbial Vegas wildlife, like hunters have to in order to obtain their license to hunt prey. That's what this place is like. A jungle. During mating season.

"Got a name?" he calls out before I can take more than a few steps.

"Yup," I shout over my shoulder with a smirk. "Thanks for checking."

"You're not going to tell me?" he yells when I continue to squeeze my way through the hordes of people. "What am I supposed to call you? Dick Girl?"

His words seem to carry over the beat of the music and I stop in my tracks, sensing curious eyes watching our interaction. I spin around, stalking toward him.

"Dick Girl? Why? Because I'm wearing a short skirt and my hair's a little different so I must really enjoy dick? I'm pretty sure there are lesbians out there who wear short skirts and color their hair differently, too. That doesn't mean they like the dick, does it? Or is it just because we're in Vegas?"

He's about to respond, but I cut him off before he has a chance to utter a single syllable. My presence in my least favorite city for a ritual I find cliché, trivial, and ordinary, all things I try to avoid being, causes the thin filter between my brain and mouth to evaporate.

"I get it. Some guy who probably considers himself a marketing genius concocted a brilliant ad campaign all those years ago when he came up with this city's tagline. Can you imagine being in the room when the creative team discussed that gem as an option? It's almost like their mission was to come up with the slogan most likely to result in surprise pregnancies, STDs, and infidelity, all of which do *not* stay in Vegas."

He tries to speak again, but I hold up my finger, silencing him.

"So, as tempting as the idea of living out my wildest fantasies is...and truthfully, you're not so bad to look at, and I do have quite an active imagination...I do not hook up with random strangers, not in this town anyway. But fear not." I give him a trite smile. "This city is full of bachelorette party attendees who would love to have a piece of you. Hell, you could probably even score a threesome or foursome. Maybe even a fivesome, like a sorority porno gone incredibly wrong. A simple online search will lead you to any number of sex clubs within a short Uber ride from here. But that shit won't be happening with me." I gesture to my crotch area. "This pussy is on a much-deserved break."

I remain in place as my words seem to ring out between us. I expect him to be stunned and unsure how to respond, maybe offer an apology for his assumption about me. Instead, he reaches out. I attempt to step back, but before I can, he toys with the chain dangling from my neck.

Smirking, he says, "I was referring to your necklace. Dick. Girl."

A tingle sweeps across my cheeks as my shoulders drop. Thankfully, it's too dark for him or anyone else to see my complexion turn red. "Oh."

"Yeah. Oh." He chuckles as his full lips curve in the corners. He flashes his white teeth, his smile exuding a confidence I'm not used to seeing. Something about it intrigues me. It's such a simple thing. The flexing of muscles to turn up your lips, demonstrating happiness, amusement, or any other number of positive emotions. But with that one smile, I feel something I've avoided for years now...

Vulnerability.

"Have a nice night... Dick Girl."

He turns from me, the crowd seeming to part to allow him passage. Then he stops, facing me once more.

"And, for the record, I didn't ask your name as a preface to sleep with you. I did so because my mother taught me manners, to treat everyone with respect." He keeps his dark eyes locked with mine, allowing his statement to sink in. "Stay safe tonight. It's a jungle out there." He treats me to one last smile, then disappears into the crowd, leaving me bewildered.

Has being single in New York so long jaded me to the point that I assume every straight man only approaches me because they want to get into my pants?

At one point, I dreamed of having the love story I read about in fairy tales...until I realized all fairy tales eventually end. Soon, the Prince will question Snow White's devotion to him whenever she runs off to the forest to spend time with the dwarfs. Prince Phillip will accuse Aurora of always just lying there, practically asleep, during sex. And poor Aladdin and Jasmine... He'll never stop feeling emasculated every time they have an argument and she so kindly reminds him that if it weren't for her, he'd still be a street rat.

If that's a fairy tale, I want nothing to do with it.

# Two

The spicy, robust flavor of red wine dances on my tongue as I relax into my barstool, savoring these last few moments to myself before embarking on another night of bachelorette party fun. About to flag down the bartender for the check, I stop when my phone pings with an incoming text.

NORA:

On a scale of one to murder, how's the bachelorette party?

I laugh at how well Nora knows me. After all, she was my college roommate. Even though I ended up leaving before the end of my second year, we've managed to remain friends.

ME:

Let's put it this way... Most would consider Ted Bundy a compassionate serial killer compared to my brutality. However, any murder I commit would probably be excused as justifiable. Or, at least, I could plead not guilty by reason of insanity. I believe the courts recognize the bachelorette party defense in homicide cases.

Her response comes almost instantly.

NORA:

I'm not so sure that's a thing.

ME:

It should be. And in case I haven't told you, I'm so glad you don't want any of this stuff for your wedding. It makes my job as your maid of honor much easier and won't require me to resort to murder.

NORA:

Blech. The last thing I want is to make my friends suffer through a night of penis jokes and scavenger hunts that border on sexual harassment. Try to have a little fun while you're there, although I know how much you despise Vegas. New York misses you. See you in a few days.

I sigh as I lean back in my chair, typing out one last text.

ME:

And I sure miss New York. See you soon.

I close out of our message and open my email, scanning my inbox. As a celebrity news columnist for one of the top women's magazines, I'm required to keep a constant pulse on what's going on in the world of the rich and famous. But this weekend has been quiet. No big breakups. No pregnant celebrities giving birth. No arrogant has-been who thinks he's above the law getting arrested for drinking and driving.

"For you, miss."

I snap my head up just as the bartender places a martini in front of me. "I didn't order this." I start to push it across the bar, but he smiles, leaving a cocktail napkin beside the glass. Scribbling in blue ink catches my attention, the pen stroke masculine, but still legible.

*Thought I'd make up for the martini you didn't get to enjoy last night.*

There's only one person who could have sent this. On a sharp inhale, I scan the lounge. It's on the darker side, the lighting dim, votive candles placed sporadically on the bar and each table to add to the romantic ambience, despite being mere feet from a roulette wheel.

As I search for familiar green eyes, I sense a warmth approach from behind. The hairs on my nape stand on end, and I freeze.

"I wasn't sure what kind of vodka you preferred, so I had to guess based on what little I know about you. But something makes me think you're a Belvedere girl. Smooth. Layered. Sophisticated."

I take a moment to compose myself before facing him. The instant my gaze floats to his, an involuntary shiver rolls through me. "A rather astute assessment. I prefer Polish vodkas."

"Smart woman."

His eyes dance as he gestures to the free chair beside me, silently asking permission to sit. I nod, then turn forward once more, smoothing the lines of my gray silk tank, adjusting my navy blue blazer. I'll most likely get shit from Bernadette for not wearing my "Bride's Bitch" shirt tonight, but I need to draw the line somewhere. One night was fine. There's no way I'm going to wear that sweat-stained, smoke-infested thing again.

As he assumes the chair beside me, his scent filters through my nose, addictive and mouthwatering. It's a woodsy and manly scent, reminiscent of rain on a hot summer day. He flags down the bartender and orders a few fingers of a top-shelf scotch. My assessment of him last night wasn't that far off after all. He would have fit in better at a quiet bar sipping scotch instead of a dance club where everyone was just one tequila shot away from alcohol poisoning.

Truth be told, it wasn't my scene, either. I'm not sure *what* my scene is.

Once he takes a sip and exhales in satisfaction, he returns his gaze to me. I tap my nails against the counter, the silence painfully loud. I've never felt so on edge in the presence of a man, so out of sorts. But I felt it last night. And I feel it now.

This man is different.

Despite him being a stranger.

Despite him barely uttering more than a few sentences to me.

Despite my not knowing anything about him.

When the heat of his stare becomes too much, the connection too palpable, I turn my eyes from his, taking a sip of my martini, the combination of dry vermouth, vodka, and just a hint of olive juice perfect.

"How did you know I liked my martini dirty?" I ask in a smooth voice, trying to calm the butterflies swimming in my stomach by bringing the glass back to my mouth.

He licks his lips, leaning toward me. "I had a feeling you liked things…dirty."

I choke on my drink, coughing as I struggle to breathe. He hands me a napkin and I cover my mouth. If anyone else used that line on me, I'd roll my eyes and send them on their way. But this guy isn't saying it to get into my pants. At least, I don't think he is. It's all part of his personality — cool, confident, yet lighthearted.

"Wouldn't you like to find out?" I quip once I clear my throat.

"You have no idea." His voice is guttural and wanton as he inches closer. I zero in on his lips, drawn to them like a moth to a flame.

Then he pulls back, bringing his drink to his mouth, acting as if his statement didn't leave me squirming. When he speaks again, he sounds different, his tone lighter and more conversational, a complete one-eighty.

"More bachelorette festivities planned for the evening? Or is that all over?"

I draw in a deep breath to compose myself. "Don't I wish. I stopped by here to ensure I'm in the right…frame of mind for what awaits me."

"And what is it that awaits you?"

"I'm not sure you want to know," I respond with a roll of my eyes.

"Is it as bad as doing blowjob shots while wearing a string of penises around your neck?"

Squinting, I cock my head, his statement catching me off guard. There's no way he'd know about those shots unless he were watching me earlier in the evening. I remind myself it could just be a coincidence. I *was* at a bachelorette party. It's not a big stretch to assume we'd do blowjob shots. They tend to go hand-in-hand.

"That was child's play compared to tonight's festivities." I flash him a coy smile over the top of my glass as I tilt it back, then return it to the bar.

"Do tell. You can't leave me hanging with a statement like that." His eyes sparkle with amusement and intrigue.

"What would you say if I told you I'd be learning how to strip and pole dance?" My voice comes out breathy, laden with desire, as I inch toward him.

His expression widens momentarily, muscles clenching, before he recovers, that unaffected attitude returning. "I'd say I'd love to see that."

I lean even closer, barely a breath between us. "I bet you would." I scrape my lips ever so slightly against his. The touch is no more than a whisper, yet it ignites a spark deep within. "Maybe later, I can give you a private show of what I learned."

"But I thought you didn't hook up in this town?" I can feel his mouth turn into a wry smile. "I thought you said your pussy was on a break."

Moisture pools between my thighs, the combination of his proximity and words making me want to blow off tonight and do my own private striptease with my mystery man.

"An exception can be made."

A slight growl escapes his throat, his lips about to press firmly against mine when a loud, shrill voice cuts through.

"There you are!"

I quickly tear away, snapping my eyes to my right as Bernadette rushes toward me, her blonde curls bouncing with each long stride, a woman on a mission. As expected, she's still wearing her "Bitch of Honor" tank top. I wonder if she slept in it.

"I've been texting and calling you the past five minutes. The party bus is out front. Izzy said you were coming here for a drink and a quick bite…"

She trails off, halting in her tracks the instant she notices the man beside me. The way his body is positioned makes it apparent we're not simply strangers sitting next to each other at a bar. Her eyes rake over his crisp suit, unshaven jaw, and wayward dark locks. A smirk forms on her lips as she all but salivates over him.

"I guess you *did* come for a quick bite." She flirtatiously waggles her brows.

He opens his mouth to say something, but she advances, closing in on his personal space like a lioness in heat. He scoots back in his chair to put distance between them, but she doesn't get the hint. I wonder if her husband knows how she's behaved all weekend, that she's shamelessly flirted with anything with a pulse, male *and* female.

"Want to come with us? We're about to go to a striptease and pole dancing class." She sticks out her chest, squeezing her arms against her body to make her cleavage pop. "I'd love someone to perform for."

Rolling my eyes so hard I'm confident I see my ass, I scoot off my stool, stepping between them. I hope I didn't come across as desperate as Bernadette when I propositioned the same thing. I don't think *anyone* could come across as desperate as Bernadette.

"I'm ready," I announce, pulling my wallet out of my purse. "I just need to pay for my dinner first."

I'm about to ask for the check when he places his hand on my forearm. The instant I feel his skin on mine, my pulse skyrockets, breath quickening. I look at him, questioning. I expect him to withdraw his hand. Instead, he lingers, his fingers tracing light circles.

"It's taken care of," he states with authority.

"But—"

"It's taken care of." This time, his voice is harsher, leaving no room for argument.

I part my lips, my words stuck in my throat. How can I make him understand why I don't like the idea of anyone paying for my meal or my drinks? That it makes it easier to walk away after a night, a week, a month, whatever it may be? That it's helped keep my heart guarded? It helps keep their heart guarded, too, safe from the inevitable destruction my life will unfold on them.

That it brings up too many memories of a past I want to forget.

"Say okay." His tone is a cross between a plea and demand.

Hypnotized, oblivious to everything other than giving him what he wants, I respond, "Okay." My voice doesn't even sound like my own. I'm a puppet and he my master pulling the strings.

He brings his fingers to my chin, tilting my head back. "Say thank you."

My pulse skyrockets. It's so simple, so innocent, yet has me wondering what it would be like to hear him tell me what to do in the bedroom. And based on what I've observed, he'd do just that.

"Thank you," I whimper.

His lips inch toward mine, every synapse in my body firing. "You're welcome."

I close my eyes, bracing for his kiss, but it never comes. Instead, he drops his hold on me, the warmth of his breath disappearing. I flutter my eyes open, disoriented. Then I spy Bernadette standing off to the side, smirking like an older sister would when catching the younger one kissing a boy. It's not that far off. At one time, Bernadette *was* like an older sister.

Trying to settle my raging hormones, I hop off my barstool, pretending I'm a composed, professional twenty-eight-year-old woman. Bernadette's smirk only grows wider. I keep my head lowered as I loop my arm through hers, dragging her away.

"Who *was* that?" she whispers once we're outside the restaurant, glancing over her shoulder.

The realization hits and I blink repeatedly. "I don't know." I stop walking and look back to where I was just sitting. He's no longer there, as if he vanished. If Bernadette hadn't seen him, I'd think I imagined the entire thing. "I never got his name."

"Pity," she replies with a dismissive shrug of her shoulders. "He was quite the looker. But fear not. There will be more than enough eye candy for us tonight."

She grabs my hand and pulls me toward another night of bachelorette torture.

# Three

Relief rolls off my shoulders as I make my way through the quiet corridors of the hotel and toward a bank of elevators, pulling my roll-a-board behind me. I don't think I've ever been so happy about a vacation ending as I am about getting on that plane in a few hours. As much as I love Hannah, I'd rather be stuck in my cubicle at the office than in this city for another second.

Once I'm in the elevator on my way to the lobby to meet Izzy, I pull my phone out of my purse and type out a quick text to my friend and coworker, Evie.

ME:

Headed to the airport. I should be back in town around 7.

EVIE:

I can't wait to hear all about it. You should do a piece about bachelorette parties for the magazine, but in a way only your cynicism can truly deliver.

I respond, arguing I'm not *that* cynical, when the elevator slows to a stop on another floor and the doors open. Keeping my eyes glued to my phone as I finish my text, I step back to make room for anyone about to get on. That's when a familiar scent hits me, earthy and raw. I snap my head up, my body stiffening when I see *him*.

I thought the first time we ran into each other was simply a chance encounter. The second a coincidence. But a third time?

At first, he remains frozen in place, gaze glued to mine. Then a mischievous smile gradually replaces his stunned expression and he enters, standing unnervingly close as he leans toward me to press the lobby button that's already illuminated.

The elevator doors close, leaving us alone in this tiny space that's abuzz with electricity. Conscious of every sound, every heartbeat, every breath, I stare straight ahead. With each drawn-out second, my pulse increases, mouth growing dry. I shift from foot to foot, ready to burst from the tension.

When the silence becomes unbearable, I float my eyes to his, only to notice he's unabashedly staring at me. Unlike our previous encounters, he's dressed casually in a white linen shirt with the sleeves rolled up to just below his elbows, revealing his muscular forearms. Khaki shorts hang from his hips, a pair of tan flip-flops on his feet.

"Taking a day off from ruling the world?" My voice breaks through.

"Ruling the world?"

"Exactly. You always act so in charge. So…in control."

His lips curve up into one of the most sensual grins I've ever seen. Screw Matt Damon's sexy smirk, or Brad Pitt's flirtatious smile. They have nothing on this guy.

"I do like being in control."

I attempt to fight against the blush building on my cheeks, averting my gaze. All I hear is his voice from the other night.

*Say okay. Say thank you.*

And I did. It was so simple, so innocent, yet it lit me up in a way that left me craving him all weekend. His words. His presence. His…dominance.

"I didn't mean it like that." I chew on my bottom lip, fidgeting with the hem of my jacket. "I meant you look and act like you have some high-powered job. Master of the universe and all that."

"Master of the universe?" He arches a single brow.

"Yes." I return my eyes to his, shrugging. "You know, like He-man."

"Well…" Licking his lips, he closes the distance, the heat of his breath on my neck making me tremble. "Appearances can be deceiving. Wouldn't you agree?" He pulls back, meeting my gaze.

"They can be," I reply thoughtfully, masking my shaky voice. "But something tells me they're not. Not when it comes to you."

"Even the master of the universe deserves a day off to enjoy life's…pleasures."

My nerve endings tingle as that one word hangs in the air, making me hyper-aware of my heartbeat, which I'm confident they can hear in the casino. Hell, they can probably even hear it all the way at the Hoover Dam.

I swallow hard, my gaze fixated on his lips, thinking how much pleasure they could give me. Suddenly, the elevator comes to a stop and the doors open, the clanging bells of slot machines breaking our moment.

I snap out of my daze, squaring my shoulders as I scramble out of the enclosed space and into the casino, able to breathe again. Normally, I hate the loud noise that meets me every time I step off this elevator, feeling much like the Grinch when he complains about all the "noise, noise, noise" down in Whoville. But right now, I find it comforting, at least compared to the anxiety that consumes me whenever I'm in this man's presence.

"Headed home?" When I hear his voice, I look to my right to see him catching up to me.

"Thankfully, yes. One night in Vegas is too long. I've been here four." I slow my steps as I near the front doors, scanning the enormous lobby for any sign of Izzy. She's probably still in a ridiculously long line for coffee. God, I hate this city.

"Aren't you headed out?" he asks when I don't follow him outside.

"I'm waiting for a friend. We're on the same flight."

"Oh." His expression momentarily falls, but he recovers quickly, smiling, although it doesn't make his eyes sparkle as it usually does. "Well, it was nice seeing you again."

"You, too."

He hesitates briefly, and I can almost see the words on the tip of his tongue. Then he turns from me, walking out the revolving glass doors. I can't help but admire his long strides, muscular legs, broad shoulders, and what I can only imagine is a firm ass. I almost don't want to look away. But when a ping sounds from my phone, I do just that.

Unlocking the screen, I read a text from Evie saying she's spending the night at Julian's and not to worry if she's not at my place when I get home. I reply, telling her she should just officially move in with him.

When her boyfriend of twelve years broke up with her, I offered her a place to stay, considering how difficult it is to find an affordable apartment in the city. But now that she has a new man in her life, she hasn't spent much time at my apartment. I'm pretty sure she's also stopped looking for a place of her own.

As I finish my text, a slight movement out of the corner of my eye catches my attention. It shouldn't, considering it's Vegas. This entire place is a constant wave of motion. But something draws my gaze toward the doors.

When I see my mystery man standing there, his impassioned stare trained on me, I'm stunned, frozen in place, in time, in this moment. The intensity in his stormy green eyes sends a rush of exhilaration through me, leaving me breathless. No man's ever looked at me this way. Or maybe they have, but I ignored it. But I can't ignore him.

He starts toward me and everything else seems to disappear. It's…quiet. Gone are the obnoxious sounds of slot machines, the tourists rushing by, and the ridiculously loud club music filling the space, even at eleven in the morning. Reaching me, his hand palms the small of my back and he pulls me against him. A spark shoots through me, low and deep, igniting a flame I didn't think would ever be lit again.

He brings his other hand to my hair, wrapping his fingers around it, forcing my head back. I stare into his eyes, unable to escape. And I don't want to, don't want to flee this bubble.

"I can't leave," he begins, his voice husky, low, sensual.

"Sure you can," I murmur. "All you have to do is put one foot in front of the other and walk through those doors."

He slowly shakes his head. "No. What I meant to say is I can't leave without…" His mouth inches even closer.

"Without what?" My lips tingle in anticipation.

"Without kissing you."

My nerves stir as my stomach fills with the wings of a thousand butterflies, all of them screaming at him to finally get on with it.

"Then what are you waiting for?"

His grip on me tightens and he yanks my body harder against his, his eyes flaring with unyielding desire. He gradually decreases the distance, this torturous dance of seduction making me even more on edge. I'm desperate to feel his lips, to know how they taste. All weekend, I've fantasized about his kiss. Most people would probably wonder what he was like in bed, how he screwed. Not me. There's nothing personal about that. Kissing is much more intimate.

Based on what little I know of him, I imagined he kissed with all the confidence he seemed to do everything else. At first, it would be controlled and reserved, but still addictive. He wouldn't be able to hold back for long. It would explode into a passionate exchange, leaving me thoughtless, breathless, soulless, ruining me for all men who would come after him.

When his breath dances on my flesh, I close my eyes, bracing to feel his full lips on me. Instead, boisterous voices infiltrate our bubble, a body slamming into me, causing me to teeter on my heels.

Forced out of my trance, I glare at a bunch of drunk guys in their twenties, all of them carrying those huge plastic cups containing sugary, frozen drinks. It's not even noon, yet they already look like they've been overserved.

"Are you okay?" my mystery man asks, and I return my eyes to his.

"Of course." I straighten my jacket, even more happy to be going home than I was before. I'm about to ask where we were when an alert interrupts. He reaches into his pocket, withdrawing his cell.

"My Uber's here." He offers me an apologetic smile. Then he leans in, his mouth a whisper from my neck. "Safe travels." He kisses my cheek, his lips lingering on my skin for several long moments. When he pulls away, he holds my gaze before retreating, leaving me feeling like a hormonally imbalanced high school freshman who was nearly kissed by the hot senior quarterback before the prom queen pulled him away.

I exhale a breath, taking a moment to collect myself. But I don't have a moment. Izzy hurries toward me, eyes wide in curiosity.

"Who was *that*?" The tone of her voice indicates she must have seen him kiss my cheek, at the very least.

All I can do is shake my head as I shift my attention to the front doors and watch my mystery man slide into the back seat of a dark sedan.

"Just some guy."

# Four

"So you mean to tell me that, of the three times you've seen him—"

"Four, if you count him coming back to try to kiss me."

"Whatever…" Izzy waves me off. "That's not the point. The point is that you never thought to ask him his name?" Her voice is filled with disbelief at the story I just relayed to her about my run-ins with Mr. Mysterious over the course of the weekend.

"I *did* think of it." I relax into my plush lounge chair, bringing my espresso to my lips as we sit in a quiet corner of the airline club. The hectic atmosphere of the airport is nowhere to be found. No screaming children being ignored by their parents who are exhausted after a long day of traveling. No annoying businessmen who feel the need to shout on their cellphones in the hopes that someone thinks they're important. No assholes bitching out the poor airline employee who had nothing to do with the delay of the flight going to Denver, where there's probably snow. In here, I'm able to have a moment of peace.

"A name is usually the *first* thing I ask," she interjects before I can say anything else. "You'd think with all the time you spent 'bumping' into each other this weekend, you would have gotten that much."

"It's just… Every time I saw him…" I shake my head, struggling to come up with the words to describe how his mere presence consumed me. Normally, *I'm* the confident one. *I'm* the one calling the shots. *I'm* the one saying whatever's on my mind without a care for what anyone thinks about me. But not around him. "It was quiet," I finish thoughtfully.

"Quiet?" Izzy gives me a sideways glance. "What do you mean?"

I place my espresso on the table separating us and lean closer, lowering my voice. "All the noise of my life. It was…gone."

Understanding immediately washes over her, and her expression relaxes.

Izzy's one of the few people who truly knows me, all my secrets, all my scars. Yes, Nora's been a great friend since we were college roommates, and once Evie was assigned the cubicle next to mine at the magazine, we formed a quick bond, considering she lacks any brain-to-mouth filter, much like myself. But Izzy knew me *before*. She knew me when my parents were still together. She knew me when it all fell apart, when I had to lie to my father about being sick so I could miss my weekend with him to take care of my mother during another one of her drinking binges. Something no teenage girl should have to do. But what choice did I have? She was the only family I had left after my father upgraded to a new one.

"Sometimes you just need someone to quiet it for a minute," she remarks.

"Because of that, I didn't think a name was necessary." We share a look before I curl my lips into a wicked grin, lightening the mood. "You *do* have to admit the entire scenario is kind of hot. Not knowing his name, anything about him…"

"*Kind of* hot?" She fans herself, giggling. "Try off the charts! I noticed the chemistry between you two right away, even if all he did was kiss your cheek. It was incredibly… sexy. I can't imagine how it made *you* feel."

"Like I could let go," I reply without hesitating. "For once, I didn't worry about the fact that we're polar opposites. That he's presumably this guy who has his shit together, whereas I'm lucky if I don't lock myself out of my apartment on a daily basis. But each time I saw him, I didn't think about any of that, didn't try to distance myself because of how it would play out. It's almost like we were in our own little bubble."

"Bubbles can be good." Then her eyes turn conniving. "Especially a bubble that sexy."

We both break into laughter. I lean back into my chair, at ease with the familiarity of joking with one of my oldest friends. If nothing else, at least I got to spend a little more time with Izzy this weekend than I usually do. While we both live in New York, her job as a nurse in the pediatric oncology unit at one of the local hospitals doesn't give her much time off. Izzy's one of those friends who you can go months without seeing, then pick back up as if you just saw them yesterday.

"So, what do you think the girls are up to today?" I ask after a few minutes.

"Knowing Bernadette, something cliché and inappropriate."

I roll my eyes. "Promise me if I ever get that lonely and desperate for attention, you'll smack some sense into me and tell me I don't need to stay in a loveless marriage. That there's better out there for me."

"You know I will."

A chiming cuts through and I float my eyes to the coffee table to see a text from my mother wishing me safe travels. I grab my cell and fire off a quick response, not wanting her to worry.

"She doing okay?" Izzy asks, obviously having seen who the text was from.

"Yeah." I take another drink of my espresso, finishing it. "She's been dating this guy who works in the same building." I stare into the distance, smiling. "It's actually a sweet story. Somehow, they kept riding up to their floors in the same elevator. After about a week, he mentioned it to her. Said he couldn't ignore it anymore, that it was a sign."

"Hmm... A sign?" She smirks knowingly.

"That's not the same thing," I argue, fully aware what she's referring to. "Mom works in the same building as Aaron. There's a decent likelihood of running into him again. This thing with me and...whoever he is, well...it's different. I have a better chance of winning the lottery than seeing him again."

Izzy shrugs. "You're probably right, but what if you do?"

"It'll never happen," I say incredulously. "I'm about to get on a flight back to New York. He was headed..." I wave my hand around, "wherever. So yeah. Not going to happen."

"But if it does?"

"It won't," I insist.

"But if it does?" she presses again.

"It won't."

"Yeah, but if it does?"

I groan, remembering how persistent and annoying Izzy can be. This could go on for hours, even days. "Fine. If by some miracle I *do* see him again, maybe I'll admit there might be a reason for it all."

She nods, leaning back in her chair, happy with herself.

"But it won't happen."

She glares at me, feigning annoyance. "Always have to have the last word, don't you?"

I grin. "Always."

My phone dings again and I reach for it, assuming it's a reply from my mother. Unlocking the screen, I see an alert from the airline.

"Shit," I mutter as Izzy's phone begins to beep.

"What is it?" She scrambles for her cell, presumably reading the same message I received. "Dammit."

"Yup. Flight to JFK is canceled."

She groans, closing her eyes in frustration. "Just how I want to spend my day. Stuck in the airport."

"And not any airport," I remind her, pointing at the busy terminal that resides just outside the lounge, the subtle sound of slot machines inching their way into our peaceful recluse. "McCarran Airport in *fabulous* Las Vegas." My voice is laden with sarcasm. "If the Strip is the tenth circle of hell, this place is purgatory."

"Glad to see all those literature classes paid off."

"What flight did they rebook you on?" I ask, opening the airline's app on my phone to get my new flight information.

"Red-eye. Eleven PM. And here's the kicker. No seat assignment available." She holds out her phone so I can see her new itinerary.

"Me, too." I mirror her movement.

"It looks like they're cramming everyone onto that flight. What are the chances of us actually getting on?"

"I'd like to say they wouldn't rebook us just to tell us no in ten hours."

"My mother used to work for an airline. They absolutely *would* do such a thing." She pinches her lips together, deep in thought, then jumps up. "I'll be right back." A woman on a mission, she starts toward the front desk of the lounge.

While Izzy speaks to an agent for what I presume to be a solution, I return my attention to my phone, opening the web browser to see if there are any other options. Despite it being a Tuesday and a light travel day, most of the flights to JFK are sold out or, if there are seats available, are way out of my price range. Not to mention, it's after one in the afternoon. The next flight into New York doesn't leave until later tonight, even on a different airline.

"Hey," Izzy says breathlessly. I look up from my phone, eyes brimming with hope. "I can get us guaranteed seats on the noon flight tomorrow. The red-eye is oversold and they'll most likely be forced to rebook again if they can't get enough people with confirmed seats to give them up. You in? Guaranteed seats or take a risk on the red-eye."

I push out an aggravated breath, pinching the bridge of my nose. As much as I hate the idea of staying in Vegas another night and having to waste even more vacation time, it doesn't seem like there's an option.

"Guaranteed seats."

"Give me your boarding pass and I'll get you rebooked."

I grab my phone and find my boarding pass, then hand it to her.

"Thanks. Be right back."

I watch as she scurries back to the front desk. She's come a long way from the little girl who was too scared to approach Hannah and me when her family first moved into the neighborhood. Now, Izzy's a typical New Yorker. Confident. Assured. And always gets her way.

After a few minutes, she returns and hands me my phone along with a new airline printout. "Here you go. You're all set."

"Thanks," I say, surprised at her efficiency. If she weren't here, I would have sucked it up and hung around the airport in the hopes of getting on the red-eye. But now that we're flying out tomorrow, there's another problem.

"Umm… Izzy, we can't go back to the same hotel, not unless we want to get roped into day 317 of the never-ending bachelorette party."

A sly smile builds on her lips. "Don't worry. I've got that covered, too."

# Five

"Where the hell are we?" I ask as our Uber driver slows to a stop in front of a gated driveway on the outskirts of Vegas. "David Copperfield's house?"

"No." Izzy rolls her eyes. "But my sources say he lives around here somewhere."

"Sources? What sources? *I'm* your source for all things celebrity."

"Maybe there are some things about me you *don't* know." She passes me a devious grin before opening the door, stepping onto the street. A little bewildered, I take a minute to collect my things. When she said she had a friend who was more than happy to let us stay the night, I didn't expect to pull up in front of a piece of property that looks like it belongs in Bel Air.

A knock on the window rips my attention away from the impressive entrance and I snap my eyes to Izzy as she opens my door.

"Are you coming? Or do you want to call Bernadette and see if you can crash with her tonight? Maybe stay up and do a makeover, then go to some Pure Romance party."

"I wouldn't mind going to a Pure Romance party." I scoot out of the car. "I'm all for women exploring their sexuality. But I'd pass on the Bernadette makeover," I say as I head toward where our driver stands, holding the handle of my suitcase for me. "With the amount of makeup she'd cake on my face and the revealing outfit she'd stuff me in, I'd come out of there looking like a blowup doll." Smiling, I take my bag from the driver as he eyes me up and down, discreetly adjusting the waist of his pants.

The Vegas sun beating down on us, I follow Izzy toward the front gate, watching as she enters a code into a box. I can't help but feel like she hasn't been forthcoming about who we're staying with. Granted, I'm not as close to her as I once was, but she would have mentioned knowing someone who owned a palace in Vegas, wouldn't she?

"Are you coming?" she asks when the gate opens and she continues up the elaborate drive.

"I suppose…," I respond in a drawn-out voice, taking slow steps toward her as I absorb my surroundings. The driveway is made of pavers, the brick matching that of the flowerbeds lining it, which are filled with succulents. Palm trees shade the path, as well as offer privacy to the occupants.

As we round the corner, the house finally coming into view, my jaw drops. I knew we were in a wealthy neighborhood, but I didn't expect this. The sprawling two-story house looks like a snapshot from a home design magazine, a rare peek into how the rich and famous of Las Vegas live and play.

I glance at Izzy, my curiosity increasing with every step. She knew the exact house we were going to, told the driver to stop when he was about to pass it. That means she's been here before.

"Iz?" I say as we approach the short flight of steps leading to the front door.

She stops, flashing her eyes to mine, a single brow raised.

"Who lives here?"

"Just an old friend from my undergrad days." She avoids my inquisitive stare, smoothing a lock of nearly jet-black hair behind her ear, her olive-toned skin becoming flushed.

"A...friend? Does this 'friend' happen to be of the male persuasion?"

"Yes." She holds her head high, but still doesn't look directly at me.

"Call me crazy—"

"You certainly are."

"But I get the feeling there's more to the story than this guy..." I wave my hand around at our surroundings, everything pristine and glamorous, "being just a 'friend'."

Her eyes finally meet mine, a flash of indecision filling them. I can physically feel her turmoil, like she wants to tell someone whatever this is, but is scared of the potential backlash. Izzy has a habit of taking everyone's feelings into account with every decision.

I rest my hand on her arm. "What is it? You can tell me anything."

"I know that. But this..." She shakes her head, conflicted, pulling her lip between her teeth. When she looks at me again, a hint of shame covers her expression. Her shoulders fall. "It's Asher York."

I remain motionless as the name rings out between us. "Asher York as in Jessie York's older brother?"

She blows out a nervous laugh. "It's not exactly a common name, is it?"

"Asher York, the handsome, struggling musician?"

"Yup."

"The Asher York with a singing voice that makes you forget your name?"

"That's the one."

"The Asher York who looks like a fucking Adonis with a guitar strapped to him?"

"Yes, Chloe. *That* Asher York," she admits, her voice growing louder, her face blushing even more as the tension momentarily lightens.

"The Asher York who would have been your brother-in-law if you hadn't smartened up and called off your engagement to Jessie?"

Her expression falls and she slowly nods. "Exactly."

I stare at her, unsure how to react to this. She still didn't admit anything's going on between them, but she doesn't have to. I can see it in her eyes as she silently pleads with me not to make a big deal out of this. And I won't.

I never liked Jessie to begin with. He was arrogant, pompous, and conceited. They dated in college. Got engaged young. I pretended to be happy for her. She's my friend, after all. Deep down, I questioned whether it would last, considering they were both so young...*too* young to decide to get married. Thankfully, she realized that before it was too late, thanks to Jessie not being able to keep his dick in his pants.

"Well..." I take in my surroundings, my voice brightening. "It looks like Asher's not a struggling musician anymore, is he?"

"Oh, this isn't *his* place. He's just kind of...staying here."

"Like, house sitting?"

"Not exactly. He, uh..."

Before she can finish her sentence, the door swings open and we both snap our heads to the entryway. I almost can't believe my eyes when they fall on Asher York leaning against the doorjamb, arms crossed in front of his chest, his biceps stretching the fabric of his shirt, a wicked smile on his full lips as he admires Izzy.

This is not the same Asher York I remember from all

those years ago. He's more mature, more muscular, more… experienced. There are hints of the man I saw a handful of times during some of Izzy's pre-wedding festivities, but his short, dark hair is now longer, the strong jawline sporting a sexy five o'clock shadow. It's only been six or seven years, but he seems like a different person. Then again, he could probably say the same about me.

"When I told you it was okay for you both to crash here, I meant *inside* the house. Not on the front stoop," he jokes, his eyes never leaving Izzy.

"Hey, Ash." A blush blooms on her cheeks, her lips kicking up into a brilliant smile. Then she looks away, nervously pushing her hair behind her ear. "Thanks for this."

"It's nothing, Iz. You know that." His words are laden with a sincerity I feel deep in my core. "I was thrilled to hear your voice, considering I thought you'd be 35,000 feet in the air by now."

"I guess the universe had different plans."

"I guess so."

Izzy peers up at him through thick lashes, her chest rising and falling in a quicker pattern. Something about the way Asher holds her gaze makes me think he doesn't want to look away. Then he glances in my direction, clearing his throat.

"Chloe. Good to see you again. I like the hair. It suits you."

I pass him a wry smile. "Thanks for letting us stay here."

"Anytime. I'd never turn away a friend in need." He steps back, gesturing for us to enter the house.

I lean into Izzy. "Hear that? He'll never turn away a *friend* in need, Iz." I waggle my eyebrows at her as we walk into the magnificent foyer complete with high ceilings and modern chandelier hanging overhead.

"Oh, hush. It's not like that."

I grin. "You want it to be like that, though, right?"

Chewing on her lower lip, she shrugs. "Maybe."

---

"All right, Asher," I say when Izzy and I step into the kitchen after getting a brief tour of the luxurious house and changing into our bathing suits. "Whose house is this?" I turn around slowly, craning my head back, my voice seeming to echo against the tile in the cavernous space. "Izzy said you're not house sitting, so what *are* you doing in a place like this?"

"Don't think I can afford it myself?" He looks up from forming a mixture of ground beef and onions into patties.

"Last I heard, you were playing bars in LA, trying to make it big."

"Maybe I've made it big."

"Have you?" I place my hands on the large island, leaning toward him, my lips pressed into a tight line. If he'd made it big, I would have heard.

He considers my question for a moment, then shrugs. "Not yet, but I'm one step closer."

"What do you mean?" I look from him to Izzy, an amused expression on her face. I notice her eyes shift ever so slightly and I follow her line of sight, my gaze falling on a glass case in the living room.

I walk toward it, my brow furrowing when I see six Grammy awards enclosed within. Squinting, I read the gold plate, then whirl around, my expression wide.

"You're in Fallen Grace?" I can't hide the disbelief in my voice.

Fallen Grace is this decade's most popular boy band, five twenty-something-year-old guys from London who girls scream and fawn over everywhere they go. I would have noticed Asher York standing amongst their numbers. I notice *everything* about *everyone*.

He shakes his head, laughing. "Certainly not. They're not really my style."

"Then what—"

"They hired me to work on their new album with them, and to help with their engagement here in Vegas."

"If they're not your style, why are you working with them?"

"They're going for a more mature sound…less pop, more rock."

I absorb what he's saying, my mouth agape as I shake my head. "How the hell did you even land this job?"

"Dumb luck," he laughs. "About six months ago, I had a gig with my band in Hollywood when one of the guys came by. He grabbed one of our download codes, listened to the tracks, then played it for the rest of the band. After doing a bit of research, they found out I wrote all the songs. Their manager called to see if I was interested in helping on their next album."

"So you're… What? Writing their songs for them?"

"More or less. Some of them write their own stuff, too, but I'm helping fill in the gaps and produce the record." He smiles, a hint of nostalgia in his eyes as he stares into space, his expression thoughtful. "Before I got their call, I was months behind on my rent and facing eviction. I was ready to throw in the towel, tell my parents they were right and I should never have left my teaching job. It goes to show that sometimes good things happen when we least expect it."

He looks from me to Izzy, admiring all five feet, seven inches of her slender physique, which is now on display in just a black bikini and sheer coverup. She pulled her dark locks into a messy bun, a pair of oversized sunglasses pushed up onto her forehead.

His Adam's apple bobs up and down in a hard swallow before he returns his attention to the burgers, his hands shaking slightly. It's adorable how nervous she makes him. That's all any woman wants. To know she affects a man in such a way as to completely fluster him.

"So…" He clears his throat. "What can I get you to drink? Beer? Wine? Cocktail? You name it, and it's yours, unless you ask for something strange. I may not have all the ingredients. But considering the parties the guys throw here, I'm pretty well-stocked."

I lean toward Izzy, whispering into her ear. "He certainly is, isn't he?"

She slaps me away, hushing me. "I'm happy with a beer." She looks toward the rear wall that consists of floor-to-ceiling windows overlooking the pool area. "It's a beer kind of day."

"A woman after my own heart," he comments with a wink, causing the blush on her cheeks to build even more. Then he lifts his eyes to mine. "Chloe?"

"Beer's fine with me, too."

With a nod, he turns toward the refrigerator and opens it, taking out two Coronas, popping the top off them. "Lime?"

"Yes," we answer simultaneously.

He retrieves a couple lime slices from a bowl on the island, sticks them into the neck of the bottle, then slides the beers toward us. We get to work pushing the lime past the neck, plugging the bottle with our thumbs, and flipping it so the lime sinks toward the bottom.

"Here's to making the most out of a canceled flight." Izzy raises her beer.

I mirror her movements. "I'd much rather be here than stuck at the airport."

"I'll drink to that," Asher agrees, bringing his beer toward ours. We clink bottles, then tilt them back, taking a sip.

"Is there anything we can help with?" Izzy asks.

"I have it all under control. You ladies are guests here. Just relax and enjoy yourselves. Come on."

He grabs the plate of burgers and starts toward the open French doors. We follow him, emerging onto the back patio area, the aroma of burning charcoal filling the air.

"Lincoln!" Asher calls out as he strides toward the grill off to the left, leaving the plate on a table beside it. "Get off your phone and be social."

I scan the pool area, following Asher's line of sight. A tall man with dark hair holds up a finger, not looking in our direction as he walks toward a fence beyond the pool, leaning his arms against it as he admires the view of the Vegas skyline from this vantage point on the outskirts of the city. It is quite impressive. I can only imagine how incredible the view must be at night. As much as I hate Vegas, I can certainly appreciate the beauty of it, especially from afar.

"He'll be done soon, I hope."

"Who's *he*?" I don't actively follow Fallen Grace, but I don't recall any of them being named Lincoln.

"Lincoln Moore," Asher answers, placing the burgers onto the grill. It instantly sizzles. "We went to college together. In fact, he was a workaholic back then, too, constantly studying. He was one of those guys who lived according to the motto 'work hard, play hard'."

"I like to think that now it's 'work hard, play even harder'."

When I hear that deep rumble, every muscle in my body tenses, my breath leaving me. It couldn't be, could it?

I slowly turn around, momentarily disoriented as I stare into those green eyes once more. Izzy pinches my side, just as surprised as me.

"Chloe, Izzy…," Asher begins, oblivious to the tension. "This is my friend, Lincoln."

I stare, seeing him differently now that I know his name. It suits him. Strong, yet flirty.

"Lincoln, this is Izzy and—"

"Dick Girl."

"Dick Girl?" Asher looks between us, confused. "Do you two know each other?"

Lincoln subtly nods. "We've had the…pleasure." The way that word leaves his tongue has my nerve endings stirring. "Or perhaps I should say *I've* had the pleasure of experiencing her sharp tongue."

"Yes." I offer him a flirtatious smile, extending my hand toward him. "It's nice to see you again, to *formally* meet you, Lincoln."

He takes my hand in his, raising it to his lips, his pupils dilating as he feathers his mouth against my skin. The touch is subtle, yet it has my stomach doing backflips.

"Likewise, Chloe." He passes me a devilish grin, then lowers my hand. "I didn't think we'd see each other again."

"Either did I."

"Funny how that keeps happening, isn't it? How we keep…bumping into each other. If I didn't know any better, I'd think someone, some*thing* wants us to keep seeing each other."

I lift my beer to my mouth. "I'm beginning to think I should buy a lottery ticket."

# Six

"Careful. Careful," I caution, biting my lower lip, my breathing ragged, wracked with nerves. "No, not there." My voice is frantic as I meet Lincoln's fervid eyes, his concentration so intense I fear it may be our undoing.

"This isn't my first rodeo," he reminds me.

"I figured as much, but you have to watch what you're doing or it won't end well." My words come out husky, my body taut with anticipation. "One wrong move and it'll all come tumbling down."

"I've got this," he insists through clenched jaws, his nostrils flaring.

Licking his lips, he pauses, the pressure so thick I could almost burst. My chest heaves, the seconds seeming to stretch as I watch his every move. He inches closer and closer and I brace myself, my hands forming into fists, the past several hours, hell…days, culminating in this moment.

Then he pushes a finger in, his motions measured and practiced. I exhale, the tension rolling off me.

"See, Chloe." He meets my eyes, waggling his brows. "I told you I knew what I was doing."

He waves the Jenga block in my face, jutting out his chest. With his head held high, he barely pays attention as he places the block on top of the tower we've spent the past hour building. It instantly falls, the pieces scattering across the table and the ground, the sound echoing throughout the patio.

Groans emanate from everyone as we watch our hard work topple over.

"See! That's what you get for being so cocky," I taunt.

"Don't you know it, baby," he says with a wink before turning his attention to the mess, picking up the blocks.

I can't remember the last time I've played this game. It was probably in college. Back then, of course, it was more of a drinking game. When I stumbled on a collection of board games in the living room, I figured it would be a better way to spend our time than sitting around and drinking.

"What's next on the agenda for game night?" Izzy asks once all the Jenga blocks are back in their box.

"Game night?" I repeat.

"Yeah." She gives me a knowing look. "Game night."

"Oh, no." My response comes quick. "This isn't game night. That's something bored, married couples do to mask the fact that they have nothing in common with each other. The arrogant husband acts as if he's a know-it-all anytime his wife answers a question wrong in Trivial Pursuit. And she realizes exactly how little her husband listens to her during a rousing game of Taboo. No thanks. Not interested."

A sly smile crosses Izzy's mouth, her eyes alight with excitement. "Not all games are boring."

I've seen this look before, the most recent being when she dragged me to what she thought was an intimate Cher concert at a club in the Village. It sounded too good to be true. And it was. The "Cher concert" was a drag show. Regardless, we had one hell of a time.

"What did you have in mind?"

Her grin widens. "You'll see." She stands and heads back into the house, a bounce in her step.

"I'm not sure if I should be scared or intrigued," Asher says, keeping his eyes trained on her.

"The one thing I've learned about Izzy is that she's rather unpredictable."

He blows out a laugh, nodding. "Truer words have never been spoken."

Izzy reappears in the doorway seconds later and walks toward us, a box in her hand. She places it on the wicker coffee table between us, her expression smug.

"I told you, Chloe. Game night doesn't always have to be boring. What do you guys think? Want to take things up a notch?" She grins mischievously. "Or are you too chicken?"

That's all it takes for the guys to puff out their chests, raw masculinity oozing from them. I almost expect them to bang their fists against their pecs and roar like cavemen.

"Never Have I Ever?" I say, reading the words on the box. I didn't realize they'd made a board game out of it.

She shrugs. "Why not? I thought you were an open book, that you had no shame."

"I don't."

"Then what's stopping you?" She smirks, briefly shifting her eyes to Lincoln before returning to mine.

"Fine," I relent with a sigh. "But if we're going to play this, I'll need another beer." I begin to stand from the couch when Lincoln places his hand on my arm, gently pushing me back down.

"I got it." He meets my gaze, which seems to linger on my lips. Then he drops his hold on me, looking at Asher. "I'll grab another round for everyone. I have a feeling we all may need it." He focuses on me once more before disappearing into the house.

"I might as well take advantage of this break and go change." I stand, stretching my arms over my head after sitting for the past hour.

We spent all afternoon lounging by the pool, drinking beers, eating burgers, and playing board games. But now that the sun has disappeared beyond the horizon, the temperature has fallen, making it a bit too cold to be out here in just a bathing suit and a flimsy coverup.

"Are you sure you're not planning to take advantage of something else?" Izzy calls after me as I start toward the house.

I roll my eyes, ignoring her comment, and continue into the kitchen, glancing back at them to see Asher stealing my spot next to Izzy. I'm definitely intrigued by their obvious connection, wondering how long this has been going on. At least I have a five hour flight tomorrow in which to get some answers.

Distracted by concocting a plan to pry this information out of Izzy, I don't pay much attention to my surroundings... Until a movement catches my eyes. I attempt to halt in my tracks, but velocity from my quick strides prevents me from stopping and I crash straight into Lincoln, the beers in his hands jostling and splashing.

"Oh, my god." My face reddens as I stare at his linen shirt, which is now soaked with beer. "I'm so sorry." I rush to take the fizzing bottles out of his hands and place them on the island. Grabbing a kitchen towel, I bring it to his shirt, dabbing at it.

"Don't worry about it." A smile illuminates his face as he looks down at me. "It's just beer."

"I know, but I—"

He wraps his hand around my arm, preventing me from fussing over him any longer.

"Chloe…"

I straighten, swallowing hard. "Yes?"

While we've spent all afternoon together, this is the first time we're alone. The atmosphere is just as charged as it has been the previous times we've seen each other. I have to remind myself to breathe.

"I said it's okay. Nothing a blow dryer can't fix." He pauses, pulling his lips between his teeth. "You wouldn't happen to have a blow dryer, would you? All my stuff is back at the hotel."

I pinch my lips together. "A girl never leaves home without her favorite blow dryer. Come with me."

I leave the towel on the island and lead him up the stairs, doing everything to settle my overwrought nerves. When we reach my room, I walk to my suitcase sitting on an ottoman by the window.

"Please don't tell me that's how you pack," he comments as I rummage through my haphazardly arranged things.

"What's wrong with it?"

He shakes his head. "It's so…unorganized."

"Perhaps to some people…" I grab the dryer, a satisfied look on my face as I wave it in front of him. "But I thrive on the chaos. If you think that's bad…" I spin around and head into the bathroom, "you should see my desk at the office."

He follows, leaning against the doorjamb, observing me as I plug in the dryer.

"And what is it you do?"

"I work at a magazine."

He raises his brow, obviously surprised. "Doing what?"

"I'm a celebrity news columnist." I offer a forced smile.

He studies me for a moment, gaze narrowed. "Why do I get the feeling you wish you were doing something different?"

My posture stiffening, I peer at him. This guy barely knows me, yet he's picked up on something my close friends haven't. That Evie never picked up on, even though she works at the same magazine.

I shrug. "It's a good job. It pays the bills. That's the important part. And I don't hate it. People would kill to have the job I do."

I'm not ungrateful for the opportunity I have at the magazine, but I didn't exactly get it on my own merits. My father's the only reason I'm lucky enough to have that job.

After I was forced to drop out of college to support my mother, who'd been fired because of her alcohol problem, I begged him to help me out with money. Instead, he called in a favor.

I thought I'd eventually go back and finish my degree, be able to get a job at a different magazine because of my own qualifications. Maybe *Rolling Stone*, or even *Time*. But life always seemed to get in the way.

Correction.

My *mother* always seemed to get in the way. I'm just waiting for the bottom to fall again. That's why I'm only taking a few classes at a time, inching toward my degree. I figure even if the bottom *does* fall, it won't be impossible to juggle my job, a couple of classes, and my mother.

"Chloe? You okay?"

I snap out of my thoughts, meeting Lincoln's concerned eyes.

"Sorry. Just thinking about…work." I clear my throat, then turn on the blow dryer. "Come here," I order, and he walks toward me. I point the air stream at the beer stain on his shirt.

He instantly flinches. "Damn. That burns."

"Well, what do you expect? The only way to dry something is with hot air." I return the dryer to the spot, and he cringes again. Men. No wonder women are the ones who get pregnant. They probably wouldn't survive period cramps, let alone pushing a watermelon through a straw.

"Enough." He steps away and I turn off the blow dryer. "New idea."

He unbuttons his shirt, allowing it to fall open, which has the unfortunate side effect of my mouth growing dry. I'd be lying if I said I hadn't fantasized about what he'd look like without a shirt. The reality certainly lives up to the fantasy. Broad shoulders. Sculpted biceps. Firm abs. And a little trail of hair disappearing into his shorts.

"Fuck me," I murmur, entranced with the thought of what he has farther south.

He lifts his eyes to mine, his lips curving into a flirtatious smile.

"I mean…" I look away, flustered, trying to come up with an excuse for my verbal vomit.

His grin widens as he steps toward me, his gaze narrowed. Warmth spreads through me, my heart drumming a feverish rhythm. It's so intense, I expect it to leap out of my chest at any moment. I remain locked in place, unable to move, fearing my knees would buckle if I tried to walk. He curves toward me and I swallow hard, barely able to breathe.

When his mouth is a whisper from mine, my eyelids flutter closed and I crane my head. My body aches in anticipation of his kiss, desperate to finally know how his lips taste.

"Allow me," he murmurs in a seductive voice that makes me even more light-headed. Then he removes the blow dryer from my hand. I fling my eyes open as he pulls back, a smirk on his lips.

In an attempt to steady myself, I place my hand on the vanity counter, drawing in several deep breaths as I try to make sense out of what just happened. What *did* just happen?

"You're familiar with the story of the tortoise and the hare, correct?" He glances at me before returning his attention to his shirt. Flicking on the blow dryer, he aims the air at the material.

"Yes…," I answer in a drawn-out voice, confused about this line of questioning.

"My litigation professor in law school often spoke of it in relation to a trial."

"So you're a lawyer." I place a hand on my hip.

I'm not sure what I thought Lincoln did, but I didn't expect him to say he's a lawyer. I grew up around lawyers. My father's chief general counsel for the biggest newspaper in the country, if not the world. None of the lawyers on his staff ever looked like Lincoln. If they did, I might visit him more often, attend more of his work functions.

"Not master of the universe. Master of the courtroom."

"In a manner of speaking, yes. But that's beside the point."

I saunter toward him. "Then what *is* the point?"

He shuts off the blow dryer, running his hand over the fabric to check for any dampness. Content, he shrugs his shirt back on, much to my disappointment. A shirtless Lincoln Moore truly is a sight to behold. In the shirtless Olympics, he'd wow the judges with a near perfect score.

"Do you know what the hare's mistake was?"

"Yes." I smirk. "He was cocky. Thought he'd get what he wanted no matter what."

He laughs, the sound causing my demeanor to momentarily crack. "That's true. But his problem was sloppy execution."

"Sloppy? How so?"

"He went out of the gate at full speed. There was no warm-up…" Fire builds in his gaze. "No buildup. And when he saw he was in the lead, he took a break."

"You don't think it's okay to take a break?"

"I think it's lazy. Certain aspects of life require a bit more finesse, a bit more planning, a bit more…effort. And let's not forget the most important part."

"And what's that?"

"That the tortoise is the one who crossed the finish line first." He leans toward me, so close I can taste the sweetness of the beers he's consumed. "And I am *very* interested in crossing that finish line."

A shiver rolls down my spine, the double meaning in his words driving me wild with need.

Then he straightens, buttoning his shirt the rest of the way. "But not until I've fully run the race."

"Well… I guess it's time for me to fire the starter pistol."

I start to walk past him, but he grasps my arm and yanks my body against his. It feels like all the air's been sucked from my lungs as I stare into his striking green eyes.

"Haven't you figured it out by now?" His lips skim against mine.

"What's that?"

"I already fired that pistol Saturday night, Chloe. We've just been running laps around each other since then."

"But even when you run laps, you need to stop for a drink of water. You need to quench your thirst."

"Is that what we're doing now? Quenching our thirst?"

"Why don't you tell me?"

His grip on me tightens as a groan falls from his throat, heady and sexy, forcing a stirring deep in my core. He licks his lips, yearning covering his expression as he closes the distance. I brace myself for his kiss, mouth tingling, synapses firing, when every light in the room suddenly snaps off, shrouding us in darkness.

We both stiffen, remaining still, waiting for the lights to come back on. When they don't, he pulls away, releasing me. I look around, but the bathroom is pitch black. Of course, we'd be stuck in the one room with no windows.

"I'll go see what's going on," he states with authority. "The door's around here somewhere."

I put my hands out in front of me, reaching for something to tell me exactly where we are in this ridiculously opulent bathroom that's probably bigger than my entire apartment.

"Why did you close it to begin with?"

"In case we needed a bit of privacy."

I follow Lincoln's scent, confident we must be near the door. "And why would we need a bit of pri—"

My leg hits something, the velocity of my strides catapulting me forward. Without being able to see, I wave my arms around, grasping onto the first thing my hand finds, which also happens to be Lincoln, and we land on the floor with a loud thump. At least my fall was cushioned by his body. He, unfortunately, didn't fare as well and grunts.

"You okay?"

"Great," he answers in a high-pitched falsetto.

"Did I…" I trail off, noticing my knee's putting pressure on something. "Shit. I'm sorry." I adjust my position and hear his exhaled breath.

"I had a feeling you were a ball buster," he groans. "I didn't think you'd literally bust my balls."

"Want me to massage them to make them feel better?" I joke.

He's silent for a moment, then breaks into a throaty laugh. It echoes against the tile, filling the space. "Thanks for the offer, but right now, I'm pretty sure my dick is shriveled up. It'll need some coaxing to come out and play again."

I run my hands up his firm chest, the sensation of being this close sparking a need for even more. To feel more of him. Bringing my mouth toward his, I murmur, "Challenge accepted." He instantly hardens beneath me, and I crook my mouth into a smile, feeling powerful that I have this kind of effect on him.

Cautiously raising myself back to my feet, I step around the room, extending my arms in front of me. When my hand brushes against a metal object, I stop, wrapping my fingers around it. I turn the knob and open the door, the light of the moon illuminating the bedroom through the windows.

"There you are!" Izzy says breathlessly as she rounds the corner into the room. Asher follows, carrying a flashlight. When Lincoln steps into the bedroom, she halts. "Both of you," she adds, her tone not quite a statement. Not exactly a question, either.

"Did we blow a fuse?" I ask in an attempt to steer the conversation away from the curiosity in her gaze.

"I don't know," she responds slyly. "Did you?"

"I don't think it was a fuse," Lincoln interrupts.

I look in his direction to see him staring out the back window that displayed a beautiful view of the Strip earlier. Now the only lights visible are those of cars snaking up Las Vegas Boulevard. No green glow from the MGM Grand. No Eiffel Tower at the Paris Hotel beckoning people to have their photo taken. No gigantic Ferris wheel spinning a slow circle. It's all dark, the sky black, apart from the moon and stars.

"Like I said," Lincoln continues when we all remain silent, congregating around him and staring into the darkness. "I don't think it was a fuse."

# Seven

"Wait a minute. Wait a minute," I say, struggling to capture a breath, my stomach aching from laughing so much over the past hour as we played a toned-down version of Never Have I Ever on the back patio under the light of the moon.

After realizing there was nothing to do but wait for the electricity to come back on, we decided to continue on with our game night. What else could we do? It took our minds off what could have happened to cause all of Las Vegas to lose power.

"You were cursed by a...cat?"

"Fluffy was not a normal cat." Lincoln sips on his beer, but keeps his eyes focused on me.

"The cat's name was Fluffy?"

"Should have been Satan," he mumbled.

"What did the cat do to make you so terrified of it?"

"Existed."

"One of his girlfriends adopted the dang thing from the shelter," Asher pipes in, sharing the story of Fluffy, the devil cat.

"She was nuts," Lincoln adds. "Certifiable."

"Are we talking about Fluffy or the girlfriend?" I ask.

"The girlfriend," he answers, then pauses. "Well, both. I'm pretty sure Mia's psychosis rubbed off on Fluffy."

"What could a cat do that's so bad to make you think it cursed you? I love cats," I offer. "They're the perfect pet. They shit in a box and clean up after themselves."

"They're nature's little serial killers. You cannot trust a cat. Or a cat person."

"Well then…" I settle into the couch. "I guess you can't trust me. Because I'm a cat person."

"Were any of your cats cockblockers?" he presses.

"Umm…no. But I never bring guys to my place to begin with."

This piques Lincoln's interest and he tilts his head. "Ever?"

"It's one of her rules," Izzy states. "Don't shit where you eat or something."

His brow furrows. "Doesn't that phrase refer to sleeping with a coworker?"

"To some, but I expand it to mean not wanting to ruin anything that's important to me."

"And not bringing a date home is important."

"It complicates things. And I like…uncomplicated. The rest of my life is difficult enough. So rule number one is never let them into my home."

"After all…," Lincoln begins, "home is where the heart is."

I peer at him, my mouth falling open. People I've known most of my life don't fully understand why I refuse to invite a guy to my apartment. But Lincoln gets it. Maybe we're not as different as I originally believed.

"This isn't about me," I say quickly. "This is about Fluffy."

"Right. Fluffy. Like Asher pointed out, my ex adopted

him. Referred to him as our 'baby'. When I ended things, she went a little crazy."

"How crazy? On a scale of one to *Single White Female*."

"She would have been more than happy to pin some murders on me," he replies, understanding my movie reference. "At least she never attempted to adopt my appearance. Suffice it to say, she didn't deal with the breakup well. One day, I got home from work to find she left the cat on my front stoop with a note saying she couldn't handle being a single parent and I needed to step up my game."

I choke on my beer at the ridiculousness of it all. I've done some crazy things in my life, but nothing like this.

"Sounds like you found yourself a clinger."

"I think she was just lonely and looking for attention," he responds thoughtfully. "Because once she started dating someone new, she forgot about me…and Fluffy."

I can certainly understand that. My mother's the same way.

"At first, I couldn't believe she'd leave the cat outside for what could have been hours in the middle of winter in Manhattan."

"Wait a minute." I shoot my eyes to his. "You live in New York?"

There's a sparkle in his gaze as he nods, brushing the pad of his thumb against his bottom lip. "Chelsea."

"I'm in the Village."

"Hmm… What are the odds?"

I sip on my beer, hiding my smile. "I'm thinking I *really* need to play the lottery now."

He smirks before continuing his story. "So I took the cat in. As much as I'm more of a dog person, I wouldn't abandon an animal. He was a pretty easy-going cat. Like you said, he shit in a box and took care of himself. But that first night…" He trails off.

"Yes?"

"I woke up in the middle of the night to use the bathroom. That's when I noticed him sitting on the opposite side of the bed, staring at me."

"He was probably curious," Izzy offers.

He slowly shakes his head. "No, because he would have eventually gotten bored. But he just sat there, watching my every move. And it happened night after night after night. Then, about a month later, I started seeing this new girl. Things were going pretty good, so I brought her back to my place."

I ignore the pang of jealousy at the idea of Lincoln bringing a girl home. I have no stake over him. Hell, we haven't even kissed. There's no reason for me to be jealous of any women in his life, past or present.

"Things started heating up and we were about to…"

"Cross the finish line," I say, completing his thought, giving him a knowing look.

"Precisely. And that's when they waved the red flag."

"On what grounds?"

"Due to the cat staring at us. It was creepy, and I couldn't…"

"What?" Asher laughs. "You couldn't get it up?"

"It's not that I couldn't get it up, but knowing that cat was looking at us with his beady eyes… Nothing helped. It's almost like Mia knew that would happen. Like the cat had some mystical powers and she purposefully left him to live at my place so I'd never have sex again."

We all burst out laughing, and I swipe the tears forming in my eyes.

"Well, I hope you found a way to get rid of the curse." I look at Lincoln beside me on the couch.

"I sure did. About three months later, my boss was going through a tough time because the family cat was hit by a car and his kids were distraught over it. I said I had a cat I could part with if he thought it would help. He refused at first, but I insisted. So now I'm free to… Ya know."

"See the checkered flag."

"Precisely."

"But what about your boss and his wife?" Izzy asks. "Don't they—"

"That's the thing!" Lincoln interrupts excitedly. "I asked him about it."

"You *asked* him? How does that even come up in conversation? I'm not quite sure a cockblocking cat is a normal topic."

He waves me off. "He invited me over for a dinner party. We both had a bit to drink, so I asked. He was convinced I was messing with him. Which leads me to the only possible conclusion. My ex tried to curse me with her cat."

We all roar with laughter once more, and it's a remarkable sound, particularly against the emptiness. It's strange how silent everything becomes when there's no power or cell service. No constant pings or vibrations from phone alerts. No hum of electricity. We've been forced back to simpler times when we actually have to communicate face-to-face, our only source of light and heat the fire pit we're sitting around.

"Okay. Who's next?" Izzy returns her attention to the coffee table, then frowns. "We're out of cards."

I chew on my bottom lip. "Maybe it's time we go off script. We stopped with the board game part of this a while back." I gesture to the game board where all the pieces were abandoned long ago in favor of just going through the stack of cards containing different scenarios. "Maybe it's time to make things more interesting and ask different kinds of questions."

"What kinds of questions did you have in mind?" Izzy waggles her brows, grinning mischievously.

"I don't know. Something deeper. A little more…personal."

"Therapist personal or *sexy* personal?"

"Therapist personal," I answer confidently. Then I catch Lincoln's gaze. "And sexy personal."

There's an instant shift in the atmosphere. Until now, we've all been relaxed, just a bunch of people getting to know each other, or catching up with old friends. But with those two words, we're about to change the rules.

"I'm okay with that." Asher takes a swig of his beer, his demeanor giving off the impression that he has nothing to hide. "We're all adults. Not much makes me uncomfortable."

"We *are* all adults, aren't we?" Izzy comments, her mouth a tight line as she taps a fingernail against her upper lip.

"What's going through that brain of yours?" I ask guardedly.

Instead of sharing, she jumps up, grabbing one of the flashlights off the table, then proceeds into the house.

"What is she doing?" Asher floats his gaze to me.

"Your guess is as good as mine."

We sit in silence, apart from the music coming from Asher's phone, all of us curious as to what Izzy's up to. Finally, she reappears, a wide smile on her face.

"What's going on?" I ask as she approaches.

"Like Asher said…," she begins with authority, "we're all adults, correct?"

"Yes…," we mumble, more or less at the same time.

"I'm declaring a circle of trust...a bubble, so to speak."
She waves her arms in a circle through the air around us,
enclosing us in an invisible dome. "I submit for your consideration a new take on Never Have I Ever."

"I'm not sure I want to know what this new take is,"
Asher jokes.

"You probably don't, considering it's how I met your
brother, but..." She holds out her arms, wavering slightly,
physical proof of how much she's had to drink. "Circle of
trust." She pauses, waiting for us to agree, which we all do
with a quick nod.

"We'll go around in a circle, saying something we've
never done. If someone says they've never done something
and you have, you drink. The changed rules apply to the
person speaking. For example, if I say 'Never have I ever shot
Abraham Lincoln', obviously, no one here will drink. In that
case, we go to the penalty round."

She opens her palm, revealing a pair of dice I recognize
from the goody bags we received this weekend. But they're
not your traditional dice. Instead of little dots indicating a
number, they have words. One is an action, the other a body
part.

"How do we know whose..." Squinting, I read off the
first words I spy on the dice, "thigh we have to bite?"

She grabs her nearly empty beer and drains it before
waving it in front of us. "That's what this is for. Whoever the
bottle lands on is the lucky winner... Or perhaps *unlucky*."

"I am *not* biting Asher's thigh," Lincoln says in a voice
that sounds even deeper than his usual one.

"And I am not..." Asher grabs the dice, watching as they
roll across the surface of the table, "sucking his finger."

Izzy sighs an exaggerated sigh, flopping back onto the
couch beside Asher. "Men. This game is much more fun with

only girls. They don't care about this shit. We have no problem licking each other's tongues."

Both guys instantly snap their eyes to her. It's so adorable that just the idea of two women making out gets their hormones running wild.

"But fine," she continues, ignoring the way Asher adjusts his shorts. "How about this? Everyone gets one free pass. Of course, just say something you know at least one other person sitting here has already done and you won't have to worry about spinning the bottle. Unless you *want* to…" She scoops up the dice and rolls, "blow on someone's neck." She looks around, lifting her bottle. "Are you all in?"

Lincoln flashes his eyes to me, a devilish glint in them. It is a bit juvenile and reminiscent of drinking games we played in college. But we're in the city of sin. What fun is being here during a blackout if you can't sin a little?

"Blackout Club," I say.

"What?" She scrunches her brows.

"The first rule of Blackout Club…"

"You don't talk about Blackout Club," Asher and Lincoln finish in unison. Every man in their twenties and thirties knows a *Fight Club* reference when they hear one.

"Exactly." I raise my beer, meeting Izzy's eyes. "Like you said, this is a bubble. We're all consenting adults… *Single* consenting adults. I'm in."

"Me, too," Asher says, lifting his own bottle.

We all shift our attention to Lincoln. He raises his beer and we all clink bottles, sealing the deal. "Let the games begin."

# Eight

An hour and two beers later, Asher confidently says, "Never have I ever gotten so drunk I had to be carried out of a bar."

I glance around our little party, our circle of trust. Neither Lincoln nor I raise our beer to our mouths. I've carried more than my fair share of drunk people out of a bar, but I've never been carried out myself.

When I look at Izzy, she smirks, slowly bringing her bottle to her lips. Something about the smug expression on Asher's face leads me to believe he was aware of this incident.

"Okay." I place my lukewarm beer on the coffee table and lean across it to where she sits next to Asher. "There's obviously a story here. I need to hear it."

"Fine." She takes another sip of her beer, then faces me. "It was Christmas break my junior year of college. I was spending it in Connecticut with my family. Jessie was in Massachusetts. I had planned to visit him, but decided to surprise him and go early."

"Jessie? Your brother?" Lincoln asks, looking to Asher.

"Yes. They were, well... They were—"

"Engaged," Izzy finishes. "Until that night." A flicker of heartache passes across her expression before she recovers.

"Their parents are snowbirds who flee the cold north for the south every winter. The guys usually went down to Florida for Christmas. Well, Jessie was getting back into town that day. Asher was already back, since he was a music teacher and school had resumed. Anyway, I told Asher my plan to surprise Jessie when he got home that day. I had this entire scenario in my head.

"At first, it all *did* go according to plan. Asher left me a key to Jessie's place so I'd have enough time to freshen up after the two-hour drive. I even made him the lasagna he loved, thinking he was probably going to be hungry after traveling all day. When I heard the car pull into the driveway, I went into the dining room, taking a page from Julia Roberts in *Pretty Woman.* You know, when she surprised Edward wearing a tie…and that's it. Sexy, right?" Her expression falls. "Until Jessie walked into the house and I could hear moans and giggles."

"Oh, Iz," I exhale, my hand covering my heart. I may not have the healthiest approach to relationships, but I've never cheated. I've never been anything but honest about what they were getting into with me — laidback, no strings, uncomplicated fun. Nothing more. Still, a pang squeezes my chest, thinking how Izzy must have felt at that moment.

"He tried to apologize, promise it was just a one-time thing, but in my heart, I knew that wasn't the case, that it had probably been going on a lot longer, especially considering *she* was the one he ran to the second he landed in Boston, not me. So I stormed out of there. After getting dressed, of course," she says, her voice lightening.

"I was a mess and not thinking clearly. I was so convinced he was the perfect man for me, although hindsight's always twenty-twenty. As I tried to figure out what to do, I passed a bar."

"Which just so happened to be where my band was performing that night," Asher continues. "Around the time we finished our first set, I looked up to see her sitting at the bar, some punk putting his hands all over her. But she was too drunk to realize what was going on."

"Not one of my finer moments."

"I knew some kind of shit had to go down for her to be there when she was supposed to be with Jessie. So I hauled her out of there before something untoward happened. Canceled the rest of our gig that night, much to the displeasure of the bar's owner, and took her to my place to sober up."

"The next morning, as he helped me nurse one of the worst hangovers of all time, I told him what happened. To which he said—"

"You deserve to be with someone who looks at you every day as if they won the lottery." He meets her gaze, a tender moment passing between them before Izzy quickly averts her eyes, clearing her throat.

"So that's how I was carried out of a bar. Who's next?" Her voice brightens, an obvious attempt to get the focus off her and Asher. "It's your turn, isn't it, Chloe?"

I stare at her, dozens of questions on the tip of my tongue. I want to know why she never told me about this, why she never mentioned Asher at all. Did they hook up that weekend, but she hid it because of how Jessie would react? Despite the heartache and pain he'd caused her, she'd still care about him. She probably still does. That's the type of person she is.

Izzy narrows her gaze on me, wordlessly telling me not to press the topic. So I don't. Not now. I don't want to ruin the fun we've been having. And I do admit I've had a lot of fun. I suddenly have a new appreciation for game night.

"Okay then." I adjust my posture. "Never have I ever given or received a lap dance."

"Try again," Izzy sings. "Already asked."

"Crap. That's right."

I pull my lips between my teeth, trying to come up with something that hasn't already been said *and* at least one person has done. This has proven to be the difficult part of the game, considering Izzy's the only person I know well and I'm running out of risqué things I'm confident she's done. Factor in the rule that you must say something before time is up, added after Asher took several minutes during one of his turns, and it's a bit more stressful, yet exciting.

"Ten seconds, Chloe," Lincoln taunts, waving his phone in front of me, displaying the countdown.

"Okay, okay." I bounce on the seat, adrenaline filling me as I wrack my brain. Then I look back at Lincoln, the timer only showing two seconds, and say the first thing I think of. "Never have I ever gotten freaky in an elevator."

My voice rings out as I bring my own beer bottle to my lips, taking a small sip. I expect someone to drink with me, indicating they've done it, but no one does.

"Remember, we're in a bubble. Circle of trust. Blackout Club and all that. It's okay if you have." I shift my eyes around, everyone shaking their heads.

"Looks like you earned a penalty round." Izzy pushes the bottle and dice my way, her lips kicking up into a sly grin.

So far, everyone else has done this at least once. The first time, Izzy had to touch Lincoln's finger. We all laughed when they did a little E.T. finger touch with each other, Izzy fanning herself afterward, pretending to be all hot and bothered from the contact.

A few minutes later, Lincoln had to roll after he couldn't come up with something in enough time. Lucky him. He had to blow on Asher's chest. Things started to heat up a little when Asher had to bite Izzy's ear. The instant his teeth clamped onto her lobe, her face flushed and lips parted as her eyes fluttered closed. She can insist they're just friends all she wants. There's more going on.

Doing my best to push down the nervous flutter in my stomach, I reach for the dice and toss them onto the coffee table. They teeter on their edges before falling over, landing on SUCK and TONGUE.

A chorus of "whoa" and a few whistles fill the night sky as I swallow hard.

"Looks like things are about to get *very* interesting," Izzy comments.

"I suppose they are." I grab the bottle and give it a spin. Now I know how contestants on *The Price is Right* must feel when they spin the wheel, trying to get as close to a dollar as they can without going over. The anticipation and tightening in their body as it nears that magical number, then the despair when it lands on a nickel. I wonder if Lincoln is *my* dollar, or if he's simply a nickel and I should spin again.

The seconds seem to stretch as the bottle takes a few more turns around the circle, each journey getting slower and slower until it gradually bypasses Asher, then stops close to Lincoln, which causes Izzy to whistle.

With all the confidence I've found sexy since the beginning, he leans back, draping an arm along the back of the couch.

"You can use your pass if you want," he says flirtatiously, raking his gaze over my body before zeroing in on my lips. "I'll understand."

"Rules are rules," I reply in a throaty voice, batting my lashes. "Plus, I'd rather save my pass for when I have to suck on Izzy's chest."

Both men groan. I can't help but laugh. What is it about two girls together that always seems to force men to revert to hormone-crazed teenagers?

"Please don't," Asher begs. "Use your pass if you have to touch her ear, but not that. *Anything* but that."

"We'll cross that bridge *if* we get to it. But for now…" Smiling a coy smile, I turn to Lincoln, crawling across the couch and into his lap, my legs straddling him. He stiffens beneath me, jaw clenching, eyes darkening as they remain focused on me. Inching my mouth toward his, I murmur, "I believe the dice have spoken."

"I believe they have."

"And that red flag that was being waved earlier?"

"It's green, baby." He brings his hand to my head, digging his fingers into my scalp. "Conditions are *very* favorable."

"I can feel that."

Slowly, I erase the last bit of distance between us, pressing my mouth to his. The kiss is soft and reverent at first, neither one of us pushing forward. I can't, not yet, breathless from the sensation of this first touching of our lips, my body buzzing to life. If this is how I react from an innocent kiss, I shudder to think what will happen when he deepens it.

As if able to read my thoughts, a groan rips from Lincoln's throat, his hold on me tightening as he yanks me harder into him. I gasp at the feel of him, how excited he is. He takes advantage of my open mouth and swipes his tongue against mine. Instant fireworks erupt in my stomach, the raw need making me kiss him with more urgency, more desperation, more unsatisfied hunger.

I grasp at him, subtly circling my hips to relieve some of the pressure building inside me. But I fear nothing will extinguish the match he lit at our first meeting, the spark he's flamed with each subsequent encounter, so much so that the fire won't be put out easily. Not anymore.

He brings his hands to my face, our fevered kiss turning into something sweeter, more ardent, more personal, offering me a different side of him. An unexpected side. He exhales, breathing into me. It's such a strange thing, feeling another person's air expand in your lungs, giving you life. I don't even know this man, but that's what he's doing — making me feel alive.

He sensually caresses my tongue with his, heat curling down my spine as I try to remember the last time a kiss made me feel *this*. I don't even know what *this* is. And for once, I don't care. I'm just enjoying the moment before our bubble bursts.

Our motions slowing, I gradually pull back, still resting my lips on his. I don't want to stop feeling them, tasting them, savoring them. Not yet. His kisses are the sweetest drug and I an addict, wanting to squeeze every last drop I can.

"Say you want more," he whispers, his grip on my head keeping me from escaping his demand. I wouldn't try to escape him even if I could.

"I want more."

A smile slowly curves his mouth. "I want more, too. I want so much more."

# Nine

"Mmm…," I moan, squirming in my seat. My breathing is labored as I run my hand down my chest and along my stomach. "That's it. I've always wanted someone to blow on my finger."

I stop moving, opening my eyes to Lincoln's and Asher's disappointed pouts, Izzy's giggles echoing around us.

As the night wore on, it's become increasingly difficult to come up with something original before time's up, which has resulted in more throwing of the dice and spinning of the bottle. When Izzy spun and it landed on me, Asher's and Lincoln's eyes lit up like a kid running downstairs on Christmas morning. But when they looked to the dice and saw all she had to do was blow on my finger, both wore a similar expression, this time of a little kid who was told they're about to go to Disneyland and end up at the dentist instead.

"What? Were you hoping for something hotter?" I smirk as Izzy returns to the couch, Asher draping his arm along her shoulders.

As things got more personal and heated, the sexual tension within our little bubble has become palpable. Where Izzy and Asher once kept some space between them, they're now practically on top of each other. And Lincoln and I… Well, I'm desperate for another lap around the track. I get the feeling he is, too, considering last time I excused myself to use the bathroom, he waited for me in the hallway, where he proceeded to slam me against the wall, stealing another kiss. But when I attempted to drag him up to my room, he resisted, said we weren't there yet. If nothing else, the man has incredible restraint. I imagine when we finally *do* make it to the bedroom, that restraint will make things even more mind-blowing.

"Honestly, yes," Asher responds, tearing me out of my hormone-filled thoughts. "We've been waiting for one of you to spin the other and it hasn't happened. When it finally does, all you have to do is blow on her finger? I feel short-changed."

"Rules are rules," Izzy sings. "We can't just make out because you want us to, hornball." She playfully jabs him in the stomach. "If you want to see girls make out, go watch a porno."

He waggles his brows, giving her a mischievous smirk. "Want to join me?"

"Maybe later," she murmurs seductively, inching even closer to his mouth. The raw need I see coming off Asher has me wanting them to kiss, too. I can only imagine the sparks that will fly when they finally do. "Too bad there's no power. It's your turn."

She abruptly pulls back, leaving Asher momentarily bewildered, and grabs Lincoln's cell from the table. Opening the timer, she hits START. "Go."

Asher takes a beat to compose himself, then says, "Never have I ever taken a sexy selfie."

"Nope!" Izzy responds, then imitates an annoying buzzer. "Already asked. Try again."

Asher leans his head against the back of the couch. "Never have I ever slept with someone whose name I couldn't remember the next morning."

"Try again!" Izzy shouts once more. For being as buzzed as she is, she has an incredible ability to recall everything that's been said. Then again, she's always been ridiculously smart.

"Shit," Asher mutters as he licks his lips, squeezing his eyes shut.

"Tick-tock," Izzy teases.

"Never have I ever..." He runs his hand through his hair as he struggles to come up with something.

"Five seconds," Lincoln taunts.

"Never have I ever...," Asher says again, but still nothing.

"Four. Three."

"Never have I ever...," he repeats once more.

We all join in with Lincoln's countdown, shouting, "Two. One!"

Izzy grabs the bottle and thrusts it into his hand. "Spin it, baby!"

He groans in playful irritation as he places the bottle back onto the table. Taking the dice, he rolls as we all lean closer to see under the dim lighting of a few flickering candles and the firepit. When they land on KISS and LIPS, Izzy and I erupt into cheers and whistles.

"I'm so looking forward to watching you two make out," I joke, jabbing Lincoln playfully in his side.

He wraps his arm around my shoulders. The heat of his breath against my neck makes my heart skip a beat. "I'd much rather make out with you again," he murmurs in a barely audible growl that has me involuntarily squeezing my thighs together. "I'd much rather do a lot *more* than make out."

"Like what?"

He leans closer. "Be a good girl and you'll find out."

I float my eyes to his, closing the gap between us, our breath intermingling. "Maybe I like being bad."

"Is that so?"

I slowly nod, my lips hovering near his. "Oh, baby. You have no idea how bad I can really be."

He shifts in his seat, a low groan escaping his throat, just as Izzy says, "Time to spin, Asher."

Reminded we're not alone, we tear away from each other, returning our attention to the game. At first, it thrilled me, the promise of what could happen. Now all I want is to go to my room and have a different kind of game night with Lincoln.

Asher grabs the bottle and gives it a spin. Every time it closes in on Lincoln, Izzy's eyes brim with hope.

As it slows and inches toward me, Lincoln's hold on me tightens. His reaction to the mere thought of me having to kiss Asher is endearing. Then again, I doubt it will be a problem. He'd use his pass, just like Izzy used hers when she was supposed to suck on Lincoln's earlobe. I wouldn't have minded. But we don't exactly have the same history Izzy and Asher apparently have.

Finally, the bottle rolls past me and lands on Izzy. She gives him a flirtatious smile. They've had to do a few risqué things over the course of the evening, like sucking on an ear or biting a neck, but nothing more than that.

"Well then…," he begins smoothly, a smirk tugging on the corners of his lips as he looks her up and down. "I suppose it's time we finally kiss."

His statement momentarily surprises me. I'm not sure what I thought. I guess I assumed they already had.

"Unless—"

Before he can say another word, she clutches his cheeks. "I suppose it is." She lowers her back onto the couch, bringing him on top of her.

"I suppose it is," he repeats, brushing his mouth against hers, nipping on her lower lip.

"The dice says kiss my lips, not *bite* them."

"I know, but I've imagined this for years now. I need to take advantage of it while I can, while we're still in the bubble."

Izzy tenses below him. "*Years?*"

Asher nods, rubbing his nose against hers. "Yes, Iz. Years."

All the tension seems to roll off her as she hooks a leg around his waist, yanking him even tighter against her.

"What are you waiting for?"

Their kiss starts out simple and innocent, just a light meeting of mouths. But it doesn't take long for it to become more intense, more heated, more…greedy.

A finger trails down my neck as I watch them, feeling like a voyeur, but I can't look away. When Lincoln brushes my hair behind my shoulder, exposing my skin, I crane my head, silently giving him permission to keep touching me. His soft lips feathering against me causes a shiver to roll through me.

"I don't recall you rolling the dice," I whisper.

I feel his mouth curve into a smile. "It'll be our little secret." He brings his hand to my leg, brushing up and down my thigh.

"Our little secret," I repeat.

Glancing across the table to see Asher and Izzy still going

at it, oblivious to the world around them, I part my legs, an open invitation for Lincoln to continue.

His teeth clamp onto my neck and I struggle not to yelp. His hand inches higher and higher, my chest rising and falling in a quicker rhythm. When his fingers ghost against my center, sparks shoot through me. I really wish I hadn't changed into jeans. If I still had on my bathing suit, this would be even more erotic, if that's possible.

"I want you," he says gruffly.

I swallow hard, biting back my moan.

"Do you want me?"

"Yes…," I whimper.

He steals a glimpse to make sure Izzy and Asher are still occupied, which they are. "Here's what I want you to do. When the two lovebirds break away, you're going to excuse yourself. Say you're tired. I'm sure they'll want to have some privacy themselves. Once they head up, I'll come to you. Okay?"

I stare straight ahead as Izzy and Asher's passionate exchange wanes, their kiss slowly coming to an end.

Lincoln squeezes my thigh. "Okay?" he asks again, more forceful.

"Okay," I answer in a breathy voice.

"Okay," he repeats, removing his hand from me, increasing the distance between us.

A giggle bursts through, and I glance up to see Asher helping a rather flushed Izzy back into a sitting position.

"Well, that was unexpected."

"Hopefully in a good way." He wraps his arm around her, pulling her close.

"In an amazing way." She beams, fanning herself. "Now, I believe it's Lincoln's turn. Or is it Chloe's?"

"Actually…" I stand up. "I hate to be the one to put an

end to game night, but I'm beat. It's been a long day. And tomorrow will be another long one with heading home, provided the power comes back on."

Izzy pouts playfully. "Always the responsible one, aren't you?"

"Always."

Her expression brightens. "It's okay. I'll probably be going to bed soon myself."

"Alone?" I lift a brow.

She bites her lower lip, flicking a mischievous grin to Asher as she squeezes his thigh. "Only time will tell."

After saying my goodbyes to Asher, thanking him once more for allowing us to crash here, I start to head inside.

"Let me walk you," Lincoln offers, surprising me. This certainly was not part of the plan.

"I'll be fine," I insist.

"I'm sure you will, but I'd feel better if I walked with you." The tone of his voice makes it clear that this isn't up for debate. I actually like the idea of him walking me to my room. I've never been with someone who so much as walked me to my Uber or the subway station after a date. Hell, a lot of them couldn't even be asked to get out of bed to walk me to the door of their apartment.

"Okay," I say.

"Okay." He places his hand on the small of my back, shining the flashlight of his cell in front of us, illuminating our path.

Once we reach my room, I turn to him, about to thank him, when he advances toward me, pressing me against the wall, his mouth covering mine. Momentarily caught breathless by his sudden invasion, I still. But the shock eventually wanes and I melt into him, grasping his face, needing more of him.

Lincoln tears his lips from mine, growling like an animal starved for too long. "You're incredible, Chloe."

Throwing my head back, I revel in his unshaven jaw scratching against the flesh of my neck. I scrape my nails down his back, wrapping a leg around him, pulsing against him as he nips at my shoulder. Our heavy and labored breaths fill the silence, every synapse in my body firing.

His hand roams my frame, his touch needy and reckless. As he reaches my waistband, I inhale a sharp breath, my core clenching when he unbuttons my jeans.

He kisses a hot trail along my collarbone, inching his way back up my neck. His fingers swipe a line along my stomach, teasing me. Finally, he lowers the zipper and brushes the top of my panties. My muscles tighten in anticipation. He bites my earlobe, tugging at it. A bolt of need shoots through me as I struggle to maintain my composure.

"Keep going," I murmur, a slave to his touch. "Don't stop."

Growling, his teeth bite down harder as he sweeps a finger under the line of my panties.

"Do you feel what you do to me?" He subtly thrusts against me.

"Yes," I moan, my eyes rolling into the back of my head. "Yes."

He inches his hand farther south, my muscles tightening as he nears the spot I need him to touch. When he finds my center, I sigh. "And I can certainly feel what I do to you."

I bring his lips back to mine, my tongue plunging in his mouth, fireworks erupting in my core. Finally, he pushes a finger inside and I relax, bliss filling me.

"You're so wet. So tight. So fucking sweet."

"Just wait till you get a taste. You'll never want another pussy again."

"Is that right?" He arches a brow, his expression playful as he continues stretching me.

"That's right," I exhale as I move with his motions. "God, that's so right." I grab his head again, bringing his mouth to within a whisper of mine, my breathing becoming more erratic with each push, each thrust, each drive. My teeth chatter, my entire body trembling, close to unraveling.

Instantly, he pulls his hand away, releasing his hold on me. I fling my eyes open, staring at him incredulously, a panting bundle of hormones.

"What are you—"

"Suck," he demands, interrupting me, touching a finger to my lips.

My eyes remaining glued to his, I slowly open my mouth, swiping my tongue against the tip of his finger. The contact is subtle, barely there. But the way his pupils dilate tells me he's on edge, that he needs more, that he's been fantasizing about this as much as I have.

With a a moan, I wrap my lips around his finger, sucking every last drop of me off his flesh, giving each of his fingers the same treatment.

"Tell me how you taste."

Flirtatiously batting my lashes, I pass him a demure look. "Why don't you find out for yourself?" I force his lips against mine. The second our tongues touch, he groans. He tastes of need, of want, of unmatched desperation.

Too soon, he tears away, chest heaving, eyes dark. "Go. Get in your room. I'll be with you shortly."

Before I can do or say anything else, he spins around, heading toward the stairs with determined strides, leaving me a quivering mess.

"Oh, and Chloe?"

I meet his heated stare. "Yes?"

"You'd better not even think about getting yourself off while you wait for me. Tonight, I own you." His voice becomes deeper, more demanding. The hairs on my nape rise. "And that includes all your orgasms. Do you understand?"

I swallow hard. No man has ever spoken to me this way, so brazen, so confident, so…hot. There's only one way to answer him.

"Yes, Lincoln," I respond in a sultry voice as I walk the few feet toward where he stands at the top of the staircase. "I completely understand." When I reach him, I stand on my tiptoes, skimming my lips along his neck. "Hurry back."

I remain motionless for several protracted moments, my breath warming his skin. His chest rises and falls quicker, and I notice him clench and unclench his fists. I can't help but grin at how much he wants me. Then I lower my heels to the floor and turn, walking into my darkened room and closing the door behind me without a single look back.

Game night really is a lot of fun.

# Ten

I've officially worn a path in the lush carpet.

I thought Lincoln would only be a few minutes, especially once I heard Izzy come upstairs. I took a lukewarm shower, needing the tepid water to dull the flames building inside me. I figured he wouldn't be much longer once I got out, considering how needy he seemed.

But as I pace in front of the window overlooking the patio, I can still make out the gentle sound of Asher and Lincoln each strumming a guitar. As if Lincoln weren't delicious enough, he has to play the guitar, too. My ovaries all but exploded when I peered down into the yard and saw how effortless he made it look. Yet another piece of the Lincoln Moore puzzle.

Finally, the music stops, as does my pacing, my libido perking up. Any other time, I'd be upset over that, but not tonight. Not when that means Lincoln's that much closer to knocking on my door. If he's even planning on doing that. I wouldn't be surprised if he simply barges in.

I walk up to the window, doing my best to remain out of view so neither one of them realize I've been snooping. I strain to listen for the telltale sound of the French doors closing. When they do, I light up, turning to look around the room.

Should I lay on the bed in a provocative pose, beckoning Lincoln to come in if he knocks? Should I put on something sexier than my t-shirt and yoga pants? Should I be wearing anything at all?

As turned on as I am about the prospect of answering the door naked, I don't want to miss out on Lincoln undressing me. We only have one night together. I need to experience everything he has to offer.

When I hear footsteps growing closer, my heart ricochets into my throat and my eyes zero in on the door. Then the knock I've been waiting for echoes.

I rush over, pausing to inhale a calming breath. But the instant I open the door and see Lincoln holding a bottle of wine and two glasses, I can't stop my stomach from doing backflips.

"May I come in?" he asks politely, yet seductive at the same time.

"Of course." I step back and allow him to enter. Using the flashlight on his phone to light the way, he walks toward the desk by the window, placing the bottle and glasses on it. He yanks out the cork and pours a deep red liquid into each glass, handing me one.

"To blackouts," he offers as he raises his wine.

"To blackouts." I clink my glass against his, then take a sip.

"I hope you like it. I wasn't sure what kind of wine you prefer, but remember you drinking a red when I saw you Sunday night."

I allow the robust flavor to dance on my tongue, a nice change after the beer. "This is more than acceptable," I say with a smile, unable to mask the tremble in my voice. "Shiraz?" I arch a brow.

He smiles over his glass, lowering it, licking the wine off his lips. "How could you tell from just the taste? Apart from a professional sommelier, I don't know many people who could do that."

I shrug nonchalantly. "I know my wine."

"Really?"

I hold his gaze, trying to act serious. Then I laugh as I nod at the bottle, the light from the moon casting a glow over the label. While most people would have to get a better look, I'd recognize the familiar script of that logo anywhere.

"Penfolds," I say. "If there's one thing Australian wine-makers are known for, it's a fantastic shiraz."

"They certainly are." He brings his glass back to his lips, but his gaze never leaves mine. I've never felt so exposed, as if Lincoln's doing more than mentally undressing me. Maybe that's what makes him so different. He *looks* into my eyes, instead of everywhere but, as I'm accustomed to.

I take another sip of my wine as I attempt to calm my racing heart. This isn't the first time I've slept with a guy I just met. But I've never been this jittery, this desperate.

When I lower my glass, he reaches for it, not saying a single word. I allow him to take it and he places them on the desk, then faces me. My chest expands with my increasingly irregular breathing, my body aching to feel him. Finally, he palms my lower back and tugs me against him. He leans down and I crane my head, inching my lips toward his. But instead of feeling his mouth cover mine, he changes course at the last second, bringing his lips to my neck, clamping down his teeth.

I yelp, struggling to make sense of the sensations filling

me, the pleasure, the pain, everything in between. I now know where that saying "it hurts so good" comes from, because Lincoln... He definitely hurts so good. I don't even care that the harshness of his bite will most likely leave a rather prominent mark. I want him to mark me. I want to walk around, have people stare and know what I did, what I let this stranger do to me. The idea makes me burn even hotter.

When his lips finally make their journey to mine, his kiss is jarring, intense, lust-filled. He tastes of mint, spice, wine, and a flavor I surmise is uniquely Lincoln. One I fear I'll crave for weeks to come.

He clutches my face, keeping me in place, his grip powerful, demanding, confident. Everything I believe this man is. Then his eyes lift to mine, the fire in his gaze replaced with a hint of amusement.

"What?" I ask, pinching my lips together.

His smile only grows as he reaches into the pocket of his shorts and pulls out something. He opens his palm, revealing Izzy's dice. "She let me have them. Said she already has some of these back home."

"Is that right?" I pass him a flirtatious grin.

He nods. "That's right."

"Well then..." I lift myself onto my toes and brush my lips against his. "Let the games begin."

I abruptly spin from him, sauntering toward the bed. When I feel the heat of his stare on me, I glance over my shoulder, a shiver rolling through me from the lust in his eyes.

"Coming?"

"I hope to." With determined strides, he walks toward me, only needing four steps to close the distance.

I lower myself to the mattress, scooting up toward the headboard, the only light coming from the moon. Lincoln's hooded eyes lock on mine as he crawls onto the bed, advancing toward me like a lion stalking its prey.

Apart from our breathing, not a single sound can be heard in the room, the lack of any power leaving everything silent. You don't realize how many noises a house makes — air conditioning, refrigerator, whirring hum of computers — until you no longer have electricity. Every little thing seems more noticeable, more intense, more amplified. Like the way Lincoln stares at me in a way I can't recall a single person ever admiring me. Like the way our chests seem to rise and fall in perfect rhythm with each other. Like the way his tongue swipes along his lips, causing them to glisten, leaving me desperate for another taste.

Clutching his cheeks in my hands, I pull him closer and press my mouth to his, exhaling into the kiss. It's gentle, yet bubbling with a passion that's been missing from my life for too long now. He threads his fingers through my hair as I wrap my legs around his waist, needing to feel all of him. When I circle my hips against him, he groans, his tongue brushing mine with more need, more ferocity, more desperation.

"I don't remember you rolling the dice," he murmurs, throwing my own words from earlier back at me.

"Those dice don't have what I want to do on them."

"Is that so?" He lifts a single brow. "And what's that?"

I run my fingers up and down his back, my nails digging into his skin. He arches into my touch, biting his lower lip as he closes his eyes, a look of bliss washing over him. The rippling of his muscles against my hands makes me want to explore every single inch of his warm, firm body.

Curving toward him, I nibble on his earlobe. "I want to taste you."

He stares down at me, his expression playful. "You can taste me if you roll LICK and FINGER." He winks.

I slowly shake my head, my gaze unwavering. "That's not what I want to taste."

He takes my bottom lip between his teeth. I grow light-headed, wanting him to keep doing that, but harder, and to other parts of my body.

"Tell me what you want to taste, Chloe," he demands.

"You."

He loosens his bite, shifting position. "Oh, come now. I didn't take you for being shy, Pixie."

"Pixie?" I lift my brows in question.

"Exactly. You're so tiny, like a fairy, or an angel." The mood changes as he touches his lips to mine, treating me to a delicious kiss, so different from the way he just had his teeth clamped on me. "*My* angel."

"I'm not shy," I insist, pressing my hand to his chest, forcing him onto his back. Straddling him, I circle him, my motions greedy, insatiable, wanton. "And I am certainly no angel. Especially not in the bedroom."

He cups my face in his strong hands. I can't help but marvel at how big they are. Everything about us seems to be polar opposite.

He's larger than life with an intimidating physique. I'm tiny with a stature that makes me often feel overlooked.

He's a professional, intelligent man who seems to have his life together. I'm a bit of a drifter who's still trying to figure out who she is.

He looks like the quintessential all-American boy who probably played football in high school and could have his pick of any woman. I was the troublemaker, the promiscuous girl with piercings in her eyebrows, nose, and tongue.

He probably has a family who loves him, who's always

supported his decisions. I often feel like my mother blames me for the divorce, a heavy burden to bear as a teenager. And it's only grown heavier now that I'm an adult.

"Is that right?"

I nod. "That's right."

"Prove it. Tell me what you want, what you want to taste."

I open my mouth to respond when he cuts me off.

"And don't just say 'you'. I want to know *exactly* what you want to do."

I briefly press my mouth to his, then meet his gaze. "I want to suck your dick."

He stares at me for several seconds, his jaw hardened, eyes on fire. Then he slams his mouth against mine, his tongue pushing through my lips, his kiss ravenous and greedy.

When he pulls away, he grabs my hips, lifting me off him and onto the mattress beside him. Standing, he extends his hand toward me, and I allow him to help me off the bed.

"Lift your arms."

Not saying a single word, I simply follow his demand. I'd normally protest, insist on remaining in control. But we're in the bubble. Maybe the bubble's my own personal Wonderland, a place where I can lose all control and live out the fantasies I've been too scared of in the real world.

He grabs the hem of my t-shirt and pulls it over my head before tossing it to the floor. His Adam's apple bobs up and down as his eyes zero in on my bra. "Turn around."

Excited nerves simmer in my veins as I obey, facing away from him. When his lips feather that place where my neck meets my shoulders, I moan.

"That's the spot, isn't it?" he murmurs, his fingers traveling toward my bra, unhooking it with practiced expertise.

His hands go to my shoulders and he pushes the material down my arms. "Does that turn you on?" He returns his mouth to me.

"Yes." I subconsciously squeeze my legs together as his hands find their way to my stomach, the pressure building to a level I didn't think possible.

He takes his time caressing my flesh. Whenever he nears the swell of my breasts, I hold my breath, only for him to change direction and return to my stomach. I squeeze my thighs together tighter, biting down on my lower lip. I'm on the brink of telling him to bend me over the desk and fuck me already, seduction be damned. But he won't do that. He's the tortoise, not the hare. This is a marathon, not a sprint. And I have a feeling he wants this race to last all night long.

"Spread your legs," he orders when I continue to squirm. I don't immediately comply, needing something to dull the ache. He tugs my body against his, pushing a knee between my thighs, parting them. "I need you as desperate for me as I am for you." He brings his hands to my breasts, tugging at my nipples. "Because I've spent the past weekend desperate for a taste of you, Chloe."

He removes his hands from my chest, his motion quick as he spins me around. Stepping back, he crosses his arms and stares at me with a menacing gaze. "Take off your pants, but leave on your panties."

I peer at him through my lashes. "Any reason for that?"

"A magician never reveals his secrets." He winks, a hint of playfulness amidst the sexual tension.

More curious than anything, I lower my yoga pants down my legs and step out of them, waiting for Lincoln's next directive. But it doesn't immediately come. He simply stares at me in wonder, his expression softening. There's something incredibly tender about this moment as we admire each other, the moon casting a serene glow in the room, illuminating pieces of us.

"You are so beautiful." He reaches for my face, brushing a tendril of hair behind my ear. The gentleness of his statement and touch has my knees growing weak. I search my memory for someone else who looked at me the way Lincoln does, for someone else who called me beautiful. Nothing comes to mind. Sure, I've been called hot, cute, even charming, but never beautiful.

Needing to break the intensity of the moment before I allow his compassion to burst through my walls, I dig my fingers into his chest, leaning into him. "Now it's your turn."

"Yes, ma'am." He unbuttons his shirt and shrugs out of it before pushing his shorts down his strong legs.

"And Lincoln?" I arch a brow.

"Yes?"

"No need to keep on your boxers. Not for what I have planned."

"Yes, ma'am." With haste, he rids himself of his boxer briefs, and they join the rest of our discarded clothes.

Approaching him, my eyes don't waver, the atmosphere shifting from playful to sensual. His taut skin is warm as I run my fingers along his chest, savoring the little tufts of hair that dot it. Soft lips skate against mine, but I pull back, depriving him of a full kiss.

"Do you want me?" I murmur, feeling unusually powerful as I scrape my hand down his torso, wrapping my fingers around his erection.

"Fuck," he hisses, his eyes squeezing shut. I study his expression, ecstasy and need filling the lines of his face, his muscles tensing.

I raise myself onto my toes. "Say you want me." I feather my lips against his neck, my touch barely there.

"You know the answer to that."

"Oh, I know," I respond coyly. "I can feel the answer to that. But I want to hear you say it." Bringing my mouth back to his ear, I nibble on it. "Two can play your little game, ya know."

When I pull away, he opens his eyes, his stare intense and bold.

"Is that what you think this is? Just a game?"

Unwrapping my hand from his arousal, I bring both of them to his chest. "Isn't that all life is? Just a game?" I drag my tongue along his lips, retreating when he parts them for a taste. "Tell me you want me."

He jerks my body against his, grinding his hips. "I want you, Chloe. So fucking much."

The look of pure torture on his face is almost more than I can stand. Almost. But he deserves a taste of what I had to endure.

"How do you want me? What do you want me to do?"

"What do *you* want to do?"

"I already told you what I want to do. But I don't want to presume you're agreeable."

"Presume away, baby."

The intensity monetarily cracks, and I laugh. I love how he's seductive, sensual, and carnal one minute, then lightens the mood the next. I never thought it would be possible to have both. Then again, I've never met anyone like Lincoln.

Recovering, I pass him a heated stare. "Tell...me... what...you...want."

"Your mouth."

I'm about to ask him where, when he interrupts.

"On my cock. Now."

His hands land on my shoulders, putting pressure on them. Happy to oblige, I rake my fingers along his chest, allowing him to push me to my knees. When I dig my nails into his skin, he releases a growl, his nostrils flaring. Not out of anger. Out of unbridled need.

Keeping my eyes locked on his, I kneel before him, taking his erection in my hand once more. He holds his breath, every muscle in his body becoming even more rigid. And I do mean *every* muscle.

I run my tongue over my lips, my heart hammering in my chest as I pause. I may be on my knees, but I've never felt so powerful. When I slide my tongue along his length before taking him into my mouth, tension rolls off him.

"Damn, Pixie..." He digs his fingers into my scalp as he begins pumping into me, his rhythm slow at first. "You have some mouth on you, don't you? I knew that about you the instant you went off on me at the bar, but this..." His grip on my hair tightens as he wraps his hand around it, pulling it. So hungry. So desperate. So determined. "This is something I only fantasized about."

His hold becomes more forceful, guiding my head. I swirl my tongue around his tip, savoring the taste of pre-cum before relaxing my throat, taking him even deeper.

"Fuck," he groans, on the brink of unravelling. He drives harder into me, then releases my hair, suddenly stepping back.

"Wha—" I begin, but I'm soon interrupted.

"Get on the bed."

I arch a single brow, confused why he pushed away when he was seconds from his release.

"Now, Chloe," he demands.

I scramble to my feet and hurry toward the bed, scooting up to the headboard. I stare at him, expecting him to join me, but he doesn't. Not right away. He simply admires me. I grab the duvet to cover myself, but he shakes his head.

"Don't. Let me look at you."

I swallow hard, feeling exposed, but I follow his command, keeping my arms to my sides, allowing him to examine every inch of me. His admiration gives me an added boost of confidence and I prop my legs up, spreading them, an invitation to see even more of me.

His green eyes darkening, he stalks toward the bed, his steps deliberate, drawn-out, measured. When he lowers himself onto the mattress, he rests his elbows by my head and finds my lips, his kiss sweet and addicting, at complete odds with the way he just fucked my mouth. I fear this strange dichotomy will be my undoing. As much as I love being spontaneous, I prefer being able to read people, determine their next move. With Lincoln, I never know what he has planned, what his intentions are.

He moves along my jawline, down my collarbone, hovering over my alert nipple. I squirm, bracing for his touch. *Desperate* for his touch.

"Something you need, Pixie?" His voice is deep and soft.

"Yes."

"And what's that?"

I lock eyes with him. "For you to taste me."

"With pleasure." When he covers my breast with his mouth, I throw my head back, my body fusing to the mattress. "With immense pleasure."

His teeth tug on my nipple, his tongue circling it, driving me wild. I'm not sure how much more of this teasing, this buildup, this foreplay I can take before I explode. I'm on edge as it is. I've *been* on edge all day. Hell, all weekend. Now isn't the time for teasing. I'm already at my breaking point.

As if able to read my thoughts, he traces soft, tantalizing lines along the curve of my breasts, down my stomach, circling my belly button before settling between my thighs.

He hooks his fingers into my panties, and I lift my hips to allow him to lower them down my legs. Instead, he grabs my ass, propping me up. I furrow my brow, unsure what he's doing. But before I can utter a single syllable, his mouth covers my panties, the warmth of him against me driving me crazy. My underwear could be a pane of bulletproof glass instead of just a flimsy piece of fabric, for all I care. It's still a very unwelcome barrier.

"Please," I moan as he continues licking and sucking on me through my panties.

"Something I can help you with?"

"Yes." I narrow my eyes. "I need your mouth on me."

"It is on you."

"No. On my skin. No panties."

He studies me for a moment, then shakes his head. "I told you before that all your orgasms belong to me tonight, did I not?"

"You did," I exhale, desperate for release, to have him consume every inch of me.

"That means I get to decide exactly *how* you come. And I want you to come like this." He brings his mouth back to me, sucking and nibbling, and I melt into it, moving with the rhythm he sets. I have to admit, there's something incredibly erotic about this.

It doesn't take long for that familiar sensation to bubble in my core. My muscles tense as I pulse against him with more urgency. He moans, the vibration pushing me higher and higher. Then he scrapes his teeth on my clit, sucking, and I scream, waves of ecstasy washing over me as I come undone, riding out one of the most intense orgasms for what feels like hours, but is probably only a minute or two.

When I finally start to return to earth, he meets my eyes and smirks, hooking his fingers into my panties and sliding them down my legs. Then he returns to me, burying his mouth between my thighs. I exhale in utter bliss, savoring in how expertly he tastes me, his tongue drawing out my orgasm even longer.

"Fuck, you're wet."

"It's what you do to me." I lower my hand, toying with my clit, spreading my juices around. Bringing my finger to my mouth, I suck on it, recalling how much it turned him on before. And that's all it takes to turn him on again. He grabs my hips, his movements quick as he flips me onto my stomach. His arm snakes under my waist and he props me onto my knees.

He leans over me, his chest hair tickling my back. "Is this okay? Having you from behind?"

"Y-yes," I stammer.

While I prefer being on top so I can be the one in control, I'll take Lincoln however he wants. This position is probably better anyway. I won't have to look him in the eyes. I'll be able to stay detached. I'll be able to walk away and carry on with my life when the blackout is over.

"Good." He straightens himself and steps off the mattress. I watch as he grabs his shorts, pulling a condom from his wallet.

Not saying a word, he returns to the bed and grasps my head, forcing my eyes forward once more. I don't argue. Don't protest. Don't return my gaze to his. I stare at the headboard, every noise putting me more on edge.

Finally, the bed dips and I feel his erection against me, teasing me. I close my eyes, rocking back into him.

"You're greedy, aren't you?"

"Yes." I bury my head into the pillow.

"Tell me what you want." He inches himself inside. I

sigh, bracing for him to push the rest of the way. But he doesn't. Instead, he pulls out, waiting for my response.

"I want you to fuck me," I pant, aching for him.

My desperate plea ringing in the air, he slams into me. Both of us still as he fills me to the hilt, savoring this sensation of fullness that's so new, so unexpected, yet so satisfying. He exhales, as if also surprised at how incredible it feels.

Then he covers my body with his, his hands gliding up my arms, his fingers linking with mine. When he moves, gently at first, I sigh, matching his rhythm. He kisses my shoulder blade, skating his teeth against my skin.

"And for the record, I'm not fucking you, Chloe."

"Then what do you call this?"

"Possession, plain and simple."

I moan at his gravelly voice, losing myself in this erotic moment.

"Possessing your mind, your soul…" He clamps his teeth onto my neck, pain pulsing through me momentarily before being replaced by the unmatched pleasure building from his measured movements. "Your body."

"Oh god…" I ball my hands into tighter fists, my grip on his fingers intertwined with mine growing stronger. I bury my head into the pillow, biting down on it.

I can honestly say I've never been with a man like Lincoln, a man so practiced in the art of seduction. Sex is supposed to be an act that tantalizes your senses, hypnotizes your mind, captures your heart, breathes life into your soul. But not for me. I've made sure of that. Until now.

He moves with greater urgency, his own breathing erratic and uneven. With each thrust, he drives deeper and deeper, forcing my body to climb higher and higher until I scream, falling apart, my mind becoming hazy, unable to form a coherent thought.

"That feels incredible," Lincoln exhales, his voice strained as he pumps faster, drawing my orgasm out. When I'm not sure whether I can take any more, he grunts, thrusting deep into me, holding my hips in place as he jerks through his own release.

We remain motionless for several long moments, both of us struggling to get our breathing under control. As his body covers mine, I feel his heart beating violently in his chest. Satisfaction fills me at the idea that I did this to him, that I worked him up to this point of exertion.

"Goddamn," he says, slowly withdrawing and peeling off me.

His touch is gentle as he supports my stomach, helping to lower me onto the mattress. My legs have never shaken or quivered as much as they are right now. I've never been this sated after sex. A woman could get used to this.

Once he's certain I'm okay, he pushes off the bed, grabbing the duvet and covering my body with it. He rids himself of the condom, tossing it into the nearby trashcan before returning to me. Without saying a word, he crawls in beside me, pulling me into his arms, my back to his front. I need to clean up, but I'm content in this moment, my brain quiet for a change.

"I don't remember inviting you to stay the night," I tease in a lazy voice.

"You didn't." He plants soft kisses along my neck and shoulder, causing that fluttering to erupt in my stomach once more.

"Then what makes you think I want you to stay?"

"Because I know something you don't."

"And what's that?"

"That I'm a huge fan of morning sex. If you thought that was incredible…" He circles his hips. Moisture pools between my thighs and I'm instantly ready for round two, or three. I've lost count at this point. "That was just a warm-up for tomorrow."

I turn around to face him. "You think so, do you?"

"I don't think…" He brings his lips toward mine. "I know."

When he leans in to kiss me, I press my hand against his chest, pushing him away. Taking advantage of his momentary surprise, I force him onto his back and crawl on top of him.

"Well, *I* know something you don't, too." I bring my mouth to his.

"And what's that?"

I bite his lower lip and tug at it before releasing it. "That I'm not done with you yet."

"God, I love blackouts."

# Eleven

An obnoxious pinging wakes me from one of the best night's sleep I've had in a long time. Then again, Lincoln worked me to the point of utter exhaustion. I've never been with someone as enthusiastic and salacious. And let's not even talk about his stamina. With him, it certainly is a marathon. Slow and steady won the race. Again. And again. And again.

It takes me a few moments to register what I'm hearing, the sound strange against the silence. Then it hits me — my cell phone.

I bolt up, grabbing it off the nightstand, surprised to learn I have service again and am being bombarded with texts from my concerned friends.

NORA:

Ohmigod. I just saw the news. A blackout in Vegas? What happened? You'd better text and tell me you're okay. You guys better be okay. Please text. Like now.

EVIE:

Hey. I heard about the blackout in Vegas. I know you and Izzy are still stuck in that shithole. Just let me know you're okay. The news says cell towers have been affected so I don't expect an immediate response, but I promised Nora I'd text. You know how she can be about stuff like this. There's no reasoning with her. Love you. Stay safe.

Flopping back onto the bed, I check my flight status to see it's not canceled, then type out a quick text to both of them to let them know I'm okay and that I'll be getting into New York later today. Curious as to what happened to cause the loss of power for a little over twelve hours, I open the web browser and run a quick search. Unfortunately, there's not much information, apart from the fact that Vegas lost power for a period lasting a little over twelve hours, but that all power and cell service is now restored.

I'm about to check my email, cringing at the idea of all the unanswered messages waiting for me, when an arm snakes around my waist. If it were anyone else, I'd shrug them off, make up some excuse, like needing to get to the airport to catch my flight, which I do, but I crave one last taste of Lincoln before our bubble bursts.

Moaning, I melt into him, craning my neck to give him better access. He feathers light kisses against my skin, his touch different from the commanding, dominant lover he was last night. Now he's gentle, tender, affectionate. Truth be told, I like this side of him just as much. Maybe even a little more.

His hand roams from my stomach, creeping its way up to my chest. As his fingers ghost over one of my nipples, I whimper, my body coming alive. He pushes me onto my back, then crawls between my legs. His vibrant green eyes are lazy in the light of day, his exhaustion from our night of sin evident. But that doesn't stop him from wanting me again.

Lowering his mouth to my breast, he delicately scrapes his teeth along the sensitized flesh of my nipple, and I lose myself to his touch yet again. Synapses firing, I wrap my legs around his waist, thrusting against him, my body a slave to sensation.

"Say you want me." His voice is raspy from broken sleep.

I smile, running my hands through his hair. Every time he woke me up in the middle of the night, he demanded the same thing. Now, whenever I hear those words, I'll only think of Lincoln, of his desperation to have my desire.

"I want you."

"Say you need me." This time, his plea is filled with more urgency.

"I need you."

Groaning, he pulls away. I loosen my grip around his waist, allowing him to lean back and roll on a condom.

"And I need you. More than I've needed anything." He covers my mouth as he pushes into me, filling me to my breaking point before retreating, continuing the same torturous, yet satisfying rhythm. Over. And over. And over.

Unlike last night, there are no carnal words, no harsh, punishing motions. It's sweet and affectionate, making me feel more fulfilled than any previous sexual encounter. My body quivers, my heart quickening as I struggle to think of something else, *anything* other than the amazing way Lincoln seems to strum me, like a practiced musician would his instrument.

He lowers his mouth to my neck, licking and biting before he murmurs, "Let go, baby. Let me have it."

My breathing grows ragged when his motions increase.

Before I can fight against it, I unravel, a kaleidoscope of lights blinding me. He moans my name, finding his own release before collapsing on top of me, nuzzling his head against my chest.

I run my fingers through his wayward hair, swiping at the sweat on his brow. My eyes shift to the window, sunlight beaming into the room. Everything seems so different in the light of day. I'm not sure if it's a good different or bad different.

"Come to dinner with me." Lincoln's voice cuts through the tranquility.

I smirk. "Did you forget I'm headed home today? My flight's still showing as being on time."

"Not here. Back in New York. I want to take you out."

My heart catches in my throat, my body becoming rigid, my brain unable to tell my lungs to breathe, to perform that simple task of drawing in air, then exhaling.

Noticing my reaction, Lincoln pulls back, meeting my eyes, his brow wrinkled in confusion. "What is it?"

I shake my head, my lips parting. Most normal people would agree, would want to see if these feelings were real, if they'd survive outside the bubble. But I'm not most people. I don't have the luxury of being able to pursue a fantasy.

Pushing against him, I free myself from his hold and roll off the bed, scrambling around the room for my discarded clothes.

"Chloe, what is it?" He stands, stepping toward me. "I thought you—"

"Trust me," I interrupt, finding my yoga pants and tugging them on after the search for my panties ends up being fruitless. "You don't want that. We're not exactly compatible, are we?"

I stumble across my t-shirt and yank it on, feeling much

more comfortable having this conversation now that I'm dressed. Lincoln doesn't seem to mind his lack of clothes, though. He's still as confident as he was last night. As he was yesterday when he gave me that lame tortoise and the hare analogy. As he was that first night I saw him.

"We're as opposite as they come," I continue, my tone frantic. "Not just in physical appearance, but in personality. There's no way this…" I gesture between our two bodies, "would ever work out. We don't even know each other."

This was never an issue with any of the other guys in my past. But they were aware of the score going in. They were *happy* with the score going in. I broke one of my rules. I failed to have that important conversation with Lincoln. I didn't think I had to. We all agreed last night. What happens in the bubble stays in the bubble.

"And once you get to know the real me, you'll—"

"Do you always try to control everyone else's decisions?" he interrupts, his voice calm.

"I don't try to control everyone else's decisions."

"You're doing it right now. You're standing here, claiming I'd never want to be with you, the real you, but you won't even give me a chance to get to *know* the real you. That's all I want. A chance."

I wrap my arms around my torso, shrinking into my tiny frame. "Once you get to know the real me, you'll understand how much of a mistake it is. Last night was great. Better than great. But we were in the blackout bubble."

"What about this morning? The blackout bubble is gone, yet I still want to know you. I still feel the same thing I did last night. That hasn't changed just because the power's back on. I still feel this connection. And I know you do, too."

"That wasn't a connection. That was just the result of

too much alcohol, being stuck in this house, and a pair of dice."

"You're wrong. I felt it the instant I touched you Saturday night. The entire time you were going off about how much you loathed Vegas, all I could think was that I wanted to know you, but that I'd never get the chance. And then I did. We kept running into each other. Over. And over. And I knew it wasn't a coincidence. That it wasn't just a chance meeting. I didn't even know your name, yet what I felt for you was stronger than anything I've felt for anyone in a really long time. It makes no sense, and I can't even attempt to explain it without sounding like I'm fucking crazy, but there it is... I just..." He licks his lips, his chest heaving as he collects his thoughts.

It takes every ounce of resolve I possess not to avert my eyes to steal a glimpse below his waist. But that's not a solution. Not here, not now.

"I'm not asking you to move in," he says, his voice softer. "Hell, I'm not even asking you to be my girlfriend. I'm just asking you to take a chance on getting to know me, on allowing me to get to know you. To see if this has the potential I feel in my heart it does."

On a long inhale, I close my eyes. Maybe if my life weren't so complicated, I'd be able to say yes. Just like it takes a certain type of person to date a woman who already has children of her own, it also takes a certain type of person to date a woman who has an alcoholic mother. When she falls, I'm the only one who cares enough to catch her. And when I do, Lincoln will just let me fall, too.

I open my mouth, wanting to tell him all of this so he'll understand. Instead, all I can muster is, "I'm sorry." I hold his gaze for a moment, then dash into the bathroom, closing the door behind me.

Seconds stretch as I lean against the wall, hyper-aware of every sound. Every heartbeat. Every breath. Every frustrated sigh. Finally, after what feels like an eternity, I hear his footsteps retreat, the door to my room closing. I exhale deeply in what should feel like relief, but it isn't. It's something else.

Regardless, I shake off the exchange, convinced I made the right decision. As great as last night was, it wasn't real. We were in a fantasy world where nothing else existed outside the bubble. Fantasy and reality don't mix. Lincoln and I in the real world won't mix.

Not wanting to get stuck in Vegas yet another night because I missed my flight, I turn on the water and take one of the quickest showers of my life. As I rush around the room, throwing my few belongings back into my suitcase, I spy a piece of paper placed on the desk next to the full wine glasses from last night.

I stop in my tracks, my heart thumping as I walk toward it, admiring Lincoln's neat, yet masculine scrawl.

*Dear Chloe,*

*I meant what I said. I do believe we have a connection. This connection won't go away simply because the blackout is over. I felt it before. And I still feel it now. There's a reason we kept running into each other. The universe has a plan for us. You just need to finally realize that.*

*Until then, I'll be yours...*

*Lincoln*

*P.S. - I took your panties. If you want them back, meet me at The Living Room in the Park Hyatt. Thursday night. 9 o'clock.*

The sound of a door slamming reverberates through the house, and I snap my eyes away from the paper, dropping it on the desk. I listen as heavy footsteps storm from Izzy's room, past mine, continuing down the hall. I get the feeling things didn't end well between Izzy and Asher, either.

My phone dings, alerting me to a text message and I rush to it, finding a message from Izzy.

IZZY:

Requested an Uber. Will be here in ten. Meet me by the front gate.

I type out a quick reply.

ME:

Okay. Just packing up.

I hit send, then finish throwing all my things into my suitcase. Once I'm confident I have everything I came here with, well...*almost* everything, I open the door to head out to catch our ride to the airport. Glancing behind me one last time, I spy Lincoln's note, taunting me.

"Oh, fuck it," I exhale, rushing to the desk and stuffing the paper into my bag.

The house is silent as I make my way down the steps, everything about this place different from the day before. It lacks life, vitality...hope. All the more reason I need to get out of this town as quickly as possible.

I step out the front door and walk down the long drive toward where Izzy's already standing, looking down the street for our ride.

"Hey, Iz."

"Hey, Chloe."

Neither one of us says anything else for several long moments. Despite the silence, our thoughts are deafening. I glance at her, catching her eyes. We both shrug at the same time, then say, "Vegas."

Our laughter fills the air as we wrap our arms around each other, offering the comfort we know we both need.

When our laughter dies down, Izzy comments, "So you're not going to see him again." It's not a question. She knows me, is fully aware of my reasons for not getting involved.

I pull out of her embrace. "What choice do I have?"

She pinches her lips together, nodding. Thankfully, she doesn't press the issue.

"You're not going to see him again?" I ask.

She meets my eyes. "What choice do *I* have?"

# Twelve

"Nothing interesting happened in Vegas? At all?"

I smile at Nora's doe-eyed expression, grateful to be back in New York and doing something I do every week — Thursday happy hour with two of my best friends.

"It was just an uneventful weekend in the tenth ring of hell," I say dismissively, taking a sip of my martini.

"Apart from the blackout," Nora says. "Do you have any idea how worried we were?"

"I read the texts," I respond, rolling my eyes. "All 187 of them, Nora."

"I did *not* send 187," she scoffs, indignant, smoothing her strawberry-blonde hair. Then she gives me a devious smile. "It was more like 186."

The sound of our laughter carries through the trendy bar. This is exactly what I needed after my weekend. A night with my girls. As I take in my surroundings, it's almost like I never left New York. The city's still the same. Nora still gets distracted anytime I ask her a question about her own wedding plans. Evie is still madly in love with her boyfriend, Julian. And I'm the perpetual single girl. Same as it was last week, and the week before that, and the week before that. My experience in Vegas didn't change any of that.

At least that's what I tell myself.

"So, tell me…" Evie squares her shoulders. "How *was* the bachelorette party? Did you have to wear something ridiculous, like a crown of penises?"

"No crown of penises, but I did have to wear a necklace of phalluses." I furrow my brow, deep in thought. "Phalli? Phalluses?"

I look between my two friends as we all murmur amongst ourselves, as if trying to answer a riddle.

"Actually, it can be either," Aiden, our bartender, interjects with a wink.

I turn my attention to him and tip my glass toward him before taking a sip. "Thanks, Aiden. What would we do without you?"

"Pay a lot more for your drinks than you do."

"I'll drink to that." Evie salutes him with her manhattan before sipping it.

"Please tell me there are pictures of you wearing a line of phalluses around your neck." Nora's eyes all but plead with me to admit there are.

"Probably. But that's not even the worst part."

"There's something worse than wearing penises around your neck?" Evie asks in disbelief.

"Oh yes. We all had tank tops. *Bedazzled* tank tops."

"Oh god," she laughs, a devilish glint in her eyes. "What was on it?"

"Mine said 'Bride's Bitch'. And the maid of honor wore one that said 'Bitch of Honor'."

They look equally horrified at the thought.

"I can promise we won't be doing anything that cheesy for my wedding."

"And this, my darling Nora, is why I love you." I raise my martini glass, toasting her.

"You'd love me even if I made you wear a crown of penises."

"You're right. I would." I pass her a sincere look, then bring my drink to my lips, sipping on it. When a song I recognize from Fallen Grace comes over the speakers, I choke on it, liquid shooting out of my mouth.

Before Vegas, I never paid much attention to the band. In the past twenty-four hours since I landed back at JFK, I feel like I see and hear them everywhere, a constant reminder of what I did in their Vegas house while they were back in London.

Almost like the universe refuses to let me forget it.

"What is it?" Evie asks in concern.

"Nothing. Drink went down the wrong pipe. That's all."

At that moment, a bar back rushes behind the counter, his arms filled with bottles. "Here's the Belvedere you need-ed," he says, handing them over to Aiden, who gets to work on restocking the shelves. All I can do is stare at the sleek bottle, trying to convince myself it's just a coincidence. It has to be. I'd purposely ordered a different kind of vodka for my martini to avoid the memory of Lincoln. Yet someone, some*thing* doesn't want me to forget.

"Chloe?" Nora says.

I whip my eyes to hers, my expression panicked, confused, and everything in between. "I—"

A flicker from the large screen television hanging over the bar catches my attention. I lift my eyes, scrunching my nose at the low-budget commercial for a used car dealership. Normally I wouldn't give it a second glance, but I can't stop staring at the actors dressed as George Washington, Benjamin Franklin, and you guessed it…Abraham Lincoln.

I could deal with hearing Fallen Grace. The radio stations play them at least once an hour. But the Belvedere vodka and a commercial with Abraham Lincoln? It's too much. Maybe Lincoln was right. Maybe the universe *does* have a plan for us.

Pushing out of my barstool, I grab a few bills to cover my drink and throw them onto the bar. I check my phone to see it's just a few minutes after nine. If I hurry, I can still make it.

"Where are you going?" Evie asks as I shrug into my jacket, then pull on my gloves and wrap my scarf around my neck.

I meet their curious expressions, parting my lips as I struggle for a way to explain this. There's so much I *should* tell them, but time is not on my side. Instead, I give them the short answer.

"I need to go see a man about a pair of panties."

Then I turn from their confused faces, running as fast as I can in my rather impractical boots away from the bar and toward the Park Hyatt, pushing through the crowded sidewalks, tourists and locals not moving as quickly as I want them to. At least Lincoln chose somewhere close to our usual Thursday evening spot. I would've been screwed otherwise.

The air is frigid, the wind whipping my face, but I've never felt so warm, so sure, so happy. When I reach the hotel, I momentarily pause, staring up at the tall building. Everything's about to shift. I'm taking a risk if I walk inside. And I'm taking a risk if I don't. But now I know which risk I *want* to take. I can no longer deny there's a reason our paths crossed. The universe made that loud and clear tonight.

Resolved, I step into the foyer, then take the elevator to the lobby. The ride seems to last an excruciatingly long time instead of the few seconds it actually does. When the doors open, I exit and am instantly swallowed up into the frenzied atmosphere of the lobby in the Manhattan luxury hotel.

Spying The Living Room past the check-in desk, I move

toward it, my heels seeming to echo in the cavernous space as I cross the threshold into the swanky lounge. Couches and chairs fill the area, giving it the feel of being an actual living room instead of a bar.

My eyes float between the tables, looking for a familiar face. But I don't see one. I grab my phone out of my purse to check the time. 9:30. Maybe I'm too late. Maybe he's already left, thinking I wouldn't show up.

My shoulders dropping, I turn around, hoping the universe will ensure our paths cross again. At this point, it's all I can do. Or Facebook stalk him. Thank god for social media.

Just as I'm about to head out, my gaze settles on a pair of familiar green eyes at a table in a secluded corner, and my mouth ticks up into a smile, a tiny exhale of air escaping. He's dressed similarly to the way he was during our first few encounters — tailored jacket, crisp shirt, designer shoes. It's been less than forty-eight hours since I last saw him, but it feels like it's been an eternity.

His stare unwavering, he slowly stands, buttoning his suit jacket as he makes his way toward me. You know those scenes in movies when everything else falls away, leaving just the two main characters? That's what happens here. The world around us instantly disappears. We're no longer in a popular lounge in Midtown Manhattan. I'm no longer thinking about all the stress in my life. It's just Lincoln. Just us. Just this bubble. An incredibly sexy and addictive bubble.

As he approaches, his scent grows stronger, wrapping me in comfort. I thought it would be strange to see him anywhere other than Vegas, but it's not. It feels...right.

"You're late." His deep voice sends heat curling down my spine.

"I'm rarely on time."

Several silent heartbeats pass as he peers at me, almost convinced I'm not real. "These panties must be pretty special if you came all the way here just to get them back."

I slowly shake my head. "You can keep them."

"Then why are you here?" He arches a single brow.

I stand on my toes, my mouth feathering against his. "For you."

He brings me into his warm body, enclosing me in his perfect embrace. "God, I was hoping you'd say that."

He's about to kiss me when I press my hand on his chest, stopping him. "But this doesn't mean I'm going to move in with you," I say, repeating the same words from his own plea. "This doesn't mean I'm going to be your girlfriend... Not right away. All this means is that I'm willing to get to know you. That I'm willing to let you know me. That's all this is. Just a chance."

"That's all I ever wanted with you, Pixie. A chance."

# Thirteen

I 've often wondered what heaven would be like.

Not really as motivation to live a virtuous life. More like…curiosity.

Is it like floating on clouds with beautiful music playing in the background, St. Peter welcoming you with open arms, as is depicted in popular folklore?

Or maybe everyone's heaven is personal. Maybe Mother Theresa's heaven is filled with all the people she strove to help, no more signs of hunger or abuse. Robin Williams is probably free from depression, cracking jokes about anything and everything. And Steve Jobs' heaven is probably a replica of that garage in Los Altos where he built the first Apple computer.

Just like my heaven is wrapped in the arms of a man who was a mystery mere days ago, one I never planned to see again. But I couldn't stay away.

Yup. I have found my own personal slice of heaven here on earth. And his name is Lincoln Moore.

An arm snakes around my midsection, pulling me against a large, firm body. Chest hair tickles my back as I relax into him. Nuzzling his nose into the crook of my neck, he inhales, then moans. The deep, guttural sound sparks my libido to life, although it doesn't need much help. Not after our night of some of the most amazing sex I've experienced. Of acting like two long-time lovers who haven't seen each other in months, maybe years.

In reality, we're practically strangers. All I know about Lincoln Moore is he's a lawyer I kept running into while I was in Vegas for the bachelorette party from hell.

Oh, and that he's incredible in bed.

And against a wall.

And on the kitchen island.

I'm looking forward to finding out how amazing he is in even more places and positions.

"How are you feeling?" he rasps out as his tongue traces a circle on that spot where my neck meets my shoulder, causing a shiver to trickle down my spine.

It's amazing how he's learned to read my body in such a short amount of time. What I like, what turns me on. A trained musician playing an instrument, familiar with the exact spot that makes me hum, makes me vibrate, makes me sing.

"Horny."

It's silent for a beat. Then his throaty laugh echoes against the walls of his bedroom. "What am I going to do with you?"

I shift in the bed, peering into his lazy eyes, the green still dazzling first thing in the morning. Hooking a leg around his waist, I subtly circle my hips, his need for me already prominent.

"I have a few ideas."

In one swift move, he rolls onto his back, pulling me on top of him. My legs fall on either side of him and I lean down, allowing my hair to form a curtain around us. I feather my lips against his, then retreat. He cranes his head, chasing my kiss, but I remain just out of reach.

"Do you like being a tease?"

Readjusting my position so I'm sitting upright, I bite on my lower lip, smiling coyly as I move against him. "I think *you* like it when I'm a tease." My voice is demure as I bat my lashes.

With a growl, he grabs the back of my head, his fingers digging into my scalp as he brings my mouth within an inch of his. My breathing becomes ragged, raw hunger flowing through me.

No man has ever turned me on to the level Lincoln has. No man has ever brought me to the brink of the kind of pleasure I didn't think possible, then pushed me over the edge to the point of oblivion. No man has ever brought me to my knees, made me want more.

But I do.

I want so much more from him.

I lick my lips, then plump them out, encouraging him to dive in for a taste. Instead, his teeth clamp onto my lower lip. The ache hits me in my core, making me burn even hotter for him. He wraps his arm around me and flips me onto my back, covering my body with his. Brushing my hair away from my face, his eyes lock with mine, vibrant green to my lackluster gray. I wonder if he can read my thoughts, if he knows I'm mentally comparing him to every man in my past, every mistake, every reminder of why I've always done things my way.

"Don't." A single word is all I need to confirm my suspicions.

I part my lips, but he captures my protest with a mind-erasing kiss.

In my lifetime, I've been treated to thousands of kisses.

Not one of them has touched me like Lincoln's do. Have made me feel like they were invading my soul. Like I needed them to breathe. Like I'd perish without them.

"I don't want you to think about anything else when you're with me," he whispers against my mouth, the roughness of his unshaven jawline invigorating as he leisurely makes his way down my body. "Like we said last night." He floats his eyes to mine as he settles between my legs. "I'm just asking for a chance. We'll take things slow."

When his tongue lands on that spot that brings me extraordinary pleasure, I sigh, succumbing to him. I doubt this qualifies as taking things slow.

But it feels too good to tell him to stop now.

---

"Shit. Shit. Shit." I check my watch to see it's almost eight in the morning, then drop to my hands and knees and search under Lincoln's bed for my panties. It's a mystery how they always seem to disappear around this man. Then it hits me.

Jumping to my feet, I grab my boots and head down the hallway of his apartment in the heart of Chelsea's art center. The exposed brick, combined with steel accents and reclaimed wood furniture, give it a masculine vibe. It's not a huge place, but given the real estate prices in this part of the city, it's probably valued at a couple million. Yes, he's a lawyer, but he's still young. At least he seems young. I'm not sure how old he is. I'm not sure I *want* to know how old he is.

I round the corner into the living room and skitter to a halt, the scene that greets me leaving me breathless.

From the instant I met Lincoln, I found him attractive. Dark hair. Mesmerizing green eyes. Muscular build. A perpetual five o'clock shadow that had me fantasizing about what it would feel like scraping on my thighs.

When I was treated to the vision of him playing guitar, I didn't think anything could top that in terms of sexiness.

I was wrong.

So fucking wrong.

Because I've discovered something even sexier than Lincoln Moore, all six-foot-three of pure masculinity, playing guitar.

And that's him sitting at the round bistro table in his breakfast nook, an impressive view of the Manhattan skyline visible in the wide expanse of windows behind him, reading the *New York Times*, a pair of dark-framed glasses on his face.

"Fuck me," I murmur, then slap a hand over my mouth.

He looks up, a brow cocked. With a smirk, he folds the paper and pushes back from the table, standing. I don't think I'll ever tire of seeing him dressed this way. Something about the dark jeans and tweed blazer makes him look like a sexy college professor. Maybe if my professors were as attractive as Lincoln, I would have been more excited about learning. Hell, I may have even taken them up on their offers of extra help.

"I think I did." He leans toward me, his lips brushing against my cheek. It's an innocent gesture, but it still leaves me lightheaded. "Quite a few times, if I'm not mistaken."

He pulls back and winks. I briefly consider dragging him back into the bedroom for one more quickie.

With the glasses on.

Increasing the distance before I make us both late for work, I cross my arms over my chest, pinching my lips into a tight line.

"On that note, you wouldn't know where my panties are, would you?"

"Why? Have they gone missing?" he asks in faux surprise.

"Indeed." My hands rest of the lapels of his jacket, able to make out the defined muscles even through the few layers of clothes.

"Hmm. It's quite the mystery, isn't it? We should open an investigation into the matter."

I shake my head, inching my lips closer to his. It doesn't matter how many kisses he showered me with over the past twelve hours. I still need one more.

I have a feeling I'll *always* need one more.

"That's unnecessary. I already have a suspect in mind."

He playfully arches a single brow. "Is that right?"

"That's right."

He palms my lower back, yanking me hard and fast into his body. "And who is this panty thief?"

"You," I breathe.

"Prove it."

"I can't. Not yet. But it fits your M.O. You *do* have a track record of stealing my panties and using them as a bargaining chip."

His lips feather against mine. "You know what they say, don't you?"

"What's that?" My husky voice is unrecognizable. I suppose that's the Lincoln Moore effect. He has me acting like a completely different woman.

Or maybe being with him allows me to be myself for a change.

"Desperate times call for desperate measures." His lips move from mine, trailing hot kisses along my jawline, settling in that spot where my neck meets my shoulders. He nibbles as I throw my head back, allowing him to push me against the floor-to-ceiling windows. The chill of the January air on the other side of the pane tempers the heat coiling in my veins.

"And what had you desperate enough to steal my panties?"

"It worked last time, didn't it?" His gaze locks with mine, his smile revealing the devil hiding beneath the tweed jacket. "I had to make sure you came…" He smirks, then finishes, "back."

I thread my fingers through his hair, pulling him to me. "I knew I could get you to admit you took them."

A beat passes before he groans, grinding his body against mine. "Naughty girl. You play a wicked game, don't you?"

"It's how we got here, isn't it?" I say breathlessly. "By playing wicked games?"

"There's no one else I'd want to play these games with, Pixie." The sincerity in his voice almost has me running for the hills. Instead, I lean in, savoring in the heat of his mouth pressed firmly against mine.

When he retreats, I avert my eyes, out of my comfort zone. I've never stayed the night with a guy before. Well, I suppose I did Tuesday night when I let Lincoln sleep in my bed during the blackout. But there was no awkward goodbye. I ran off and locked myself in the bathroom before we could get to that point.

But now, I'm at that point. What do I do? What's the proper protocol? Do we make plans to see each other again? How soon is too soon? I wish I'd asked Nora or Evie. But that would mean telling them about Lincoln. I'm not sure I'm ready to share him with anyone yet. I'm not sure we're at that stage in…whatever this is.

"Well…" I clear my throat, pushing against him. "I should get going, so…" I arch a brow, expectant.

"So?" he says when I don't finish my thought.

"My underwear?" I hold out my hand.

"What about them?"

"Aren't you going to give them back?"

"I wasn't planning on it." There's an arrogance about him as he retreats from me, bringing his now empty coffee mug into the open kitchen area. I look around his clean apartment, marveling at the simple act of him washing out his coffee mug. I tend to allow mine to collect for days before I finally throw them all into the dishwasher.

"Why?" I follow on his heels. "Concerned the only thing of value you can offer me is my own underwear?"

He ponders my question for a moment, then advances toward me as I stand near the island, a hand on my hip. "I'm more than confident I can offer you something else of value."

"And what's that?"

He shrugs, the heat that was present in his eyes turning into something...more. "Me."

"I— " I stammer, words escaping me. I've never met anyone so transparent, someone who laid it all out there for the world to see. In a way, I envy that about him, wish I could be more like that. But I can't. Not with my past. Or my present.

Able to sense my unease, he covers my mouth with his. "Whenever you're ready. No pressure. Like I said—"

"I know," I breathe. "Just a chance."

"Exactly. Just a chance." His reassurance lingers as he places a hand on my lower back and leads me toward the foyer. "But I'm still keeping your panties."

Huffing, I playfully roll my eyes. "I'm going to run out of panties soon. Then what are you going to do to lure me back to your lair of sex?"

"I'll figure something out." When we reach the door, I face him, and he curves into me, our lips meeting. "I can be pretty resourceful."

"I've heard that about you."

# Fourteen

The familiar drone of a frenzied newsroom meets me the second I round the corner behind the reception desk of *Blush* magazine. Nails click at keyboards. Phones ring incessantly. Low music plays from some cubicles...except those belonging to the fashion department. Their little area is often akin to a rave.

Glancing at my watch to see it's five minutes before ten, I hurry to my desk and drop my bag before continuing through the open space, a woman on a mission.

I duck into the breakroom to find it empty, considering most of the editors are probably already in the conference room waiting for the weekly meeting. I'll need to pull some sort of story out of my ass to pitch today. It won't be the first time.

I make a beeline to the Nespresso machine, pop a pod into the brewer, and place a cup beneath the spout. The instant the nutty aroma fills my senses, my shoulders relax. After my night of little sleep, I need this magical concoction. Espresso is the perfect pick-me-up when you want something stronger than coffee but weaker than cocaine.

"You needed to see a man about a pair of panties?" a familiar voice cuts through my moment of peace.

I curse under my breath, then whirl around, meeting Evie's hardened expression as she leans against the door-jamb, arms crossed over her chest, an inquisitiveness in her green eyes.

How was I going to explain my sudden retreat from the bar last night? And the panties? I hadn't given it much thought this morning, thanks to the spell Lincoln cast over me.

With my head held high to make my five-foot-two frame appear bigger than it is, I grab my espresso and walk toward her. "One of my hook-ups kept a pair of my underwear. I wanted them back."

I avoid her stare as I skirt past her, heading toward the conference room. I've never looked forward to our Friday staff meeting as much as I do right now, if for no other reason than to give me a few minutes to figure out what to tell my friends.

I should be able to gush about this new guy in my life. But that's never been my thing. In fact, there's never been a guy in my life *to* gush about. Isn't there a waiting period required by law before doing that or something? Lincoln and I aren't even an item. At least, I don't think we are. I'm not sure *what* we are. All I know is he's got me all out of sorts.

And he likes stealing my panties.

"I wasn't born yesterday, Chloe." Evie's right on my heels. Relentless, as always. "We've known each other over five years now. Hell, we practically worked on top of each other until last week when I moved into the assistant editor office. If you think you can say you went to get a pair of panties back from one of your 'hook-ups' without me calling bullshit..." She steps in front of me before I can disappear into the conference room. "You'd better think again."

I take a sip of my espresso, doing my best to remain confident.

"There's no way this was just a hook-up," she continues. "Not with that shit-eating grin that was plastered across your face last night. I know that look. It was the look of someone *excited* about something. You had a glow about you. Come to think of it…" Squinting, she scans my body.

I wonder if this is how criminals feel when they've finally been apprehended and try to convince the officer the bag of drugs in their coat isn't theirs. Except I wasn't caught with drugs, although Lincoln's more addicting than even the most potent narcotic.

"You *still* have a glow about you." Her eyes brighten. "You had sex last night!"

"Evie," I hiss, trying to hush her.

While I've never been one to keep my sex life to myself, this is different. I *care* about Lincoln. I don't want to broadcast our fantastic sexcapades for all to hear. I don't want to share him with anyone. Not yet. I want to keep him all to myself for a little longer. I fear the second I talk about him, it'll make it real. I'm not ready for that yet.

"I have sex a lot… Well, not *a lot*, but enough that going to see some guy isn't a big deal." I straighten my spine. "It's not the first time I left you and Nora at the bar to hook up with somebody."

"No, it's not." She wraps a strand of her striking red hair around a finger, toying with it as she continues assessing my demeanor. "But I don't think last night was just a hook-up. I think you *like* someone."

I open my mouth to protest when the conference room door swings open, Maggie, the editor-in-chief's assistant, standing there, an air of superiority about her. "Are you two coming? Viv's waiting on you." She spins around. "As usual," she adds under her breath.

My expression brightens as I smile cheerily. "Come on, Evie. We don't want to be late," I chirp as I head inside.

She leans toward me. "This conversation isn't over," she murmurs, her voice low.

"I didn't think it was."

---

Thankfully, after the pitch meeting, Evie's too busy with assignments to continue to press me about the new man in my life, which gives me time to figure out how to address the elephant in the room.

Or at least the very large cock in my life.

As I attempt to catch up on all the work I missed while I was out of the office, as well as come up with a way to spill the beans about Lincoln to my friends, my phone dings with an incoming text. At first, I ignore it, assuming it's a tip about a breaking story in the world of the rich and famous. I can't be bothered with that stuff, not with a deadline looming on articles that go to print in just a few days.

But when it beeps again, I float my eyes to the screen, smiling when I see it's not from a source, but from my very own panty thief.

And that smile only grows wider when I open the text, which reveals a photo of a familiar pair of panties.

LINCOLN:

Missing you like you wouldn't believe. But at least I have a souvenir. And the scent is intoxicating.

ME:

> You really do have a fetish, don't you? Is it
> 'bring some random girl's panties to work'
> day? I didn't receive the memo.

I hit send, relaxing into my chair as I focus all my attention on my phone. One text, yet I've forgotten everything I'm
supposed to be working on. Hell, if Lincoln asked, I'd probably sneak out of work to meet him for a quickie, although
I'm not sure Lincoln's capable of a quickie. His bedroom
skills are those of an expert, a man who's made sex an art
form. He's a masterpiece I doubt I'll ever tire of experiencing.

LINCOLN:

> You're not just some random girl, Chloe. You
> never have been.

My heart warms as I read his words. Then the text
bubble appears, indicating he's typing more.

LINCOLN:

> And to answer your question, I do have a bit
> of an underwear fetish. At least when it
> comes to your underwear.

ME:

> Well then, I hate to disappoint you. I haven't
> had time to do my laundry since returning
> from Vegas, so I had to go commando today.

LINCOLN:

> Fuck...

A part of me wishes I were with Lincoln so I could see
his expression. Pupils dilating. Green eyes darkening with
unbridled lust and need. Jaw clenching. Muscles tightening.

God, I love that look on him, knowing I make him react that way.

LINCOLN:

You really know how to torture a man, don't you, Pixie?

ME:

Only you.

LINCOLN:

I like the sound of that.

I want to say I like the sound of that, too, but I don't, responding with something safer instead.

ME:

Think of me today.

LINCOLN:

I haven't been able to stop since the moment I saw you.

ME:

Me, either.

I hope that's enough to make him believe I'm willing to try, even if my words aren't overly amorous. I'm just a work in progress.

When no additional texts arrive, I return my attention to my computer, concentrating on my work once more, hours passing. I'm so focused, I don't tear my eyes away from my screen until I hear a slight knock on the exterior wall of my cubicle, the receptionist holding a large white box with a pink bow wrapped around it.

"A courier just dropped this off for you." She places it on my desk.

I eye the box much like one would glare at a device with a timer and wires attached. "What is it?"

"I'm sure if you open it, you'll find out," she snips, then whirls around.

I've always wondered how some of our receptionists got their job, since they all seem to have a stick shoved up their asses, unless a handsome man walks through those doors. I can't really complain. I started at that desk myself. I'd like to think I wasn't so bitchy, but I probably was.

As I look back at the box, a suspicion it's from Lincoln forms in my gut. Who else would send me something at work? How does he know *where* I work? I don't think I told him, apart from the fact that I work at a magazine. But there are hundreds of magazine offices in New York City.

After loosening the ribbon, I lift the lid and pull back pink tissue paper, laughing when I see what lies beneath it. I reach for the envelope placed in the center and slide out the small card, Lincoln's familiar scrawl greeting me.

*My dearest Chloe,*

*I've worked out a solution to our little...dilemma. And your lack of undergarments for the day.*

I glance at the contents, my cheeks flushing at the dozen or so pairs of panties before reading the rest of the note.

*They're all laundered and ready for you to wear. It was torture sitting here, thinking about you not wearing any panties. No one's allowed to steal a glimpse of what's mine. And rest assured, Chloe, you will be mine.*

*I'm already yours...*
*Lincoln*

*P.S. - In addition to the panties, there's a little extra some-*
*thing for you. I'd love to see you in it. Whenever you're*
*ready.*

I place the card on my desk and rummage through the box, pushing the panties aside. My pulse increases when I find a sexy black lace negligee with a matching thong. The thought of Lincoln's reaction to seeing me in this has my blood pumping, electricity coursing through my veins.

Phone in hand, I type off a quick text.

ME:

> What makes you think I'm interested in seeing you again? A little cocky, don't you think?

LINCOLN:

> Not a little cocky. At least I think it's impressive. It gets the job done.

I burst out laughing as my fingers fly over the screen.

ME:

> It certainly does.

I'm about to type out another reply when my cell rings, Lincoln's name appearing on the screen. My heart catches in my throat, face heating as I bring my phone up to my ear.

"Hello," I answer as seductively as I can get away with at work.

"Say thank you."

His deep voice murmuring those words brings me back to that bar in Vegas when he picked up my tab.

*Say okay. Say thank you.*

It hypnotized me, and I succumbed to his request without a moment's hesitation. That spell is still cast over me.

"Thank you."

"Good girl."

A shiver rolls down my spine, renewed desire igniting deep within. This feels so surreal. How far will I take this? Will I always do what he demands? The idea doesn't scare me. It excites me. I *want* him to tell me what to do. I like not having to think about all the potential ramifications of every single one of my actions. It's refreshing to turn it off for a minute. To quiet all the noise and drama that usually clouds my mind.

"Now, tell me… *Do* you want to see me again?" he asks, his voice as calm and collected as ever.

I picture him in a large office sitting behind an impressive wooden desk, one wall lined with AmJurs and the CJS, much like in my father's own office, despite no one using hard copies of legal encyclopedias these days. Everything is probably impeccable. It's not stacked high with boxes containing evidence or notes or other case material. There's a place for everything, and everything's in its place. A far cry from my cubicle, which on a good day looks like a bomb went off.

"Or are you having second thoughts about giving me a chance?"

"Never," I admit breathlessly.

"Good answer. Then I look forward to seeing you…soon."

"You're not going to ask me when?" I blurt out after a beat.

"No, I'm not. I understand this is new territory for you, so I won't push. When you're ready, so am I." His tone lightens. "Although I hope you don't wait too long, because now that I've had a taste, I'm not sure how long I'll be able to go without you in my arms."

A flutter erupts in my belly and I feel like I'm floating, the force of the butterflies' rapid wings lifting me up.

"Have a good day, Pixie."

"You, too." I linger on the line a moment longer, about to hang up when I call his name. "Lincoln?"

"Yes?"

I chew on the inside of my cheek. "How did you know where to send my…gift?"

It's quiet for a beat before he answers, "What would you say if I Googled you?" I can hear the smile in his voice.

"You…Googled me?"

"I wanted to surprise you. I don't know much about you, other than your name, what you do for a living, and that you make the most adorable sound when you're about to come."

"Yeah. It's called a moan."

"No. It's not that. It's more like a…mewl." His voice grows heated, wanton, lustful. "This excited mewl I can't get enough of. So please, don't make me wait too long to hear that again."

"I won't," I respond before I can stop myself. "Promise."

I imagine him smiling at my response. Hell, *I'm* smiling at my response.

"Goodbye, Pixie."

"Goodbye, Lincoln."

I stay on the phone a moment longer, then end the call. With a sigh, I try to return my focus to what I was working on, but all I can think of is Lincoln.

There's this mysteriousness about him, which makes me want to learn even more. Was he born in New York? Where did he go to law school? Does he have brothers? Sisters? What's his family like?

These are all things I've never cared enough to learn about any other man. Now I'm desperate to have a fuller picture of Lincoln Moore.

Navigating to my Internet browser, I type his name into the search bar. I hit enter just as a voice startles me.

"What is this?"

I quickly close out of my browser before I have a chance to look at the results, snapping my eyes up to see Evie hovering in my cubicle, staring at my gift.

"I was low on underwear and didn't feel like doing laundry," I lie nonchalantly.

"Bullshit." When she reaches for the card, I don't fight her. It was only a matter of time before she found out anyway. We spend over forty hours a week together.

She takes a few seconds to read. Then her wide eyes dart to mine. "Who's Lincoln? How does he know you're not wearing any underwear? Is he the one you went to go see about your panties last night? And why is he…yours?"

"He's…a guy."

"I gathered, but—"

I hold up my hand, cutting her off. I take a deep breath, summoning the strength for the conversation that's about to follow. "He's a guy I like. And yes, he's the panties guy." My lips quirk into a smile. "A panty thief."

Evie stares at me, her mouth agape, her response similar to one she'd have if she just learned I'd been leading a double life as a sex abstinence advocate. Then she squeals, her words coming out a mile a minute.

"Who is he? Where did you meet? What's he like? What does he do? What does he look like? Where's he from?" Her questions come like rapid gunfire.

"Evie… Evie… Evie!" I say in between each question, having to shout the last one to get her attention.

She snaps her mouth shut. "You're right. This calls for reinforcements."

"Reinforcements?"

"Exactly."

# Fifteen

"Oh my goodness!" Nora squeals, placing her hand over her heart as we sit in a row of spin machines, sweat dripping from our bodies. Upbeat music blares, overpowering the sound of wheezing breaths and the whirring of the wheels on the stationary bikes. "It's better than any movie! It was meant to be!"

I roll my eyes at her reaction to the story I'd just told, slightly breathless, about meeting Lincoln in Vegas.

"It's a total fairy tale."

"Fairy tales all end with 'And they lived happily ever after'," I taunt, using air quotes, imitating her light, dream-like voice. "That's not us."

Nora scowls, an adorable pout on her face, as if she'd just learned a car had hit her childhood dog. "What makes you think that?"

"It's too soon to be planning a future with him." I pedal harder, pretending to focus on my workout when, in reality, I want to flip off the instructor, who seems to get off on people's anguished expressions. If I hear her say "Pain is weakness leaving the body" one more time, I'll show her some real pain. "We agreed to take things slow."

Evie snorts a laugh. "Yeah. Him practically telling you he owns your pussy is *really* taking things slow."

"He didn't say he owns my pussy," I protest, somewhat loudly.

A few people glance in our direction, the women scrunching their nose in disgust at my use of the word "pussy". It makes me want to shout it repeatedly at the top of my lungs.

"He'd stolen yet another pair of my panties, and I haven't been home long enough to drop off my clothes at the laundromat, so I had to go commando."

When an attractive man in his thirties looks our way, I flash him a smile, then notice the wedding band on his hand as he not so subtly adjusts his shorts. Facing my friends, I lower my voice to avoid any more stares.

"Once I told him that... Well, you can fill in the blanks. He didn't want anyone to catch a glimpse of what *could* be his. But don't worry. It's not his yet. I still own this pussy."

"And his cock, by the sounds of it," Nora chimes in.

"I don't own his cock."

Evie and Nora share a look before fixing their gazes back on me. "You do," they say simultaneously.

"Impossible. We haven't even known each other a week. Not to mention, I didn't know his name until Tuesday. That's only three days ago! Hell, the only thing I know about him is that he's a lawyer. I don't even know what kind of law he practices..." I trail off as I shift my eyes to the large mirrored walls, the reflection of dozens of people's legs cycling on their spin machines dizzying. "But there's one way to find out." I grab my phone off the bike and navigate to the browser.

"What are you doing?" Evie asks, a brow quirked up, slowing her pedaling.

"Googling him."

Her eyes widen as she shares a look with Nora yet again. In a heartbeat, she snatches the phone out of my hands. "No. Don't."

"Wha—"

"I get that you're a curious person by nature, that you love digging for dirt on every celebrity out there. And you're damn good at it." She waves my phone in front of me. "But don't do that here."

The instructor increases the resistance on the bikes and we all pedal even harder, the ache in my legs a temporary distraction.

"When I agreed to that first non-date with Julian," Evie continues, panting, "I had no idea who he was. And it's probably a good thing. I'm not sure I would have gone. I probably would have second-guessed the entire scenario. Hell, I did that anyway, but having no clue who he was allowed me to relax and get to know him. I never looked him up, apart from that one time you showed me his Wikipedia page. I got to learn about Julian from him, not the Internet."

She exhales a breath, her face reddening. "And who the fuck decided spin classes were a good idea?" Her eyes dart to Nora. "It was you, wasn't it? Sadist. Why can't we have girls' time with ice cream instead?"

"That's a different situation, E," I argue when Nora simply shrugs in response to Evie's accusation. "Julian Gage is well known. Lincoln Moore isn't."

"How do you know?" Nora asks, then does a double take, brows furrowed. "Wait a minute. His name is Lincoln Moore?"

"Yes…," I answer in a drawn-out voice.

She stares at me, mouth agape. I brace myself to find out he's now officially off-limits due to the girl code. Before she settled down with Jeremy, her fiancé, she was a date-aholic. We often compared "war stories" about what it's like finding someone you feel a connection with in the New York City wildlife. I never cared about the connection, not like Nora, although she claims she didn't, either. That she was simply enjoying her twenties. Secretly, I could tell she was looking for more than a fleeting romp in the sack.

Maybe I was, too, but I didn't realize it.

"Damn, that's a great name. Lincoln Moore." She fans herself, continuing to pedal, making it appear effortless when everyone else in the class is ready to stick the instructor's head on a spike in revolt. I suppose running a yoga and meditation studio has its benefits. "Does he have you begging for *more?*" She grins mischievously.

"No." I pause before breaking into a smile. "More like screaming."

"That's my girl." Nora reaches toward me and we bump fists. Some may find our conversation inappropriate, but we've never shied away from topics some consider taboo. That's probably why I've remained friends with Nora and Evie…and even Izzy…for as long as I have. They're as comfortable with discussing sex as I am.

"Scream for more all you want," Evie interjects. "Just promise you won't Google him."

"He Googled me first."

"I bet he did," she says under her breath.

"To send you underwear," Nora reminds me. "Not to figure out who you are. I know how you work. You'll find something random and convince yourself not to pursue him. Don't. Get to know him. Don't assume he has some weird fetish because you misread something while stalking his social media profiles."

"Well, he *does* have a weird fetish."

They perk up.

"For my panties."

We all erupt in laughter, eliciting a few glares, but we ignore them.

"I'm happy for you, Chloe," Nora says in all sincerity.

"Me, too," Evie adds. "And, for the love of a magical penis, will you take some of your own advice?"

"My own advice?"

"Exactly. When I wasn't sure what to make of Julian going from hot to cold in three point five seconds, do you remember what you told me?"

I don't immediately respond.

"You told me to enjoy the ride."

"On his rocket," I add to cut through the tension.

She smiles for a second before fixing her expression once more.

"Yes. And I'll give you the same advice here. Chloe, I've known you five years."

"And I've known you ten," Nora pipes up. "I've never seen you this excited about a guy."

"I don't think I've *ever* seen you excited about a guy, period," Evie offers, then adds quickly, "Don't get me wrong. It's not a bad thing. I just... I want you to be happy. If that means pursuing something serious with Lincoln Moore, great. If you want to keep things casual, that's great, too. Don't think too much. Let life lead you down the path you're meant to travel."

I take a swig of my water, giving her a smug grin. "Strange words coming from a woman who, six months ago, used to plan every minute of every day down to the nanosecond."

Evie playfully punches my bicep. "I did not. At least not

down to the nanosecond." She winks. "But you know what I mean. I understand how it is when you find yourself in uncharted territory. You over-analyze everything. I know *I* do. And as much as you'd like to think we're opposites, we're more alike than you think. So have fun with Lincoln Moore—"

"You can just call him Lincoln."

She pauses, her eyes scrunched together in contemplation, before she quickly shakes her head. "Nope. Can't do it. His name rolls off the tongue too perfectly."

"She's right," Nora agrees. "It does."

"It really is the perfect last name for a sex god." Evie giggles.

"I never said he was a sex god."

"You didn't have to," Nora states. "It goes with the territory."

"What territory?"

Nora and Evie share yet another look. It makes me wonder if they have a secret code when it comes to me. I've never exactly given them a reason to focus on me.

For the past five years, our friendship has focused on Nora's seemingly never-ending search for Mr. Right while insisting all she cared about was a decent lay, although we all knew she wanted more. To our surprise, she met someone on Tinder who felt the same.

Then there was Evie's breakup with her long-time boyfriend and her whirlwind fake relationship with one of Manhattan's most eligible bachelors, which ended up being a lot more real than either intended. Compared to them, my life is boring, mainly because I tend to keep the details to myself.

Evie pinches her lips together before answering. "You have high standards."

"Says the girl who once berated me for sleeping with anything with a pulse."

"To which you replied you were sampling the buffet before you went back for seconds."

"Precisely."

"My point exactly, Chloe. You *rarely* go back for seconds."

"I've seen a few guys more than once," I argue.

"True," Nora says, finally piping up. "But I think this time's different."

I roll my eyes. "All I promised him was a chance to get to know me. He left the ball in my court, so to speak."

"Well, if I were you," Evie begins, "I wouldn't wait to throw that ball. I'd toss it now. Hell, I'd spike it to show him you're not stringing him along."

"He knows I'm not."

"Trust me," Nora interjects. "A single, attractive man who's interested in more than a quick fling is a rarity, especially in New York. Most men you'll meet are either married to their career, married to their bachelorhood, or married to their wives. Yes, you say all he's asking for is a chance to get to know you, but he's giving *you* a chance, too. Don't fuck it up."

"Gee, thanks for the words of encouragement." My tone oozes sarcasm.

She shrugs. "What are friends for?"

---

Nora's and Evie's warnings seem to play on repeat in my mind for the rest of the afternoon and evening, festering, making it impossible for me to concentrate on anything other than Lincoln and what he's doing. Is he out with friends? At work? Having dinner with another woman he's also sent panties to?

The idea of him stealing another woman's panties is all the motivation I need to get off the couch, shower, and make my way to his apartment. He surprised me with a present at work today. What better way to spike the ball back onto his side of the court than by showing up at his apartment wrapped in a present for him?

Bringing my hand up to the door, I knock softly, my insides vibrating with anticipation of how Lincoln will react. I strain to listen for any sound coming from within. At first, there's nothing but silence. Then I hear a faint rustling. Shoe-less footsteps gradually grow closer. There's a pause, and I assume Lincoln's checking to see who could be here at ten on a Friday night.

When the door opens, he peers at me with a furrowed brow. He parts his lips, presumably to ask me what I'm doing here, but I place a finger over them, silencing him.

Without saying a word, I loosen the belt on my coat and slowly unfasten each of the buttons, allowing my jacket to fall open, exposing my body clad in the negligee he'd sent me earlier.

"Fuck," he hisses, his jaw clenched, nostrils flaring, a bull in heat. His gaze rakes over me, calculating, agonizing, as if imprinting every inch of me to memory.

Approaching him, I stand on my toes, my lips ghosting against his. "That's the plan, Mr. Moore."

A growl rips from his throat as he tugs my body hard against his, his mouth covering mine, devouring, possessing, consuming. I curve into him, signaling with my acquiescence to his touch that I'm his for the night.

Maybe longer.

# Sixteen

**M**y heels skid on the tile in the lobby of the journalism building on campus as I rush to the elevator, checking my watch. Ten minutes past three on Thursday afternoon. Meaning I'm ten minutes late for my first day of class. I shouldn't be surprised. I'm notorious for being late, especially when sexting with Lincoln Moore.

*Lincoln. Just Lincoln.*

Ever since I appeared at his door last Friday, scantily clad, we've seen each other every day. And every day, I grow more and more addicted to his touch, his essence, his everything.

Once the elevator doors close, I pull out my phone and read through our most recent exchange, unable to stop the smile from tugging on my lips.

LINCOLN:

> Have I mentioned today how much I love your legs?

ME:

> My memory's not what it used to be. I am closing in on thirty. Why don't you refresh my memory?

LINCOLN:

You're still a baby. And I love your legs.
Actually, I'm not so sure love is the correct
word. I think about them nearly every waking
moment.

ME:

Nearly?

LINCOLN:

Yes. Nearly. Except when I'm buried deep
inside you. Then I can only think about how
amazing your pussy feels when it clenches
around me.

Desire, thick and intense, coils in my core as I attempt to come up with a response, having left him hanging once I realized I was running late. The elevator doors open and I scurry down the hallway toward my classroom, typing out a quick reply.

ME:

Sorry to leave you with your dick in your
hands. Lost track of time. Have class. Maybe
I can come over after and you can feel my
pussy clench around you. You know, so you
can take a break from thinking of my legs.

Once I hit send, I shove my phone into my bag, slowing when I reach the classroom. Fixing my frantic expression, I open the door and do my best to slip in unnoticed without interrupting class, smiling at a few familiar faces who don't seem surprised to see I'm late on the first day.

I make my way toward one of the vacant seats in the middle of the room, trying to be as quiet as possible. It's obvious by the stiff posture and annoyed breathing of the professor he's not exactly pleased with my disruption.

When I'm about to slide into my chair, he finally turns

around from where he's written out the text of the First Amendment, and our eyes meet.

Ever have one of those dreams where everything seems perfect? Maybe your boss called you into his or her office and gave you that promotion you've been hoping for. Maybe Publishers Clearing House, if that's even still a thing, showed up at your door with one of those oversized checks. Or maybe you ran into one of the hottest guys you've ever seen while grabbing your morning coffee. All great things, right?

Until you look down and realize you're naked.

That's what this moment feels like.

Correction.

This is worse.

Because this isn't some dream.

This is real.

Lincoln Moore is my college professor.

I've been sleeping with my college professor.

Without knowing it.

*Fuck...*

A throat clearing cuts through the heavy silence. Unsure what else to do, I slink into my chair, doing my best to hide behind the girl sitting in front of me. Even so, the slight tremble in Lincoln's hand as he writes on the board doesn't escape my attention, evidence he's as surprised about this turn of events as me.

Had I walked into this room and one of the other men I'd slept with had been lecturing the class, I wouldn't have been so dumbfounded. But this is different.

*Lincoln* is different.

I try to convince myself this is for the best, that this never would have worked out. Listening to his lecture solidifies this assessment. He needs someone who can be his intellectual equal. Someone he can debate about what should be classified as obscene and not deserving of First Amendment protections. I'd barely be able to get out a few words without stumbling over them.

Conversation breaks out in the room and I glance up from the blank page of my notebook to see the other students packing up their things. When I glance at my watch, I'm surprised to see it's fifteen minutes to six. I'd just sat through almost an entire three-hour class without hearing a word, too consumed with this strange, new reality.

Snapping out of my daze, I scramble to shove my belongings into my bag and leave without having to confront Lincoln and endure an awkward conversation where we pretend we don't know each other. I'm not sure what I'm supposed to do, but I'll figure something out. Try to drop the class. Do an independent study. Something...*anything* so I don't have to come back to this classroom.

My eyes averted, I attempt to escape unnoticed when a familiar deep voice foils my plan.

"Miss Davenport."

I stop in my tracks, my shoulders tensing as I exhale a frustrated breath. I hate that he used such a formal tone. It's one he's used with me in the bedroom, but it was part of our game. This isn't a game.

In an effort to appear unaffected by this turn of events, I fix my expression and slowly face him, staring into green eyes that mere hours ago looked upon my naked body with an unmatched hunger. "Yes, Professor Moore?"

When I address him this way, he flinches. "I'd like a word."

"I have somewhere I need to be."

"I insist." He widens his stance, his gaze darkening. It's not quite a glare, but it's not a compassionate look, either. It's a new expression, one that tells me not to test him, that this isn't something we can avoid discussing. "Just a few moments of your time, then you can go on with your life."

His statement hits me hard. By the way his Adam's apple bobs up and down in a thick swallow, I get the feeling it was just as difficult for him to say as it was for me to hear.

On a deep inhale, I nod, trailing a few steps behind him as he leads me toward the faculty corridor. This entire scenario makes me feel like an errant teenager who acted out in class and is being handed off to my guidance counselor, who will press me to talk about my parents' divorce and how I'm "coping".

Except I'm an adult.

Who just found out she's been screwing the professor of the one class she needs to finally graduate this spring.

So much for proving to my father I'm not a complete fuck-up.

Once the door to the office closes behind us, allowing us to talk in private, he heads to the window, peering at the city surrounding us. I simply stare at him, unsure what to say. Then he glances over his shoulder.

"Did you know?" There's a hint of pain in his tone.

Aghast, my eyes widen. "What?"

"When you saw me in Vegas…" He fully faces me. "Did you know who I was and not say anything in the hopes of getting me in bed?"

"Of course not! Why would you think that?"

"How could I *not* think that, Chloe?" He runs his fingers through his hair, tugging at it. "This seems to be *too* much of a coincidence."

I cross my arms over my chest. "Yeah. Because I'd go through the trouble of starting to fall for a guy, only to have to walk away when I learn he's my goddamn professor!"

"I don't know. I—" He stops short, inhaling sharply. "What did you say?"

"That you're my professor…," I answer in a drawn-out voice.

"No." He shakes his head, licking his lips. "Before that." His tone becomes tranquil, expression softening.

I replay the words and stiffen at the truth that poured so freely from my mouth. His eyes plead with me, and I can't deny him this.

"That I wouldn't fall for a guy if I knew there was zero chance of survival."

"You were falling for me?" He steps toward me, his gaze raking over me, as if searching for something. What, I'm not sure.

"It doesn't matter anymore." I tear my eyes from his.

A part of me wants him to tell me we'll make it work. That the connection between us is too strong to throw away over something as trivial as this. But he doesn't, the compassionate Lincoln transforming back to the man he was the past three hours as he lectured the class.

"You're right. It doesn't matter anymore. It *can't* matter anymore."

He walks to his desk and pulls out a thin book, Policies and Procedures written on the front in bold letters. He flips to the table of contents before turning to the appropriate page, scanning it.

"Right." His tone is firm when he looks up. "According to the conduct code, as long as the previous relationship is disclosed, it's not a big deal."

I hug my jacket tighter around my body, my stomach queasy as I listen to Lincoln talk about me as if I'm just a problem in need of fixing, not a person he once cared for.

"I'll go to the dean and let him know, assuring him we

ceased all contact once we learned the truth. I'll request a third party grade all your papers and exams, and I'll forego having class participation be a part of the final grade this semester in order to appear neutral."

I nod, still having difficulty coming to terms with this new reality. My eyes scan his desk, everything about it as neat and orderly as I imagined it would be. As I continue looking around, I spy a copy of the syllabus he probably handed out before I'd arrived. I pick it up, my throat tightening even more.

"And you're only going to disclose this to the dean, right? No one else?"

"Of course not," he insists, then corrects himself. "Well, there are ethical concerns, so to err on the side of caution, I'll be informing my boss at the newspaper where I work."

"You're an associate attorney at the *Times*," I state, reading his credentials listed at the top of the paper.

"Yes," he answers, ignoring the forlorn expression on my face. "My boss *is* friends with the dean and is actually the one who recommended me for the adjunct position here, so…"

Our eyes lock. "I can't let you do that. Can't let you tell either of them."

"I don't have a choice," he whisper-shouts, placing his hands on the desk and leaning toward me. "This is my career."

"That may be true, but your boss at the newspaper? David Jensen?"

Lincoln's expression blanches, seeming to sense I'm about to drop yet another bomb on him. Which I am.

"He's my father."

# Seventeen

The surprise that covered Lincoln's expression when he turned around and realized I was one of his students is nothing compared to the utter and morose shock now plastered on his face. His jaw drops open, his eyes scanning me, probably for any hint of resemblance to the man who hired him…and could fire him.

"But your last name is Davenport." He shakes his head, brow furrowed, as if hoping the fact I don't share his last name will negate the DNA running through me.

"After he divorced my mother, I took her last name. I didn't want a reminder of that man attached to me for the rest of my life."

He exhales, pinching the bridge of his nose. "Chloe, I—"

I step toward him, folding my fingers together as I beg for him to keep this quiet. "Please, Lincoln. Maybe if it were just the dean, it wouldn't be so bad. There'd still be a chance he'd mention it to my father, since they're friends, but this… With my father being your boss? There's no way the dean *won't* tell him. And my father can*not* find out."

"It's not up to me! I *have* to report this. It's right here in black and white." He points to the book in front of him. "I'm obligated to report any prior relationship with a student to the dean."

"Who will tell my father since you work for him," I hiss back. "Please. I am *begging* you." Tears dot my eyes, my throat closing up.

"Why don't you want him to know?"

I wrap my arms around my stomach, warming myself against a sudden chill enveloping me. Do I feed him some line in the hopes he'll grant my request? Or do I tell him the truth, revealing another fragmented piece of myself?

"Help me understand." His voice softens, reminding me of the way he'd whisper sweet words in my ear as I drifted off to sleep in his arms. I want to curse the world for being so cruel. For giving me a taste of something I never thought possible, never thought I wanted, only to rip it away, dangling it in front of me like a memento of something I can never have again.

"You never could. You probably had the perfect life. The perfect fucking family who supported you through everything."

He parts his lips, but I hold up my hand.

"Well, I didn't. As you've figured out, my father's a bit of a hard-ass."

He snorts out a laugh, the tension momentarily cracking. "You can say that again."

"And he's always been that way." I draw in a deep breath, attempting to compose myself, swiping at the few tears that had managed to escape. "All my life, I've been nothing but a disappointment to him and his impossibly high standards. I get that all parents want their children to succeed. But nothing I did was ever good enough. Nothing I *do* is ever good enough."

I pull my lips between my teeth. "For once, I'm close to finishing something on my own." I lower my voice. "I'm close to finally being able to prove to my father I'm not just a massive disappointment."

"Chloe, I—"

"I know it makes no sense," I interrupt before he can utter a single word of sympathy for my fucked-up childhood and adolescence. "Why should I care what he thinks? I ask myself that same question constantly. A part of me doesn't care. But as you've learned, my father is extremely stubborn. And that stubbornness is genetic. So instead of writing him off like I should have years ago, I keep trying. Just to say I proved him wrong."

I meet Lincoln's eyes that are awash with compassion. Something about the way he gazes upon me makes me think he's dying to wrap me in his arms and comfort me. But he can't do that. Never again.

"If you report this and he learns I had a prior relationship with my professor, with one of his employees, he'll never let it go. He'll always think I only passed because I screwed my way to a passing grade. Just like he thinks the only reason I was promoted from receptionist to columnist at the magazine is because I was the only one willing to trade my body for tips on celebrity comings and goings. While there may be *some* truth to his opinion, it's not the only thing that's gotten me to where I am. If he finds out about this…" I shake my head, swallowing. "If you report this, he'll always see me as the naïve twenty-two-year-old girl who made a terrible decision and got herself in a bad situation just to prove she could do more than answer a phone."

He stares at me for what feels like an eternity, dozens of questions on the tip of his tongue after this admission, something I didn't think I'd ever share with him, or anybody. Finally, he blows out a long breath, his shoulders falling.

"I can't believe I'm about to do this, but okay." He brings his eyes back to mine. "We'll keep this between us."

All the tension rolls off my body, gratitude filling me. "Thank you."

His expression hardens, his jaw tightening, nostrils flaring. "But if I hear the faintest hint of whispers about us, it will leave me no choice. So do *not* speak a word about this to anyone. Do not say anything during class that would lead anyone to believe there has ever been anything between us."

The compassionate Lincoln is gone, serious and stern Lincoln taking his place. "For all intents and purposes, the relationship happened before you were my student anyway, and once we were aware of the situation, we ceased all contact. Neither one of us is taking advantage of the other, so if we keep it quiet, no one will ever know about it, considering I have no intention of continuing this relationship."

"Such a lawyer," I comment, his words stinging more than I thought they would. "Trying to get off on a technicality."

"Do you see any other option?" He pinches his lips together. "Need I remind you, I'm the one whose ass is on the line here. I'm doing this as a favor to you. I can go down the hall and report this right now. I *should* go down the hall and report this."

"No," I respond urgently, advancing toward him, desperate. "It's okay. You're right." I swallow hard as I straighten my spine. "There *is* no other option."

We stare at each other in silence for several moments. Then he nods. "So we're in agreement. We'll continue on with our lives as if this never happened. We'll forget about everything." His tone rises in pitch at the end, his words neither a question nor a statement.

I bite on my lower lip to prevent Lincoln from seeing how difficult this is.

"It's already forgotten."

# Eighteen

I barrel into our normal happy hour meeting spot and make a beeline for the bar, plopping into the empty barstool to the right of Evie, Nora and Izzy sitting on the other side of her. While I'm thrilled Izzy was able to find time in her schedule to come out with us, seeing her only reminds me of Lincoln, considering she was present during the blackout that started it all.

Fuck Vegas.

And fuck whoever's responsible for that damn blackout.

Why couldn't Vegas have lost power and cell service one day later? Better yet, why couldn't our flight not have been canceled? Why did Lincoln have to steal my panties? And why did I have to go get them back?

I should know better. Hell, did I not learn anything from the story of Orpheus and Eurydice? He lost everything that was important to him because he looked back, a lesson to all to only look forward. Not only did I look back, but I made several return trips to the all-you-can-eat buffet. Now the hostess is telling me I've overstayed my welcome.

"Is everything okay?" Evie's brow wrinkles as her analytic eyes survey me.

"Fucking marvelous." I wave down Aiden, our handsome, yet very gay bartender. He begins pouring my usual martini. "Get me a shot of Jameson, too."

He peers at me quizzically, as do my three friends, particularly Izzy, who's more than aware of my reasons for not drinking much. I need it today, though.

"What's going on?" Izzy asks once I slam back the shot.

"Did something happen at class?" Nora chimes in.

"Did you get kicked out for being late?" Evie presses.

I draw in a deep breath, placing my palms against the cool wood of the bar. "No, I didn't get kicked out for being late. This is undergrad, Evie. Not the fucking Marines." I playfully roll my eyes, which elicits a laugh from Nora and Izzy. "But something *did* happen at school."

"What is it?" She leans toward me.

"I—"

She holds up her hand. "Wait. Are we talking 'need to take the edge off' kind of something? Or is it more like 'line 'em up and let's get wasted'?"

"It's more along the lines of 'I don't think there's enough bourbon in all of Kentucky to handle this'."

The girls look at each other, eyes widening, before zeroing in on me, sitting on the edge of their seats.

"Okay. Spill." Evie fishes the Maraschino cherry out of her manhattan and tugs it off the stem with her teeth.

I bring my own drink to my mouth, taking a sip of the smooth vodka. And of course, being a martini, it only serves as another reminder of Lincoln. I've known this man less than two weeks, yet I find pieces of him in every part of my life. Is that how it will always be? God, I hope not.

Exhaling, I place my glass back on the bar, squaring my shoulders to address my friends, their expressions akin to children meeting Santa for the first time.

"When I got to campus today, I was only about ten minutes

late. No biggie. At least for me," I add when I see the absolute horror on Evie's face at my admission. "So I snuck into the classroom and grabbed a seat in the middle of the lecture hall." I bring my drink back to my mouth with a trembling hand, forcing a smile. But even a fake smile can't mask the hurt in my voice. "And that's when the professor turned around and I found out *who* would be teaching my First Amendment class."

"Oh god," Nora exhales. "It's your father, isn't it? Did you not check the schedule to see who it would be?"

I wave her off. "It wasn't my father. Thank fuck for that."

"Then who?" Izzy asks.

On a hard swallow, I allow his name to roll off my tongue. "None other than Lincoln Moore."

"Holy shit." Nora takes a big gulp of her drink, as if she were the one who'd walked into class and learned the guy she'd been sleeping with was her professor.

"Oh, my god," Evie exhales.

"Hold on a second," Izzy says, her mouth agape as she stares at me, knowing I wouldn't have told Evie and Nora about Lincoln if there weren't still something there. "You've been seeing Lincoln Moore and never said anything?"

"His name is just Lincoln," I respond, not wanting her to pick up on Nora's and Evie's habit of referring to Lincoln by his full name. "And you'd know about it if you stopped working long enough to meet me for coffee. I haven't seen or talked to you since Vegas, so I didn't exactly have a chance to tell you."

She waves me off. "Whatever. That's not important right now. What *is* important is what's been going on with you and Lincoln."

"Nothing now."

"Well, before."

I shrug. "We…reconnected."

"Reconnected how?"

I chew on my lower lip. "He kind of took my panties. And I kind of went to get them back."

"And what? You kind of slipped and fell on his dick?"

"It *is* an impressive dick."

It's silent for a moment. Then the girls' laughter carries through the bar, overpowering the chatter and music.

"Guys," I whine. "It's not funny. This is serious!"

"I know, I know," Nora says, tears forming in the corner of her eyes. "We're not laughing at the situation."

"Then—"

"You tripped and fell on his dick?" Evie giggles.

"Kind of. I mean, that guy has some serious game."

"What are you going to do?" Nora asks the question on everyone's mind.

I shrug. "Hope my advisor agrees to let me fulfill these credits with an independent study instead. This is the last class I need to graduate, but I don't want to sit in that room every Thursday for fifteen weeks or however long the semester is."

"I'm sure she'll agree," Evie assures me. "After you disclose your relationship to Lincoln, there's no way they'll let you stay."

"Right." I avert my eyes, taking another large gulp of my drink.

"What is it?" Izzy tilts her head.

I glance at her sideways, then blow out a breath. "We kind of agreed to keep it quiet."

"You *what?*" Evie shrieks, aghast.

"That's crazy," Nora adds.

"Not to mention a horrible idea," Izzy offers. "No matter

what you may think, these kinds of things never stay quiet forever."

Briefly closing my eyes, I clench my fists. "I understand that, but there's no other option."

"Yes, there is," Nora pushes. "My replacement roommate after you dropped out made the mistake of hooking up with her TA. It went on her record. On *both* their records. And it affected him for years, all because they got drunk one night, messed around, and someone eventually found out about it."

"It's not optimal, but…" I release a heavy sigh. "It's not just the fact he's my professor. I knew he was a lawyer, but I assumed he worked at some high-power law firm."

"Is he some ambulance chaser instead?" Evie presses.

I bury my face in my hands, shaking my head. "No. Worse." When I finally lift my eyes and stare at my friends, the truth is plastered in my expression, at least enough for Izzy to put the pieces together. Who better to teach First Amendment Law than someone who practices it on a daily basis?

"He works for your father, doesn't he." It's more a statement than a question.

I slowly nod.

"And you're worried if Lincoln reports this it'll get back to your father."

"It's not a question of if. It *will* happen. My father and the dean golf together. Plus, Lincoln teaches at the university *because* of his experience as a lawyer for the newspaper. *Because* my father recommended him for the job. He was adamant about telling his boss…until he found out my relationship to his boss."

"And your father cannot know," Izzy says in understanding.

"Precisely."

"I don't follow." Evie scrunches her nose. Out of the three of them, she's known me the least amount of time, coming in at a point in my life when I'd already distanced myself from my father.

"We have a…difficult relationship."

"Difficult? How? He's your father."

I can understand how she'd be confused. She comes from the stereotypical family. Two loving parents. An older brother who adores her and most likely put the fear of God into all the boys she'd dated in her past. Hell, they probably even have a cookie-cutter house with a picket fence, à la *Leave it to Beaver*.

"He may be my father, but that always came second. Maybe even third or fourth on his list of priorities. His job always came first. Always. It still does."

While he did remarry soon after divorcing my mother, it's a strange marriage. I don't feel any love between him and Tiffany. No passion. No intense need to be with each other. I think my father simply wanted to have a woman on his arm during important functions. And Tiffany was more than happy to have a career as a housewife. It's not like it was with my mother, a woman who had strong aspirations of her own.

"He's always had impossibly high standards."

"So did my parents," Evie offers, still trying to understand this.

"Nothing I did was good enough. If I won the class spelling bee, he'd point out I failed to win the school-wide competition. If I won a fencing match, he'd comment how my opponents weren't well-trained. If I were cast as the lead in the school play, he'd mention all the flaws in my performance. All of this in the hopes of encouraging me to work harder."

"Did it?" Evie's voice is hesitant.

"At first, yes. I worked my tail off trying to make him happy. Then I discovered boys. And I mean *really* discovered boys. Do you know what I discovered about them?"

Evie and Nora shake their heads, transfixed. Izzy listens with polite attention, fully aware of this part of my life.

"That they were nothing like my father. That they didn't put me down after we kissed by telling me my technique could use some work. And I liked that feeling. Of course, my father hated the fact I became more focused on boys than school. Why should I care, though? No matter what I did, it wouldn't be good enough, so why try?" I take a sip of my drink, needing the liquid encouragement to share this piece of myself with my two friends. "Despite it all, there's still this part of me that wants to make him proud, to prove to him that I *am* good enough."

"And if he learns you slept with your professor…," Evie begins, putting the pieces together.

"He'll never think you earned this degree," Nora finishes.

"I know it sounds stupid, that it shouldn't matter."

"We all want to make our parents happy." With a smile, Evie places her hand over mine, squeezing. "Or we want to prove them wrong."

"And I'd love to prove my father wrong, make him see I'm not a failure."

"So if you're keeping it a secret," Nora begins after a brief pause, "will your advisor agree to an independent study?"

"All I can do is hope she does."

"If she doesn't? Do you think you'll be able to handle him teaching the class?" she asks in all seriousness. "I mean without picturing him naked every time he talks about briefs, or penal violations, or getting a client off."

I lift my eyes, staring at her for a protracted moment,

then burst out laughing, grateful for the break in the tension. It's a relief, especially after the day I've had.

I fidget with the stem of my martini glass, a pang squeezing my heart as I watch a couple walk into the bar holding hands, an obvious affection between them.

"Actually, I *don't* think I'll be able to deal with it, so I'll just pray my advisor is on my side and allows me to do an independent study." I swallow thickly. "Then I can forget about Lincoln Moore."

# Nineteen

My stomach roils as I look up at the journalism building on campus, the structure feeling more like an unwelcome fortress than a place of higher learning. A chill washes over me, having nothing to do with the frigid January temperature and everything to do with what awaits me inside those doors. The last thing I want to do is walk into this building and sit through class with Lincoln — *Professor Moore*. But I no longer have an option. Not if I want to graduate this semester.

Because I'd taken this class twice before with less than stellar results, thanks to problems with my mother, my advisor refused to sign off on an independent study. I'd considered withdrawing from the class altogether, but like Izzy reminded me, it's my last one. There's no guarantee someone different will teach it next semester, either, so I may as well get it over with.

Spine straight, I summon the determination to walk into the lobby, my steps quickening when I see the elevator doors begin to shut. Thankfully, someone notices me and places their hand on the door.

"Thank you," I say breathlessly as I sneak inside, keeping my head lowered.

"You're welcome."

As the doors close, my breath catches, every muscle becoming rigid. I fling my eyes to my left to see Lincoln standing there, all poised and confident.

It's official. The universe is out to get me. I wrack my brain to think of what I could have done to piss it off this much. I consider finding the nearest Catholic church, despite not being religious, just to go to confession. Then again, I doubt any priest would be prepared to listen to the number of sins I've committed. He'll probably say a plethora of Our Fathers and Hail Marys to cleanse my soul, too.

"Professor Moore." I stare ahead, pretending this isn't anything more than a teacher and student sharing an elevator. It's not the first time I've shared one with a professor of mine. But they weren't Lincoln.

"Chloe." When he says my name, it's soft, compassionate, endearing.

"Don't," I snap, refusing to so much as glance at him.

In the silence, I can sense his turmoil. Sense he wants to say something but doesn't know what. I doubt they teach this kind of thing in whatever law school he attended. Probably Harvard, just like my father. Another reason this is for the best. Lincoln would turn out just like him — in love with his career and nothing else. Better to cut my losses now.

"For the record," he states as the elevator slows to a stop on our floor, "I'm sorry things had to end this way."

The sincerity in his voice forces my eyes to his, and I look at him. Actually look at him. I'm not sure what I expected to see. Maybe the same demeanor I've come to expect from him — self-assured, bold, a hint of arrogance. But that's not what I see at all.

The way his sad eyes trace over my face with longing is all the proof I need that this has been as difficult for him as it has for me.

The green is lackluster, the circles under his eyes evidencing lack of sleep. It could be due to having to pull extra hours at work, but the wistful expression as he focuses on my lips makes me think he's been tossing and turning at night, cursing fate, just like me.

The doors open, breaking our moment, and he scurries off. I watch his long strides as he continues down the hall, turning into the faculty wing just as I whisper, "Me, too."

Pulling myself together, I shake off the interaction and head toward the classroom. It's relatively empty when I arrive, a handful of ambitious students discussing the assigned reading.

I assume the same seat in the middle of the lecture hall and pull out the few notes I jotted down as I attempted to absorb this week's material. It turned out to be a lost cause. Whenever I tried, all I could think of was Lincoln. I fear I'll be faced with the same problem every time I open the textbook. I pray Lincoln won't be cruel enough to call on me to discuss the reading. I can only hope he'll avoid bringing attention to me these first few weeks while we attempt to find a new normal in this strange dynamic.

"Is all this legal talk as much a foreign language to you as it is to me?" a smooth voice asks after several minutes.

I glance to my right as a man I estimate to be in his thirties sits down in the empty chair beside me. I thought I was one of the oldest students in the department, considering most everyone else isn't even able to legally drink yet. How did I not notice him last week? Oh, yeah. Because I was dealing with the fact that I'd been fucking my college professor. Another day in the life of Chloe Davenport.

I meet my fellow classmate's eyes. They're a dull combination of brown and green, completely uninspiring. "You have no idea."

"That's a relief." He pretends to swipe sweat from his brow, his smile comforting. "After the last class, I thought I was the only one who felt lost."

"I barely retained anything." It's not a complete lie. I couldn't tell him a single thing that was discussed last week.

"Right? I get that all this First Amendment stuff is important as a journalist, but can't they teach it to us in simpler terms?"

I smile politely. While I find it difficult to concentrate on the material because of *who* is teaching it, it is fascinating. I can understand why my father chose the path he did. Spending your time ensuring people's First Amendment rights aren't infringed unnecessarily is certainly admirable. Why couldn't he exhibit that kind of enthusiasm toward his family?

"I'm Owen," he says, extending his hand toward me.

I eye it before placing mine in it. "Chloe."

"Nice to meet you, Chloe." He keeps his grip firm on my hand, holding it a little longer than socially appropriate. When he finally lets go, my skin tingles with his phantom touch.

Part of me wants to feel something — desire, craving, lust. Owen *is* an attractive guy. Sandy hair with hints of copper. Deep-set eyes. Full lips. Clean-shaven jawline. I estimate he's about six feet tall, and based on the muscled forearms I see, the sleeves of his white shirt rolled up, I assume he has a nice physique.

Regardless, my body has no reaction to him. Almost like my ten days with Lincoln have now ruined me for any man who's to come after him.

"You, too," I say, although it's more of a polite formality than a truthful statement.

"So, what's your story?" he asks as I turn my attention back to my notes.

"What do you mean?"

"The usual. What do you do for a living? Why are you studying journalism? What's your favorite sexual position?"

I dart my wide eyes to his, unsure how to respond to this inquiry.

"You know. Those usual ice-breaker questions people don't give two shits about but ask each other in an attempt to make inane conversation." He winks, his smile growing wide.

I don't know what it is, but something about his cavalier attitude is refreshing. He *does* have a point.

"Well, since you're not going to pay attention anyway," I begin with a grin, "I work at a magazine as a celebrity news columnist. Started as a receptionist just trying to make a living wage and worked my way into the newsroom. So I guess that's why I'm studying it. I've got a foot in the door of an industry that's notoriously exclusive. I figure having a degree will only help me move on to something bigger and better."

"You mean you *don't* enjoy reporting on what celebrities had for lunch or whether they're good tippers?" He looks at me aghast, a playfulness about him.

I chuckle, tension rolling off me. Maybe having a friend in this class is exactly what I need. If nothing else, Owen makes me laugh, something I haven't done in days.

"Shocking, I know. So, how about you?"

"Oh, I'm not too complicated. I tend to follow my part-ner's lead."

I furrow my brow.

"Favorite sexual position," he clarifies, his tone light. "Whatever my girl wants, my girl gets."

I stare at him, assessing. If some random guy at a bar said that to me within seconds of learning my name, I'd write him off. But something about Owen's good-natured demeanor makes it more than clear he's using humor to break the ice. So, instead of being turned off by his statement and doing everything to avoid him in the future, I laugh, the sound carrying through the room, echoing against the walls. I don't even care that I'm drawing attention to myself.

Until a loud, booming voice cuts through.

"Miss Davenport!"

I fling my gaze to the front, seeing Lincoln standing there, his arms crossed, stance wide, expression severe.

"If you don't mind, I've called class to order. Or is your conversation more important than the First Amendment?"

I blink, my heart caught in my throat. I consider arguing that I was exercising my own First Amendment right, but decide against it. "Of course not. I apologize."

Several protracted moments pass as he stares at me, making me feel small and insignificant. Then he flits his glare to Owen, his jaw clenching as he does so. To anyone else, his actions wouldn't be seen as anything other than a silent warning to him, as well. But I know Lincoln. There's jealousy in those green eyes.

Finally, he breaks his attention from us and turns toward the whiteboard.

Owen leans close, whispering, "I'm sorry."

I nod, but remain silent, not wanting to draw any more attention to myself.

"And for what it's worth...," Owen adds. I glance at him as he passes me an encouraging look. "You have a beautiful laugh."

I smile. It doesn't reach my eyes, but it's something. "Thanks."

"You bet." He winks, and I feel the tiniest flutter in my chest.

If nothing else, Owen could serve as a very welcome distraction. Maybe this class won't be so bad after all.

# Twenty

"God, I hate the suburbs," I exhale as the Uber driver comes to a stop in front of a well-maintained three-story house in an upper middle-class neighborhood in Greenwich. A thick layer of snow covers the front lawn, making the property look even more picturesque. Even more perfect. Even more idealistic. The quintessential place to raise a family.

I should know. It was once my home.

Until my father realized he didn't get it quite right the first time around and started over again from scratch. New wife. New kids. Kept the house. At least he got *that* right.

Prick.

You'd think Tiffany, my father's new wife, would have wanted to move, start their lives in a new house where they could make memories of their own. That didn't seem to matter to her. I wouldn't be surprised to learn she'd insisted he keep the house just to be able to gloat that she took my mother's place.

"You're doing this for Midge," Izzy reminds me.

I float my eyes to her and nod.

Midge, my half-sister, is the youngest of the four children Tiffany pushed out after marrying my father fifteen years ago. The first one appeared less than nine months after my parents separated, so it didn't take a genius to solve that little mystery. But one kid wasn't enough. So they kept having them. I thought they were trying to form their own basketball team. It seemed like every time I saw them, Tiffany was pregnant. In the end, she simply wanted a girl.

It must drive her crazy that the girl she so desperately wanted looks up to me. It's a mystery how the little pipsqueak formed an attachment to me, but when I show up for holidays and parties, she shoves everyone aside, clinging to me as if *I* pushed her out of my hoo-ha. It's probably the only reason I was invited today. Probably the only reason I'm ever invited.

"But if it'll help, we can make a pit stop at my parents' house and sneak some of the liquor bottles my mother stole from the airline." She waggles her brows.

"Iz, didn't she quit the airline, like, ten years ago?"

"Fifteen, but last I checked, she still has those mini bottles."

A horrified expression crosses my face at the idea of drinking anything that's been sitting in a plastic bottle that long. "Gross." I try not to gag. "That stuff wasn't good when it was fresh. Can you imagine how disgusting it would taste now? Not to mention…" I gesture toward the house. "My father has a *very* well-stocked bar." I slide out of the back seat of the Uber and step onto the street, meeting Izzy as we walk up the driveway together, the March air crisp on my cheeks. "Sharing his DNA has its benefits, like being able to steal some of the thirty-year-old scotch he keeps hidden away for special occasions."

"And you just so happen to know his hiding spot?"

I pass her a mischievous look as we approach the front porch, the sounds of children laughing and screaming filtering out, as I suspected it would. "His youngest daughter's sixth birthday should be a reason to celebrate. Don't you think?"

"I suppose you're right." About to open the door, she pauses, looking to me, silently asking if I'm ready.

I nod, steeling myself. At least Izzy agreed to come with me, since she knows how uneasy being in this house makes me. She was there when I learned my parents were separating. When I packed up my room. When I got into my mother's car and left this neighborhood behind. Regardless of the months that would sometimes pass without speaking to each other, our connection has remained strong. She'll always put her life on hold to help me out, especially when it involves my father.

We walk into the house, my eyes immediately going to a series of framed photos on the entryway table showcasing my father and his new family. I can't remember ever seeing a photo of my parents and me. Sure, there are photos of my mother and me, as well as some of my father and me. But I don't think there's anything in existence of the three of us, like we never were a family.

"Chloe!" an excited voice calls out, followed by two small arms flinging around my mid-section, squeezing me tightly. "I was worried you weren't going to make it!"

I briefly close my eyes, relishing in Midge's unbiased love. Regardless of her mother's feelings toward me, it hasn't rubbed off on her. I wish she could stay this innocent the rest of her life. It's only a matter of time until she picks up on her mother's animosity. After all, we're not born programmed to hate. We're taught that. And I know her mother will eventually teach her to despise me, even if she doesn't do it deliberately. All I can do is savor the fact that Midge hasn't learned to hate me yet.

"I wouldn't miss this party for anything. It's not every day my favorite sister turns six." I tousle her perfect blonde curls as she releases her hold, looking up at me.

"I'm your *only* sister."

"But you'd still be my favorite," I sing.

"Midge, sweetie," a high-pitched voice calls out, the sound of heels clicking against the hardwood growing closer. "Where did you—"

Tiffany stops in her tracks when she sees Izzy and me in the foyer. Her dyed blonde hair doesn't have a single strand out of place. I imagine she went to the salon early this morning to have it styled and her makeup applied so she'd look impeccable in the presence of all the other house vultures she invited.

"Oh… Chloe. You made it."

She leans in, pretending to kiss both my cheeks before pulling back. It must kill her to have to be nice to me because of Midge.

"Unfortunately, you missed all the cake and presents. Perhaps we should start telling you to be here an hour earlier so you'll show up on time."

For Midge's sake, I bite my tongue at her passive-aggressive statement. "I'd figure it out, then show up two hours after you said it started." I look down at Midge, handing her the gift bag. "Happy birthday, pipsqueak."

Tiffany huffs, crossing her arms in front of her chest. She's made it more than clear she doesn't believe in pet names for her children. But I do.

"Is this for me?"

"Of course it is, silly."

"Can I open it?"

"Absolutely."

With pure joy in her eyes, Midge plops onto the floor and tears at all the tissue packed inside the bag. She shrieks as she pulls out her gift. I steal a glimpse at Tiffany, who feigns enthusiasm. I saw the wish list she put together for Midge's birthday. Books about important figures in history. Educational toys. Computer programs to help her learn a foreign language. Nothing any young girl would be remotely excited about.

At Christmas, Midge had asked me if her parents were actually Santa, since he seemed to get her the same kinds of toys they did, while other kids at school received fun things to play with. So, I asked what she really wanted, then knew exactly what I'd be getting her for her birthday.

"You got me an American Girl doll?" She jumps to her feet and squeezes her arms around me as I crouch down to her level.

"You deserve it, pipsqueak. One of these days, I'll take you into the city so you can go to the American Girl store yourself. You can bring your doll, pick out some clothes for her. We can even take her to lunch there."

She squeals even more, hugging me again. This makes it all worth it, being able to give her something she really wants. Giving her one moment of happiness.

"Yes, well, we'll have to see about that," Tiffany snips, head held high. "Chloe does have a very busy schedule."

"But I'm never too busy for you," I tell Midge directly. "Okay?"

"Okay." She beams, looking from me to her doll. I sense she's itching to show off her new toy to her friends.

"Go play."

"There are a bunch of accessories and other things to use with your doll in here," Izzy offers, handing Midge a second gift bag.

Midge's gray eyes light up again and she wraps her arms around Izzy. "Thanks, Auntie Izzy."

"You bet. Now go."

Grinning, she spins, hurrying into the living room, excited shrieks coming from all the girls.

Able to feel the heat of Tiffany's glare on me, I shift my eyes to hers. "I thought we were clear that only gifts on the pre-approved list were to be purchased for Midge."

"Oh, you were clear. But as I'm sure you've learned, I don't exactly like rules." I return Tiffany's condescending smile, then spin from her.

The instant I enter the living room, all conversation ceases among the house vultures, as I've affectionately referred to them for years. I've never quite understood this group of women. They're all in their forties. All happy not to have a career, to be completely dependent on their husbands to provide for them. Granted, each is married to someone who does well for himself, all of them having married a man in their fifties or sixties, but I'd never want to be known as "Adam's wife" or "Joe's wife" or "Nathan's wife". No identity. So handmaid-ish.

Perhaps that was why my father wasn't happy with my mother. She was ambitious. Didn't want to sit at home and raise children. She wanted to show me that women could be just as successful as men. And she did, as much as she could when forced to sacrifice her own career to take care of me as a child.

"Chloe," one of the house vultures says, smiling and pretending they hadn't spent the past several minutes talking about me.

If I remember correctly, her name's Stephani-with-an-i, as she introduced herself to me when we met a few years ago. Not sure why it mattered, but apparently, that unique spelling was important enough that she was no longer Stephani, but Stephani-with-an-i.

"So glad you could finally make it. We were beginning to worry."

I meet her fake smile and raise her a fabricated grin. "The trains out of the city were running behind schedule."

Izzy and I move toward a few vacant chairs, and I take a minute to absorb my surroundings, the place barely recognizable as the home I remember from my youth. The furniture and window treatments are so over-the-top, probably meant to be a display of wealth but missed the mark and are downright gaudy.

"I don't know how you can stand living there," another one of the women offers, dressed almost identical to Tiffany and Stephani-with-an-i.

I wonder if there's an unspoken rule that every housewife in Greenwich must adhere to the same uniform. Hair just past their shoulders, preferably blonde, with perfect beach waves. Skin bronzed year-round, despite the fact it's only March and not yet beach weather. Pastel-colored sheath dresses showing off the figures they pay personal trainers thousands of dollars to help them achieve. I must stand out with my skinny jeans, oversized cardigan, and knee-high boots, not to mention my gray and lilac ombre hair.

"I know," Denise, another one of the house vultures, adds. "It's so big. And noisy. And chaotic. Not a place I'd ever be proud to live in."

"Well, I could never live in the suburbs," Izzy states in my defense, as she's prone to do whenever I leave Manhattan and come out to this place that often feels like a foreign country after living in the city so long. The fresh air, chirping birds, and large expanses of open space make me uneasy. I much prefer concrete, tall buildings, and a barrage of honking horns.

Denise looks at her with a wavering smile, then shrugs, sipping on her Champagne, oblivious to the children running around the house.

Izzy leans toward me. "Drink?"

"The stronger, the better." I'm usually not one to drink during the day, but there are exceptions to that rule. And today is an exception.

"You got it." She squeezes my side, then heads toward the kitchen.

"So, Chloe," Stephani-with-an-i says. I look in her direction. "The barista at the Starbucks by the elementary school recently colored her hair similar to yours. What's her name?" She scrunches her brows, glancing at a few of the other women.

"Lottie," one offers.

"No. I think it's something like Lauren."

"No," another woman says. "It's something strange. Like a stripper name. Lola maybe?"

"Possibly." Stephani-with-an-i still doesn't look convinced. "Or is it…" She pulls her bottom lip between her teeth. "Not Lola. Poppy!" She tilts her head and looks at me as all the women nod in agreement. "Do you know her?"

"I don't live here," I remind her. "So I haven't had the pleasure of having suburban Starbucks."

"Oh, I know you don't live here. I figured since your hair…"

I blink repeatedly, trying to mask my utter shock at the stupidity spewing from Stephani-with-an-i's mouth. This conversation further proves we need to put more money into our educational system and encourage women to have a career, instead of aspiring to be a trophy wife.

"So, since our hair is similar, you figure we…know each other?"

She peers at me like it's not a ridiculous idea. "You don't?"

I have to bite back my laughter, desperate for Izzy to return with that drink. "Simply because we have similar attributes doesn't mean we're BFFs. I doubt you're BFFs with every woman who's had a shitty blonde dye job." I pause, smiling as I glance around the room at the sea of blonde. "Actually, I stand corrected. It appears you are."

Her expression falls, her nose turning up in disgust. "Well, you don't have to be nasty about it. I was only trying to make conversation. Apparently, your mother never taught you manners."

"She was too busy teaching me common sense."

"Here you are," Izzy says breathlessly as she flies into the room, handing me a glass. She meets my eyes, her expression a look of warning to play nice for Midge's sake.

With a smile, I take it from her. "Saved by the martini," I mumble under my breath.

If nothing else, being here does have a certain entertainment value. Whenever I attend one of Tiffany's parties, I often feel like a prostitute who just walked into church.

And not one of those "we accept everyone regardless of your sexual orientation, past failings, and current drug habits" kind of churches. More like those judgmental, holier than thou churches that quote the Bible when it suits them but refuse to practice any kind of forgiveness, humility, or charity.

Hypocrites.

"As always," Izzy sings.

"Is Hannah coming?" Stephani-with-an-i inquires in an attempt to recover from her earlier blunder.

"I believe she's still on her honeymoon," Tiffany pipes up. "And her parents are decompressing in Fiji now that the wedding's over. A gift from Hannah and her husband."

All the women *ooh* and *aah* over their generosity.

"It was a beautiful wedding," Denise comments.

"Just perfect," Theresa adds. "And her husband will be able to provide such a wonderful life for her. She's so lucky to have found a man so successful. She'll be able to quit her job and focus on raising their children."

I snort-laugh as I bring my drink back to my mouth, taking a long sip to cover my reaction.

"Something funny?" Tiffany asks in a pleasant voice, a smile plastered on her face as she exudes all the manners she was taught during the years of etiquette lessons her upper-class family insisted she attend.

"The idea of Hannah staying home and raising children."

While she *did* marry a very successful man and the wedding a few weeks ago *was* gorgeous, Hannah's not the kind of woman who would be happy adhering to such a societal role. Whenever she comes to one of Tiffany's parties, mostly as moral support for me, she rolls her eyes at the ridiculousness of these women. How they have no drive to have a life of their own. To have an identity of their own. Plus, for as long as I can remember, Hannah has wanted to be a teacher. I don't see her giving up that career anytime soon. Or ever.

"Who else will raise her children when she has them?" Carrie asks.

"She gets summers off."

"Yes. But what about the rest of the year?"

"Gosh, that *is* a problem, isn't it?" I scrunch up my brow, pretending to be deep in thought, as if this predicament is one no one has considered before. Then my expression brightens. "Actually, I read about this new concept that's been around for...oh, probably only forty or fifty years. What is it called?"

I glance at the ceiling, pinching my lips together. Izzy stifles a laugh, the only one amused, since I can feel the daggers the rest of the women are shooting at me. "That's right." I snap my fingers and return my gaze to them. "Day-care. Hannah can put her spawn in daycare. That's assuming she even *wants* to have children."

"Why would you get married if you didn't want to have children?" Stephani-with-an-i asks.

"I don't know. Maybe because you're in love and want to commit your life to each other." I take a sip of my drink, many of them still looking at me like I'm crazy, so I go in for the kill. "Plus, Hannah mentioned wanting to adopt. She works with a lot of kids in the foster care system. Some of them get moved around so much that their education suffers. It's a noble thing."

"That is true," Tiffany says, always trying to be diplo-matic. "But aren't a lot of kids in foster care..." She trails off, wanting us to fill in the blank so she doesn't have to say it. But I'm not going to let her off so easily. She's always been prejudiced against anyone who isn't white and what she considers perfect.

"What?" I press.

"They're... You know."

"I don't think I do." I smirk. "Perhaps you should embellish so there's no misunderstanding."

"Just say it," Izzy interjects harshly, her dark eyes growing even darker.

She has very strong opinions on this subject. After all, she *is* Hispanic. And adopted. But it seems they all forget that

because, as Tiffany puts it, she doesn't "act" Hispanic, whatever that means.

"They're something other than white," Izzy states firmly
when she remains silent.

Tiffany's eyelids flutter as she holds her head high,
placing her hands in her lap. She steals a glance at the children. I wonder if any of these sheltered kids have ever seen a
person of color.

"Well, yes. Wouldn't she want her child to look like her?
What will people think when they see their mismatched
family?"

I've always found it odd that as staunch of a defender of
the First Amendment as my father is, often filing suits against
our own government when they try to suppress the media, he
married someone as closed-minded as Tiffany. Then again,
I'm not sure my father's ever loved her. I'm not sure he's
capable of loving anything other than his career. And I
doubt Tiffany's capable of loving anything except a large
bank account.

"Oh, I don't know," Izzy mocks. "Maybe that Hannah
has a heart of gold. So much so that she'd jump through
hoops to take in a child who isn't her own and love him or
her like they were. Do you have any idea how difficult it is to
adopt?"

All the women stare at her in silence.

"It's damn near impossible. Most people give up after so
many years because they can't take the constant roller-
coaster ride anymore. I would never prejudge a family
because they don't fit into some mold. It's the twenty-first
century, for crying out loud. I see all walks of life come
through the doors of the pediatric oncology wing at the
hospital. And yes, some of those kids are adopted. It's heart-
breaking to watch those parents struggle to find their child's

birth parents to have any hope for a bone marrow transplant. But you know the one thing that's universal. The only thing that matters in any family?"

The room becomes eerily still, her voice seeming to reverberate against the walls. Izzy darts her eyes to the kids who've stopped playing and are focused on her. She briefly pulls her lips between her teeth as she regains her composure.

"Love. Regardless of whether you're related by blood, *love* is all that matters. *Love* makes a family."

I reach for Izzy's hand, squeezing it, offering her a comforting smile.

"Like how I love Chloe, even if she's only my *half*-sister," Midge's voice breaks through the awkward silence.

"Exactly." Izzy smiles at her. "And you don't only love her because you're related, right?"

"No. I love her because she wears cool clothes, has awesome shoes..." She grins, lowering her voice to a dramatic whisper. "And she swears a lot."

A few women snicker, but quickly cover their mouths when Tiffany shoots a glare their way. In my defense, I've made a conscious effort to curtail it when I'm around Midge. I've yet to drop an F-bomb. I think.

"Just like Daddy," she finishes. "So they probably *are* related. Where else would Chloe have learned to swear if she didn't learn it from Daddy? That's where *I* learned."

I glance at Tiffany over my martini glass to gauge her reaction, an odd sense of satisfaction filling me at the sight of her squirming. After the number of kids she's had, she should know you can't say anything in front of them. At least nothing you want kept private.

"The apple certainly doesn't fall far from the tree," she says in a saccharine voice, neither confirming nor denying

Midge's statement. "Speaking of which, how's school going?" She smirks at me, probably expecting to hear I've withdrawn from yet another class because outside obligations interfered with my coursework.

"It's been an…interesting semester." I glance at Izzy and we share a knowing look. "But I'm happy to report it will be my last. I filed my graduation paperwork a few days ago."

I leave out the part about nearly dropping the class earlier in the semester. But as I'd hoped, Owen has made my situation increasingly tolerable. There's still a bit of awkwardness anytime my eyes meet Lincoln's, but it's not as thick as it was in the beginning.

"Is that right?" a deep, booming voice cuts through.

I whip my head toward the foyer to see my father standing there, much to my surprise, considering I'd assumed he was working today, as he always is.

But his presence here isn't what has my heart ricocheting to my throat, all the air sucked from my lungs.

It's *who* stands beside him that makes me feel like the walls are closing in, suffocating me.

Izzy nudges me, silently reminding me to pretend like it's a normal occurrence for Lincoln Moore to be in my child-hood home. Based on the familiar greetings from many of the house vultures, it might be. Many of them fawn over him, batting their lashes, sticking their chests out a little. But he doesn't notice them.

Just like that night at the club in Vegas, just like when he sent that martini over, just like when he nearly kissed me in the lobby of the casino, he looks at me as if I'm the only person who matters. Or maybe he's just as surprised to see me here as I am to see him.

"Let me get you another drink," Izzy murmurs, forcing my attention back to her.

I nod, swallowing the rest of my martini in one gulp before handing her the glass. I meet my father's expectant stare beckoning me toward him, probably so he can demean me in front of his employee in a show of superiority.

On a long exhale, I raise myself from the chair and walk across the living room, skirting discarded shards of wrapping paper and boxes filled with clothes.

"Hey, Dad." I float my eyes from his, looking at Lincoln. "Professor Moore."

"Miss Davenport."

"So I take it you're giving your First Amendment class yet another try?" My father lifts a single brow. He's always had a distinguished look to him. Tall and lean. Salt-and-pepper hair. Clean-shaven, apart from the times he's working on a big case and foregoes normal grooming to pull all-nighters. Smartly dressed, even when he keeps it casual with a blazer and jeans, like today.

"I *do* need it to graduate." I fold my arms in front of my chest, casually leaning against the wall, trying to appear unaffected when, in reality, my heart thunders against the walls of my chest, threatening to burst through.

"I won't pop the Champagne bottle just yet. It's your fourth time taking this class, isn't it?"

"Third." I grit a smile. "There were extenuating circumstances preventing me from completing the course the previous two times."

"There are *always* extenuating circumstances with you. It's your *tenth* year, isn't it? In my experience, people who've been going to college as long as you would be graduating with their doctorate, not merely a bachelors." He laughs jovially, as if his humor rivals that of a comedian.

That's how it's always been. He makes snide comments about everything I've done that fails to live up to his expectations, shrouding them in humor. But he means every biting comment, even if made in a light tone. If making passive-aggressive remarks were an Olympic sport, he'd be more decorated than Michael Phelps.

I clench my teeth, my jaw tensing. Yet I still smile. It's my last line of defense to act as if I don't care what my father thinks. That his statements have no effect on me.

"What can I say? I've never been one to stick to the rules."

"Rules are there for a reason, which I'm sure you're learning from Lincoln... Professor Moore here," he corrects quickly.

I look at Lincoln, a hint of sympathy in his gaze as he witnesses this strange dynamic, observing the exact reason I begged him to keep our past a secret.

"He's only thirty-five, yet he's accomplished so much. Graduated at the top of his class at Tufts, then went onto Yale Law. Worked for an advocacy group in the city before I stole him away. He's one of the top constitutional scholars in the country, a remarkable feat for someone so young. And you know why he's already achieved everything he has?"

"Because he's a white man?" I quip, partly joking, partly serious.

He rolls his eyes. It's something my protest-happy, political strategist mother would say.

"Because he knows about dedication. About having a strong work ethic. About putting in the time and effort to achieve goals, even if the path might be hard."

I inhale a deep breath through my nose, my lips pinching together as I do everything to maintain my composure and not completely lose it.

"Actually, Chloe is a wonderful student. The faculty

speaks very highly of her, particularly her advisor, Lara Stone."

I whip my eyes to Lincoln.

"Lara Stone isn't exactly a pioneer of hard-hitting journalism," my father scoffs. "But I suppose I can understand why she'd say that, considering she ended her career at a daytime talk show. That kind of thing is right up Chloe's alley, not real journalism. Simply reporting on celebrity gossip. No wonder they get along so well."

"We all have to start somewhere." Lincoln's tone is polite, despite my father's clear displeasure over the idea of anyone standing up for me. "At least she's working in the industry and learning how a magazine runs."

He gives me a reassuring smile before looking back at my father. A part of me wants to stop this, to tell Lincoln I don't need him to stand up for me. I stopped standing up for myself in this man's presence ages ago. But that's at odds with this small part that wants him to keep going. To hear the kindness and compassion in his tone.

"Not everyone is fortunate enough to land a desk at the *Times* right out of undergrad," he continues, referring to my father's dumb luck. "But Chloe's been in my class for six weeks now. In those six weeks, she's demonstrated an incredible understanding of the First Amendment that would rival that of any law student. In fact…" He glimpses at me. "She'd make one hell of a lawyer."

My father peers at him with curiosity. Can he sense there's a history between us? Don't fathers have this kind of sixth sense about men who've been intimate with their daughters?

"Chloe in law school?" He bursts out laughing, the gritting sound making the hair on my nape stand on end. "That's rich. It took her ten years to finish her bachelors.

Could you imagine how long it would take her to graduate law school?" He wipes at his eyes. "Come on. Let's get to work."

Jovially slapping Lincoln on the back, he forces him away from me. He probably thinks the longer he stays in my presence, the greater the chance of my inferiority rubbing off on the man who's obviously his star attorney. I remain frozen in place, summoning all my strength to pretend my father's comments have no bearing on me.

As they're about to disappear into my father's office, Lincoln glances over his shoulder, his eyes locking with mine. Then he mouths, *I'm sorry*.

That could have so many meanings. Is he sorry for what my father said? For not standing up for me more? Or is he sorry for us?

# Twenty-One

I make a beeline for Izzy, ignoring the curious eyes from the house vultures, and snatch the martini from her. Shakily raising it to my lips, I gulp down a large swallow, the liquor burning my throat.

"Come on." She loops her arm through mine, pulling me out of the room. "Let's see what kind of food's left over. I saw a few of my mother's famous tamales." Her voice is bright, a stark contrast to the warring emotions filling me at not only seeing Lincoln unexpectedly but hearing him stand up for me.

Izzy doesn't release her hold on me until we're out of earshot and in the large eat-in kitchen. At least she didn't lie about her mother's tamales. As expected, they were barely touched, most likely because it's "ethnic food", as I'm sure Tiffany referred to it. At this point, Izzy's mother probably sends it to piss her off, considering my father loves her tamales.

I grab a plate and pile on one pork and one chicken tamale, peeling back the corn husk before slicing into it. Once I've taken a bite, I look at Izzy, my muscles relaxing. We stare at each other for a few seconds before simultaneously breaking out in laughter at the ridiculousness of the situation.

"The only thing that would make this even more awkward is if Asher shows up." I shove another heaping forkful of "ethnic food" into my mouth, moaning at how delicious it is.

"Considering I haven't spoken to him since we left Vegas, there's a greater chance of this house being struck by lightning." She grabs a plate, assessing the options, settling on a few tamales, as well. "What are the chances Lincoln would be here?"

"He *does* work for my father. I guarantee Dad tried to go into the office today, but Tiffany undoubtedly threw a fit of epic proportion. So work coming to him was probably the compromise."

"What did your father say?" She leans closer, her voice barely audible. "Did he pick up on anything?"

"No. As usual, our conversation revolved around the fact I'm a complete failure who doesn't follow through on anything. All jokingly of course."

She rolls her eyes. "God, I hate that. I don't know why you put up with it. If it were anyone else, you'd give them a piece of your mind, then knee them in the junk to make them think twice about speaking that way to anyone else again."

Shrugging dismissively, I glance at the refrigerator, the surface devoid of anything personal. No birth announcements. None of Midge's artwork. Not even her latest spelling test because it wasn't good enough, even though she'd received a high mark.

"I've learned to pick and choose my battles. It's like he *wants* to piss me off. *Wants* me to lose my temper with him. Why give him the satisfaction? It's best to suck it up for the ten minutes a year we actually *do* speak to each other, then go back to my normal life he no longer has any say over."

It's silent for a moment as she assesses my statement. "And what did Lincoln have to say?"

My cheeks warm as his deep voice complimenting me echoes in my mind. I smooth a strand of hair behind my ear. "He told my father I was one of the smartest students he's ever had. That my understanding of the material would rival that of a law student. Of course, my father nearly dropped dead from a heart attack at the suggestion of me going to law school."

"So Lincoln stood up for you."

"I suppose," I answer nonchalantly.

"That's sweet."

I shoot my eyes to hers. "What? No, it's not. It's demeaning and chauvinistic. I don't need Lincoln to protect me from my asshole father. I've done just fine handling him for the past almost twenty-nine years of my life. And I'll do just fine the next twenty-nine years." I shove more tamale into my mouth, barely chewing before swallowing and inhaling deeply, using the food as a distraction from the conversation.

"He could have simply said you were doing well in class. He didn't have to go the extra mile and say you're exceptional, yet he did." She narrows her eyes, pinching her lips together. "I think he's struggling with this as much as you are."

"What?" I practically choke on my food. "I'm not struggling with this."

Izzy bursts out laughing. "Nice try, Chloe. You wouldn't be eating your emotions right now if you didn't still have feelings for him."

I pause with my mouth wide open, about to shovel in

even more food. "I'm not eating my emotions." I put down the fork, pushing the plate away. "I'm just hungry."

"Whatever you say."

"Like I said, we've agreed to pretend that Vegas never happened, or the few days that followed. It's for the best."

"Do you really believe that?"

"Of course I do!" I retort loudly before lowering my voice. "Even if I didn't, it doesn't matter," I remind her.

"I get that. I just…" She trails off, blowing out a long breath.

"Do you remember what you said while we waited for our flight out of Vegas before it was canceled? When I told you about the man I kept running into whose name I didn't even know?"

She subtly nods. "That maybe there was a reason you kept running into each other."

"The same can be said here. Maybe this is the universe's way of telling me it would have never worked out anyway. That we really *are* too different to be compatible. You should see the man's apartment! There wasn't a speck of dust anywhere. And his closet?"

Izzy smirks, crossing her arms in front of her chest, clearly amused. "Yes?"

"The clothes were actually hung up. On hangers."

"What?" she shoots back in faux shock, bringing her hands to her cheeks. "You mean they weren't thrown all over the bed and floor? This isn't right. It must be some sort of witchcraft."

"You know what I mean," I whine.

Her joking expression lightens, and she looks upon me affectionately, placing a hand on my bicep. "I don't know Lincoln all that well, but there's something to be said about playing Never Have I Ever with complete strangers. You learn things. I don't think you two are as opposite as you believe."

Footsteps sound from the hallway, and I snap my head up, expecting Tiffany to come in and berate me for being antisocial by hiding away in the kitchen and stuffing my face with food.

Instead, Lincoln rounds the corner, coming to an abrupt stop when he sees Izzy and me. He hesitates, forehead wrinkling as he seems to weigh his options.

"Lincoln," Izzy greets, breaking through the silence. "What a surprise to see you, and here, of all places."

I pinch her side, an unspoken warning.

He pulls his lips between his teeth, and I sense him mulling over his words. Then he recovers his composure, posture straight, eyes distant.

"David said there's coffee?"

Pushing away from the counter, she passes him a sly smile. "Chloe can show you while I use the little girl's room."

I dart my wide gaze toward her. But even with the death stare I give her, she doesn't change course, floating out of the kitchen without a single look back as she sings, "Good to see you again, Lincoln."

He remains silent, not acknowledging her. Once we're alone, he brings his eyes back to mine. But I can't bear to look into their depths, spinning him, my purposeful strides taking me toward the coffee bar in the corner of the kitchen.

"I can do it."

"It's fine," I practically bark out, grabbing a pod and placing it into the one-cup brewer. I groan, realizing someone turned it off so now it needs to warm up and heat the water, drawing out Lincoln's presence even longer. I press the power button, staring at the machine as it hums to life.

"I'm sorry about what your father said before," he offers after several moments of strained silence.

"Don't." I whirl around, my hardened stare cautioning.

"I just—" He steps toward me, but I hold up my hand, preventing him from coming any closer.

"I don't need your help," I seethe, my nostrils flaring. "I've been dealing with that man fine my entire life. Got it?"

He stares at me for several intense moments, then nods, his shoulders falling. "Got it."

"Good." I spin around, staring at the screen on the brewer, willing it to stop preheating.

"Has he always been that way?" he asks after a pregnant pause.

I shrug.

"You mentioned he's why you didn't want..." He trails off. "I guess a part of me thought you were over-exaggerating. I didn't realize how..."

"What?" I face him once more. "How much of an asshole your boss is?"

He shoves his hands into his pockets. "I knew he was a hard-ass. He has a reputation for being one, but that's what makes him a great lawyer. He doesn't stop pushing, even when facing adversity. But..."

"You assumed he'd leave the job at the office?"

He brings his bottom lip between his teeth. I look away, the memory of how those lips felt against mine only making this more difficult. It's one thing to have to watch him during class, but at least there's distance between us. Now that distance seems to evaporate with every beat of my heart.

"Yes, I did." He takes another step toward me. My brain tries to tell my body to retreat, but I'm still drawn to him, the magnetism I felt that first meeting ever present. "That's why you're here, isn't it?"

"You think I come here so he can use me as a verbal punching bag? Hell, I'm only here because I assumed he'd be working. Like he always is. If I had known he'd be here, I never would have made the trek out of the city."

He peers at me thoughtfully, peeling away layer after layer. "I don't think that's true. You do this for her."

"Who?"

He floats his eyes to my wrist where the beaded bracelet Midge made me sits. She put so much effort into it, telling me how she learned to spell "sisters" so she could make it. It's the most thoughtful gift I've ever received. But it allows Lincoln a peek into who I am, even more so than he's already had.

"Your sister."

I quickly cover the bracelet with my free hand, shifting my feet.

"Midge, right?"

I nod, the movement borderline imperceptible.

"You come here for her, don't you?"

"It *is* her birthday party." My tone is sarcastic as I try to shrug off his insinuations. "*Everyone* is here for Midge."

Slowly shaking his head, his eyes rake over my face. "That's not what I'm talking about. You leave the city and come to suburbia, which probably stands for everything you despise, just so Midge feels loved. You'll do whatever you can to make her realize she's perfect, that everything she does is perfect." He smiles, laughing slightly. "Even if she misspelled sisters and mixed up two of the colors in the bead pattern, you'd never point it out to her. You probably told her how much you loved it, how you'd always treasure it, more so than some ridiculously expensive piece of jewelry from Cartier or Tiffany's some guy bought you just to have a shot with you. Isn't that right?"

Bewildered, I stare at him, his words so accurate it's frightening. "Maybe."

He forms his mouth into a tight line, squinting, as he continues to analyze me, the space between us decreasing. "You're quite the conundrum, Chloe Davenport."

"What makes you say that?" My voice is low, wanton, husky, his nearness casting a spell over me.

"That morning in Vegas, you made it sound like you were incapable of being loved. That you were incapable of loving anyone. You may not have come right out and said it, but I've been practicing law long enough to know how to read between the lines, to make educated assumptions."

"And what assumptions did you make?"

"That you wanted to take a risk but were scared of the potential ramifications. Worse, that you were scared people would think you aren't as strong as you want them to believe because of your feelings. But you can love someone and still be strong."

"I don't see how," I manage to croak out. "Love makes you weak."

"No. It makes you human." His breathing increases as his lips hover even closer, barely a whisper away. "Don't you want to feel human again? Don't you want to *feel* again?"

I close my eyes, convinced this is a dream. There's no other explanation for this conversation, for this moment. Not after he insisted we keep our distance, that we forget each other, that we pretend we don't know each other. But if it *were* a dream, I wouldn't feel the heat of his breath ghosting against my lips. I wouldn't feel the tingle of what's to come overtaking me. I wouldn't feel my knees growing weak in anticipation.

I lift my chin, my heart drumming violently in my chest as we flirt with the devil. The fact that touching Lincoln is forbidden only makes me want him more. Makes me want him in ways I've never craved another man.

"I do want to feel," I whimper, the past several weeks of not tasting his lips pushing me past my breaking point.

"Then feel me." His voice is a low growl as he erases the final distance between us. Suddenly, footsteps echo, growing closer, cutting through our trance.

My eyes widen, breath catching, at the same time Lincoln jumps back, the tenderness mixed with yearning that covered his expression replaced with fear…and regret.

"There you are," my father's familiar voice bellows. He comes to a stop when he sees me. "Oh, I apologize. Was Chloe bothering you? She should know better than to try to butter you up just because she's realized you work for me."

I turn around, taking a moment to settle my flushed complexion as I finish preparing the coffee. "I wasn't buttering him up. I offered to make him a coffee since he's a guest in this house." I whirl around, gritting a smile. "Then again, I suppose I am now, too. Here you go." I hold the mug out toward Lincoln. "I prepared it how—"

His sharp intake of breath, coupled with his frantic expression, cuts my statement short. I snap my mouth shut, horrified at what I was about to say. The last thing I need to mention is that I know how Lincoln likes his coffee. That's not exactly something a professor includes on the class syllabus.

"How I like it," I finish, recovering. "I hope only a hint of sweetener is okay."

"That's fine." His lips curve up in the corners. I wonder if he's recalling the few times I brought him coffee in bed. Along with another kind of morning "pick me up".

"Tell her if it's not," my father insists. "You shouldn't

have to drink something you're not happy with because Chloe wasn't paying attention. I taught her better than that."

"Actually, it appears I take my coffee like she does." His eyes remain locked on mine. "Even if I didn't, I'd never depreciate someone's kindness and generosity that way," he adds, but my father glosses over his comment.

"Right. I just got off the phone with the legal department of a small newspaper down in Texas where that school shooting happened."

Lincoln nods. Normally, I tune out once my father discusses anything work-related, since it acts as a reminder of how he'd never love anyone as much as he does that job. But something about watching the wheels spin in Lincoln's head turns me on, has me glued to him. The same way I find myself mesmerized in class when he plays devil's advocate with the other students, sometimes to the point of almost being an asshole. The passion he exudes for the subject is unmatched by anything I've ever witnessed.

"The court sealed the criminal record of the accused's father, from whom he stole the gun he used in the massacre. They've asked us to help prepare an emergency motion unsealing it. I don't have to tell you the importance of this information, so let's get back to work."

He spins on his heel, walking out of the kitchen, past the living room, not acknowledging Midge. I wonder if he even wished her a happy birthday. Based on my experience, he most likely didn't.

Lincoln hesitates, his gaze locking with mine, and I can sense a part of him wants to stay to clear the air we've now muddied.

"Are you coming?" my father calls from down the hallway once he realizes Lincoln didn't immediately follow him.

My eyes beg him to tell my father no, to ask me to go somewhere with him, regardless of how wrong it is. This once, I want a man to choose me, to want me, to *fight for* me. But he doesn't. Instead, he shakes his head, turning from me without a single glance back.

# Twenty-Two

"Earth to Chloe," Owen sings. I lift my eyes to his, wondering what we were talking about, having zoned out. "Welcome back, sunshine."

"Sorry." I offer an apologetic look. "I'm a bit preoccupied." I shift my attention to the front of the room where Lincoln will deliver his lecture. It'll be the first time I've seen him since our near kiss this past weekend, and I'm not sure how to act.

I've spent the past several days convincing myself that everything having to do with Lincoln Moore has been one big mistake. From sleeping with him in the first place, to agreeing to give him a chance, to nearly kissing him during Midge's birthday party.

With a few sweet words, I allowed him to see behind the mask, to peer into my soul. Never again. From now on, I'll treat Lincoln exactly how he'd asked when we started this charade back in January. I'll act as if I have nothing more than cold indifference toward him.

"Everything okay?" Owen asks.

"Yeah. I've had a lot on my mind. The last thing I want to do today is sit through this class."

"Well, you might get lucky." He gestures to the clock

right above the doorway. "It's ten minutes after. Five more minutes and we get to leave."

"That's odd. Li— Professor Moore is usually punctual."

"True. Unless he got distracted with Professor Gordon." He playfully nudges me in the side. "If you know what I mean."

Heat washes over my face, my heart plummeting. "Actually, I don't."

"*Everyone* knows about Professor Gordon and Professor Moore." He looks at me as if I just asked what color the sky was, as if it's a fact that just is. No explanation necessary.

"Professor Gordon and Professor Moore are an item?" My voice comes out more like a squeak.

"I figure you knew. Like I said—"

"Yeah, yeah. *Everyone* knows." I chew on my lower lip, doing my best to pretend this news has zero effect on me. It shouldn't, but I can't stop the myriad of questions that pop into my mind. Was he dating her when we met? When he begged me for a chance? When I gave him that chance?

The relationship makes sense. He's ridiculously handsome. Intelligent. Successful. And Professor Gordon is what many of the guys in the department refer to as a solid eleven on a scale of ten. Like Lincoln, she's young and incredibly ambitious. In fact, she's the driving force behind a website, the sole purpose of which is to give unbiased news in an age when corporations and big money buy newspapers and television stations in order to skew the message.

"I guess I just kind of tune out all the gossip here at school," I add, my voice lacking any emotion. Owen doesn't seem to pick up on my sudden change in demeanor, though.

"I can understand that, considering you must get your fair share at work."

"Yeah."

When the door opens, all eyes shift in its direction, watching as Lincoln walks into the room. His hair is a bit disheveled, his tie not as tight and straight as it normally is. I do my best not to glare, but fail miserably.

"Well, I guess he was able to pull himself away, after all," Owen mutters.

Jealousy, raw and ugly, rears its head. There could be a perfectly reasonable explanation for his harried appearance and tardiness. Maybe an emergency filing at the paper. But a sinking feeling forms in my stomach that it has nothing to do with work.

"I apologize for the delay. I had something to take care of. Now, who wants to tell the class about the infamous 'cake' case?"

Owen leans toward me. "I bet he did." He waggles his brows.

"Mr. Campbell."

"Dammit," Owen utters under his breath, barely audible.

"Why don't you tell us the background of this case."

Owen straightens in his chair, looking through his notebook. When he speaks, his voice evidences his nerves. It doesn't matter how often he gets called on in class. It's more than apparent he hates public speaking.

"A couple went to a popular local bakery to discuss a design for their wedding cake, but the owner refused to serve them because they were gay."

"Did the owner refuse to *serve* them?" Lincoln shoots back. "Or was it something else?"

"Well, he refused to make the cake for them."

"Better, Mr. Campbell. It may not seem it, but there is a difference. Technicalities are extremely important in the law. Now, what did the couple do?"

He hesitates, flipping through his notes, searching for the

answer. I shift my notepad so he can see, subtly pointing to my own scribblings on the case.

Owen offers me a grateful smile as he glances at my notes, which are surprisingly much more organized than his. "Filed a complaint with the local anti-discrimination commission."

"And why does that matter?"

Owen looks at his pages again, but it won't be in there. He can talk about social injustice and current events with an understanding and expertise I doubt I'll ever possess, but when it comes to the law, he has trouble wrapping his head around procedure and how it all fits together.

I tap loudly on my notebook, getting his attention once more, and he steals a glance.

"Oh," he says after reading, lifting his eyes to address Lincoln. "Because the state had enacted an anti-discrimination statute, preventing any business from discriminating on the basis of race, gender, or sexual orientation, among other things."

"Correct. So it sounds like this is an anti-discrimination suit. Then why are we studying it in a First Amendment class?"

Owen stares, uncertain, pulling his bottom lip between his teeth as he attempts to formulate a response. "I—"

"I'll wait while Miss Davenport gives you the answer." His tone is biting, and I hate that he seems to pick on Owen disproportionately to the other students in class simply because we've formed a friendship over the past several weeks. Well, I'm done playing this game. Done letting Lincoln use Owen as his own verbal punching bag.

"The owner of the bakery argued the anti-discrimination law violated his First Amendment rights," I say without raising my hand.

Lincoln shoots his eyes to mine, as does everyone else, considering I've yet to speak in class.

"More specifically, the Free Exercise Clause. He claimed the state overreached in commanding him to make a cake for a wedding he objected to on religious grounds."

"Thank you, Miss Davenport. Should I assume you're Mr. Campbell's mouthpiece now?"

"I suppose that's better than the other way around." I pinch my lips into a tight line, crossing my legs.

Lincoln scowls, an unspoken warning in his eyes, before he shifts his attention back to Owen. "Now, Mr. Campbell, what did the court decide?"

I don't even give Owen a chance to respond before answering. "They sided with the asshole baker. But not on the bigger issue of the intersection of using the First Amendment as a defense to an anti-discrimination statute, but because they believed the commission exhibited hostility toward the baker's religious beliefs in its decision."

"Thank you for that rather astute analysis, *Mr. Campbell*," he barks out in a condescending tone. "As you so succinctly put it in a voice that's much more feminine than your normal one, the court never decided the issue of the intersection of anti-discrimination statutes and the Free Exercise Clause. So why would I require you to read this?"

"To demonstrate the lack of balls the court exhibited," I quip sarcastically.

"Lack of...balls?" Lincoln repeats. Several of the other girls in class giggle at his statement.

"Exactly."

He folds his arms in front of his chest, widening his stance, turning his attention fully to me. My pulse increases as I focus on his biceps, the flexing muscles stretching the material of his suit jacket. I push down the memory of having those arms wrapped around me, how it felt to be enclosed within them.

"And if *you* were on the court, what would you have decided, Miss Davenport?"

All eyes in the room shift toward me. Most every other student would probably say something well-thought-out and educated, based purely on legal precedent. But that's not me. I've always been much more emotionally driven.

"That the baker shouldn't be permitted to not serve a customer just because of his bigoted view, which he shrouded in religion. I'm not an expert, but I'm pretty sure Jesus would be pissed. Or God. Or whomever makes the rules."

The corners of his lips curve up. "So you wouldn't afford him his constitutional right to the free exercise of religion?"

"Where would it end?" I counter, everyone's attention shooting back to me. "Should we allow restaurant owners the ability to refuse service to gay couples, too?"

Lincoln grins. I thought he'd be upset by my persistence. Maybe he was at first. But now I can't help but feel he's getting some kind of satisfaction out of me arguing with him like this.

"Then let's take the anti-discrimination law out of it. Let's just look at this from a First Amendment standpoint. Should a state be able to force a citizen to create art for someone else? Regardless of whether they're straight, gay, black, white, woman, man. Take away all the complications here. Shouldn't people who create have the right to decide which commissions to take?"

I smirk. "So baking a cake is a protected form of speech now?"

"Art is considered speech. Just a different form."

"But where does it end?" I say once more. "Going back

to my example from before. A chef could consider plating his entrees art. Does he get to deny people service?"

"That's not the same thing. Those entrees, although pleasing to the eye, aren't created for their aesthetic qualities."

"And a cake is?" I arch a brow.

He shrugs. "While I've never been married myself, I have plenty of friends who have. Choosing the wedding cake is one of the most important items on their to-do list. They go over designs for what seems like days. Hell, some of these people aren't even called bakers or pastry chefs, but cake artists. These cakes can take days to finish. If we were discussing a simple sheet cake with a layer of plain frosting, like one you'd buy at a local grocery store, I'd be inclined to agree with you. But that's not a wedding cake. At least no woman I know would ever stand for something so ordinary and trivial. You may not like it, but these distinctions are important. These lines are important."

"Of course," I shoot back, my voice growing louder and increasingly annoyed. "I understand how important it is to have *clearly drawn lines*."

My words come out biting, causing Lincoln's eyes to darken and narrow on me in a look of warning. I should stop right now. Get back on track and apologize for my outburst, make up some story about having a gay friend who should be able to have the wedding cake of his dreams. But I don't. All the heartache at having to sit in Lincoln's presence for weeks and not be able to touch him, feel him, kiss him has come to a head. Add in the knowledge that he's been seeing someone else, and I've lost the ability to give a shit about keeping my mouth shut.

"I'm sure your anal-retentive nature needs the ability to put everything into boxes. Boss. Employee. Male. Female.

Rich. Poor. Teacher. Student." I pause briefly, noticing Lincoln shift uncomfortably, the cords in his neck straining, his fists clenching. When I continue, my voice becomes increasingly agitated with each word. "No gray area. No crossover. No risk. But lines sometimes get blurred. Sometimes those blurred lines are okay because you finally feel something so perfect and beautiful and you just want to tell society to fuck off and let us be together."

My voice rings out as shocked gasps fill the space. Lincoln's posture stiffens as he gives me a death glare. It's not until I see his reaction I realize exactly what I've said in front of a class of several dozen journalism students who love nothing more than a juicy story.

"Them," I correct softly, my tone wavering. "Let them be together."

His jaw twitches as his lips curl almost into a snarl, his stare cold and vindictive.

"Class is dismissed. Miss Davenport, my office. *Now.*"

Without another word, he collects his things and storms out of the room, leaving everyone in stunned silence. Including me.

# Twenty-Three

T he walk from the classroom to the faculty corridor seems to be miles instead of the dozen or so yards it is. I can't help but feel like a condemned prisoner heading to the gallows. Hell, I can practically hear the warden yelling "Dead man walking" in the recesses of my mind.

I almost turn around countless times, deciding it isn't worth it, that I should withdraw. But my father's biting comments and my drive to prove him wrong push me forward.

With my head held high, I steel my resolve, about to knock on Lincoln's door when it swings wide, my executioner standing before me, his anger having only increased in the past several minutes.

*Oh shit.*

He yanks me inside, closing the door behind me. I barely have a minute to catch my breath before he leans toward me.

"What the fuck was that?" he seethes, the vein in his neck engorged. "Are you out of your goddamn mind?"

He paces, tugging at his dark hair, more frazzled than I've seen him before. A part of me wanted this reaction, wanted to see this passion, this intensity, this humanity, instead of the unfeeling, unaffected human who's been standing in front of the class for weeks, doing everything to ignore me, to pretend he never met me.

"What were you thinking?" He stops, turning toward me, his voice choked. "I promised I'd keep whatever we had a secret. *For you.*"

I blow out a laugh. "Right. For me. Not because you didn't want a certain someone to find out about us." I roll my eyes, allowing my heavy bag to fall to the floor with a loud thump.

He advances on me, his expression flashing with rage, jaw tense, lips achingly close. "What's that supposed to mean?"

"Exactly what I said." I step back, increasing the distance between us, my mouth formed into a tight line. "Did you not think I'd find out?"

"Find out what?"

I place my hands on my hips. "About you and Professor Gordon," I hiss. "Why did you beg me to give you a chance when you were already getting a piece of ass? Or is this part of your game?" With every word, my voice becomes more strained, the hurt that he was never serious about me causing my fists to clench, my body to quake with anger. "See how many women you can get to fawn over you as some boost to your fragile male ego?"

I fight back the tears threatening to fall, hating that this man has brought out these kinds of emotions in me. I've often prided myself on not allowing anyone to get to me. But Lincoln has. It makes me despise him even more.

"What are you talking about?"

"Oh please… Don't play dumb now. It doesn't suit you, *Professor.*"

"I'm not playing dumb. I… You think I'm dating Tess? I mean, Professor Gordon?"

"Not just me. The entire student body of the journalism department claims you guys are an item. Apparently, it's common knowledge."

"And what makes them say that? Because I agreed to talk to her students about defamation one day?"

I shrug, not answering. The truth is, I'm not sure of the details, didn't stop to verify any information, not like I normally would, the shock of it rendering me momentarily incapable of doing so. Stealing a glimpse at his face, I study his features, searching for any sign he's playing me. But all I see is genuine confusion.

"Or maybe because I've been seen having dinner with her on occasion, considering she often reaches out to the *Times* for help with FOI filings when they affect matters of national importance."

Lowering my head, I pull my lips between my teeth, my confidence waning with every reasonable explanation he gives.

"Or maybe it's because I genuinely like her as a person and can trust her, so when we're seen having lunch together before class, it must be a precursor to something more. Because certainly men and women can't be friends. One must be interested in the other. Is that right?"

I shake off my indecision, turning my resolute gaze back to him. He can come up with different explanations all he wants. After all, he *is* a lawyer. That's probably one of the first things you learn in law school. How to bullshit. But he can't fool me.

"You haven't denied it."

When he steps toward me, his green eyes darken as he studies my face, taking his time to appreciate the curve of my cheeks, the heart-like shape of my lips, the fire in my stare. The heat radiating from him is reminiscent of our first night together. When he came into my room and looked upon me with so much hunger, wanting the night to last an eternity for fear that what we had would vanish the instant the lights came back on.

"Chloe…"

The way my name rolls off his tongue makes it sound like a prayer. A benediction. A supplication. I've missed the intonation when he says my name. My *real* name. I'm so tired of having to be Miss Davenport around him. Of him having to be Professor Moore. There have never been two lines I wanted to blur more than those.

"How can I date someone when I'm still hung up on the last woman in my life?"

I release a tiny exhale of air, blinking repeatedly, taken aback by his admission. "And who's that?" I barely manage to squeak out.

"This incredible woman I've been unable to stop thinking about since the moment I laid eyes on her when she was stuck at a bachelorette party in Vegas, where she was obviously miserable."

"Sounds like a smart woman," I retort, my tone lightening. In the blink of an eye, Lincoln's able to shift my outrage into something else, something much more electrifying. "Bachelorette parties are akin to torture."

"Then you'd probably like this woman. I know I did from the instant she finally spoke and told me off because she thought I was trying to hit on her."

"But you weren't?"

"No," he answers smoothly, then quickly corrects himself. "Well, I mean, in a way, I suppose. I don't know. But something drew me to help this stunning woman when some drunk guy, who thought she was a prostitute, wouldn't leave her alone. Regardless of whether I was lucky enough to find out her name, I needed to go to her, to remind her there are decent people in the world." He leans toward me and cups my cheeks in his hands. "That there are people who think the world of her, regardless of what others have led her to believe."

As I relish in the heat of his rough skin on mine, I whimper, not wanting this moment to come to an end before it has a chance to begin.

"That *I* think the world of her, regardless of what my behavior has led her to believe."

All sense of where we are, *who* we are, flees from my mind at his captivating words, and I grab the back of his neck, forcing him to erase that final bit of space between us. The instant his lips press against mine, sparks shoot through me. Every inch of me floods with warmth, with desire, with need, our bodies molding together as we greedily reignite this connection we've done everything to pretend never existed.

I swipe my tongue along the seam of his mouth, begging to taste what I've been deprived of for too long. With a growl, Lincoln deepens the kiss, enclosing me in his firm body.

His hands move to my hips and he lifts me with ease, forcing my legs around his waist. Losing myself in him, I remain oblivious to how wrong this is. In this beautiful moment, nothing else matters. That he's my professor. That I'm his student. That we've just eviscerated any line we had drawn. But the truth remains. There is no line. Not when it comes to Lincoln. Not when nothing else has ever felt so fucking right.

A man obsessed, he deposits me on the desk, sending neatly stacked files and papers to the floor. Tearing his lips from mine with a heady groan, he trails a hot path along my jawline, sucking and biting on my neck. The scruff of his trim beard is jarring and bruising, yet so wanted, making me feel more alive than I have in weeks.

"I could never forget you," he assures me, his voice laden with desire. "You're all I've been able to think about, Chloe. Every time I walk into class and see how incredible you look, all I can focus on is getting you alone again. Of feeling you again."

"Then feel me."

Pulsing against him, I reach for his pants, unbuckling his belt, desperate for him. As I'm about to lower his zipper, he grabs my wrist, stopping me. My eyes dart up, meeting his. I brace myself for him to tell me this is a mistake, that he lost his head. But he doesn't. Instead, he brings his lips to mine, feathering soft kisses.

"I don't have a condom." He chuckles, the deep rumble electrifying. "I don't exactly make a habit out of bringing girls back to my office for this sort of thing."

"I don't care," I breathe. "Let me feel you."

His mouth slams against mine once more as he squeezes my thigh, the pressure leaving no question there will be a mark. And just like our first night together, I'm confident that's exactly what he wants. That every time I look at my body and see the bruises on my thighs and bite marks on my neck, I'll be reminded of who put them there, who marked me, who branded me as his.

"I'm yours," I exhale, giving him the confirmation I know he needs.

"Mine," he snarls, an animal in heat.

"Yours. Always."

"Mine," he says again, this time softer, more heartfelt.

His hand moves up my leg, disappearing under my dress. When he pushes the skirt up around my waist, I meet his eyes. A devilish glint appears within as he hooks his fingers into the band of my panties…ones he bought for me. With quick movements, he lowers them down my legs before shoving them into his pocket.

"And those are mine, too." He kisses me, starved and greedy.

"Yes. Yours."

His teeth clamp onto my bottom lip, the pain dueling with the pleasure of what's to come. Then he leans back, his eyes locking on mine. He runs his hand along my collarbone, traveling between the valley of my breasts, down my stomach, coming to a stop just shy of that place I'm desperate to have him touch, explore, command.

I should feel cheap and dirty, considering he has me on his desk, legs spread, leaving me exposed to his fully clothed body, but I don't. I just want Lincoln. Any way I can get him.

He brings himself out of his pants, raising his arousal to me. My pulse skyrockets and I hold my breath, bracing to experience him with no barrier. He looks at me, an unspoken question in his tender gaze. I nod.

His pupils dilate, about to drive inside, when a knocking rips through the space. "Linc? It's Tess."

Every muscle in his body grows taut, all the color draining from his face. "Shit."

Eyes that overflowed with primal heat mere seconds ago widen, filling with remorse and disgust. In a heartbeat, the Lincoln I met in Vegas is gone, transforming into the Lincoln I saw the first time I stepped foot in his classroom. Into Professor Moore.

"Just a minute," he calls out, his voice trembling with anxiety as he hurriedly shoves himself back into his pants, readjusting his suit.

"I heard you ended class early." There's a pause before

she speaks again, her voice lower. "That you got into it with Chloe Davenport. I wanted to make sure everything's okay."

"I'm in the middle of a phone call," he replies as he practically throws me off the desk, pushing my skirt down to hide any hint of impropriety. When I remain in place, shocked from the sudden shift in demeanor, he grabs my bag and thrusts it at me.

I blink repeatedly, feeling like an errant child who was caught with her hand in the cookie jar when she knows it's off-limits.

Like I know Lincoln's supposed to be off-limits.

That doesn't make this any easier.

"It was a misunderstanding. We've straightened it out. I can assure you it will *never* happen again." His eyes narrow on me, his expression severe. It doesn't take a genius to hear the true meaning behind his words.

"Okay," Professor Gordon's sweet voice carries through. "I'm around if you want to grab a drink."

"Sounds good. I'll be with you once I put out this fire."

I listen as her footsteps retreat. Heat covers my face, making me momentarily oblivious of the consequences, and I reel back, landing a hard slap against his cheek, the sound seeming to reverberate in the small space.

At first, he's stunned, his body frozen. I gave Lincoln a chance because I thought he was different. Thought nothing would turn him into an asshole. Thought he wouldn't become like every other guy who made me feel cheap, useless.

But he's just like them. Willing to get a piece until they're reminded they have a wife, a girlfriend, a life they don't want to lose. Maybe my father's been right all along. Maybe I'm *not* good enough. Maybe I'll *never* be good enough.

Lincoln's expression softens as he licks his lips. "Chloe, I—"

I quickly shoot up my hand, cutting him off. I want to tell him I'm going to the dean with the details of our relationship to spite him, but he'll know it's an empty threat. *I* was the one who didn't want him to tell anyone.

"You're right." I square my shoulders, my words straining past the lump in my throat. "It was a misunderstanding, one that will absolutely never happen again. No matter what." I storm toward the door, about to open it when he calls out to me.

"Chloe…" The timbre of his voice is tender, a complete contradiction to the way he just spoke to me.

As much as I know I shouldn't, I look over my shoulder. Turmoil covers his expression and he moves toward me, his eyes pleading. I fully face him, hope building inside me that he's about to apologize, say he made a mistake. Then he slowly reaches into his pocket, pulling out my panties.

"These are yours." He holds them out toward me, swallowing hard, a hint of reluctance on his face.

Remember in elementary school when your teacher tried to shape your behavior toward others and promote kindness by saying that actions speak louder than words?

Well, this moment proves that's true. Because this one action obliterates my heart more than any words ever could.

# Twenty-Four

"Wait a second," Nora says the following Wednesday as she zips up the back of one of the bridesmaid gowns she's considering for me.

Pulling the material to make it tighter, she glances at my reflection as I stand on a pedestal in front of a three-way mirror in the middle of a posh bridal boutique in Midtown. It's a silver dress that hugs my body through my hips to where it falls a few inches above my knees. Thankfully Nora's not sticking us all in the same color and style. We'll all be wearing different tones and cuts, based on our body type and coloring. Better than Hannah's wedding, when Izzy and I were forced to wear identical pink chiffon gowns that looked like a bottle of Pepto-Bismol got freaky with a cotton candy machine.

"You had sex in his office?"

Her voice carries through the space and I glare at her, but she doesn't seem to care. I doubt any of the ladies who work here will flock to social media to dish about whatever hot gossip they overhear. They've probably heard much juicier stories than one of the bridesmaids almost sleeping with her college professor.

"We didn't have sex," I correct. "We *almost* had sex."

"How close are we talking here?" Evie pipes up from her position on one of the uncomfortable looking chairs that would be more fitting in a Victorian tea room than a dressing room at a bridal boutique. "Are we talking 'about to rip open a condom' close? Or 'a little tip action before the first thrust' close?"

"There was definitely some tip. Although I'm not sure I'd call it just some." My cheeks heat. "Lincoln is rather...gifted."

We all giggle as I fan myself dramatically. As angry as I was initially, discussing everything with my friends is exactly what I need. They're better than any therapist. They make me believe I'll get through this little rough patch.

"What are you going to do?" Evie asks once our laughter dies down.

"What *can* I do? I should have stayed quiet. This never would have happened if I kept my mouth shut in class and pretended we have no history, just like he's done."

"And what? Risk an even bigger blow-up down the road?" Izzy quips before glancing at Nora. "By the way, that's a good style choice for Chloe. Simple, straight lines work best since she has... What?" She looks back at me. "Size A boobs and no waist?"

I stick out my chest a little, but she's not far off. "For your information, I'm a B-cup."

"So you *have* graduated from the training bra."

"Ha. Ha. Ha. Sorry I don't have triple D boobs like all of you."

"I'm only a C," she argues back. "Now, getting back to Lincoln Moore—"

"Just Lincoln," I correct.

"Whatever. This was bound to happen. Especially after the way he looked at you during Midge's birthday party."

"What?" Nora and Evie simultaneously fling their eyes toward me.

"He was at Midge's party?" Nora spins me around to face her. "When were you going to share this with us?"

"Eventually… Maybe."

"Why was he there?" Evie presses.

"Because instead of taking the day off to celebrate, my father had work come to him. Just like he did when I was growing up." I grit a smile.

"Did you talk to him?" Nora asks, her voice lower.

"It was impossible *not* to. He was right there."

"What happened?"

"What usually happens whenever I'm around my father. He made his usual cracks, how most people who go to college for ten years are doctors. And, of course, after learning I'll graduate this May, he said he'd wait to pop the Champagne. He's great for an ego boost, isn't he?"

"How did Lincoln react to all this?" Evie asks.

A smile lights up my face. "Actually, he defended me. Said I was one of the most promising students he's had the pleasure of teaching."

The girls look at each other and sigh.

"Aww…" Nora places her hand over her heart. "So sweet. Your knight in shining armor coming to your rescue."

I place a hand on my hip, fixing my expression. "I don't need a knight in shining armor to come to my rescue. And I told him as much when he came into the kitchen later on."

"I never asked what you guys 'talked' about." Izzy waggles her brows, grinning deviously.

I stare into space, recalling with striking clarity the conversation I had with Lincoln. We talked about a lot of things, but one stands out.

"Love," I murmur.

Three pairs of eyes instantly widen.

"What?" Evie gasps.

"In what context?" Izzy inquires, always the pragmatic one.

"Did he tell you he loved you?" Nora bounces on her feet.

"No, no, no." Since it appears we've settled on this dress for me, I head back into the fitting room. "Not like that."

"Then how?" Evie asks.

I pull on my jeans, then yank my top over my head before tugging my boots up my legs. Satisfied with my appearance, I walk into the sitting area, plopping down on a chair. "It was more in the context of my relationship with Midge and how he thought I was a conundrum."

"Which he's spot-on about," Nora comments.

"I'm not that difficult to figure out."

"Oh, come on." She exaggeratedly rolls her eyes. "You're hot, then cold. I can understand how Lincoln would be confused. You give off the impression you're this tough bitch who doesn't let anything get to her. And that's probably exactly what Lincoln thought because he didn't have a chance to get to know the real Chloe. Not like we do. So I can only imagine his surprise when he walked into your father's house to see you at a birthday party for the spawn of the man you loathe and his replacement wife, as you've always called her."

"It's not Midge's fault she has a father who will never be happy with anything she does."

My words linger in the air for a moment before Izzy speaks once more. "What happened next?"

I shake my head, trying to piece it all together. "I told him love makes people weak, to which he argued it makes you human. And then…"

"And then?" They all lean toward me, sitting on the edge of their seats. Literally.

Staring into the distance, a shiver rolls through me as I recall that exact moment. "He asked if I wanted to feel human. If I wanted to *feel*. He was so close. The closest he'd been to me in months. And then…"

"Yes?" Nora encourages as they all inch even closer, desperate for my story.

"We almost kissed."

"Almost?" Izzy asks.

"My father came in talking about some emergency filing they needed to get done. So Lincoln went back to work."

It's silent for a moment. I don't expect anyone to come up with a solution. This isn't a problem that can be fixed. It's just something I need to learn to live with for the next seven weeks. Then I'll never have to see Lincoln again. At least I get a break this week with it being spring break.

"That's it!" Evie slams her hand on the side table, startling us.

"What?"

"That's what this is all about."

"What is?" I scrunch my brows together, tilting my head.

"This whole thing with Lincoln. You're worried he'll choose his job over you."

"He *has* chosen his job over me. But it wasn't like he had a choice. It's right there in the code of conduct."

"Exactly." She shoots up, tapping a finger against her lower lip. I can see the wheels spinning in her head. Never a good thing. "*You* were the one who insisted he not tell anyone about your relationship. *He* wanted to report it. Then after the semester, if there was still something there, you'd be free to pursue it. But you made sure there was no chance, under the guise of your father not finding out for fear he'd think you didn't earn your degree."

"And if he knew, that's precisely what he'd think."

"I don't think that was the reason at all. Sure, that may be what you told Lincoln, but—"

"It was a preemptive strike," Nora breathes, turning her wide eyes to me, as if a puzzle piece just snapped into place.

"A preemptive strike?" I counter dismissively, averting my gaze. "You two are crazy. You've been reading too many romance novels. Or watching too much daytime TV. I did *not* tell Lincoln to keep this a secret as a preemptive strike against..." I wave my hand around. "Whatever you've concocted in those twisted brains of yours."

"Maybe not at the time," Izzy interjects thoughtfully. I shoot my eyes to hers, glaring at my traitorous friend. She's not supposed to take their side. She's supposed to support *me*, have *my* back. "Maybe at first, you genuinely *were* concerned about your father. But I also think, deep down, you were hoping Lincoln would fight for you."

"What? I didn't—"

She stands from her chair, walking toward me, squeezing my biceps. "I know you, Chloe. Probably better than anyone else. For you to take a chance on Lincoln, you must have seen something in him that made you believe he was different."

"Well, thank you, Dr. Nolan. Should I book my next session with you or your receptionist out front?" I joke, trying to lighten the mood, but Izzy doesn't let up. She never does.

"Your father was a crappy male role model. He still is. Which is why, when Lincoln didn't even try to fight for you, it broke something inside you."

I push out of her hold and cross my arms in front of my chest. "He didn't break me," I insist, but I can't look her in the eye.

"I think he did. I think he showed you what was possible. I think you felt hope that not all men are like your father or any of the other assholes you used to sleep with. So when he didn't fight for you, it reminded you too much of how your father chose his job over you and your mom. But I think if Lincoln knew how much you still want to be with him, things might be different. I think he *would* fight for you."

"I'm pretty sure lying on his desk with my legs spread sends that message loud and clear."

"That just shows you were willing to *sleep* with him. Maybe he needs to know you're willing to take a risk, like he'll have to. I doubt you've ever given him any indication you were serious about him."

"Since it appears you haven't been following along, I'll say it again. I never had the opportunity. I found out he was my professor before we could take things to that level."

"Or are you using that as an excuse?"

I open my mouth, trying to come up with some argument in my defense. I want to deny her words hold even the faintest hint of merit, that Lincoln wrote me off the instant he learned who I was, but I can't. His pained expression as he handed back my panties is still ingrained in my mind. A person who feels nothing but indifference doesn't look at you that way.

A loud ringing rips through and I blow out a breath, saved from having to respond. I rummage through my bag, pulling out my phone, a number I don't recognize appearing on the screen. Inwardly grateful for the reprieve, I offer the girls an apologetic smile, then bring my cell up to my ear.

"Chloe Davenport," I answer with all the professionalism I can muster, assuming it's a lead on a story.

"Chloe, it's Louise."

"Louise?" I wrinkle my nose, trying to place the name. I

usually pride myself on my memory, but I'm drawing a blank here.

"Yes." She lowers her voice to almost a whisper. "Your mother's sponsor at AA."

I inhale sharply. In all the years I've played lifeguard to my mother's alcoholism, her sponsor has never called me, even when things got a little hairy. We took it in stride, simply trying to keep any temptations or triggers as far away as possible.

"I'm sorry. Of course." I give Izzy a knowing look, then stand and slip out of the sitting room, making sure I'm out of earshot before continuing our conversation. "Is everything okay?"

"Yes. It's just… Your mother hasn't attended her normal meetings the past two weeks. And she *never* misses a meeting without letting me know. I've tried calling, but she hasn't answered. I thought of phoning her work to see if anyone there knows anything, but I'm not sure what her co-workers know of her recovery. I didn't want to overstep, so that's why I called you. Have you spoken with her recently?"

I pinch the bridge of my nose, releasing a long sigh. "No, I haven't."

Guilt forms a knot in my throat at how I've dropped the ball these past few months. Apart from a few texts and phone calls, I've barely spoken to her since I got back from Vegas. It sounded like things were going great with Aaron, her boyfriend. I didn't think I needed to keep a close eye on her.

"I've had some personal stuff going on myself and I guess I kind of fell down on the job, so to speak."

"It's not your job to take care of her," she reminds me. "I'm sure it's nothing. I can be a bit of a worrier."

While I may not know Louise well, I can tell her concern

goes above being a worrier. She's a recovering alcoholic herself. She knows how quickly someone can regress.

"You're right. She's probably fine, but I'll make some calls anyway."

"And you'll let me know?"

"Of course."

I hang up and draw in a long breath, fighting against the headache I feel coming on. Like Louise said, it's probably nothing. But I've been in this place before. It's never nothing, not where my mother is concerned. So I return my attention to my cell and call my mother's work number. On the first ring, a bright voice answers.

"Carsdale Associates. How may I direct your call?"

"Hi. It's Chloe Davenport."

"Hello, Chloe. How can I help you?"

"Is my mother around?"

"I'm sorry," the receptionist says with fake sympathy. "She's not. Actually, your mother hasn't been to work in about ten days or so. Said she needed some time away from the office to recenter herself after the last big PR nightmare she had to deal with."

"Of course she did," I mumble under my breath. "Do you know how long she'll be out of the office?"

"She didn't say," the receptionist answers, and my suspicions only grow.

It's not like my mother to take extended periods of time off, not now that she's working in crisis management and doing something she enjoys again. A part of me hoped that would be enough to keep her happy, to keep her from regressing. But I've also learned that, regardless of how put together someone may appear on the outside, they might be battling demons no one else can see.

"I'll call her cell instead."

"Okay," the receptionist chirps, unaware of any troubles. "Have a great day, Chloe!"

"You, too."

I hang up just as light footsteps sound from behind me. Whirling around, I meet Izzy's concerned eyes. I don't even have to say anything for her to know what's going on.

"Oh, Chloe…"

I shrug, doing my best to hold it together. Like I always have. "What can I say? When it rains, it fucking pours."

# Twenty-Five

I climb out of the cab and glance up at the shotgun-style house in the East Flatbush neighborhood of Brooklyn where my mother lives. It's a quaint house in a quiet neighborhood. Well, as quiet as you can find within a short commute to Manhattan.

Ten years ago, I didn't think my mother would ever be able to hold down a job for long, let alone afford a house in this neighborhood. But once she started taking her twelve-step program seriously, things turned around for her. I just pray she hasn't fallen that far again.

Hesitantly, I climb up the stairs and pull back the screen door, the hinges groaning. I consider knocking. There could be a perfectly reasonable explanation my mother missed her meetings and didn't answer her cell when I called. Experience tells me otherwise.

Pulling my keys out of my bag, I find the one I'm searching for and insert it into the lock. The instant I step inside, my suspicions are confirmed. The scene is the perfect example of what it's like to have a high-functioning alcoholic in your life. The house is decorated with expensive furnishings, artwork hanging on the walls, high-end appliances in the kitchen. A demonstration of success.

But the wine bottles littering the island, kitchen counter, and living room coffee table tell a different story.

I curse under my breath. I should have known something like this was bound to happen. I've been so consumed with work, school, and all the drama going on with Lincoln, not to mention helping Nora with the final stages of planning her wedding. Most nights, I'm barely able to sleep more than a few hours. I thought my mom was doing good. She *had* been doing good. Better than good. So good that I made the mistake of moving her down my list of priorities. Now I'll have to suffer the consequences of that.

"Mom?" I call out timidly, stepping farther into the house. I walk to one of the windows and crack it open, allowing some fresh air to fill the place.

A crash sounds from the basement, the sound ominous against the quiet. I whirl around, darting down the stairs. When I round the corner, I expect to see her lying on the floor, having fallen in a drunken stupor.

Instead, I come face-to-face with a do-it-yourself nightmare. The walls have been repainted from the previous drab eggshell color to a deep gray, droplets splashed on the laminate wood flooring, since my mother didn't think to lay down any plastic first. Bubbles and streaks abound on the walls from the shoddy paint job. Various fabrics and cuts of wood are strewn all over the place, along with power tools I wouldn't trust this woman with sober, let alone in her current state.

My mother's personality when she drinks can range from happy to angry and everything in between. Over the years, I've learned to prepare myself for a wide variety of personalities, thanks to the alcohol. If she was drinking because she had a good day at work, she'd shower me with love and praise. But if something happened in her personal life, she'd curse and demean me in a way that made my father seem like an amateur.

But I'd take an irate drunk over a home-renovating drunk any day. I can handle her mood swings. I can't handle her with power tools.

"Mom?"

She spins around, her mouth falling open, eyes widening. She blinks, remaining still, trying to figure out her next move. Her gaze briefly floats to a corner of the room where several cans of paint sit. Beside them is a glass of red wine, the bottle next to it nearly empty. At three o'clock on a Wednesday. I'm not saying I'm perfect and never occasionally have a few drinks during lunch. But I'm also not a recovering alcoholic who shouldn't be drinking at all.

At. Fucking. All.

My glare narrows, lips forming a tight line, nostrils flaring. I don't even know what to say. As always, I want to blame myself. How much longer can I do that?

I'm about to ask her what she thinks she's doing, but when she sees the outrage in my expression, she attempts to distract me.

"Chloe!" Her movements are overly dramatic as she takes the cigarette out of her mouth, opening her arms to me, a lazy smile on her face. Her silver hair is pulled back, paint dotting her tanned complexion as well as the jeans and t-shirt she wears. "There's my baby girl!" She steps toward me, wrapping her arms around me. I can smell the liquor coming off her.

"What are you doing?" I push out of her hug before she burns me.

Taking the cigarette from her, I extinguish it in a nearby ashtray. I've never been a fan of her smoking. She picked it up when she finally got serious about getting sober, trading one vice for another, but I'd rather have her smoke than be drunk.

"What does it look like I'm doing?" She waves her hand around.

"Making a mess out of the basement?" I shoot back.

She jabs me playfully. "Oh, stop. No. I'm surprising Aaron with a man cave."

"A man cave?" I lower my voice. "Has he moved in with you?"

"Not yet, but he does spend a lot of time here, so I thought I'd do something to surprise him when he gets back from his business trip later today."

She looks around the space, scrunching her nose at the utter chaos surrounding us. The basement looked infinitely better when it still had its dreary wall color that lacked personality.

"I'm not sure it'll be done in time, though." She blows out a breath, then straightens, her voice brightening. "I'll tell you something. All those home improvement shows that make this kind of thing seem easy are full of it. This shit is hard. But look…"

She grabs my wrist, pulling me toward the far wall where it appears she attempted to install a custom entertainment center. I shudder at the idea of my mother using a circular saw and nail gun. She's lucky she didn't lose a finger. I steal a glimpse at her hands to make sure, counting ten.

"Isn't it incredible? I did that myself! Who would have thought?"

"It certainly is incredible." Feeling like I've stepped into an alternate universe, I wonder if my mother thought to use a level in her infinite wisdom. By the looks of the lopsided shelves lining the place where a TV would eventually sit, I assume the answer is no.

"Well, I'm glad you're here. I can use an extra set of hands if I'm to finish this before Aaron's flight lands in…" When she brings her watch to her face, her eyes bulge. "Shit. Is that the time already? His flight's supposed to land in a few hours and I haven't had a chance to start the coffee table. Come on." She clutches my arm again, dragging me toward several pallets, all in various stages of disrepair.

"Do I even want to know what this is supposed to be?"

"This is what we're going to make the coffee table out of," she answers proudly.

"Pallets?"

"Apparently, it's a trend. I printed out some instructions." She glances around, wavering slightly from the sudden movement. "They're around here somewhere." She begins moving piles of wooden slats, paint cans, and brushes.

"Mom…"

"Not now, Chloe," she barks, probably sensing what I'm about to say. "I don't have time."

"And like I had time to come here today?"

"Then leave," she snips, growing defensive.

"Mom, please," I implore, my voice strained as I try to take the wheel when the world spins out of control around me. "Just tell me what the hell is going on!"

"I told you. I'm renovating." The vein in her forehead pulses as she shuffles things around with increased annoyance. "Doing something nice for Aaron. Something you wouldn't know about since you can't exactly keep a man for longer than a few weeks, can you?"

My jaw tightens and I take a deep breath, counting to ten in an effort to stop myself from going off on her. I'd like to say this is the first time she's spoken to me like that, but it's not.

I wish I could say it'll be the last, but I know it won't, although I wish it were.

"This isn't about me." I keep my tone calm and even, despite the frustration bubbling inside me. She wants me to engage. Wants to shift the focus off the fact her house is littered with empty alcohol bottles. "It's about you."

"I'm doing just fine. So if you're not going to help me build this coffee table, you can help by finding your way out the door."

"Mom," I warn.

"What? It's not hard. You found your way in, didn't you?"

"Mom," I say again, this time louder.

"Chloe," she taunts, mimicking my tone.

"You are *not* doing fine."

"Why?" She whirls around. "Because I'm happy? You just can't *stand* the fact I'm doing well, can you? You're just like your father. You're not happy unless I'm miserable."

Hearing her compare me to my father sends me past my breaking point. As it always does. I can handle a lot of verbal abuse, but I refuse to be compared to a man I've spent the past twenty-odd years of my life ensuring I'm *nothing* like.

Heat flashes across my face and I ball my hands into fists, my body tensing. "Mom! Look at you!" I shriek before I have a chance to keep my temper in check. "When I walked into this house, it was worse than a fucking distillery. There are empty wine bottles everywhere." I spin in a circle, quickly counting four bottles tossed aside. "What happened? You were doing so good! I honestly thought this wouldn't happen again. That you cared enough about yourself and the people in your life who *love* you that you weren't going to drink anymore!"

"Don't speak to me like I'm a child!" she shouts back,

indignant. "You seem to have forgotten that *I* gave birth to *you*. *I* raised *you*. *I* nurtured *you*."

"Yeah, you did. Until getting drunk became more important. I was the one who covered for you so Dad didn't know how bad it was. If it weren't for my constant lies to him, do you honestly think he would have allowed you to keep custody of me? Then what would you have done without his child support payments financing your addiction?

"Maybe that's where I fucked up. Maybe I *shouldn't* have kept this a secret. Maybe you would have gotten the help you needed earlier and we wouldn't be going through this cycle that doesn't seem to ever fucking end! But no matter the price everyone who loves you has to pay, you don't seem to care!" I bellow, tears streaming down my face.

"I *care!*" she snips. "I care so much that I'm renovating this entire basement for Aaron! So if you don't mind, I need to finish!" She storms toward the pile of pallets.

I briefly close my eyes to calm myself and inhale a deep breath. On a long exhale, I approach her.

"Mom." I soften my tone, hoping she'll relax enough so we can have a rational conversation.

"What, Chloe?" She spins around, her motions quick. Too quick.

Everything seems to happen in slow motion as the sound of an air compressor firing a nail echoes, followed by a sharp pain in my thigh just above my knee.

Darting my eyes up, I see the nail gun in her hand and collapse to the floor, clutching my leg as blood blooms on my jeans.

The sight is all it takes to push my mother over the edge. She loosens her grip on the nail gun and it falls with a clatter just as she passes out, her body slumping to the floor.

"Of course," I grit out through the pain. "It's not like she could have driven me to the hospital anyway."

Pulling my phone out of my back pocket, I unlock the screen and call the only person I can in this situation.

"Izzy, I need your help."

# Twenty-Six

"How's she doing?" I ask several hours later when Izzy reappears around the privacy curtain in the emergency room where I'm lying on a bed, my leg propped up.

"She's fine. Had to get a few stitches over her eyebrow and suffered a mild concussion from the fall, but she'll survive. How are *you* doing?" She heads toward me, pulling off the thin blanket, revealing my heavily bandaged knee and thigh. "Is the local wearing off?"

"Yup. But they gave me some painkillers." I shoot up in bed. "You didn't let them prescribe any for my mom, did you?"

"No. I apprised the attending of her history, but it was in her chart already. Her injury is minor anyway. She'll just have to suck it up with regular ol' ibuprofen."

"Good." I relax back into the mattress, checking the time to see it's after seven. "I can't believe I wasted my entire fucking day on this. And for what? For my mother to shoot my knee with a nail gun?"

Izzy assumes the chair beside the bed. "Not *quite* your knee. She's lucky her aim was off. A few centimeters down and you could have faced some major reconstructive surgery. At least it didn't nick any bones and the doctor was able to yank the sucker out." She grins a devilish smile. "Did the doc let you keep it?"

"Why would I want to keep a bloody nail?"

"As a souvenir," she says, as if it's obvious.

I playfully roll my eyes. "I'd rather not have a reminder."

She shrugs. "To each their own. How long will you be off your feet?"

"Doctor Warren said I should be back to my old self in a week or so, but to take it easy and listen to my body, since the stitches need to stay in for about two weeks. Speaking of the handsome doc, is it a requirement for every doctor here to be ridiculously good looking?" I narrow my eyes at her. "Please tell me you've taken advantage of working here."

"I'm on the pediatric oncology floor."

"So? They have doctors there, too, don't they?"

"They do, and I'm sorry to disappoint you, but most of the hot doctors also have hot wives at home."

I sigh dramatically, leaning back against the pillows. "Yeah. Doctor Warren told me he was happily married during my attempts to flirt with him after I was given anesthesia."

Izzy straightens her spine, her brows furrowing. "Chloe, they only gave you a local to numb the area."

"So?" A mischievous smirk skates across my lips.

She stares at me for a moment, remaining silent. Then she bursts out laughing. It's a strange sound in a hospital, as out of place as a nun in a strip club, but maybe we all need to laugh more. After this afternoon, *I* need to laugh more.

"You really have no shame, do you?" she asks, wiping at her eyes.

"I figure he probably sees enough depressing shit working here, so I may as well do something to make him laugh. Consider it my civic duty."

"Civic duty," she repeats, shaking her head, giggling even more.

"Excuse me, Chloe."

At the sound of a serious voice, I whip my eyes from Izzy, my own laughter ceasing when I see my mother's boyfriend, Aaron, standing in the opening of the privacy curtain. His graying hair is slightly disheveled, worry and guilt etched in the lines of his face. He's on the tall side, around six feet, and in great shape, considering he's in his sixties. But the energy and liveliness he usually exudes is lacking, his tie loosened, his suit wrinkled. Based on the suitcase beside him, I gather he took a cab straight here from the airport.

"Aaron." I sit up in the bed. "My mom is—"

"Actually," he interrupts, "I'd hoped to talk to you first." He shifts his attention, noticing Izzy at my side. "Thanks for taking care of my girls, Iz."

"You bet." She stands from the chair and walks to him. They hug briefly and he kisses her cheek. "I'll give you two a few minutes." She looks back at me. "You should have your discharge papers soon, but if you need anything in the meantime, shoot me a text."

"I will." I watch as she leaves, grateful to have a friend like Izzy, who immediately left Nora and Evie to get me to the hospital. Then I turn my attention to Aaron, apprehensive about his reason for wanting to talk to me.

"This is all my fault." He slumps into the chair, burying his head in his hands.

I exhale, knowing all too well what he's going through. I've done this same thing myself more times than I can count. Hell, I did this same thing earlier today when I walked into Mom's house and was met with the smell of alcohol.

"No, it's not," I say with all the compassion I can. "I promise you, nothing you could have done—"

"No." He darts his eyes to mine, his gaze intense and remorseful. "It *is*. I could have stopped it. I could have prevented it from starting in the first place."

I open my mouth, about to reassure him once more, when he says, "I gave it to her."

I shake my head. "I don't—"

"Alcohol. I gave her the alcohol."

His admission is a punch to the gut, the air knocked out of my lungs. "You...*gave* her alcohol?" I'm barely able to get the words out.

With a deep sigh, he closes his eyes, his shoulders drooping.

"How long has this been going on?"

He runs a hand over his face. "For a little while now."

"How. Long?" I demand again through clenched teeth.

Hesitant, he licks his lips. Then his unwavering gaze meets mine. "About three or four months."

His admission hits me hard, my jaw dropping, the world feeling like it's giving out from beneath me. My mother's been drinking for three or four *months*? I'd hoped maybe he'd brought over a bottle of wine a few weeks ago. But three or four months? So much could happen in that timeframe. So much could go wrong in that timeframe.

"I didn't expect it to get this out of control," he offers in a misguided attempt to not seem like the villain in all of this. But even if he'd only given her a sip, it would be one sip too many.

"Oh, you didn't? What *did* you expect when you gave alcohol *to...an...alcoholic*?" I hiss, trying to keep my voice low.

A part of me feels bad about speaking to him this way. It's one thing to have a shouting match with my mother when she's in one of her stupors. Sometimes it's the only way to get through to her. But Aaron is basically a stranger to me.

"It's not like I showed up at her door one day and force-fed her a bottle of vodka. It started out relatively innocent. A sip out of a glass of wine I'd order at dinner."

"That's the same thing as force-feeding her! And what were you thinking ordering wine when you were with her? You've been to meetings with her, haven't you?"

He nods, his eyes glassy from unshed tears.

"Then you know being around other people drinking could trigger a relapse."

"I didn't think it would be that bad. She's around worse stuff with some of the clients she works with, helping them cover up their own alcohol or drug abuse issues. I thought she could handle it." He blows out a long breath. "I guess I was wrong."

"Ya think?" I glare at him, a tightness in my chest. "Do you have any idea the damage this has caused?" I manage to say through the frustration building in my throat.

"But I read that most alcoholics who suffer a relapse come out stronger afterward."

"That would be true if her *boyfriend* hadn't been giving her the goddamn alcohol!"

"I wanted to tell you a few months ago, especially when the occasional sip turned to drinking half my glass, then a full glass, but I didn't want you to hate me. I care about your mother. You need to believe I'd—"

"You have a funny way of showing that."

He pinches the bridge of his nose, his jaw tightening. "I know I fucked up. And I don't expect you to forgive me. That's not what I'm asking for." His eyes float to mine, imploring. "I love your mother. Tell me what I can do to make it right. To help her get back on track."

I stare at him, sick to my stomach. "You want to know how you can make it right?"

"Yes." He clasps his hands in front of him. "Anything. Tell me and it's done."

"Leave her alone."

My words cause him to instantly straighten. "Wha— "

"*You* are her trigger." I lean as close as I can in the hospital bed, my gaze unwavering. "If you really do care about her, you'll keep your distance. She needs to get sober, something that won't be easy if the person who constantly fed her alcohol is around."

"I…," he stammers, chewing on his bottom lip. "Do you think that's best? Won't that upset her? Make it even worse?" He blinks repeatedly, grasping at the last straw he can pull. "Getting her sober again will put enough stress on her. Shouldn't she—"

"Not have a daily reminder of the man who gave her alcohol? Absolutely. She may love you, but now you're just one giant alcohol vending machine. And that's all you'll ever be to her. That's all she'll ever see when she looks at you. A man who will cave and feed her addiction when the people who truly love her would never have even imagined giving her so much as a sniff of their wine. So if you truly do love her, you'll walk away and let her heal."

Jaw tight, I glower at him, my chest heaving. I'm sure this conversation isn't good for my blood pressure. This entire scenario is shit for my blood pressure. Briefly closing my eyes, I suck in a steadying breath before looking back at him.

"I can't make you do anything you don't want to," I continue, my voice softer, more controlled. "I can beg for you to walk away, but you're two adults. It all comes down to how much you love her. Are you selfish enough to stay with her, knowing you're a crutch? Or are you self*less* enough to allow her the opportunity to recover, something she'll never have otherwise?"

He stares at me for what seems like an eternity, indecision flickering in his gaze. My heart thrums in my chest, my breathing echoing in my ears, my lips pinched tight.

Finally, he lowers his head, nodding in resignation. "Okay." His agreement comes out as a strained whisper.

I offer him a compassionate smile. It doesn't go unnoticed how difficult this must have been for him. I hate that I even had to force him to make this decision. But he forced me to put him in this position.

I just pray my mother understands why this was the only option.

# Twenty-Seven

I stretch my leg out in front of me as I work on the couch Saturday evening. It's been an interesting couple of days since the incident in my mother's basement. Upon being discharged, she apologized profusely, even went so far as insisting I stay at her house that night. I took her up on the offer. Partly because I was recovering. Partly so I could keep an eye on her.

To my surprise, the instant we got back to her place, she cleaned up all the empty bottles, then proceeded to pour every last drop of alcohol down the drain, all without me asking her to. The following morning, she was up bright and early, getting ready for work. She even attended an AA meeting on her lunch break. It gave me hope that this little relapse may not be as bad as all the others, which was why I felt comfortable enough to stay at my apartment tonight, since the weekends tend to be busy in my line of work.

If my mother weren't coping as well as she is, I would have been at her place. But she went to her normal Saturday Book Club meeting with some of her other AA friends, then texted afterward to say she was crawling into bed and relaxing for the rest of the evening. She even sent a photo as proof. I hate that she thinks she has to provide photographic evidence to back up her statements, but there's a certain level of trust that's broken whenever she has a relapse. She's used to it as much as I am.

Just as I'm about to stand and hobble into the kitchen to make a coffee, my phone rings, a number I don't recognize appearing on the screen.

"No rest for the weary," I murmur to myself before answering. "Chloe Davenport."

I'm instantly met by loud music, coupled with raised voices. "Is this Chloe Davenport?" a man practically bellows.

"Yes," I respond hesitantly.

"I need you to get to Spring Lounge in SoHo. There's a woman here. Very intoxicated, argumentative. I was about to call the cops when she begged me to call you instead. I'm assuming this is your mother since you have the same last name. Short. Silver hair. Mouth like a trucker."

With a heavy sigh, I pinch the bridge of my nose, fighting against the frustration filling me. Like the other day, I start to blame myself for this, but I can't keep doing that. I can't keep putting my life on hold to babysit her. When will it end?

"Yes. That's my mother."

I briefly entertain the idea of not bailing her out this time. Maybe a night in jail and criminal charges are exactly what she needs. But what will that do to her career? In her line of work as a crisis management specialist, they deal with enough scandals from their clients. The last thing they'd want is a scandal from one of their employees, as well. And I refuse to go back to the way things were years ago when I had no choice but to find more creative ways to earn money to help her pay the mortgage. It takes everything I have to afford my own rent.

"I'll be there as soon as I can."

"Don't take all night. There's only so long I'm willing to babysit her."

"All right. All right." I jump to my feet, wincing from the pain. "I'm on my way."

Yanking on a pair of sneakers, I limp out of my apartment without grabbing a jacket, despite the snow beginning to fall, and hail a cab. The drive takes a little longer than normal, thanks to the weather, but after fifteen minutes, the cab pulls up in front of the neighborhood dive bar.

When I step inside, I'm grateful to see my mother sitting at the end of the bar, a full glass of water in front of her, seemingly calm. I limp toward her, doing my best to forget about the pain shooting through my leg.

"Mom?"

Her movements are slow as she lifts her lazy eyes toward me. Then a wicked smile curls her mouth. "There she is. The prodigal daughter. This is her, everyone!" she shouts.

Several people look in my direction, more out of curiosity than interest. And maybe a little pity.

"My lovely daughter who asked my boyfriend to break up with me!"

"Mom," I hiss, grabbing her arm in an attempt to yank her to her feet. But my injury prevents me from being as strong as I usually am. I wish I'd taken this into consideration and called someone for help. But who? This has always been my burden, and mine alone.

"You just can't let me be happy, can you?"

"Come on. Let's get you out of here." I ignore her statement, attempting to pull her off the barstool, to no avail. "The bartender was nice enough to call me instead of the cops. The second we're outside, you can tell me all about how I'm a horrible daughter for asking the man who provided alcohol to an alcoholic to keep his distance if he really cared about you and your recovery."

"Well, your little plan backfired," she sneers.

"You've got to get her out of here," the bartender warns as his eyes float to patrons who start fleeing in droves. "I'm losing customers because of her."

"I'm sorry." I wrap my arm under her shoulder blades, but she's dead weight. There's no way I'll be able to get her out on my own. "Can you help me get her outside? Please. She has a problem—"

"No, I don't," my mother interrupts. "*You're* the one with the problem." She shoves a sharp finger into my chest. "You can't stand anyone being happy."

I clench my jaw, drawing in a deep breath before I do or say something I'll regret and make an even bigger scene, resulting in both of us getting arrested.

Looking back to the bartender, I implore one final time. "Please. I'm begging you." My voice trembles, a lump forming in my throat. I've been in this situation with my mother more times than I can count. I've had to drag her out of numerous bars before they called the cops. But I've never felt as helpless as I do right now.

The bartender blows out a long sigh, throwing the dishtowel hanging over his shoulder onto the bar. "Fine."

Gratitude fills me, the bald man akin to a guardian angel at this moment. "Thank you."

He simply nods, then comes out from behind the bar and hoists my mom to her feet with ease. Thankfully, she doesn't fight it. Once we're outside, I gesture to an empty bench at a nearby bus stop, and he brings her over, depositing her onto it.

"Thanks," I say again.

"You bet." He begins back inside before pausing,

looking over his shoulder. "You did the right thing by asking that guy to stay away from her. I would have done the same."

I smile, savoring his words. It may not seem like much, especially considering he's telling me something I already know to be true, but living with an alcoholic, *loving* an alcoholic is a constant battle of doubt, second-guessing yourself, and wondering if you handled a situation correctly.

When he retreats into the bar, I dust some of the snow off the bench, then plop onto it, ignoring my mother's venomous stare. Opting to order an Uber instead of trying to hail a cab, I pull my phone out of my purse. Maybe if I offer a big tip, the driver won't mind helping a severely inebriated woman into the car.

"You must feel proud of yourself," she taunts. "Huh? You're responsible for Aaron leaving me, then decided to come here to gloat."

I shake my head, looking at my Uber app to see the estimated arrival time of the car, as well as the model and license plate. Thankfully, it's only a minute away.

"You're the one who called me," I remind her through gritted teeth. "If I didn't come, that bartender was going to call the cops."

"I should have let him." She wavers on the bench as she tries to sit up straight. Placing my hand lightly on her shoulder, I push her back. She barely notices. "I would have been better off spending the night in the drunk tank instead of having to sit next to someone who only wants to ruin everything good in my life because she can't hold down a relationship for anything."

I pinch my lips together, briefly closing my eyes, just wanting to get her home so I can put this night behind me. Like so many similar nights that came before it. Thankfully, the Uber I'd ordered turns the corner, and I wave the driver over.

"Okay, Mom. I need you to cooperate for a minute and get into the car."

"You want me to cooperate?" she retorts, barely able to even enunciate the word. "Like you wanted Aaron to cooperate with your plan to destroy my life?"

My hands ball into fists as I remind myself not to apologize for any steps I take to remove a trigger from my mother's life. Instead, I try to focus on the immediate task at hand. There's no rationalizing with her when she's like this.

"I understand your frustration. And I'm happy for you to make a long list of all the ways I'm a shitty daughter—"

"And you are."

"But when we're home," I plea in a strained voice, feeling like I'm trying to bargain with a three-year-old who doesn't want to take a nap. "Okay?"

"Hey, lady," the driver calls out. I lift my eyes to his. He points to my mother. "Is she drunk?"

"She's just a little under the weather." I return my attention to my mother, ignoring the curious stares from passersby on the street of the popular restaurant and bar area in SoHo.

I wrap my arm around her body and use every ounce of strength I possess to pull her up, gritting through the ache in my leg. When I realize I'm successful, I exhale, holding onto her as tightly as I can to prevent her from falling.

But the massive quantity of alcohol she consumed, coupled with my unsteady balance from my injury and the snow-slickened sidewalks, makes this a difficult task. She wavers on her feet before crashing to the ground, taking me with her.

When I land with a hard thump, I cry out in pain, which only causes my mother to laugh hysterically.

"This ain't worth it," the driver says. "Find another ride."

I don't even look up to watch him drive off. I can't. I fear I'll lose what little hope I've miraculously held onto through everything.

I've dealt with my mother in this condition for what feels like most of my life. I never thought twice. It was just always something I had to do. I honestly believed if I did everything right, if I focused on keeping the stress out of her life, regardless of the personal cost to myself and my own dignity, she'd eventually get back on her feet, eventually stop drinking.

But now I'm exhausted. Broken. Defeated. And for the first time since I realized my mother had a problem, I allow my tears to fall, allow the emotions I've kept locked inside to flow out.

"What did I ever do to deserve this?"

Despite the pain, I clutch my legs to my chest, wanting to hide from the world, to press that imaginary reset button on my life. Sirens wail, horns honk, happy voices converse as people pass, not one soul stopping to help the poor, injured twenty-something struggling with a drunk. I shouldn't be surprised. I learned long ago the only person I can count on is myself.

"Karma really is a bitch, isn't it?" my mother slurs. "This is what you get for ruining my life. For *always* ruining my life."

I shift my eyes to hers, tears obscuring my vision. I should just leave her here, should let her fend for herself, but I can't. No matter what she's done, no matter the vitriol she spews, I've always put up with it, refusing to abandon her like my father did.

"I would have been better off if you were never born.

Then your father never would have left me. We were happy until you showed up."

"I know." I nod, swiping at my cheeks, my throat closing up. I don't have the strength to fight her anymore. Life has sucked everything out of me. I don't even have the energy to return to the bench, my limbs too heavy to move.

Instead, I stay on the sidewalk, my teeth chattering, my fingers growing numb from my lack of any winter attire. Another reminder of how I can't do anything right.

I pull my legs tighter against me, feeling like it's the only thing keeping me glued together. I try to cover my hands with the sleeves of my thin shirt, but my clothes are wet from the snow, my body shaking from the combination of my sobs and frigid temperatures. I'm not sure tonight could get any worse.

"Chloe?" a deep voice cuts through.

I stiffen, unable to breathe, to move, to think, wanting to wake up from this nightmare that keeps getting worse with every passing heartbeat.

I thought I'd hit the lowest of the low, sitting on a dirty New York sidewalk, too weak to drag my drunk mother into a cab, snow falling around me, my body shivering because I didn't have the wherewithal to protect myself from the elements. But no. Fate or karma or whoever had to make sure the one man I didn't want to see me like this bore witness to my breakdown.

"Chloe," he repeats when I don't react, keeping my head buried in my legs. This time, his tone is less confused, more sympathetic.

"Please go," I manage to get out through my wheezing breaths, my tears falling even more relentlessly.

His hand touches my shoulder. I snap my head up, shrugging him off. I have no idea what I did to deserve being saddled with an alcoholic mother for the past fifteen years of my life. But I took it all in stride. I didn't break down when my mother failed to show up for my high school graduation. I didn't break down when I had to quit college to work so she didn't lose the house. I didn't break down when I saw that first property tax bill and knew I no longer had a choice but to sacrifice the last shred of dignity I had in order to pay it. But this right here, having Lincoln look at me this way, his eyes glassy with emotion… It fucking destroys me.

He licks his lips, shaking his head, speechless.

"Please. Go," I say again, this time louder, my words drawing the attention of several passersby. "The last thing I need right now is you gloating about what a fuck-up I am," I sob, my entire body quivering, but no longer from the cold. From the raw emotions filling me. "I know I am. I'm trying so fucking hard. I just… Please. Leave me alone."

When he doesn't make any move to retreat, I bury my head back in my legs. "You're the last person I want to see right now."

"Chloe," he says again, just as Professor Gordon's familiar voice calls out to him.

"Linc, the car's here."

Without looking at him, I can sense his hesitation. I bring my legs closer to me, sending a silent prayer to the big man upstairs to grant me this one favor and make Lincoln leave. Seconds pass, seeming like hours. Finally, he exhales deeply. When I hear the crunch of his footsteps retreating in the snow, I steal a glance and watch him walk away. It's what I wanted, but it makes me cry even harder. Makes me feel even more alone.

Burying my face once more, my tears continue to fall, releasing everything I've kept hidden for years. It doesn't seem to faze my mother. She keeps her head on my shoulder, berating me. I tune it out. I can't listen to it anymore.

Officially out of options, I'm about to reach into my purse to call Izzy when I feel a warmth wrap around me. A weight lifts off me and I dart my eyes to my left, disoriented, watching as Lincoln hoists my mother off me and carries her down the block toward a yellow cab idling in front of an upscale French restaurant.

Once she's secure in the back seat, he returns to me. I want to scold him for not listening when I told him to leave me alone, but the comfort of his wool coat surrounding me is too inviting.

Fishing a handkerchief out of the inside pocket of his suit jacket, he hands it to me. I dab at my eyes and cheeks as he wraps his arms around me, helping me to my feet.

When I limp, he glances down at my leg, but doesn't ask what happened, as if he can tell I don't want to talk about it. It only makes him hold me even tighter as we make our way to the cab and he helps me inside before sliding in next to me.

"Where to?"

"My place." The last thing I want is to sit in a cab all the way out to Brooklyn when my apartment is mere minutes away.

"Which is?" Lincoln arches a brow.

I blink, caught off-guard that he doesn't even know where I live. I guess we never got to that point.

Turning my attention to the driver, I rattle off my address in the West Village. With a nod, he merges into traffic.

I relax into the seat, closing my eyes as a shiver rolls through me. Lincoln pulls me against him, rubbing my arm, and I rest my head against his chest, the metronome of his heartbeat offering a brief escape from my reality.

"I've been where you are," he says after a beat.

I raise my eyes to his, my brow wrinkled.

"Exactly where you are," he emphasizes, then looks forward, keeping me in his warm embrace.

# Twenty-Eight

"I got her," Lincoln assures me, adjusting his grip on my mother's inebriated body as I lead him toward my building. "Go unlock the door, but try not to kill yourself while you do it."

"Are you her boyfriend?" my mom slurs, her eyes mere slits. The alcohol coming off her breath is pungent. It's a miracle she didn't throw up in the cab. Then again, she passed out the second the driver pulled into traffic, not waking until Lincoln started to get her out.

"No, I'm not." His tone isn't exactly friendly, but it's not icy either. Just…indifferent.

"Figured as much. Did he get tired of you like the rest of them?"

"Mom," I grit out in warning as I climb the front steps, searching my purse for my keys, grateful when my frozen fingers land on them. "We've never dated." I insert the key into the lock, pushing the door open and stepping inside, Lincoln close behind. I head into the living room, kicking off my shoes.

"Now that I *do* believe. All these years, you've claimed you weren't interested in settling down. But I finally figured it out. It wasn't *you* who wasn't interested in settling down. It was everyone else."

I draw in a slow, steady breath, keeping my eyes forward, biting my lower lip to prevent myself from flying into a seething rage.

"They saw you for what you really were," she continues, relentless as always. "Someone who would spread her legs for a story, or a great pair of shoes, or the latest designer purse."

"That's enough," Lincoln barks, his voice echoing. I spin around to see his expression tight, his lips pinched together as he glares at her, not allowing her to escape his words. "Your daughter is the *only* reason you're not sleeping on the street or sitting in a jail cell right now. She didn't have to help you tonight. Or any other time you found yourself in a similar situation."

"It's okay. I'm used to it." I give him a small smile, then limp from the living room and into the den to make up the pull-out couch.

"That's right. She's used to being nothing but a disappointment. All she does is ruin things. You're smart you didn't get involved with her. She would have found a way to ruin your life, too."

I peek at Lincoln, the vein in his neck throbbing, his nostrils flaring. The temperature in the apartment seems to rise several degrees. With determination in his stride, he brings my mother over to the reading chair, depositing her harshly onto it. Then he glowers, pointing a finger in her face.

"Don't. Move."

A chill runs down my spine. It has nothing to do with my damp clothes, but everything to do with the power and dominance in his voice. I swallow hard, my own heart thumping in my chest, observing my mother snap her mouth shut, nodding quickly.

My mother's always been tenacious, tough as nails. You don't get to be a political strategist, then work in crisis management unless you have thick skin. Seeing her obey Lincoln's command is somewhat surprising.

Although it shouldn't be.

I couldn't resist obeying him, either.

I watch as Lincoln stalks toward me, every muscle in his body taut. I return my attention to the task at hand, grabbing a cushion off the couch and tossing it into the corner. As I'm about to add another one to the pile, he stops me, grabbing my hands in his.

"This is *not* okay, Chloe," he says in a choked voice. "Nothing about this is okay." He drops his hold on me, ripping the remaining cushions off the couch before yanking out the mattress, taking out his aggression on it. Pausing for a beat, he runs his hands through his hair before facing me. "Nothing about the way she spoke to you is right. Don't you realize that?"

I'm about to argue once more that it's not a big deal, when he cuts me off.

"I know. She's your mother. If you don't take care of her, who will?"

I shrug. It's the truth.

His jaw twitches and he shakes his head, his distressed expression hitting me hard. Why does he seem so invested, so hurt by the things she said?

"Go change into some warm clothes. I'll get her comfortable. You've done more than you needed to."

"*You've* already done more than you needed to. I can handle this. This isn't my first rodeo." I start to turn from

Lincoln when his fingers wrap around my arm. I lift my eyes to his, so much hurt and understanding within.

"I *haven't* done enough. And for that, I apologize. Let me do this for you." His Adam's apple bobs up and down in a hard swallow. "Please."

I part my lips, struggling to form a response. I should stand my ground, insist I'll be fine on my own, that it's not the first time I've been here. But the idea of having someone to lean on, even if for just a minute, lifts a weight off my shoulders.

"Okay," I murmur.

"Okay." He smiles a small smile, but doesn't release me, lightly dragging a finger down the length of my arm. My gaze remains transfixed on his, the feel of his touch sending a bolt straight to my core. When he reaches my hand, he squeezes, his thumb brushing across my knuckles.

"Okay," I say again, hypnotized.

"Okay," he whispers, curving toward me, his lips lingering just above my forehead, grazing my skin. I don't move. Hell, I don't even want to breathe, blink, anything. "Okay," he repeats, almost like an affirmation to himself. Then he releases me, heading to where he'd left my mother on a chair in the living room.

At first, I remain still, the tingle of his small kiss still trickling through me.

"I told you." He glances over his shoulder as he's about to hoist up my mother, who's passed out once more. "I've got this. You need to warm up."

Snapping out of my stupor, I limp toward my bedroom, hyper-aware of the heat coming off Lincoln's eyes as I pass him. Once I'm alone, I blow out a long breath.

I'm still not sure what to make of tonight's dramatic

events, of Lincoln being in my apartment, but I'm not going to think about it. Right now, I just want to slip into something warm and allow someone else to shoulder the burden for a change.

# Twenty-Nine

Bottles clanging against each other rouses me from sleep. I bolt up, my eyes flinging wide. Disoriented at first, I hurriedly scan the living room, trying to remember how I'd fallen asleep on the couch. Then the events of the night trickle back. Working. Getting a phone call. Having to drag my mother out of a bar yet again...

*Shit.*

I jump to my feet, wincing as I hobble into the kitchen, expecting to see her raiding all the booze I was too tired to get rid of just yet. But when I round the corner, I'm surprised to see Lincoln pouring bottles of alcohol down the drain, the sleeves of his crisp button-down shirt rolled up, his suit jacket lying neatly across the counter.

Sensing my presence, he glances over his shoulder, offering me a sweet smile as he continues to drain the contents. When he's finished, he wipes down the sink, then fully faces me.

"I'm sorry. I hope you don't mind. If I were in your shoes, this is what I'd want."

"I was planning on doing it. I just needed a minute to decompress. I guess I dozed off. Did my mother give you a hard time?"

He shrugs. "She's fine. Tomorrow will be a completely different story."

I playfully roll my eyes. "You've got that right." The last thing I want to think about is the state she'll be in when she wakes in the morning.

"I didn't wake you, did I?"

"It's okay. I need to get some work done anyway. My voicemails and inbox are probably overflowing with messages."

"Ah, yes…" He leans against the counter, crossing his arms in front of his chest. I avoid staring at his biceps as I limp past him toward the one-cup brewer, trying to ignore the heat coming off him. It's impossible to escape it in such close quarters, my kitchen no bigger than the galley of a boat. "The gossip mills must be running full force, correct?"

"Celebrities seem to enjoy getting into trouble on the weekends." I grab a mug and place it underneath the spout, popping a pod into the brewer. I glimpse at Lincoln. "Want one?"

He worries his bottom lip, seeming to weigh the pros and cons of staying for a coffee, before finally answering. "Sure."

I refocus my attention on the coffee maker, neither of us saying anything while I prepare two cups. When I'm finished, Lincoln grabs them and heads into the living room, making himself comfortable on the couch.

Once I lower myself onto the opposite end, he hands me my mug and I take a sip, the nutty flavor relaxing me. Shifting my body, I stretch my legs along the length of the couch, placing a pillow under my injured one to keep it elevated, per my discharge instructions.

"So… What happened?" He keeps his voice low so as to not disturb my mother sleeping in the den.

"Are you asking about tonight with my mother or my leg?"

"As curious as I am to know everything, I'm more interested in your leg at the moment." He inhales a sharp breath, his eyes widening, expression flushing. "I mean... I didn't mean it like that. I just meant—"

"It's okay." I smile, then take another sip of my coffee. "On Wednesday, I was trying on bridesmaid dresses for Nora's wedding when I got a phone call. My mother's sponsor. Said my mother hadn't been to a meeting in a few weeks, which is unlike her. I called her work, only to learn she'd taken some time off. I had a bad feeling in the pit of my stomach, so I went to her house in Brooklyn...where she was drunk before three in the afternoon, working on remodeling her basement into a man cave for her boyfriend, Aaron."

I lift the leg of my yoga pants, revealing my heavily bandaged knee and thigh. "We got into an argument. When she tried to continue on her project of making a coffee table out of a bunch of pallets, she accidentally fired the nail gun. This is the result."

Lincoln's eyes widen. "Holy shit. Are you okay? I mean, I see you are, but—"

"I'm fine. I'll *be* fine." I lower my pant leg. "She missed hitting any bones, so they were able to remove the nail without surgery. I should be as good as new in a few days. Apart from the nice new scar I'll now have the rest of my life."

"Battle wounds. We all have them. Some you see. Some you can't." His voice is tender and understanding. I lift my eyes to his, a dozen thoughts on the tip of my tongue. He quickly looks away, breaking the moment. "And tonight?"

"I can't be certain, but based on the slurs my mother slung my way, I imagine she found out I'd asked her boyfriend to stay away from her, considering he'd been giving her alcohol the past few months, even though he knew she was a recovering alcoholic."

He leans forward and rests his forearms on his thighs, contemplating. Then he looks back at me. "How long has this been going on?"

"Since the divorce." My response surprises me. I've always kept this private. But Lincoln's already seen me at my lowest. I have nothing left to lose by sharing this piece of me. "She drank before, but I never thought anything of it until it was just us."

"And when was that?" He peers at me.

"Fourteen."

Nodding, he looks forward again, filing this information away in whatever category it belongs. "Did your father know?"

"I don't think he cared, but I never came right out and told him." I glance at him, hesitant as I open up even more. "He still doesn't know. The only person in my life who knows is Izzy. And now you."

"Why haven't you told him?" His brows furrow, that same pained expression from before returning. "Especially when you were so young?"

"I didn't want him to know. Didn't want him to have anything he could use against her to get custody of me."

"In your mind, an alcoholic mother was the lesser of two evils." It's not a question. More a statement of understanding.

"You know how my father can be. My mother might be an angry drunk, but my father's an angry *person*. At least my mother's harsh words are limited to when she drinks."

He's quiet for a beat, then admits, "My mother started

drinking when I was in high school, too. After she found herself alone."

"Your parents are divorced?" I'm not sure why I find this more surprising than his mother being an alcoholic. I always pictured Lincoln having a flawless life and upbringing. From the beginning, everything about him was perfect. I guess no one's perfect. Everyone has scars. Some just know how to hide them better.

"No." He smiles briefly before faltering. "My father... He was killed on assignment."

"Assignment?"

"He was a bureau chief for the *Times* and living in Southeast Asia. He was kidnapped by some extremists and held for ransom."

I gasp, my hand covering my mouth. "My god. I'm sorry. I didn't know." These days, it seems we've become desensitized to these things, since they happen so often. It doesn't make them any less tragic.

"This was maybe six months after 9/11 and the U.S. government had taken a hard stance against negotiating with terrorists, given the current state of affairs."

As I listen, his story sounds achingly familiar. It was one of the first gruesome acts I'd read about in this post-9/11 world. Yes, the attacks themselves were horrific, especially for someone who's lived in the New York area most of her life. But I remember walking into the kitchen at my house one morning to see my father beside himself with an emotion I wasn't used to seeing from him. He actually hugged me. And there were tears. Later, I learned it was because he'd just received word that one of his colleagues, who'd been reported missing, had been found decapitated, his body evidencing signs of extreme torture.

"You're Elijah Moore's son," I breathe, the puzzle pieces locking into place.

He nods, his shoulders slumped slightly. "He died a few months before I graduated high school. My mom's drinking probably started much like yours did. A glass of whatever here and there. So innocuous and common you barely notice. But within a few months, one glass turned into two. Which turned into an entire bottle. Which turned into two. Like most other alcoholics, she still held down a job, made it appear to everyone she was doing fine, or as fine as could be expected when you lost a piece of yourself in such an inhumane way.

"I guess a part of me felt compelled to fulfill my father's legacy. I was originally a political science major, but added a double major in journalism. Graduated at the top of my class. Excelled in the field. Submitted articles to various papers and magazines during college. Got a job as a contributor for the *Post*, then attended Yale Law."

"That's why you're this crazy workaholic, isn't it?" I shift my eyes to him, seeing him in a different light now that I know the truth. For the longest time, I questioned what someone as put together as Lincoln could see in me. But he's as broken inside as I am. "It's the one thing you *can* control."

Children of alcoholics tend to gravitate toward one thing they're good at and put all their effort into that, since it gives us a sense of control we don't have with our parents. Of course, I didn't focus on school. Instead, my "relationships" with various men gave me that sense of control. I said when. I said how. I said where. Until Lincoln, it was the only thing I felt I had control over in my life. And I needed that control.

"You think I'm obsessed with my work?" There's a twinge of hurt in his voice.

"Trust me," I scoff playfully, trying to lighten the growing tension. "You are. I grew up with a man who always put his work before anything else. Still does." I shrug dismissively, not wanting to dwell. "Which is probably why I'll never measure up to his impossible standards."

Lincoln arches a single brow. "Yet it doesn't stop you from trying, does it?"

I blow out a breath, surprised at how forthcoming I am. Exhaustion can do that to a girl.

"Just once, I want to feel like I'm good enough."

"Chloe…" His tone is filled with compassion. He reaches across the couch, grabbing my hand in his, his thumb brushing my knuckles. "You're more than enough." Such a simple statement, but it's exactly what I need to hear. What I've needed to hear my entire life.

"You're more than enough, too," I barely manage to squeak out.

He squeezes my hand, the touch innocent, but the way he swipes his thumb along my skin has my cheeks heating. I lock my eyes with his, unable to look away. There's something new in his deep pools. Wonder. Amazement. Respect. And need. He can deny it all he wants, but people who are just supposed to be acquaintances don't look at each other the way Lincoln's currently admiring me.

The way I'm currently craving him.

Wanting to feel something good and pure, even if for a moment, I inch toward him. Hypnotized, he leans into me, his eyes focused on my lips as I part them. I promised I'd never put myself in this position again, especially after last week. Right now, I just need to wrap myself in something other than feelings of inadequacy and failure.

But am I ready for the feelings of inadequacy and failure that will follow when Lincoln realizes this is a mistake? When he looks at me with the same disgust as he did a few days ago?

Can I really put myself through that again?

I know the answer to that.

I've known the answer to that all along.

When Lincoln's a whisper away and I can almost taste his addictive kiss, I snap out of the spell, practically jumping from the couch. "You should go. I have work to do." I snatch his coffee cup and bring it into the kitchen.

Spying his suit jacket on the counter, I grab it, ignoring his bewildered expression as I shove it at him. He doesn't say anything at first. Just looks at me in a way that makes me want to wrap my arms around him and lose myself in everything he is. But that's not who we are.

His gaze trained on me, he stands, taking his jacket from me and shrugging it on. "If that's what you think is best." He arches a brow in question.

A flicker of hesitation passes. How do I answer that? Is this what I want? No. But is this for the best? It must be.

"I do," I answer with reluctance, a sinking sensation forming that this is our final goodbye. That this is our last chance.

"Understood." His shoulders fall as he retreats from me.

I cross an arm over my stomach, chewing on my lower lip. Am I ready for this man to walk away when I know in my heart we turned a corner tonight?

"Lincoln!" I call out as he's about to disappear out my door.

He pauses, glancing back at me, eyes brimming with hope.

I part my lips, struggling to form a single word.

"Your coat," I say quickly, then rush into my bedroom, grabbing his heavy wool coat off the floor. When I return, I hand it to him. His fingers delicately brush against mine as he takes it from me. A part of me thinks he did that on purpose, a reminder of the spark, the connection, the flame that hasn't dulled despite the obstacles facing us.

"Well, goodnight then?" His tone lifts toward the end, turning his statement into more of a question.

It takes every ounce of resolve I possess not to clutch his face in my hands and kiss him. But tonight's events haven't changed the fact that he's my professor and I'm his student. I need to remain firm. I need to keep that line drawn.

"Goodnight, Professor Moore," I say in as determined a voice as I can muster at the moment.

He briefly closes his eyes, exhaling a long breath. "Good-bye, Chloe."

# Thirty

As a little girl, I went through a phase when I was obsessed with all things supernatural. After learning about the folklore theory of the witching hour being a time increased supernatural activity could be present, I'd always hide under my blankets if I somehow woke up between the hours of three and four.

Tonight, as I toss and turn at three in the morning, the only increased activity is in my brain. No matter what I've tried, I can't seem to quiet my mind.

I can't seem to stop thinking about Lincoln.

I haven't been able to since we met.

I've tried closing the chapter on us, tried starting a new one, but it's hard to turn that page when the person you want won't be there anymore.

On a long exhale, I throw my arm over my head, staring at the ceiling, wondering if Lincoln is as restless as me.

If he's thinking of me.

If he wishes we could turn back the clock and take a different path.

A gentle rapping cuts through my thoughts. I still, unsure whether it's real or if I'm simply hearing things due to exhaustion. A few seconds pass, my apartment falling silent once more. Then the knocking sounds again, this time firmer.

More curious than anything, I get out of bed and limp toward the front door. Lifting myself onto my toes, I peek through the peephole, my heart catching when I see Lincoln pacing on my stoop, snow still falling around him, hair disheveled, demeanor frantic. From the looks of it, he's had as much trouble sleeping as me.

I steal a glimpse of my reflection in the entryway mirror, smoothing my hair before opening the door. The instant I do, he halts in his tracks, his wild eyes shooting to mine.

"Lincoln, wha—"

Before I can finish, he advances toward me and grips my face. All the air leaves me, the combination of his sudden movement and rough flesh on mine making me breathless. His fingers dig into my skin, a fevered energy about him as his lips inch closer, the heat of him causing my pulse to skyrocket.

"Invite me inside," he growls.

"I don't—"

"Please, Chloe." He releases me, wearing a path on my stoop again. "I've done everything in my power to stay away from you, to forget about what we shared. It was only... What? Ten days? There's no way two people can form that strong a connection in such a short period of time, right?"

"Right...," I say in a drawn-out voice, leaning against the doorjamb.

"Right." He stops pacing, peering at me through pained eyes. "So why can't I forget you?"

I stand straight. "I—"

"Why don't I *want* to forget you?"

I keep quiet, letting him get out whatever he came here to say.

"Because I don't, Chloe. Believe me…" He laughs to himself. "I've tried. I've tried dating other women. Thought it would make it easy. That it wouldn't hurt so much. But you have to know how *excruciating* it is to sit in class and watch you with Owen."

"We're not—"

He holds up his hand, and I snap my mouth shut. "It has destroyed me, Chloe, regardless of whether there's anything between you two. The idea that you can have an open conversation with him, even a platonic one, kills me."

The veins in his neck tighten as his hand squeezes into a fist, pure anguish oozing from every pore. His face reddens. His teeth clench. His body shakes.

"Because I. Can't. Do. That. I can't enjoy the luxury of making you laugh. Of taking you out and treating you like the amazing woman you are. Of kissing you in the middle of Times Square with the world watching. Not without jeopardizing everything I've worked so hard for. Without destroying my father's legacy. But I'm willing to do that. For you." Eyes focused and chest heaving, he steps toward me. "I just need to know you're all in. I need to know you're willing to take a risk. To take a chance."

"I told you I was," I reply softly.

He closes the final bit of space. "That was before. Things have changed. I need to know you're willing to do this. Right here. Right now. With who we are to each other. I need to know you're willing to lower your guard and let me past the wall you've built up throughout a lifetime of being made to feel inadequate. So please…" He lifts a hand to my nape, not blinking as he stares intently into my eyes. "Invite. Me. Inside."

I part my lips, searching his expression. It's a reasonable request, one most women would agree to without a second thought, especially with a man as handsome and addictive as Lincoln Moore standing in front of them.

But I'm not most women. Lincoln knows this.

Worse, he knows how sacred maintaining my own space is. I've never invited a man into my apartment. That meant giving them a piece of myself. It meant permitting them into my heart, something I've always avoided.

Until now.

Bringing my hands to his face, I savor the scruff of his unshaven jaw, ghosting my mouth against his. "Okay."

He vehemently shakes his head. "No, Chloe. Not just okay. Not yes. Not a nod. I need the words," he pleads with me like a man begging for his life.

Licking my lips, I focus my gaze on his. "Lincoln… Will you please come inside?"

His muscles relax, a tiny exhale of air escaping. Then he threads his fingers through my hair and crushes his lips to mine, his tongue exploring my mouth like it's the first time he's ever kissed me…sweeping, penetrating, needy.

I've been treated to my fair share of Lincoln's kisses since we met. Every single one left me addicted for more. But not one felt this electrifying. Not one had the power to hit me so deep, to fulfill me in a way I didn't think possible, to make me think we've finally found ourselves in each other.

When he tears away, he leaves me gasping for air. Peering up at him, I see his jaw clenched, eyes untamed. I remain locked in place, not moving, worried he changed his mind, came to his senses. Then a brilliant smile crosses his lips.

I cup his cheek and he melts into my touch, covering my hand with his. I pause to admire this man. The man who felt the need to rescue me from some drunk guy who wouldn't keep his hands off me. The man who smoothly sent a martini my way just so he could come talk to me. The man who begged for a chance.

His smile turning wicked, he swoops me into his arms and carries me toward my bedroom.

"Lincoln," I whisper-shout, "what are you doing?"

"Helping you follow doctor's orders by keeping you off your feet."

Once he kicks the door closed, he helps me find my footing, the playful atmosphere shifting. We stare at each other in the relative darkness, the only light coming from a streetlamp casting a slight glow into the room.

He brushes a strand of hair behind my ear, allowing him to see me unobstructed. His fingers linger on my face. I close my eyes, savoring the warmth of his skin on mine.

"You are so beautiful."

I bask in his ardent declaration, my heart expanding. Then he brings his other hand to my face, his grip becoming harsher.

"Say you want me."

"I want you," I whisper.

His lips touch mine, our kiss a tease. "Say you need me."

I grip the back of his neck, digging my fingers into his skin. "I need you, Lincoln." I move my mouth along his unshaven jawline, taking his earlobe between my teeth, his taste addicting. "I've always needed you."

With a growl, he forces my lips back to his, his tongue sweeping against the seam. His motions are the perfect combination of desperate and sweet. Greedy and reverent. Chaotic and controlled. His ravenous kiss leaves no question in my mind of how much *he* needs *me*.

His rough grip loosens, his urgent kiss becoming tender. He exhales into me, his arms wrapping around me, keeping me safe in his embrace. As much as I want more of him, *all* of him, I want this, too. These quiet moments between us. These reminders that he hasn't given up on us.

Our mouths never break from each other as I fall onto the mattress, bringing him on top of me. I can't stop kissing him even if I want to. He is the elixir for my suffering. The cure to my torment. The remedy to all the tragedy.

My perfect addiction.

As he peppers starved kisses along my jawline, I crane my head, a shudder rolling through me when his two-day scruff scrapes against my throat. I hook a leg around his waist, slowly circling my hips, my pulse increasing.

"Do you have any idea how much I've thought about this? How much I've fantasized about this?"

"Yes," I moan as his fingers lift the hem of my t-shirt, my body aching for him.

"Tell me you've thought about me."

"Every day," I answer without a moment's hesitation.

"Tell me you've fantasized about me." His voice becomes more demanding.

"Every night," I pant.

"God, Chloe. Why can't I stay away from you?"

My fingers rake through his dark locks and he arches his back, relishing in my touch. "Maybe because we're not meant to be apart."

Before I can utter another word, his lips are on mine, his hands running along my body, exploring, remembering. We only tear away from each other long enough for him to lift my top over my head. He cups my breasts, his fingers rolling my nipples, eliciting a moan from me. I claw at his own t-shirt, yanking it off.

The instant it joins mine on the floor, he wraps an arm around my waist, raising me to a sitting position, pressing my body to his. Skin to skin. Flesh to flesh. Heart to heart. We take a minute to calm our ragged breathing and temper our racing hearts.

Toying with a few tufts of chest hair, I rest my head against him, this moment more intimate than any other time I've been with a man. Because I'd never truly been intimate with anyone else. Not like this. I gave them my body, nothing more. But Lincoln captured my heart, captivated my mind, invaded my soul.

"Your heart's racing," I murmur, covering it with my hand, the pounding rhythm comforting.

"I can't help it." His deep voice is tranquil as he runs his fingers up and down my back, causing a shiver to roll through me. "It always beats faster when you're around." He touches my chin and tilts my face, bringing my eyes to his. "It's always burned for you." He brings his lips to mine, his kiss achingly perfect as he lowers me to the mattress once more.

Taking his time, he tastes me, feasts on me, experiences me, his journey down my body torturously slow. My nails scratch his scalp as I pulse against him, my muscles tightening. A low rumble vibrates from him, and I smile. Such a simple, innocent touch, but the sensation of my fingers clawing at his skin has always unhinged him.

I hope it always will.

When he reaches my breasts, he floats his gaze to mine, a hint of mischief within. Then he returns his attention to me, taking a nipple into his mouth.

I close my eyes, my body fusing into the mattress, sparks shooting through me. When his teeth gently scrape against the sensitized flesh, I yelp, then moan, my muscles clenching as I attempt to calm the myriad of sensations filling me.

His hands roam my frame, getting reacquainted with every dip. Every valley. Every curve. Each time he looms close to the waistband of my shorts, I grow hopeful, only for him to retreat.

"Please, Lincoln," I beg, my body a slave to his touch.

"Something I can help you with, Miss Davenport?" Lifting his eyes, his lips kick up in the corners.

"I need you," I pant, my chest rising and falling in a quicker rhythm, the ache in my core only burning hotter with each passing second. "I need to feel you."

"You *are* feeling me." He circles one of my nipples with his tongue, eliciting another moan, before tracing a line in the valley between my breasts, the sensation unhinging me.

"You know what I mean."

He cocks his head. "I *think* I do. But maybe you should tell me so I'm certain we're on the same page."

It takes all my resolve not to break into a huge smile at the memory of the games we played our first night together. Both outside and inside the bedroom.

His cheeks clutched in my hands, I look at him with a heated stare. "Lincoln, I need you to fuck me."

He keeps his gaze locked on mine for several seconds as my words linger in the air. Blowing out a long breath, he shakes his head.

"I'm not going to fuck you tonight, Chloe."

My heart falls as I blink repeatedly. "But—"

He presses a finger to my lips, silencing my protest. "This isn't just sex for me."

I swallow hard at his sincerity. "It's not just sex for me, either." My words surprise me. Despite trying to convince myself otherwise, it's never been just sex with Lincoln. It's always been something more.

"That's why I'm not going to fuck you. Not now that we've finally made it to this place. Tonight, I'm going to seduce you." He lowers his mouth to my neck, beginning his agonizing journey down my body once more. "Your mind." He briefly sucks on my nipple before heading farther south. "Your body." He dips his tongue into my belly button, drawing a line along my waist before meeting my eyes. "Most importantly, your heart." He holds my face in his hands, our connection strong. "Your heart is what I want more than anything."

"It's yours," I assure him, my voice a whisper as I struggle to speak through the lump in my throat. "It's always been yours."

He treats me to a sweet kiss before pulling back and lowering my shorts, leaving me in my panties.

"These look familiar." He smiles slyly, smoothing a finger along the silky material.

"They should." Not caring about the pain from my stitches, I manage to prop my legs up, spreading them. He takes the hint and brings his thumb to my center. "They're yours after all." Arching toward him, I scrape my lips against his. "Yours are the only panties I've worn since you got them for me. I never stopped being yours, even if you stopped being mine."

He presses his mouth more firmly against mine. "I never stopped being yours, Chloe. Never." He narrows his gaze on me, allowing his statement to sink in. Then his fingers hook into the waist of my panties, about to pull them off.

"Don't." I grasp his forearm, then grin deviously. "Leave them on. Like our first night together."

"You liked that?"

Biting my lower lip, I nod, my eyes heated. "You know I did."

"Well then…" He grabs my thighs, spreading them wider, positioning himself. "Who am I to disappoint?"

As he inches toward me, my pulse skyrockets, the seconds

seeming to stretch, time standing still when I need it to hurry. Finally, he presses his mouth against me and I moan, my eyes fluttering into the back of my head.

The first time he did this, the unwelcome barrier of my panties only frustrated me. But this is what I need right now. A reminder of how far we've come since that night, but at the same time how we're still the same people. That nothing's changed. At least the important thing hasn't. This connection hasn't.

"Lincoln," I moan, scraping my fingernails against his scalp.

"Yeah, baby."

The vibration of his voice pushes me higher and higher, and I move against him with greater urgency. I never thought it possible to get off without him actually touching me. He proved me wrong back then. Just like he's continued to prove me wrong.

That familiar quivering sensation fills me, my toes curling, spine tingling, and I hold my breath, my brain unable to focus on anything other than the immense pleasure this man brings me. When I don't think anything could feel more incredible, Lincoln pulls back the fabric of my panties, his tongue tracing along my center. He pushes a finger into me, then another, stretching and twisting. Lights blind my vision and I shatter, screaming his name as I convulse on my bed, not wanting this euphoric sensation to end. And Lincoln won't let it, drawing out my orgasm as long as possible until he can no longer control himself.

"I need to be inside you," he states in a gruff voice, a man obsessed.

With haste, he yanks my panties down my legs, then lowers his own jeans and briefs. I don't take my eyes off him, admiring his beautiful physique. I want to pinch myself to make sure this is really happening, that I'm not dreaming. It all seems surreal, considering a little more than a week ago, he looked at me with absolute disgust as he kicked me out of his office.

He returns to me, crawling up my body. His motions are tender as he brushes the hair away from my eyes.

"Are you okay?"

"Newsflash." I smirk. "This isn't the first time I've done this. This isn't the first time *we've* done this."

"True. But there's no looking back after this. There's a lot more at stake now."

I gaze at him thoughtfully, trying to find a way to assure him I'm ready for everything that follows. "Are you familiar with the story of Orpheus?"

He cocks a brow, releasing a small laugh. "This may be the first time someone's brought up Greek Mythology during foreplay. At least, it doesn't seem to be a common topic in my circles."

I give him a sardonic look before my expression turns serious once more. "When his wife, Eurydice, died, he went to hell to bring her back from the underworld, risking everything. Hades and Persephone were so entranced by his musical ability that they permitted him to go into hell and bring her back with him, on the condition she walk behind him and he not look back."

"I know the story."

Grabbing the back of his neck, I bring his lips within a breath of mine. "He lost the love of his life because he made the mistake of looking back." I shake my head, emotion choking my words. "I won't make that mistake here. Not now that I know what living without you feels like. You're the only one who's ever quieted the chaos, who's made me feel I have worth. I'm never looking back again."

Overwhelmed, he covers my mouth with his, his hold on me tightening in a way that makes me think he'll never let go. "I'm never looking back, either."

"Promise?" I ask, allowing him a glimpse at my vulnerable side.

"Promise." He touches his lips to mine, then steps off the bed, fishing his wallet out of his pants' pocket. A condom in hand, he starts to tear the wrapper open.

"Wait."

He stops mid-rip, giving me a questioning look.

"I want to feel all of you. Like we were about to…" I trail off, averting my eyes.

"Hey." He drops the condom to the floor before returning to me, cupping my face in his hands. "I am *so* sorry about how I treated you that day. I never should have…" He pauses, collecting his thoughts. "I guess I was just scared."

"I get it. You're risking a lot by being with me."

"That's not what scares me."

"Then—"

"I was scared of what I felt for you. What I *still* feel for you. I needed to know you were all in, that you wanted this…whatever this is. That you wanted more than you've ever wanted before."

With a grin, I pull him on top of me. "I can unequivocally say I want more. Lincoln Moore."

"Because I've never heard *that* one before," he jokes.

"Hey!" I playfully slap him. "You're not supposed to allude to past girlfriends when you're about to have sex with the new woman in your life. Didn't anyone ever teach you that?"

"Possibly." He smiles a devilish smile. "But I'm happy to have you teach me that lesson." Lifting his arousal to me, he spreads my wetness around, then pushes into me. Slowly. Deliberately. Perfectly. "Over. And over. And over."

"God, I like the sound of that." I bring him closer to me, meeting his rhythm.

I expect him to pick up the pace, but he doesn't, drawing out his motions in an agonizingly slow rhythm. He was right. This isn't sex. This *is* a seduction. Of my mind. My body. My heart.

He buries his head into the crook of my neck as I wrap my legs around him, needing him closer. But no matter how tightly I squeeze, how deep he drives, it's still not enough, still can't extinguish the flame building inside, the fire that's been burning for him since the first time our eyes locked.

I scrape my nails down his back, which elicits a groan, causing him to increase his pace. I meet him thrust for thrust, our bodies a tangled mess of legs and arms as we share this beautiful moment, propelling each other higher and higher until we both shatter in an explosion of ecstasy and bliss.

Spent, Lincoln collapses on top of me, breathing labored. I wrap him in my embrace, kissing his sweat-stained brow.

"Thank you." He brushes his lips against mine.

"For what? Not making you use a condom?"

He chuckles. "No. I mean, it's certainly much more enjoyable without one, but thank you for letting me in. For choosing me."

"It was never a choice with you."

# Thirty-One

Light filters into my bedroom as I stir from a restful sleep, my mind quiet for once. My muscles sore, I stretch, yawning, then steal a glance at the clock on the wall, expecting it to be maybe six or seven in the morning. When I realize it's after noon, I shoot up, scrambling for my phone. I never sleep in like this, especially on a weekend. Hell, most weekends I *don't* sleep. I shudder to think of all the stories I missed last night.

*Last night…*

I dart my eyes to the opposite side of the bed, finding it distressingly empty, despite the evidence of a body having slept there. Maybe it *was* too good to be true. Maybe in the light of day, the reality of the risk he'd have to take finally hit Lincoln and he left.

I can't blame him. He's seen the mess that is my life. Alcoholic mother. Disappointed father. I just thought things would be different this time. Thought we'd connected in a way we never had. In a way *I* never had. I actually fell asleep feeling something I hadn't in so long… Hope.

I bury the notion, needing to focus on the more pressing issue of my mother's current condition. I step out of bed, yanking a t-shirt over my head before pulling on a pair of yoga pants. When I spy my panties lying on the floor, I stop, a pang squeezing my heart.

On a hard swallow, I pick them up, staring at them. Every other time we've spent the night together, we didn't part ways without him stealing my panties, claiming them as his. This solidifies my original suspicion.

"You'd better not be thinking about keeping those."

I whirl around, my breath catching when I see Lincoln standing in the doorway, hair mussed, a lazy smile on his face.

His green eyes narrowed, he strides toward me. "They *are* mine, after all." With a wink, he reaches for the panties, taking them out of my hand and shoving them into his pocket. When I don't react with a snarky comment as I normally would, all the playfulness disappears from his expression. "Are you—"

"I thought you left," I admit, my voice small. "That you realized this was a mistake."

"Oh, Pixie…" He wraps his arms around me, pulling me against him. I inhale his comforting scent, savoring in his use of my nickname again. "Nothing about you has ever been a mistake. Well, except the way *I* treated *you*." Gripping my chin, he forces my gaze to his. "And I won't do it again. I will never make you feel like you're a mistake. Like you're not worth the risk. Like you're not enough."

I swallow hard at the sincerity in his promise, doing my best to stop the tears from forming in the corners of my eyes. I should hate that I'm letting him see my vulnerable side, but it's cathartic. Around Lincoln, I don't have to pretend to be someone I'm not. I don't have to be this resilient person who's unaffected by anything. I can lower my walls and let him in. I can finally be me.

"I meant what I said last night. You're more than

enough, Chloe." He kisses away the tear sliding down my cheek before bringing his lips to mine. "You're...more."

"You're more, too."

He skims his mouth against mine, the touch light, making me want it deeper. But responsibility dictates otherwise. With a sigh, I break away. "I should go check on my mom."

"She's fine," he says nonchalantly, as if it's perfectly normal for him to be here during one of her relapses. "Well, as fine as she can be." He lowers his voice. "I hope you don't mind, but I called my mother."

I furrow my brow. "Your mother?"

"She's a nurse. Used to work in OB, but once she went into recovery, she changed paths and now works in a rehab clinic. I figured it would be good to have some sort of medical professional around."

"Medical professional?"

He blows out a long breath, running his hand through his hair. "On my mother's advice, I found your mom's keys and went through her place this morning." He brings his hands to my biceps, his expression grave. "Chloe, I think your mother's been drinking a lot longer than you've been led to believe. Definitely much longer than just a few months. Possibly years."

"How? I—"

"I think she just got good at hiding it. Probably figured if she did everything she was supposed to — went to work, attended meetings, stuff like that — no one would think anything was amiss."

"But I already went through her house." I place my hand on my dresser to steady myself. "The night we were discharged from the hospital. When she was sleeping, I made sure she'd gotten rid of everything."

He arches a brow. "Hidden bottles?"

"What do you mean?"

"Even though it was *her* house, she had liquor stashed in places you never would have thought. A flask between the mattress and box spring. Some mini bottles hidden in the top of the toilet. She even cut out pages in a few of her hardcover books to fit a bottle. All places my mother also hid alcohol."

"But she promised…" I clench my fists. "After I had to quit school because she lost her job due to her drinking. After I…" I trail off, bile rising in my throat at the memory of everything I endured to keep a roof over her head. "She *promised*. Said she finally realized how it was affecting those around her."

"And she probably did…until the withdrawal got to be too severe and she started sneaking a sip here and there. Then a glass. Then an entire bottle. My mother did the same thing. The only thing that finally helped her beat her addiction was a full detox, not simply going to meetings and seeing a therapist. I won't lie to you. It's going to suck, especially with the length of time your mother's been self-medicating."

I shake my head, still trying to process the betrayal and lies, my limbs growing heavy under the truth.

He grabs my hand, running his thumb along my knuckles. "You don't have to go through this alone. I know you don't like the idea of depending on anyone, that you want to prove to the world you can handle anything and everything life throws at you, but it's okay to let someone else carry the burden for a while. That's all I want. To help you carry that burden. Tell me what you need."

"What I need…," I begin.

"Anything. Within reason, of course." He winks.

"What I need…" I meet his eyes, searching them.

"Yes?"

With a smile, I say, "What I really need is a strong cup of coffee."

He pushes out a laugh, his shoulders relaxing. Bringing me back into his embrace, he places a soft kiss on my head. I breathe him in, wishing I could stay here all day, maybe forever.

"I can do that. I already figured out how to use your espresso machine…thanks to Google." He winks.

"Good. Because you'll need to get used to making me espresso if you want to earn your keep around here." I lift myself onto my toes, brushing my lips against his.

"And I certainly plan on doing just that."

# Thirty-Two

I won't lie and say the next few weeks are a walk in the park, because they certainly aren't. In fact, I can't remember a more stressful time, a more agonizing experience. Watching my mother's body shiver and shake as it fights to rid itself of all the toxins has opened my eyes and made me come to terms with the idea that I failed her. That I should have done more than insist she go to meetings and see a therapist. That I should have demanded more than just her word that she'd quit drinking.

I still have trouble reconciling the fact that she hid it so well from me for so many years. Thankfully, Lincoln's mother, Wendy, has helped me understand better than any high-priced therapist ever has. Seeing how well she's doing has given me hope my mother will also make a full recovery. Finally.

I think it's given my mother hope, too.

"Have you left this place at all this week?" a deep voice says as I stand in my mother's kitchen, heating some soup Wendy brought over.

I look up from the stove, smiling when I see Lincoln standing in the doorway. He's been more than understanding of my need to stay with my mother these past few weeks. It's been a long process, one we've dragged out even longer by not having my mother quit cold turkey. At first, I didn't like the idea of continuing to let her drink a single drop, but Wendy eventually convinced me that stepping down her alcohol consumption over a period of a few weeks would be best. After reading up on the severity of alcohol withdrawal side effects, I have to admit, she was right, especially considering my mother's been able to detox in the comfort of her home instead of a clinic.

"I have," I insist, stirring the soup before putting the cover on it, allowing it to simmer.

He arches a brow, tilting his head. "For more than a few minutes to answer a phone call on the back deck?"

I open my mouth, then snap it shut. He's got me there.

"Chloe…" He exhales as he strides toward me, running his hands down my arms in a soothing manner. "You need to give yourself a break."

"I am."

"Really? You've been holed up here for nearly three weeks now. You've put your entire life on hold."

"I'm still working," I remind him. "My boss said it was okay for me to work out of the office." Granted, I didn't give her the exact details. Just said there was a family emergency.

When Evie heard, she'd called, wondering if everything was okay. I told her not to worry, using my mother's concussion from the nail gun incident as an excuse. I've kept her problem a secret for so long, I'm not sure *how* to tell my friends without them feeling betrayed.

"Yes, but you're sacrificing everything else." He licks his lips, hesitating before lowering his voice. "You haven't been to class in three weeks."

"Lincoln…" With a warning tone, I push away from him. I'd hoped we could leave the professor-student relationship in the classroom, where it belongs. To his credit, this is the first time he's broached the subject, although I have a feeling he's been wanting to bring it up since the first day I didn't show up.

"I'm worried about you."

"Well, don't," I snap, defensive, my face heating. I spin from him, stirring the soup with more force than necessary, the liquid splashing onto the stovetop. "Once my mom gets through these next few days, I'll go down to campus and officially withdraw from class. Your mom said the first few days without alcohol are the worst. It's Friday. We stopped permitting her any alcohol Wednesday, so I—"

"Withdraw?" he interrupts, his voice soft. He touches my shoulder, forcing me to face him. "What do you mean?"

"It's for the best."

"How?"

"If there's ever a question about us, you don't have to worry about any code of conduct." I'm unable to look into his eyes as I rattle off the response I'd prepared. "If asked, I'll say I'd already decided to withdraw. That you had nothing to do with that decision. That a family emergency prevented me from filling out the necessary forms. With me not having been in class since we slept together, it'll make any appearance of impropriety diminish."

"Why would you withdraw when you're so close to graduating?"

"Like my father loves to remind me, it's already taken me ten years to get my bachelors." Although the idea of him gloating about being right eats away at me. "What's one more? My mother needs me—"

"Are you sure that's the case? Or is it the other way around?"

"*I'm* the one who's dropped the ball on this for years now." My voice rises in pitch, my gaze fiery. "The least I can do is make sure I'm here for my mother so she knows she doesn't have to go through this alone. Like I should have been when I..." I trail off, collecting my thoughts, but Lincoln interrupts me anyway.

"And how do you think she'll feel when she learns her daughter, who's mere weeks away from graduating, withdraws to take care of her yet again?" he shoots back in an annoyingly calm tone. Which only irritates me even more.

I take several steps back as my eyes dart around the room, his analytical stare trained on me. He squints, a puzzle piece falling into place.

"Unless she doesn't know she's the reason you quit school in the first place." Advancing, he grips my chin, forcing my eyes to his. "Please tell me she knows."

"I didn't think it was important at the time." Pushing out of his grasp, I rummage through my mother's cabinets for a bowl. This is why I've avoided serious relationships as long as I have. People don't understand. Living with an alcoholic is a constant balancing act — balancing her already fragile emotional state against my needs. *All* my needs.

"Didn't think it was important?" he says incredulously, keeping his voice low. "Chloe, that is *extremely* important. Have you *ever* been honest with her?"

"What's that supposed to mean? If you're trying to tell me this is all my fault, I know it is. I should have seen the signs earlier. I should have known something was wrong the first time she supposedly quit drinking, yet didn't exhibit any of the normal traits of alcohol detox. I was barely a fucking adult, so I messed up! I get that! But now I can finally do it right! And I don't need you reminding me I ruined her life!"

Desperate for some fresh air, I storm past him, but he's in front of me before I can escape. It's hard enough dealing with the truth of how I've constantly failed my mother. How I was selfish enough to just take her word for everything, not wanting to return to the way things were when she was at her lowest because of what that would mean for me. I can't handle Lincoln's disappointment on top of this, too.

"Hey…" He wraps his arms around me, bringing me into his chest. As much as I want to be alone, I can't help melting into his embrace. "You did *not* ruin her life." He tilts my head back, our eyes locking. "I blamed myself, too. Thought if I paid more attention to my mother, maybe I would have prevented it. But the truth is, nothing either of us could have done would have stopped any of this from happening."

"But I've known she's struggled with alcohol most of my life. Hell, I lost count of the number of times I lied to my father when it was my weekend with him, telling him I was sick so I could stay and take care of my mother."

He pauses before asking his next question. "I know you've hidden this from your father and pretty much everyone else, but have you spoken to someone about everything you've been through?"

With a sigh, I push out of his embrace, heading back to the kitchen. "Izzy knows," I answer as I grab a ladle, scooping the soup into a bowl. "I talk to her about it."

"Anyone else? Maybe a professional?"

"I used to go to Al-Anon meetings, but it's been a while." I steal a glance as he lingers in the kitchen, a formidable presence. "I guess I wanted to think everything we'd been through was in the past. That it was just something I could lock away and forget happened."

"It *did* happen. You can't pretend this isn't real. You're surrounded by friends who love you, friends who would love nothing more than to help you through this. You don't have to do this alone."

I swallow hard. "I don't know how *not* to be alone," I admit. It's one of the most honest statements I've made in a long time. For as long as I can remember, it's just been me and my mom. I've kept her secret for years. Isolated myself for fear it was the only way to protect her, to keep her safe.

Lincoln approaches, enclosing me in his arms. "You are a remarkable, strong, resilient woman, albeit stubborn. But it's okay to let others hold you up once in a while." He slowly lowers his mouth to mine, his soft kiss leaving me wanting more. "It's okay to live your life."

"I don't even know how to do that anymore," I breathe.

"Then let me show you how." His lips press more firmly against mine as his hands go to my hips, their grip resolute and needy. He swipes his tongue along my bottom lip, and I open for him, reaching up and threading my fingers through his hair as I melt into the kiss, all the noise in my head alarmingly quiet.

When he pulls away, his expression is light and carefree. "You can start by finally coming back to class."

I huff. "Why do you care so much?"

"This may sound like a foreign concept to you, but I care about *you*. I want you to succeed." A salacious smile crosses his mouth as he steps back and leans against the counter, his brows waggling. "And I'd be lying if I said the past three weeks of not having you in class have been excruciating." His heated tone forces a shiver to roll down my spine. Foreign, yet so welcome.

"Is that so?" I ask in a husky voice, approaching him, running my fingers up his crisp shirt.

He slowly nods, his eyes darkening to a hunter green shade. "That's so."

"And why's that?" My hand wraps around his tie and I pull him toward me. He tries to lean in for a kiss, but I remain just out of reach.

"Even though you weren't there, I was still able to smell your perfume. Like it's permanently engrained in my senses." Looping an arm around my waist, he drags me to him, grinding his hips against me. "And I can't tell you how hard just the smell of you makes me."

"I don't think you have to." Releasing his tie, I stand on my toes and nuzzle the crook of his neck, flicking my tongue along the skin. "I can *feel* how hard it makes you."

Muscles tensing, he grips my face, fingers digging into my skin, about to press his mouth to mine when the sound of footsteps breaks through.

I jump away, snapping my gaze to the stairway at the exact moment Lincoln's mother appears. She comes to a stop, looking between us, smiling slyly. Now I know where Lincoln gets his smile from. Actually, I see a lot of him in her. While his six-foot-three frame has a solid ten inches over her, she has the same green eyes, dark hair, and compassionate personality.

"Mrs. Moore." I lower my head, shifting uncomfortably on my feet. Lincoln, however, appears just as calm and collected as ever, amused by my reaction. "How's my mother doing?"

"I told you. Call me Wendy."

"Right. Wendy."

Turning from her to hide my embarrassment, I head toward the refrigerator and hoist myself onto my tiptoes, reaching for the breakfast tray on the top, but my height works against me. Seeing my struggle, Lincoln approaches, standing unnervingly close. I attempt to get out of his way, but he places his hand on my hip, keeping me in place as he reaches past me and takes down the tray.

I expect him to let go of me once he sets it on the counter, but he doesn't, snaking an arm around me and pulling me close. Wendy's smile only grows in response.

"Your mother's doing as well as can be expected. She's had a few bouts of heart palpitations, but they've seemed to settle."

"Will we be able to keep her here?"

"She's not exhibiting any extreme symptoms that would require constant medical supervision. I'll continue to monitor her, but because we didn't detox cold turkey, I don't foresee the effects to be as severe as they otherwise would have been."

I blow out a breath, grateful I had a few voices of reason to help me make decisions about my mother's treatment plan.

"She asked to see you," she says after a few moments of silence.

"Oh. Right." I step out of Lincoln's grasp, hesitant. While I feel compelled to be here during this process, I've tried to keep my distance, not wanting to sit through another verbal battering. At least the outbursts and angry shouts have decreased the past few days. "I'll bring her soup up."

I place the bowl onto the tray, along with a bottle of water and a baguette.

"And, Chloe?" Wendy calls out just as I'm about to head up the stairs.

I glance over my shoulder. "Yes?"

"There's no need to jump away from my son whenever I

enter the room. You're more than welcome to kiss him anytime you'd like. In fact, you're welcome to do *more* than just kiss him." She gives me a conniving look.

My eyes widen, my cheeks burning, and I face forward, continuing up the stairs as Lincoln's deep chuckles fill the house with warmth. Fill *me* with warmth.

# Thirty-Three

"Chloe? Is that you?" my mother calls out as I timidly approach her room.

I push open the door, peeking inside. I swallow hard at what appears to be a shell of the woman who raised me. The strong, tenacious woman who didn't take shit from anyone. Who would fight tooth and nail for a cause she believed in. Who, on more than one occasion, had gotten arrested during a protest. It's difficult to see her so weak that she can barely support her head, her hands shaking every time she attempts to bring a sippy cup to her mouth. All from drinking too much for more than a decade.

"Hey, Mom," I greet weakly. "I brought you more of Wendy's soup."

"Thanks, sweetie." She waves me over, the motion seeming to take all the energy out of her.

I set the tray onto the table beside her and prop her into a sitting position, placing a few extra pillows behind her to keep her head upright. "Can I get you anything else?" I step back.

"Actually, yes." She pats the mattress, smiling. It reminds me of my younger days when she'd beam, bestowing praise on me for accomplishing something ordinary and unexceptional, like help her decorate a cake, or set the table, or sing a song. She never berated me for not living up to my true potential, as my father would. "Sit down, baby."

With a nod, I lower myself onto the edge of the bed. She grabs my hand in hers. I have to swallow through the lump forming in my throat when I feel how cold they are, how violently they shake. I do my best to steady them, covering her hand with my own and holding her tightly, wishing I could fast forward through this part.

"Chloe, sweetie," she begins with a sigh, peering into my gray eyes. "You remind me so much of your father."

"What?" I stiffen, heat washing over my face. "I'm not anything like that man."

"Maybe not the man he is today, but back when we first met…" Staring into the distance, a nostalgic gleam fills her eyes. "I see a lot of him in you. You'll fight for something you strongly believe in. You'll bend over backwards to help a friend in need." Her smile fades and she pulls her hands from mine, leaning back against the pillows, her gaze slowly lifting to mine. "You'll sacrifice your happiness and well-being for those you love, often without them knowing."

Unsure where this is going, I remain silent.

"I overheard your conversation with Lincoln."

I glance at her sideways, hesitant. "What part?"

"Enough to realize how selfish I've been." Her gaze searches mine before she asks, "Did you really drop out of school to take care of me? I thought you left because you got a job in the field."

"I couldn't let you end up on the streets." I lower my voice. "You're my mother."

She closes her eyes, a few tears trickling down her cheeks.

"And I've been a horrible one at that." She returns her determined gaze to me. "I want you to know that you bear no blame in any of this."

"But—"

"No. I won't have you blaming yourself. *I'm* the one who decided being numb would solve all my problems. I knew it wasn't the answer. I should have focused on my daughter, not ignore her for the bottle. Definitely not make her take care of me instead of the other way around."

"It's not your fault, Mom."

"It is. And don't you dare try to convince me otherwise. I will not let you walk out of this room thinking this isn't my fault. That you bear even a speck of blame here. You don't. So don't you even try to argue with me, Chloe Lynn, because I'll win." She winks. Then her light expression falls and she reaches for my hand once more. This time, it's a little more steady, but not much. "Promise me something."

"What's that?"

"I want you to finish this semester and finally graduate."

On a long exhale, I pull away. "It's not that easy. Things are…complicated."

"Why?" She crosses her arms in front of her chest. The way her body trembles makes it appear she's trying to warm herself, not suffering from the lack of alcohol in her bloodstream. "Because Lincoln's your professor?"

My heart drops to the pit of my stomach, eyes widening. If she knows, who else does? And *how* does she know to begin with? Yes, Lincoln's dropped by on occasion over the past few weeks, but we'd kept our conversations focused on my mother's recovery. Today was the first time he brought up class.

"When you have kids of your own, you'll understand

how mothers develop this kind of…sixth sense about things. Plus, I've spent a lot of time talking to Wendy." She looks at me thoughtfully, her smile returning. "We actually met once many years ago now. At the company Christmas party a few months before…" She trails off.

She doesn't need to elaborate. I know she's referring to the death of Lincoln's father.

"I remember talking to her about how she felt about her husband's new assignment as the Southeast Asia bureau chief, especially considering this was mere months after 9/11. She didn't seem too fazed by it, said the hardest part was being away from him. But it was a mutual decision they made so their son could finish his senior year of high school here in the States. Once he was off to college, she planned on settling in Mumbai with him."

"But she never got a chance, did she?"

"No, but that's not relevant here. The fact is I know who Lincoln is, Chloe. Wendy mentioned he worked for the *Times* and also taught at a local college. The same local college my own daughter currently attends. From there, we both kind of put the pieces together."

"Then you understand why I have to do this. Why I have to withdraw."

"No, you don't. I am more than aware that your father and I have done a horrible job at making you feel like you're deserving of this risk Lincoln seems willing to take, but you are. You are worth so much more than the hand you've been dealt. So promise me. Go back to school. Finish this semester. Graduate. Finally prove that smug father of yours wrong. Don't give him the satisfaction of being right. Okay?"

I chew on my lower lip, torn. Yesterday, this seemed like the right decision. I assumed Lincoln would eventually realize it was best for both of us, considering how much we've muddied the waters. Then again, we muddied those waters the instant I begged him not to report our relationship to the dean and he agreed. There's only four more weeks left in the semester. What can possibly go wrong?

"Okay."

# Thirty-Four

My office line ringing sounds Thursday as I catch up on all the articles I'd pitched and need to deliver in the next few days. Despite my initial reluctance, Lincoln was right, as was my mother. I needed to live my life. And that life included returning to work.

Shuffling papers around my desk, I follow the noise of my phone, finally finding it under a folder full of photos of the latest royal baby. Quickly grabbing the receiver, I answer breathlessly.

"Chloe Davenport."

"Ah, Miss Davenport." A deep, gravelly voice comes on the line, the timbre making my body buzz to life. "It's Professor Moore. I do hope it's not too forward of me to call you at work." There's a flirtatious quality to his tone that has me playing along with his little game. And if I know anything about Lincoln, it's that he loves games.

"Not at all, *Professor*," I reply softly, facing the corner of my cubicle to have a bit more privacy.

"I was calling to see if you'd be available for a bit of a chat today before class. Regarding your…past performance."

"Past performance?"

"Precisely. Fifty-two West Thirteenth Street. Near Fifth.

Meet me there in thirty minutes. Go to the front desk and give them your name."

"Not your office?" I ask in a demure voice, swiveling in my chair. "Isn't that against school policy?"

"It *is* frowned upon."

"Then I—"

"Don't play coy with me, Miss Davenport." His tone is gruff, demanding, a complete change from the flirtatious quality mere seconds ago. I snap my mouth closed, involuntarily clenching my thighs together in an attempt to dull the ache. "I see how you look at me every week."

"And how's that?"

"Like you want to part those legs of yours and let me have my way with you."

"Professor," I gasp, feigning indignation when, in reality, everything about this game turns me on in a way nothing has before. I've always craved Lincoln, am always desperate for more of him. But this… This takes carnal desire to a level I hadn't expected.

"Don't even try to deny it, Miss Davenport. Because I've been fantasizing about you all semester. How can I not when you come in and flirt with those boring classmates of yours, all to make me jealous?"

"I don't—"

"You do," he barks before softening his voice. "But I know something your male classmates don't."

"What's that?" I glance over my shoulder to make sure I'm alone. It would be just my luck that an audience of coworkers would be assembled, eavesdropping in on bits of our juicy conversation. Thankfully, that's not the case.

"That they can fawn over you all they want, then go home and jerk off as they imagine how you feel and taste. But the truth remains."

"And that is?"

"Every single one of them… They're just boys. You need a man. Someone who can satisfy even your most hidden desires." His voice becomes breathy, carnal, wanton.

"And you think that's you?"

"I don't think. I know. And you do, too." He pauses before adding, "Don't be late, Miss Davenport. You know how I feel about tardiness." He allows his words to linger for a moment before the line goes dead.

I remain motionless, staring at the wall of my cubicle, my heart racing. Then I jump to my feet, return my phone to the cradle, and hastily collect my things.

I don't want to be late for Professor Moore.

Or maybe I do.

I check my watch as I hurry down the street, the address Lincoln…Professor Moore requested I meet him at coming into view. I thought I'd be practical and take a cab instead of the subway or bus. I was wrong. I'm convinced the cab driver intentionally took the route he knew would be most congested to pad his fare. The drive, which should have only taken twenty-five minutes, took close to forty.

Frantically pulling open the door to the boutique, Georgian-style hotel, I burst down the short flight of stairs to the lobby. I scan the area for any sign of Lincoln, then remember his instruction that I give my name at the front desk.

I run my hands over my dress to calm my frazzled appearance, my heels clicking on the tile as I continue toward the registration desk. If I weren't in such a hurry, I'd take a minute to appreciate the beauty surrounding me. Brick walls. Wood accents throughout. Crown molding.

Flecks of gold. All elements I never would have thought to marry together, but it works here. The charming, yet sophisticated space fits in with the style of Greenwich Village.

"How can I help you, miss?" a blonde with a congenial smile asks.

"My name is Chloe Davenport. I—"

"Yes, Miss Davenport." She retrieves a keycard from the desk area and hands it to me. "Elevators are around the corner and to the left." She gestures in the general vacinity. "Enjoy your stay."

I offer her my thanks, then head in the direction she pointed, skirting past a family of tourists as they step off the elevator. I sneak on, glance at the room number, then hit the button for the sixteenth floor. Once the doors close and I'm alone, I rock on my heels, jittery, unsure what awaits me. But if the buildup is any indication, I have a feeling it will be better than any fantasy.

Once the elevator stops, I step off, padding down the short, quiet hallway to the correct room. I insert the key into the slot and turn the knob, stepping hesitantly onto the hardwood of the foyer, praying the woman at the front desk gave me the correct key and I'm not about to walk into some crazy swingers' party.

But if there *were* a party going on, there wouldn't be this striking silence, the only noise that of the air conditioning unit and the faint, ambient city sounds I barely notice now that I've lived in Manhattan this long.

I round the corner from the foyer and my feet meet plush carpet, the bedroom coming into view. I halt in my tracks at the sight of Lincoln sitting in a wingback chair, a view of Greenwich Village and beyond visible behind him. A leg rests on a thigh, today's edition of the *Times* spread in front of him.

My heart skips a beat as my eyes feast on him. So casual. So smooth. So sophisticated. The way he looks in a crisp, three-piece suit, coupled with his dark-framed glasses and designer tie, has my libido going into overdrive. I'm pretty sure the ol' girl is stretching in preparation for what she hopes to be a killer workout.

Finally, Lincoln's eyes lift to mine. Slow. Deliberate. Calculated. The heat in his stare sends a delicious shiver through me, ending between my legs, my core clenching.

"Miss Davenport." His voice is even, unaffected, as he folds the newspaper, placing it on the small table beside him.

"Professor Moore."

He raises his arm, using a single finger to beckon me to him, the severe expression he wears not allowing any room for argument. My eyes remain locked on his, ash gray to vibrant green. The closer I get, the more I'm attuned to the raw masculinity and sexuality coming off him.

I stop when I'm mere inches away. Closer than would be considered socially acceptable, but still far enough away that I'm not right in front of him. Not yet anyway. He places both feet on the floor, resting a hand on either thigh, but makes no move to get up, a king holding court over his subject. And I am more than willing to be his subject.

"You're late. You're aware I have a very strict policy when it comes to tardiness."

"My cab driver gave me a nice tour of Fifth Avenue, instead of taking a less congested route. Otherwise, I would have been on time." My voice is little more than a squeak, a complete shift from my normally assured tone.

"You also know how I feel about excuses, do you not?" He glares at me through condescending eyes.

"I do."

He grips my hips, yanking me between his legs in one

swift move, his hands going to my ass, squeezing. I gasp, my pulse skyrocketing, as if this is new. I guess it is in a way.

Leaning toward me, his nose grazes against my waist before he dips lower, inhaling when he reaches the apex of my thighs. He squeezes tighter, a visible shiver rolling over him before he pulls away, his eyes on fire. It sears a hole straight through me. Or at least through my panties.

He releases his grasp on me, sliding a hand along my hipbone, my muscles clenching. I have to remind myself to breathe as his touch leisurely travels down my thigh, pushing back the slit of my skirt.

"Perhaps I should teach you a lesson so you won't let it happen again." He shifts his eyes to mine, his voice becoming gruff, unable to hide his own need for me. The heat of his finger looms torturously close to my center, but still too far. He may as well be in Jersey City. "Would you like that?"

"God, yes," I exhale.

"I had a feeling you would." Abruptly pulling away, he stands, his sudden shift forcing me to step back.

With purposeful strides, he moves past me, turning to face me once he reaches the bed. Eyes narrowed, he beckons me with that same finger. I could find a better use for that finger, but damn if this entire scenario doesn't have me running hotter than any previous sexual encounter… including all the other times I've been with Lincoln.

I keep my expression even as I walk toward him, my chest rising and falling in a quicker rhythm. When I'm within reach, he spins me around, yanking my body hard and fast against his, my back to his front. He runs a desperate hand along my stomach, over my breasts, up to my mouth, never staying in one spot too long.

"Tell me, Miss Davenport. What do you think an appropriate punishment is for your tardiness?" He finds my nipple through the fabric of my dress. When he pinches, I moan, my body pulsing with need. My libido has checked the laces on her sneakers and is officially ready for that starting pistol. But I know Lincoln. He has no intention of firing it anytime soon. His self-control is excruciating.

"Whatever you think is best…" I swallow hard. "Sir."

With a hungered growl, he grips my hair, forcing my head to the side, exposing my flesh for his pleasure. He clamps his teeth down on that spot where my neck meets my shoulder, and my legs turn into jelly.

An arm wraps around my waist and tugs me even harder against him, supporting me. He knows how much his mouth on this spot drives me insane. And today is no different, but something about this game we're playing has my body more alert, more needy, more desperate for him.

Too soon, he releases his hold on me, forcing me around to face him. "Strip," he orders.

I feign shock and a hint of innocence. "But, Professor Moore, I—"

"Don't play the virtuous card with me. You've been fantasizing about this as much as I have." He curves toward me, his delicious scent consuming me. "You can't stand here and tell me you haven't. I know the truth."

His hand goes to my chin, tilting my head up, his mouth a whisper from mine. All it would take is the slightest movement and I'd taste his lips. And I want to. God, I want to. But just like the night we first connected, I want this even more. The chase. The hunt. Then the kill.

"And what's that?"

His finger draws a line down my throat, through the valley of my breasts, then circles my belly button before disappearing into the slit of my skirt. "That you can't stop thinking about me every time you touch this delicious pussy of yours." His thumb brushes against me, teasing.

"You are so wet for me, aren't you?"

"Yes...," I pant, my eyes rolling into the back of my head.

"Yes what?"

I swallow hard, licking my lips, my chest heaving. "Yes, sir."

"Good girl."

He removes his hand from me, and I snap my eyes open, watching as he steps back. His demeanor is nothing short of collected and assured, as always. This is simply a game, an opportunity to pretend to be two different people for a minute, but I doubt I could remain as composed as he. I'm already on the verge of losing what little control I have left.

"Strip."

"Yes, sir." I reach behind myself and lower the zipper of my navy blue sheath dress, the sleeves off the shoulders. I take my time as I shrug it off, addicted to the heat building in Lincoln's eyes as he watches my every move.

"No bra?"

"Benefit of having nearly non-existent boobs," I answer shyly. "You can get away without a bra instead of having to wear a strapless that digs into your skin."

Lincoln's demeanor changes as he closes the distance between us, pressing my body to his. His mouth finds mine and I sigh into his tender kiss, a break in character. He cups my breast, his touch reverent, yet still filled with so much passion.

"You're perfect, Chloe," he whispers against my mouth. "Everything about you is perfect. Don't let anyone ever tell you otherwise."

Before I have a chance to respond, he steps back. With

the flip of an internal switch, he turns into Professor Moore, stance wide, expression severe. He nods slightly, and I continue pushing my dress down my body, over my hips, allowing it to pool at my feet. I step out of it, about to kick off my heels when his voice rings out.

"No. The shoes stay on."

My libido gives me a high five. Apparently, she was hoping he'd say that. So was I.

"Yes, sir."

"But your panties do not."

"Yes, sir." Smirking, I hook my fingers in the waist of my panties, ridding myself of my last article of clothing while Lincoln remains fully dressed. I'm about to toss them on top of my discarded dress when he extends his hand toward me.

"I'll take those."

"Why am I not surprised?" I murmur in a sly voice, placing them into his palm.

He clutches my bicep, spinning me around, binding my body against his. "You're already in trouble, Miss Davenport. Shall I increase your penalty?" He slides a leisurely hand down my stomach, which only serves to heighten the pressure building inside me, growing more excruciating with the passing of each second.

When his finger slides beyond my hipbone, I discreetly part my legs. "And what penalty is that?"

"Maybe I won't let you come," he warns, his teeth skimming against my neck, a dull ache from where he'd marked me. "That should serve as sufficient motivation to follow my rules."

"No," I beg, desperate. "Not that. *Anything* but that."

"Anything?" he repeats, amused.

"Anything." The idea of being left in this state for the

next several hours is enough to drive me mad. I need to get off. And soon.

He turns me around, his grin mischievous. "I do have something else in mind. Something *I've* been thinking about for quite some time now."

"And what's that?"

"You'll see." He brings my panties up to his nose and makes a show of inhaling, shivering dramatically before shoving them into the pocket of his pants. "Have you ever used a safe word?"

"I have."

"And have you ever been spanked?"

"I have."

He nods, seemingly unaffected by my response, as if I'd just told him I've been to Florida, not that I've been tied up, spanked, or blindfolded.

"I won't be too harsh. Not today anyway. We'll start slow, since we've never really explored much of this together. If you're not ready, that's okay, too," he adds quickly, cupping my face, my sweet, compassionate Lincoln returning. "I would never force you into doing something you're not ready for. It won't make me want to be with you any less. Okay?"

I simply stare at him, my expression even, not giving anything away. Then I rid myself of his hold, stepping past him.

"Chloe, I—"

When I glance over my shoulder with a sly smile and wink, he snaps his mouth shut, his eyes filling with wanton lust as he watches me crawl onto the mattress, my ass exposed to him.

As I wait in anticipation, the room becomes eerily silent, apart from my labored breathing, and I stare at the black-

and-white print of the Brooklyn Bridge hanging over the headboard.

When I feel Lincoln's finger draw a line down my spine, I peek back at him standing to the side of the bed, his jacket and vest discarded.

"You're sure?"

I nod subtly.

"I need you to say it, Chloe. I need more than a nod."

"I'm sure. I want this."

His mouth quirks into a smile as he pulls away, loosening his tie. But just as soon as it appeared, the light expression vanishes.

"Face forward."

Like a trained pet, I oblige, jerking my eyes forward, the snap of his tie ripping from his neck as formidable as the crack of leather against skin. He brings the silk-like material up to me, using it to shroud my world in darkness. Without the sense of sight, everything else is heightened. Smell. Sound. Touch. Feel.

The shiver from his finger tracing a line from my nape down my spine nearly unhinges me. Such an innocent touch, barely there. But the depth of it hits places on my body I never knew existed.

The bed dips and my breathing increases, my heavy pants echoing in my ears. The heat of him prickles my skin as he leans over me, his teeth lightly pulling on my earlobe.

"If it's too much, say…panties."

"Panties?"

"Fitting, don't you think?"

I smile, a break in the charged atmosphere. "I couldn't think of a more appropriate word."

He turns my head toward his, covering my mouth,

treating me to a taste of him, before he pulls away, resuming the role he's here to play.

The sound of a belt buckle loosening finds its way to my ears, followed by his zipper. I hold my breath, bracing myself for whatever's to come. But nothing does, the room still.

One second. Then another. And another. When I'm about to remove the blindfold, a hard slap lands across my ass, the shock of it causing me to scream and bury my head in the pillow. Not out of pain, but in unbridled ecstasy, my body craving more of his brutal touch, his stinging hand, his punishing caress.

I don't even notice how much I'm shaking until Lincoln grips my hips, steadying me. He covers my frame with his, his hands gliding down my arms, his fingers linking with mine.

"Are you okay?" His breathing is hard, labored.

"Yes."

"Good girl." He leaves a jarring kiss on my neck before pushing himself up, his touch gone.

I take several deep breaths, moaning when he lands another blow to my other cheek, harder this time. But it makes me burn for him even more. He brings his hand back to me, massaging my ass, then sliding a few fingers between my legs, pushing inside, stretching and massaging.

"Does spanking turn you on?"

"Yes." I move against his fingers, on the brink of shattering. I'm unprepared for him to withdraw and slap my ass once more.

"Yes what?" he growls.

"Yes, sir," I yell, gripping the sheets, my muscles tight.

"Better." He slides a finger back inside me and I move against him, my mind a haze.

"Don't come," he whispers in a gruff voice. "Not yet. I

want to feel your pussy clench around my cock, not my hand."

"Then you'd better hurry because I'm ready to fall apart."

His chest hair tickles my back, his breath hot against my flesh. "Condom or no condom?"

"No condom."

"Good girl," he says again, removing his fingers.

He lifts his arousal up to me and runs his tip around my slickness, but doesn't slide inside, torturing me even more.

"Lincoln...," I moan.

He fists my hair, yanking my head back. "What did you call me?"

"I mean... Professor Moore," I stammer.

"Better. I shouldn't let you come from that little slip-up," he muses, pulling his erection away.

"No!"

He bites my neck. "Then beg for me," he orders, his mouth never leaving my skin, jarring and bruising.

I squeeze my eyes shut, my entire body stiffening as I breathe through the ache. "Please, Li... Professor Moore."

"Please what?" His bite becomes even more harsh, but still makes me hunger for him. I fear the second he pushes into me, I'll implode into a thousand tiny pieces. "Tell me what you want."

"Please fuck me." My voice is even, but still laced with desperation.

"Good girl." He loosens his grip, his tongue tracing gentle circles where his teeth just dug into my skin. "Or perhaps I should say bad girl."

"You know what they say, don't you?"

"What's that?" he asks, amused.

"Good girls go to heaven. But bad girls—"

"Bad girls make you *feel* like you're in heaven," he finishes as he thrusts into me. "And this is most certainly heaven." He kisses my shoulder blade, not moving as he fills me to the hilt. "You are my heaven."

He slowly retreats before pushing back into me, going even deeper. This torturous rhythm continues as he plunges into me in a punishing drive, stills for several agonizing moments before withdrawing, almost like he knows I'm close to losing my mind and is prolonging my pleasure.

His hand massages my ass, making me moan. Then he lands a hard blow at the same time as he pushes into me. The combination of the agony and ecstasy has my heart racing. If there weren't a blindfold obscuring my vision, I'd be blind from sensation.

The pattern continues, bringing me to the edge, only to slow down, waiting until I've recovered before thrusting and slapping again. Each thrust, each slap is more punishing, more enthralling, more addicting, making me cry out louder, my legs to shake more violently.

"Harder," I beg, so close to unraveling.

"Like this?" His breathing labored, he reels back, the force of his blow and drive pushing me forward.

"Harder!" I bite the pillow to muffle my cries.

He stills, preparing for his next assault, which is more brutal, yet erotic.

"Harder!" I scream once more, unsure how much more I can take, but I'm willing to find out, to test my limits.

Like a beast unleashed, he drives into me, pressing his hand to my back, keeping me locked in place so my pleasure is completely at his mercy. But the buildup to this moment was so intense, so drawn-out, it doesn't take long for me to fall over the edge, crying out his name as forceful waves of ecstasy wash over me, my legs trembling as I come undone.

"Fuck, Chloe." His words come out almost like a strangled plea. He increases his rhythm even more before he stills, clutching my hips as he finds his own release.

We remain motionless as we attempt to get our breathing under control, my body still shivering through the aftereffects of what is probably the most body-numbing orgasm I've ever had. Being with Lincoln has always been an adventure. He's able to satisfy me in a way I never thought possible. But this… This may be the hottest experience to date.

Looping an arm around my waist, he slowly pulls out, then helps me roll onto my back. When he unfastens my blindfold, I'm met with blazing green eyes.

"Hey," he says sweetly.

"Hey." I reach up, running my fingers through his hair, my arm quivering from muscle fatigue. Grabbing my hand to help steady it, he closes his eyes, arching into the touch before returning his gaze to mine.

"How was that?"

"Hot. Insanely hot."

"Are you sore?"

"A little." I curve toward him, brushing my lips with his. "But just think. Every time you see me squirming in class because of how uncomfortable those hard chairs are, you'll know it's because of you."

"I would offer to bring my office chair in for you, but I fear more students might expect the same treatment."

"There are quite a few girls who I'm sure would love for you to tie them up and spank them," I jest, although my statement's not a complete lie.

He wraps his arms around me, and I kick off my heels, allowing them to fall to the floor with a load thump. "I was talking about bringing a chair in. You're the only one I want to tie up and spank."

"Good," I say drowsily, closing my eyes, and he covers our bodies with the duvet.

"Good." His soft kiss on my temple is a stark contrast from his earlier dominance. I love that this man can give me both. He can be fire and ice. Harsh and endearing. Wicked and honorable.

And he's all mine.

"Can I ask you something?" I press after a few moments of silence.

"Anything. Except where Jimmy Hoffa's buried. I'm sworn to secrecy on that one."

I turn around, playfully pinching him in the side as I snuggle into his chest. "Why did you want to do this?"

"Have sex with you?" He touches my chin, forcing my eyes to meet his. "In case I haven't made myself clear, I am absolutely addicted to you."

"Not that. I meant the whole role-playing thing. Well, technically, it's not exactly role-play with us."

"True," he responds thoughtfully. "It's not. I guess I didn't want this to become an elephant in the room between us. Is our situation ideal? Far from it. When we're together like this, I want to be able to be us and not worry about life outside these walls." He returns his mouth to mine and pushes me onto my back, hovering over me, resting his weight on his forearms. "And I've been fantasizing about some role-play with you ever since I met you."

"Is that right?"

He leisurely licks his lips, his gaze darkening once more. "That's right."

"And what kinds of things did you have in mind?"

"Oh, you know…" The corners of his mouth twitch up in a flirtatious grin as he lowers himself, dragging his tongue along my collarbone, traveling farther south before tugging on my nipple. "The usual."

"And what's that?"

"Doctor-patient. Boss-secretary. The virgin college freshman." He moves to my other breast, giving it the same treatment. I close my eyes, hooking my leg around his waist, feeling his erection slowly return to life. "But I am certainly partial to professor-student, especially after today." He covers my mouth with his, trailing a hand down my torso before sinking a finger inside, my body reigniting.

"Oh, Professor."

# Thirty-Five

"Chloe," a tender voice says, rousing me from one of the most erotic dreams I've had in quite some time.

I slowly blink my eyes open, taking in my unfamiliar surroundings. The instant my gaze locks on Lincoln, I realize it wasn't a dream. This afternoon was real. Lincoln lured me into a hotel room for the sole purpose of having hot, naughty sex.

"Here." He extends his hand, revealing two ibuprofen. "This will help with, well…any discomfort."

I scoot up, wincing, my ass sore. But I'd gladly suffer through this pain again, the pleasure I experienced still making me feel like I'm on a high.

"What time is it?" I place the pills on my tongue, then grab the bottle of water he holds out, taking a sip.

"After two thirty. We need to get to class."

"Uh-oh." Passing him a coquettish look, I reach for his tie that served as a blindfold mere hours ago. "It appears I'm going to be late again." I yank him toward me, my words coming out breathy. "Perhaps I need a reminder of your rather strict tardiness rules."

"Perhaps you do." He crushes his lips against mine, his tongue plunging into my mouth as sparks shoot through me.

I rake my fingers along his back, about to push his jacket off his shoulders when he abruptly pulls away, adjusting his belt. "But at a later date."

"Oh, really?" I roll onto my side, propping my head in my hand as I narrow my eyes on his crotch. "From where I'm standing, you're hungry for more."

"I'll always want more of you." He brings his hand to my cheek, lovingly brushing his thumb along the skin. "My sweetest addiction. But we still need to go."

"Ugh…" I throw my legs over the side of the bed. "So serious."

He flashes a beautiful smile my way, then his expression falls as I turn to grab the dress he placed neatly over a chair, his attention focusing on my ass.

"Chloe, I—"

I press my mouth to his before he can utter another word. "Don't. I liked it. Actually, I *really* liked it. I don't want you to feel bad because then you won't want to do it again. And I really want you to do that again." With a bounce in my step, I head toward the bathroom. "But next time, you be the doctor. I'll be the patient, and you can give me a very thorough exam."

I close the door behind me, grinning to myself when I hear him curse under his breath.

Aware of what a stickler Lincoln is for being on time, I hurriedly run a washcloth over my body and freshen my appearance so I don't look like I've just been fucked, especially on my first day back to class after missing three weeks. A bruise has already formed on my neck, teeth marks visible, so I smooth my hair over my shoulder, covering it as best I can.

When I emerge into the bedroom, Lincoln's re-adjusting his tie. He appears just as put together as he did when I first walked into this hotel room, apart from his hair, which has a mussed-up, just-fucked look.

Sauntering up to him, I bring my hands to his neck, helping to straighten his tie. "Every time I look at you and see this tie, I won't be able to stop thinking about the things you did to me when you used it as a blindfold."

"That's the point." He waggles his brows.

I touch my mouth to his, then allow him to help me into my jacket. After a quick check to make sure I have everything, apart from my panties, he walks me to the door. "Thanks for this afternoon."

With a smile, I lift myself onto my toes, kissing him. "Thank you."

He pulls back the door, holding it open for me. I step into the hallway, turning around when he doesn't immediately follow. "Aren't you coming?"

Hesitation flickers in his expression. "I don't think it's a smart idea for us to walk out of a hotel together. We *are* only a few blocks away from campus."

"Oh…" My heart deflates.

"It's just…" With a sigh, he pinches the bridge of his nose before returning his eyes to mine. "We need to be careful. I want to be with you, but I'll lose my job. Probably *both* jobs, so…"

"Of course." I force a smile, the high I was on crashing to the floor now that reality has set in.

Will we ever be able to be seen together? Or is this all we'll ever have? A few clandestine meetings. Some really hot sex. Then being sent away before anyone realizes the truth. It reminds me a little too much of all the men who came before him.

"Well…" I hold my head high, re-securing my mask. "I'll be on my way."

He steps toward me. "Chloe…"

I hold up my hand, stopping him. "It's no big deal." My tone turns icy. "Thanks for the private session… *Professor.*"

---

By the time I step off the elevator and make my way through the familiar corridors of the journalism building, my blood is boiling. No matter the questionable things I'd done in my past, I've never felt as cheap as I just did with Lincoln. Why did I expect things would be different? It was stupid of me to think we'd ever have a normal relationship.

When I barrel into the classroom several minutes after three, all eyes go to me in expectation, then disappointment when they see I'm not Lincoln. A few of the girls rake their disapproving gazes over me. I wonder if I have a blinking sign on my forehead, advertising the fact that I'd just fucked our professor. This must be how Hester Prynne felt. Except she knew she wore a giant sign announcing her sins to the world. My sins are still invisible. How much longer will they remain that way?

I take a few seconds to compose myself, feeling unnaturally exposed without the panties I can only assume are still stuffed in Lincoln's pocket, and meet Owen's confused stare, which doesn't leave me the entire time I walk in his direction and sit down, shrugging out of my coat.

I pull a notebook from my bag, flipping to a free page, squirming in my chair. I smooth my hair over my shoulder, ensuring it adequately covers the mark Lincoln left. I should have sat on the other side of Owen so he wouldn't have as many opportunities to see it. Better yet, I should have kept my coat on.

"Where have you been?" he asks once I'm situated. "I

figured Professor Prick kicked you out. And since you haven't responded to any of my texts—"

"He didn't kick me out. I had some…personal stuff come up." I fidget with my dress, tugging the skirt to cover a few bruises on my thighs. But as discreet as I try to be, it doesn't escape Owen's attention.

"Is something going on?"

"What?" I shoot my eyes to his. I notice his gaze flicker to my neck, so I quickly hide the mark with my hair once more. "No. I just…" I stammer, needing to come up with something to tell him, to bring his attention away from the questionable bruises that cover my body. "My mom's sick." It's not a complete lie. "That's why I haven't been in class. I had to take care of her."

"Oh god," Owen responds with all the compassion I've come to expect from him, his shoulders dropping. "I'm so sorry. I had no idea." He shakes his head. "Do you need anything?"

"Thanks, but she's doing much better now. We both are."

"That's good to hear, but next time, answer your damn texts. I was worried about you." He reaches for my hand, covering it with his before I have a chance to pull away. "Worried the Big Bad Wolf ran away with Little Purple Riding Hood."

"Mr. Campbell!" A booming voice fills the room.

Owen and I jump in our seats and I yank my hand from his, hiding it in my lap. I expect Owen to shift his attention to Lincoln, but he doesn't, his analytical eyes studying me. I straighten my spine, feigning confidence, praying he doesn't put the pieces together. He wouldn't, would he? Then again, the last time I was in this very room, class ended early due to some unexpected fireworks.

"Do you mind? Or is your conversation with Miss

Davenport more important than, say, a journalist's privilege to keep their source anonymous?"

"No, sir. I apologize, sir."

Lincoln glares for several uncomfortable seconds before turning around, scribbling on the whiteboard. I keep my eyes glued to the blank page of my notebook, ignoring the way Owen steals a glimpse of the bruise on my leg, then shifts his attention back to Lincoln, as if on the brink of putting a puzzle together.

"Now, Mr. Campbell," Lincoln begins when he turns around, a cocky smirk on his face. "What can you tell the class about the Branzburg cases?"

I blow out a breath. As much as I hate when he intentionally picks on Owen because of our friendship, I'm grateful for it today, since it forces Owen to focus more on Lincoln's line of questioning and less on me.

All throughout the three-hour class, I do my best to focus on the material and compartmentalize this Lincoln from the Lincoln who called me his sweetest addiction, from the confusing Lincoln who recoiled the instant I suggested we leave the hotel together.

The more I stew over his behavior, the more my irritation grows. He can't order me to a hotel room, treat me like he's only interested in getting between my legs, then get mad if Owen, a *friend*, appears genuinely concerned about my mysterious absence. He wants to have boundaries about where we're seen together. Well, I need boundaries, too.

When the class finally ends, Owen turns to me, raking his hand through his sandy hair. "I didn't think I was going to survive that."

Thankfully, any earlier suspicion has disappeared, probably because Lincoln called on me, much to everyone's surprise. But I suppose it's best to remove any appearance of impropriety.

"You did great. You're smarter than you give yourself credit for." I playfully nudge him in the side as we walk toward the door. I pay no attention to Lincoln, pretending to be more interested in whatever Owen's telling me. If he wants to treat me like I'm disposable, two can play his game.

I know it's juvenile and a bit rash, but after this afternoon, he deserves a taste of his own medicine.

As I'm about to leave with Owen, Lincoln's voice sounds from behind me. "Miss Davenport, I'd like a word, please."

I turn to face him. "Oh, I wouldn't want to inconvenience you."

"I insist," he grits out, his jaw clenched. "We need to discuss your absences and devise a plan going forward."

"You can email me. I need to get to an appointment," I lie, although I *am* supposed to meet the girls for happy hour.

"You've already missed enough classes for me to fail you, Miss Davenport. A few minutes of your time to discuss this is the least you can do. Rest assured, despite any…connection I may have to your father, I have every right to fail you."

I clench my jaw, my hands balling into fists. The room is still, dozens of curious stares watching our conversation. The last thing I need is to draw any more attention to us. That's the last thing Lincoln needs, too. So why is he doing this?

Fixing my expression, I give him a saccharine smile. "I apologize, Professor. You're right. There are things we should discuss regarding expectations going forward."

Nodding curtly, he adjusts that damn tie, then grabs his messenger bag. "Follow me, Miss Davenport."

"With pleasure, *Professor*."

# Thirty-Six

"What the fuck was that?" I strain in an irate whisper the instant the door to Lincoln's office clicks closed. "You think you can order me around in class? Threaten to fail me just to get me alone? Like this is some fucking game?"

"I know it's not a game." His voice is soft, a complete juxtaposition to mine, which only aggravates me more.

"You don't get to treat me like that," I choke out. "You don't get to fuck me, toss me onto the street, then act all jealous when I talk to a classmate, a *friend*."

He grabs my hips, his earnest gaze attempting to put out the fire within. "I know. And I'm sorry." His lips part as he struggles to find words, a rarity for a man who always seems to know what to say. "We're skating on very dangerous ice here. One slip and we can both sink. I just…" He releases me, pacing the office, tugging at his hair.

"We don't have the luxury of being able to go out to dinner wherever we want, or going to see a show, or going away with friends for a weekend. Hell, even if you weren't my student, I still wouldn't be able to tell any of my colleagues at the paper about you because you're the goddamn boss' daughter! Did I overreact when I saw Owen squeezing your hand? Joking with you?"

I open my mouth to say something, but he interrupts me.

"Absolutely. But I can't help it around you. I can't reel in this insane jealousy that rips me apart, Chloe."

The vein in his neck throbs with the passion and intensity with which he speaks, and I remain still, speechless, my earlier anger dissipating with every word.

"I can't even hold your hand in public without worrying about who could be lurking around the corner. About someone snapping a selfie that has us in the background, then posts it on Instagram for the world to see. For the *wrong person* to see."

He clutches my hands, his expression frantic, a man on the edge. "I want to be able to take you out. I want to be able to show you off and shout to the world how fucking amazing you are."

His face falls and he drops his hold on me, heading to the window. "But I can't." He peers at the city surrounding us, his shoulders drooping as his realization this will never work rings out between us.

I stare at him, swallowing hard through the lump in my throat, my heart sinking to my stomach. It was nice while we were in our own fantasy world earlier, but the fantasy never lasts. It'll fade and all we'll be left with is the sad truth of who we are. Two people who can never be together. We were fooling ourselves to think otherwise.

"I understand." With timid steps, I turn around, heading toward the door, using every ounce of resolve not to look back. Now I know why Orpheus did. Because it is so fucking hard not to.

"But that doesn't mean I can let you go."

His emotion-filled statement reviving my hope, I pause with my hand on the doorknob.

"That night I found you and your mother struggling in the snow…" Lincoln approaches, his hands sliding down my arms. "I told you I was willing to risk it all for you, as long as you were willing to let me in." He spins me around, his eyes searching mine. "*Are* you still willing to let me in? Even knowing things aren't going to be perfect. That it's going to be hard. That we're going to fight."

I reach up, pushing back a lock of his hair. "If you ask me, perfection is grossly overrated. And let's not forget the most important thing."

"What's that?"

"That make-up sex can be really hot."

His mouth kicks up into a smile as he cups my face, a flicker of desire in his eyes. "That's all I needed to hear."

Without a moment's delay, he crashes his lips against mine, desperation and devotion and everything in between consuming him. I part my lips, treating myself to a taste of him. But like that first kiss, I won't be satisfied with just one taste. I need more.

Wrapping my arms around his neck, I arch into him, running my hands through his hair. I dig my nails into his scalp, and he emits a hungered groan, pushing me across the room.

When we reach the desk, I slide onto the edge, parting my legs as I hook them around his waist, tugging him even closer. His lips never leaving mine, he places his hand on my back and carefully lowers me onto the surface.

"Say you want me."

I grin. Some things never change. And this is one I don't want to change. I never want to go a day without Lincoln begging for my reassurance.

"I want you."

"Say you need me."

"I need you."

Tremors follow the line his hand draws up my leg, my pulse increasing as it disappears into the slit of my dress, his hold on my thigh possessive, sending sparks throughout my body.

"Do you have any idea how difficult it was to focus during class knowing you were a few feet away and weren't wearing any panties. How, if I turned your way at just the right moment when you uncrossed your legs, I may be lucky enough to catch a glimpse of what's mine."

I close my eyes as his tongue traces a line from my mouth, down my throat, then across my neck. When he reaches the tender spot where he marked me, he's surprisingly gentle, peppering the most delicate kisses on my bruised skin.

"And you *are* mine, Chloe." His hand continues traveling north along my thigh. When he hits my center, I moan, succumbing to his touch once more. "Say it." His voice isn't demanding. Not like it was earlier today. It's more pleading, as if he can't go another moment without my declaration.

"I'm yours. All of me."

His lips find mine, and he breathes into me. "And I'm yours, Chloe. Have been since I first saw you. I knew back then that there was something different about you. That I had to have you. And not just your body." He slides a hand up my torso, tweaking my nipple before he affectionately rests his palm my chest. "But your heart, as well."

I grab onto his wrist, keeping it there as his other hand continues exploring me, pushing a finger in, then withdrawing before stretching me even more.

Unable to endure another second without feeling him, I

sit up and reach for his waist. With my gaze locked on his, I loosen his belt and lower his zipper, wrapping my fingers around his erection and pulling it out. I stroke him as he continues fucking me with his fingers.

His nostrils flare, his jaw twitching, his eyes dark as they look upon me with pure lust.

"Enough," he hisses, clutching my wrist, stopping me from jerking him off. Blind to all reason, he pushes me back and enters me in one quick thrust, filling me to the hilt.

Closing my eyes, I release a low moan, forgetting where we are.

"Shh…" He brings his hand to my mouth covering it. "Quiet."

I nod. He takes his hand away, his pace slow and languid so as to not make too much noise.

"Put it back."

He pauses, furrowing his brow.

"Your hand. Put it back over my mouth."

His pupils dilating, he does as I command. "Like this?" he asks in a husky voice.

I nod again, the temperature in my body rising, my core clenching at how dark this man can be. He continues pushing into me, filling me completely, just as a knock echoes between our labored pants.

"Lincoln, are you in there?" a deep voice calls out from the other side of the door.

We freeze, neither one of us so much as breathing. His wide eyes dart to the door, the seconds stretching. My heart is in my throat, adrenaline coursing through me.

"It's John Morrison."

"Shit," Lincoln utters under his breath.

"Do you have a minute?"

He blinks, his gaze shifting between the door and me. "I —" he stammers. "I'm on the phone."

We both wait in anticipation, praying he walks away. But when no response comes, Lincoln hangs his head and reluctantly pulls out of me, offering a silent apology.

"Give me a minute to wrap things up."

"Certainly."

"On the phone? Is that the only excuse you can come up with?" I whisper as Lincoln helps me to my feet, remembering his use of the same excuse mere weeks ago when Professor Gordon interrupted us.

"Would you rather I tell the dean I was in the middle of screwing one of my students and I'd be with him when I made sure she came?"

Despite the gravity of the situation, I can't help but laugh quietly. "I'd give anything to see the look on his face when you told him that."

"You may get your wish if I can't figure a way out of this."

"Relax…," I soothe, standing on my toes and kissing his cheek. "You're lucky you chose to screw the shortest student in class. And probably the most flexible."

"Why's that?"

"I can fit in some remarkably tight spaces." I waggle my brows, grab my coat and bag, then head behind his large cherrywood desk, crawling into the alcove between the drawers on either side.

"Chloe…" His Adam's apple bobs up and down in a hard swallow. "You don't—"

"It's okay. There's no other option right now. So go see what he wants before he gets suspicious."

He readjusts his composure, straightening the lines of his suit before walking to the door and opening it. I do my best to remain still, despite my uncomfortable position. I pray it's a quick conversation. My legs are still sore from this afternoon's calisthenics, not to mention the pain already screaming from my ass. I won't be able to stay here for too long.

"Dean Morrison," Lincoln greets, his voice deep and professional.

"I hope I'm not disrupting you."

"Not at all. Just had to answer a few questions on a filing we're making at the office." His steps draw closer and I see his shoes appear a few inches from me. I glance up at his intimidating physique, oddly turned on at how commanding he looks behind this desk with me at his feet. "Won't you have a seat?"

"Thank you."

There's a slight stirring as Dean Morrison assumes one of the chairs in front of the desk. Lincoln catches my gaze as he sits, but his eyes don't linger.

"What can I do for you this evening?"

"I heard through the grapevine that Chloe Davenport is back in class."

He shifts, discreetly adjusting his belt. "She is."

"That's good. At least she'll be better prepared for next semester."

He cocks his brow. "What do you mean?"

"The school only allows students to miss ten percent of class hours. For most courses that meet for an hour three times a week, that amounts to four missed classes. But since yours is three hours once a week, anything after two is grounds for an automatic failure. Well, technically, anything after the first hour of the second missed class is, but I'm being generous. If my calculations are correct, Miss Davenport has now missed three classes."

"I understand the school policy, but I've decided to excuse the absences due to extenuating circumstances."

"I see." There's a pause before Dean Morrison speaks again. "Professor Gordon mentioned you both saw Miss Davenport outside a bar in SoHo several weeks ago."

The tension in the room thickens, his line of questioning sounding more like an interrogation than a conversation between colleagues.

"Yes."

"She also mentioned you shared a cab with Miss Davenport."

I hold my breath, the seconds stretching uncomfortably. I crane my head, stealing a glimpse of Lincoln, his expression unaffected. I suppose that's the upside of being a lawyer. He has a damn good poker face.

"I did. Again, there were extenuating circumstances."

"I see."

I hear the chair push back, followed by footsteps. I send a silent prayer that the dean isn't about to walk behind the desk. I'd never forgive myself if Lincoln lost his job, lost everything because of me. But isn't that the game we're playing?

"The same extenuating circumstances you're using as grounds to excuse Miss Davenport from missing too many classes?"

Lincoln stands, straightening his tie. "As a matter of fact, yes. Since it's a confidential matter, I'm not at liberty to discuss the exact nature of the problem without Miss Davenport's permission, but it is sufficient enough to warrant excusing her. Last I checked, the school policy allowed professors the discretion to determine whether or not to excuse absences, and I've used that discretion here. These were the first classes she's missed—"

"This semester," Dean Morrison interrupts pointedly. "She doesn't have the best track record."

"Compared to her classmates who are fortunate enough to have their parents support them financially and emotionally, you're correct. But when you factor in that she works a full-time job, I'd say she's doing pretty well. In my opinion, she's a brilliant student. One of the most promising I've had in my class."

"I don't doubt that. Her father's a brilliant man. But Professor Gordon has voiced her concerns regarding your relationship with Miss Davenport. I must admit, I find it disconcerting you would share a cab with a student, even if she *is* the daughter of your boss. You're aware this school has a policy regarding personal relationships between faculty and students."

Lincoln places his palms to his desk, leaning toward the dean, his eyes narrowed. "What are you insinuating?"

"That your behavior is raising eyebrows."

"Well, it shouldn't." Straightening, he widens his stance. "You've been in higher education long enough to know this place is often worse than a soap opera. Miss Davenport needed help. I decided to act like a decent human being instead of ignoring her simply because my actions may, as you put it, raise a few eyebrows. If I saw one of my male students in the same predicament, I'd help him, too."

"That may be true, but I'd still like to take a look at all the coursework Miss Davenport has submitted so far this year. Make sure it's on par with the level you claim."

I study Lincoln's demeanor, arms defensively crossed in front of his chest, eyes unwavering, everything about him giving the impression that he has nothing to hide.

An impressive performance, considering he's hiding me underneath his desk.

I notice Lincoln's jaw twitch slightly, then he sits, careful to give me space, and opens a drawer. Tossing a file onto the desk, he leans back into the chair. "There it is."

I hear the subtle rustling of pages as Dean Morrison presumably flips through the few papers I'd handed in throughout the semester. Seconds turn into minutes as my heart thunders in my chest. I pray the dean can't hear it in the strained silence. And that he doesn't find my high marks suspicious.

"It appears she does have a knack for the law," Dean Morrison finally says. "Much like her father."

"She certainly does."

It's silent for a moment before the dean speaks once more. "Very well. I'll let you get back to…whatever it is you were working on. I apologize for jumping to conclusions. This school takes these kinds of things seriously."

"Completely understandable, sir. I should have informed you of the incident previously. In the future, I'll be sure to report any encounters with my students outside class or office hours."

"You do that."

Footsteps echo, followed by the welcome sound of the door opening. I don't think my heart has ever pumped as fast as it has these past few minutes.

"And I'd strongly advise you to stay as far away from Miss Davenport as possible. No more requesting she come to your office to discuss her work, as I've heard has happened. Even if it's innocent, you don't need anything else to add fuel to the fire, so to speak."

"You have my word."

"Good."

When the door finally clicks closed, I blow out a breath, never having been so relieved in my life.

"Hey…" Lincoln crouches down to my level, extending his hand toward me. "It's okay. I locked the door."

Nodding, I put my hand in his, allowing him to help me to my feet. "I am so sorry." Rattled, I adjust my clothes, then collect my things. "I didn't mean for something like this to happen. You could have lost everything because of how careless I was. You should have—"

"Hey…" He grabs my biceps, forcing me to stop. "You have nothing to apologize for."

"But you're risking so much to be with me. *Too* much. It was fun role-playing earlier, but this…" I step out of his touch and gesture between our bodies. "This isn't a game, Lincoln. It's not just a fantasy, although I wish it were. You *are* my professor. If you stay with me, I will ruin your life. There's no way around it. No possible way this will have a happy ending, no matter the risk you're willing to take."

He stares at me for several long moments, and I expect him to agree and send me on my way. Instead, he smiles.

"Do you know how my parents met?"

"No." I shake my head. "I've read about your father because of what happened to him, but other than that…"

"He was the teaching assistant in one of Mom's English electives. Granted, it's not the same as our situation, but they still weren't permitted to be together. They had to wait. They weren't allowed to date while he was the TA assigned to her class."

"So he waited for her?"

He lowers his mouth toward mine, his breath kissing my lips, sending a shiver through me. "He did. Said he knew she'd be worth the wait. But that's where I'm different from my dad."

"How's that?" I murmur, craning my neck back.

"I've already had a taste. And I'm greedy for more. So

I'm not going to stand by and wait for you, Chloe. I need to have you now, even if that means we have to be careful while we figure this out." He traces my jawline with a single finger. "I already lost you once. Already pushed you away when I should have begged you to stay. It's going to take a lot more than the risk to my career for me to push you away again."

Comforted by his sweet words, I fling my arms around him, kissing him with everything I have. I've never been with a man who was willing to risk everything to be with me. I still don't know how I deserve this, but I won't question it. Not now.

"There's just one problem," I murmur against his mouth.

"What's that?"

I glance at the door. "How do you suggest we get out of here without raising any suspicion?"

A contemplative look crosses his face as he scans his office, weighing his options. "Right." He shifts his eyes back to mine. "I'll leave first. It's probably safer. When the coast is clear, I'll text you. I can't guarantee you'll have much time, so when you get my message, make it quick."

"But what about locking your office?"

"I'll double back and lock it once you're in the clear. Okay?"

"Okay."

He collects a few papers, meticulously separating them into their appropriate folders before sliding them into his messenger bag. He heads toward the door, pausing when his hand touches the knob. A thoughtful expression crosses his brow as he looks back at me.

"What are you doing tomorrow night?"

I give him a sideways glance, seeing the wheels spinning in his head. "Why?"

"I want to see you."

"What did you have in mind?" I saunter toward him.

His lips brush mine. "You'll have to wait and find out. I'll have a car pick you up at seven. Wear a dress." His eyes skate over my body before returning to mine. "And heels. Definitely wear heels."

"Any reason why?" I bat my lashes.

"Because I love the way they dig into my skin when I make you come."

I whimper, rendered speechless by his wanton and lust-filled statement, the way he says it with no hesitation. It makes me want him right now, code of conduct be damned.

Smirking, he twists the knob, pausing before opening it. "For the record, I don't regret a thing. We'll figure this out, Chloe. Promise."

My lips curve into a smile, my heart warming. "Okay."

He holds my gaze a moment longer, then says, "Seven o'clock."

"It's a date."

He beams, his eyes sparkling. "I like the sound of that." Then he disappears, closing the door behind him.

"I like the sound of that, too," I whisper into the darkness, feeling unusually content, despite our close call. He's right. Our situation isn't ideal, but it's better than the alternative of not being together at all. I don't want to go back to that. Not now that I have him again.

When my phone buzzes mere seconds later, I yank it out of my purse and read Lincoln's text telling me the coast is clear.

Drawing a deep breath, I crack open the door, peeking into the hallway. Once I confirm no one's lingering nearby, I sneak out of the office. Adrenaline pumps through me, making me hyper-aware of every sound, every cough, every sniffle. The corridors through the faculty area feel like they're miles long instead of just a couple dozen feet.

When I finally step into the main corridor, my muscles relax and I can breathe again. I pause briefly to collect myself, then continue to the elevators, grinning deviously when I see Lincoln heading toward me.

"Miss Davenport," he says as he passes, mischief in his gaze.

"Professor Moore."

"Have a great evening."

I glance over my shoulder, lasciviously licking my lips. "I already have."

# Thirty-Seven

One of my strongest childhood memories is sitting in my mother's room, watching as she got ready for some important function, usually a political rally or fundraiser. She'd always dress in smart pantsuits. Told me they made her feel more powerful, insisted skirts and dresses were tools the patriarchy used to keep women where they wanted them.

While I may not have acquired her flair for feminism, since I actually feel incredibly powerful in a skirt or dress, I did inherit a few of her other habits, like always spraying a bit of perfume behind my ears.

As I do that same thing now, peering at my reflection in the mirror, I pause. For the first time in years, I see my mother in me.

Correction.

For the first time in years, I *don't mind* seeing my mother in me.

The mass quantities of makeup I'd typically wear on a "date" is absent. Minimal contouring and eyeliner take its place, along with a bit of gloss on my lips to make them shine. But that's not the biggest change.

I wrap a lock of hair around my finger, the blonde hue

mixed with darker highlights giving me a more mature look. Gone is the gray and lilac color that's become my signature style, something I've kept simply for the attention it garnered. I liked that guys came up to compliment my bold choice in hair color, then slyly invite me back to their place. I don't want that kind of attention anymore. Lincoln is the only person I want to notice me. And I want him to know who I really am. Want to show him I'm ready to let him in, to let him see the real me. The me few people have seen over the years.

The me I haven't seen much of these past few years, either.

The knee-length dress I chose for tonight has a halter neckline that accents my back and shoulders. It's not as tight-fitting as I'm used to, but the belted waist adds a sensuality, as does the slit going to my mid-thigh. I never would have been able to pull off the emerald green shade before, since I hated how that color contrasted with my hair, but now that I'm a blonde again, I can get away with it. It actually suits me, bringing out a few green specks in my eyes I hadn't noticed before.

When I hear the buzzer, I tear my eyes away from my reflection, my heart ricocheting into my throat. With shaky hands, I grab my clutch and shrug my belted coat over my dress, then walk toward the door, smiling a greeting at the chauffeur standing on the doorstep.

"Good evening, Miss Davenport. I'm Charles, your driver." He helps me down the steps and opens the back door of the idling dark sedan.

"Thank you."

Once I'm secure inside, he shuts the door before running around the car to get behind the wheel. Pulling into traffic, he glances at me in the rearview mirror. "We should be there in about fifteen minutes."

"Where are you taking me?"

"Mr. Moore requested I not give any information away."

I can't help but grin, the unknown of what awaits causing my insides to vibrate. It's been years since I've been on anything remotely resembling a date.

Actually, I don't think I've ever truly had a "first date". Not in the adult sense anyway. My only other serious boyfriend was Parker, but we met in college. I'm doubtful a stolen kiss at the local pizza place where the entire university hung out qualifies as a date. Or going to the dining hall together. Or holding hands as we walked across campus, since we both had the same class.

As Charles maneuvers through the streets of Manhattan, I stare at the buildings as they become increasingly taller the farther away from the Village we get. Each time we pass a hotel, I perk up, thinking this is all another buildup to whatever fun role-playing game Lincoln has in store for tonight.

So when the car pulls up alongside a French restaurant in Midtown, I'm convinced I'm in the wrong place. Less than twenty-four hours ago, Lincoln and I discussed how we had to be more careful, discreet. Now he's taking me to a restaurant mere blocks from Central Park? There's no way we won't be seen. The risk is too great.

Charles opens my door, helping me out of the car and walking me toward the restaurant. I steal a peek at the windows in an attempt to peer inside, but they're all made of mirrored glass, ensuring the patrons' privacy.

"*Mademoiselle* Davenport?" a voice says in a thick French accent.

I snap my eyes to see a man dressed in a dark suit standing inside the double doors, holding one open for me.

"*Monsieur* Moore is expecting you."

Aware of the domino effect I fear tonight will cause, I look from the man back to Charles, who gives me an encouraging nod. I don't exactly have the best of luck. Hell, Murphy's Law should be renamed Chloe's Law. If something in my life can go wrong, it will.

"Enjoy your evening," Charles says before retreating with a smile.

"*Mademoiselle* Davenport?" the *maître d'* repeats, his brows raised in expectation, extending his arm into the foyer.

I chew on my lower lip, torn. Isn't this what I wanted, though? Didn't I want Lincoln to treat me like he would a normal girlfriend, not kick me out of a hotel room after having sex? But at what cost? Lincoln's always been a very rational and pragmatic person. He wouldn't bring me to a popular restaurant without some sort of safeguard, would he?

On a deep inhale, I walk through the doors, allowing the *maître d'* to take my jacket.

Once the exterior door closes behind us, I'm met with serenity. There's no ambient chatter, no clinking of glasses, no scraping of forks against plates. The only sound is that of soft music coming from a piano.

When I turn the corner, following the *maître d'* into the dining room, I know why. The entire restaurant is empty… apart from Lincoln sitting at a table in the center.

The instant he sees me, he stands, buttoning his suit jacket. It's not unusual for me to see him in a suit. But tonight, he looks…different. His hair appears damp from a shower, his beard and mustache neatly trimmed to resemble just a bit more than a five o'clock shadow. Exactly how I like him.

"Chloe…" His Adam's apple bobs up and down in a

hard swallow as he rakes his gaze over my changed appearance.

I was so wrought with nerves over the idea of being exposed that I didn't have time to obsess about whether Lincoln would like the new me. But it appears I had nothing to worry about, not with the way he currently admires me with nothing short of unabashed reverence.

"You look…"

Emboldened, I do a quick spin, allowing him to get a full view of the dress I bought just for him. For tonight. For this new me.

"You like?" I pass him a demure look.

His gaze unwavering, he takes several long strides toward me, drawing me into his embrace. "You're stunning."

I wrap my arms around his neck, toying with the few tendrils of hair that curl over his collar. "You're not so bad yourself."

He runs a finger down the curvature of my face, then grabs a lock of hair, twisting it around his digit. "You got rid of the purple."

"I figured it was time for a change. Time to be me." I pause, bringing my lips toward him. "Time to let you see the *real* me."

His mouth finds mine, the kiss ardent, yet still respectful as he communicates how much this gesture means to him. When he pulls away, he cups my face. "Thank you for letting me see who you truly are." He kisses my nose, then places his hand on my lower back and leads me toward the table. He holds out the chair, helping me into it before sitting catty-corner to me.

"Do I want to know what's going on here?" I glance around the space, still a little confused why one of the premier French restaurants in the city would be empty on a Friday night.

"What do you mean?" Lincoln responds nonchalantly.

I lean closer, lowering my voice. "This place. Being here. The lack of other diners." My brow furrows. "What's going on?"

He reaches for my hand, grabbing it in his. As he runs his thumb over my knuckles, his eyes remain focused on my skin. "I never thought I'd be able to do this in public," he remarks contemplatively, almost in awe.

"What?"

He lifts his gaze to mine. "Hold your hand. It's…everything I imagined it would be."

I'm pretty sure another piece of my heart floats across the table at his words, wrapping around him.

"I don't want to deprive you of the normalcy that goes along with a real relationship because of who we are to each other. You deserve better than that. All last night, I couldn't stop thinking about what we discussed yesterday. How we'll never be able to do normal things. Go out for a romantic dinner, hold hands, steal a kiss for no reason at all. Right now, there are definitely some complications."

I blow out a laugh. "Ya think?"

"But that doesn't mean I won't take you out. That all we'll ever be able to do is hide away in one of our apartments or a rented hotel room. Granted, yesterday, my plan for tonight *was* another hotel room. But you deserve romantic dinners. Starlit walks through Central Park. Surprise flowers at work. I promise you…" His grip tightens, his voice firm. "In time, I *will* give you everything you've ever dreamed of, and more. There will come a day I'll be able to shout to the world how fucking happy I am because of you." He moistens his lips, pausing as he collects himself, his tone softening. "But right now, I hope this is acceptable." A hint of a smile curves his mouth. "We *are* in public, even if there are no other diners present." He winks.

"You lawyers. Always trying to get off on a technicality," I jest.

"Only with you. I only want to get off with you." He waggles his brows.

"Good. And tonight is more than acceptable. Although I'm not sure I want to know who you had to sweet-talk in order to buy out this place for the night."

"No one." With a casual shrug, he leans back, releasing his hold on my hand. "I'm friends with the executive chef, so I called in a favor. He's been closed the past two weeks preparing for a menu revamp, so it worked out quite well."

"I'd say," I muse as a waiter approaches with a bottle of wine Lincoln must have ordered before I arrived. After he presents it to him, the waiter opens it, pouring a small amount into a wine glass, allowing Lincoln to taste it. When he nods in approval, the waiter fills both glasses.

Once we're alone, Lincoln raises his wine and I follow suit. "To a first date I hope you'll never forget."

"I doubt I will." I smile, then bring the wine to my lips, taking a sip of the robust red. "Although yesterday's role-playing was pretty unforgettable, too."

"I can't count that as a date. You deserve better than that."

"That may be true, but we can still play once in a while. You won't hear any complaints from me."

He grins mischievously, which makes me want to skip dinner and go straight to dessert. "I'll be sure to keep that in mind for future dates."

"A bit presumptuous, isn't it? To assume I'll agree to see

you again? This first date could be a complete disaster and I may have to cut my losses."

He takes another sip of wine, his motion slow, deliberate, meticulous as he swirls the liquid around his mouth. It's strangely erotic to watch. Such a simple thing adults of drinking age do on a fairly regular basis. But the way Lincoln takes his time to savor the liquid that winemakers spent countless hours perfecting makes my heart beat a little faster, my breathing to become a little more labored, my skin to flush under his sensual stare.

Forget Pornhub. I could watch Lincoln swirl his wine all day long and probably get off numerous times.

"It may be presumptuous," he finally says when I'm on the verge of combusting. "But something about you makes me think you like a man who's bold, who's confident, who has no problem telling you exactly what he wants. Am I right?" He arches a single brow.

"Perhaps," I flirt, pretending to be completely unaffected by his charms.

"Then trust me when I say that, if I do my job right, I'm *confident* you will be so swept off your feet after tonight that I'll ruin you for any first dates that come after me…although I hope there won't be any." He reaches under the table, his hand settling on my knee. When he grips it somewhat harshly, I jump, yelping, before regaining my composure, nervously glancing around.

"And I'm also confident that after I get you in my bed tonight, the only name you'll scream again will be Lincoln Moore." Eyes flaming with need, he brushes his fingers up my leg before pulling back, acting as unaffected as ever. But I know the truth. That he's the tortoise, and this is part of his seduction, his first lap around the track.

I curve toward him, salaciously licking my lips. "It already is, Lincoln..." I pause, then moan out, "Moore."

The grip on his wine glass tightens and I'm surprised it doesn't shatter in his hand. Now *that* would be a first date I'd never forget.

The next hour seems to fly by as we talk about anything and everything that pops into mind. I search my memory for an instance we've done this, coming up empty. We've never really talked to each other, apart from playing Never Have I Ever during that fated blackout. But that was just part of a game. Here, we're finally learning about each other. More importantly, we're no longer hiding from each other, no longer trying to keep our past inside to prevent reopening wounds that probably never healed completely.

Throughout the course of our dinner, he tells me story after story about his father. It's clear from the excitement and hint of longing in his voice that he still misses him, even though it's been nearly twenty years. I suppose time can't erase all wounds. I'm living proof of that, too.

"It's not as romantic as meeting at a club in Vegas," he says after telling me how his parents met at a blood drive on campus at the start of the semester. She was a nursing student who was helping with the blood collection. The second he laid eyes on her, he was attracted to her.

Apparently, confidence and cockiness are traits among the Moore males. Instead of taking his time after giving blood, allowing the lightheadedness to wear off, Elijah insisted he was fine and attempted to stand. Of course, dizziness instantly took over and he fell, cutting his head, which required a couple stitches. Wendy found out where his dorm was and went to check on him. And the rest, I suppose, is history. Until she walked into class a few days later and learned he was her TA.

"I guess we all can't be so lucky." I roll my eyes.

He grabs my hand in his. I've lost count of the number of times he's done that tonight. It's something so many other couples take for granted. I doubt I ever will again.

"I actually like our story. I like that we kept running into each other, as if the universe was trying to force us together."

"Bet you never expected to learn I was one of your students, though."

"That certainly threw me for a loop." He gazes at me thoughtfully. "But I wouldn't change that, either."

"Really?"

"I like to think everything happens for a reason. And I like to think there's a reason you ended up in my classroom."

"And what's that?" I lean toward him, my eyes glued to his.

"I think we both needed to fight for this. If there weren't these huge obstacles facing us, I think we would have taken each other for granted. Taken our feelings for granted. Maybe it would have eventually turned into something more, something meaningful, but I think we needed this. Because I know something I didn't back in January. Hell, something I didn't even know a few weeks ago."

"What's that?" I ask again, my voice softer.

He brings my hand up to his mouth, placing soft kisses against my knuckles. "That I'll always fight for you, no matter the battle, no matter the cost."

And that's all it takes for the remainder of the wall protecting my heart to crash down, allowing Lincoln Moore to possess it.

# Thirty-Eight

I slam my hand onto the kitchen island where I've been chopping tomatoes and cucumbers for a salad. "Oh, my god! I just thought of something."

Lincoln glances over his shoulder. "Should I be worried?"

"Fluffy!"

"Fluffy?" Facing me, he crosses his arms in front of his chest, and it takes every ounce of resolve I possess not to drag him back into the bedroom, especially when I see his muscles flex with the motion. There is nothing sexier than a man cooking in the kitchen. Except a man cooking without a shirt. And that's my current view.

Over the past several weeks, I've spent a great deal of time in Lincoln's apartment. It now feels more like home than my own place. We've gone out on occasion, usually to a late movie at a theater so far out of the way that the chance of seeing anyone we know is slim, but we tend to play it safe and have a "date night in", as he calls them. Cooking dinner together. Watching movies. Always adding a personal touch to make it more than just staying at home.

"Yes. Fluffy, your cat. The one you told us about in Vegas that you're convinced cursed you."

"I remember Fluffy." He returns to the stove to check on

the steaks searing on the burner, coating them with some melted butter from the pan.

I do my best not to gawk. Yes, I love a muscular chest and chiseled abs, but there's something incredibly sexy about Lincoln's broad shoulders and sculpted back that tapers into a defined waist. And those dimples right above his shorts beg to be licked. But I don't. That might be a little creepy. I know I'd be creeped out if I were cooking and he came up and licked my lower back. Then again…

"And it's a good thing we just had sex because bringing Fluffy up in conversation would probably curse me," Lincoln adds as he turns around, his voice and sudden motion forcing my eyes up to his. A sly smirk tugs on his mouth when he realizes he caught me ogling his physique. He stalks toward me, using his body to press me against the island. "But I have a feeling you'd be able to lift any curse." He grinds against me, making his erection known.

"Down boy. Do you need a cold shower?" I push him away. "What I meant was it just occurred to me that Midge's cat, Pigpen, is Fluffy. You said you gave the cat to your boss after they'd lost theirs."

"I did." He walks back to the stove. "And yes. Fluffy's name is now Pigpen."

"Don't you find that incredible?"

"What do you mean?"

"Think about it. If you'd mentioned the name he has now, I would have pushed to find out who your boss was. Let's face it. Pigpen isn't exactly a common name for a cat."

"It is if you're a *Peanuts* fan." He transfers the steaks to a baking sheet before placing them into the hot oven, setting a timer for six minutes.

"True, but it would have provoked a follow-up." I squint, considering all the pieces that had to fall into place for us to end up together. "And if I'd learned you worked as an attorney for the *Times*, I never would have so much as entertained the idea of sleeping with you, let alone kissing you."

"So you would have friend zoned me?" Cocking a brow, he approaches me, pushing the cutting board to the side. With incredible ease, he grabs my ass and lifts me onto the surface of the island, settling between my legs.

"No. You would have been in the no-zone."

"Not even the friend zone? At least there I could have attempted to use my amazing powers of persuasion." He curves into me, his mouth landing on my neck, the way he sucks and licks the perfect mixture of carnal and reverent.

"That would have been futile," I respond breathily. "I draw a hard line in certain matters."

"Is that right?" He slowly circles his hips, the friction jumpstarting my libido, as if the ol' girl needs an excuse.

"God yes." I throw my head back as he continues moving against me, his unshaven jaw bruising my skin. "That is so right."

He abruptly pulls away, his eyes dancing with amusement. "*Now* who needs a cold shower?" With playful arrogance, he retreats from me, heading toward the counter to take the baked potatoes out of the foil.

Refusing to let him beat me at this little game, I slide off the island, nonchalantly sauntering up to the sink. I make it look like I'm about to rinse the berries I set aside to top the cheesecake I'd brought over.

"Cold shower, huh?"

"That's right."

In one quick move, I yank the hose from the faucet, spraying him with the water.

He stiffens, spinning around to face me, but he makes no attempt to get out of the line of fire. His lips curl with a

sinister smile as he advances, his steps slow, deliberate, unfor-
giving. When he grabs the bowl of heavy cream I'd whipped
to go with our dessert, a devilish glint flashes in his eyes.

I take the pressure off the water, but that doesn't stop
him from scooping whipped cream out of the bowl and
smearing it down my face.

I stand completely still for a moment, the shock leaving
me frozen. Then I wipe some of the cream off my face,
making a show of seductively licking my fingers, even though
I shudder to think what I look like. With a devious grin, I
grab a handful of blackberries from the carton on the
counter. His gaze remains glued to mine, watching me with
interest as I smash them into his chest, rubbing the juices all
over his body.

He tries to remain serious, but I notice the faintest hint of
his mouth lifting in a smile. "You're in trouble now, Pixie," he
warns as he goes to hook an arm around my waist.

Squealing, I attempt to escape him, but slip on the wet
floor, taking him down with me. We land with a hard thump,
the room momentarily silent. Then we break out in laughter,
the sound echoing against the high ceilings.

"I've always wanted to add food into the mix," I joke.
"But I figured we'd start with whipped cream on my nipples.
Maybe a little chocolate syrup. Not sure how erotic the face
can be."

"Oh, baby, I guarantee I can make it hot for you." Grinning, he drags his tongue along my jawline, tasting the sweet
treat, and I moan, succumbing to him.

When the timer buzzes, neither one of us are interested
in those steaks anymore.

The sensation of warm lips brushing against my temple slowly stirs me from sleep. Normally I hate to be woken, treasuring every second of sleep I can get. But these days, my reality seems better than my dreams. And who wouldn't want to be awoken by such a beautiful kiss? It worked for Snow White and Sleeping Beauty. They didn't groan and roll over, pushing their Prince away, begging in a raspy voice for five more minutes of slumber. And neither do I.

"Morning," I say, melting into Lincoln's lingering kiss.

"Morning."

My eyes flutter open, but the room is still dark, day not having broken just yet, although the glow coming from the windows tells me it will soon.

"What time is it?"

"Six."

I shift, turning my eyes to his. "An emergency at work?"

A slight smile curves his lips. "No. It's my day at the university. I wanted to go early and finish grading papers so I can turn in my final grades."

"Final grades?" I arch a single brow.

Slowly nodding, he erases the distance between us. "And we'll be one step closer to finally being free. To finally being us."

A fluttering erupts in my stomach when his mouth skims mine, his kiss hesitant and soft. As much as I love his hunger-filled kisses that brim with so much desperation and passion, these are my favorite. These gentle exchanges in our stolen moments before dawn.

"I think this calls for a celebration."

I feel his lips curve up. "I agree." The scruff of his beard scrapes me as he trails kisses from my mouth and along my neckline.

"What did you have in mind?" I crane my head, allowing

him better access. His hand roams the contours of my frame, and I part my legs, moaning when he grazes against me.

"I can think of a few things," he answers coyly, nipping at my skin, driving me even more wild. "One in particular that I've been fantasizing about for months now."

"What's that?" I pant.

He pauses, and I can almost see the smile crawling across his mouth. Then he pulls back. "Meet me at The Living Room in the Park Hyatt tonight."

My eyes fly open as I prop myself up onto my elbows, searching his gaze. "Are you sure?"

"Why wouldn't I be?" he says nonchalantly, straightening himself, buttoning his suit jacket. "It's fitting, if you ask me. Starting this new chapter where it all began. Where you finally gave me a chance." Then he gently touches his lips to mine, erasing any trepidation. "Even more so considering today marks four months since the blackout that changed my life."

I sigh into him, unable to believe it's been that long. In some respects, it feels like it has been longer than four months, considering everything we've been through. In other ways, it seems like it was just yesterday that I walked into that classroom and learned the man I'd been having incredible sex with was my First Amendment Law professor.

"The happiest, most excruciating, amazing, heart-wrenching four months of my life. But I'd do it all over again if it meant I'd still be here with you." When he cups my cheek, I close my eyes, savoring the feel of his rough hands against my smooth skin. His mouth brushes mine and I melt into his soft kiss. "So, eight o'clock?"

I simply nod, ignoring my internal voice of reason that tells me we should still be careful, that we won't be in the clear just because he submitted my final grade. But when have I ever listened to reason? If I had, I never would have run out of the bar all those weeks ago, telling Nora and Evie I had to go see a man about a pair of panties. Then I wouldn't be here. Sometimes, it pays to take a risk.

"I can't wait."

"Either can I." Lincoln treats me to one last kiss, then leaves me alone in his large bed.

# Thirty-Nine

Tapping my fingernails against the bar, I check the time to see it's nearly 8:20, growing antsy with each passing minute that Lincoln doesn't show up. Did someone put the pieces together? Was my father nearby when one of my texts flashed on Lincoln's phone? Did someone see us during one of our supposed clandestine meetings and report him to the dean? Or, worse, my father?

A ding rips through the background noise of the bar and I flick my eyes to my cell, blowing out a breath when Lincoln's name pops up on the screen.

LINCOLN:

Play along. No questions.

Confused, I'm about to text back when I notice movement to my left and shift my eyes in its direction.

"Is this seat taken?"

"Fuck me," I murmur, swallowing hard as I stare at the man in front of me.

He's in a different suit than the one he wore this morning. His hair glistens, evidencing a recent shower, his beard neatly groomed. But that's not what has me squirming in my seat. It's the British accent with which he speaks. It sounds remarkably authentic. And sexy. Holy shit, is it sexy. I didn't think I could be any more attracted to this man. Didn't think it were humanly possible.

I was so wrong.

"Miss?" he says with a smirk, knowing all too well what has my panties about to combust.

Trying to play it cool, I take a moment to compose myself, then smile slyly. "It is now."

With a wicked shine in his eyes, he assumes the seat, flagging down the bartender. I simply watch him, trying to figure out exactly *what* game we're playing. No matter what, I have a feeling it's going to be a lot of fun.

"You here alone?" he asks after he swallows a sip of his scotch, his lips wet from the remnants of the liquid.

"It appears I am." I smooth the lines of my skirt.

"Is that so?"

"I was supposed to meet someone." I sigh in mock disappointment. "But it looks like he stood me up."

A salacious smile builds on his mouth. "His loss is my gain." He eyes my nearly empty martini. "Can I buy you another?"

I lean back in my chair. "I should probably just go home and forget about tonight, considering it appears my *date* has." I pinch my lips together, interested to see how Lincoln plays this.

"You're right. You definitely *should* go home." His gaze darkens, a warning. "But don't you think you'd have more fun with me than going back to your place with nothing to distract you from thinking about some prick who apparently has horrible taste."

"What makes you say that?"

"Isn't it obvious?"

I shrug. "Humor me."

"He stood you up." He rakes his gaze down my body, and desire flickers in his deep pools. I uncross and re-cross my legs, allowing the slit of my dress to reveal the skin of my thigh. Jaw tightening, nostrils flaring, he reluctantly lifts his eyes to mine. "No man in his right mind would stand up a woman as stunningly beautiful as you."

He inches toward me, his lips close. I'd give anything to erase that last bit of space between us and taste him, but I don't, remembering the game we're playing. And I certainly love these games.

"Give me one drink to prove it to you. If you're not convinced, you can go on your way."

"And if I am convinced?" I exhale.

"Then you come up to my room and I make you forget all about this man who isn't worth your time."

"And how do you hope to do that?" I bat my lashes.

"Use your imagination." His mouth skims against mine, causing a shiver to roll through me. Then he pulls back, the epitome of restraint.

"I do have a *very* active imagination."

He lifts his scotch to his lips. "That's what I'm banking on." My gaze lingers on him as he swirls the liquid, then swallows. Returning his glass to the bar, he focuses his attention on me. "So, what do you say? One drink with me, then maybe one night where you can have all your needs met? Or go home all alone?"

I pause, enjoying the anticipation in his expression before nodding. "One drink."

"Good girl." He leers at me for a moment, then waves down the bartender.

Once he turns his attention away from me, I exhale a long breath. I've shared a bed with this man numerous times, but the rush of exhilaration filling me makes me feel like we're two strangers, my heart pounding a thunderous rhythm.

When the bartender sets my drink in front of me, I offer him a smile.

"I took a guess at what kind of vodka you'd prefer," Lincoln states, reminding me of a similar conversation back in Vegas. "But something made me think you were a Belvedere girl." He leans toward me, running a finger down my arm. "Smooth. Layered. Sophisticated."

I take a sip of my drink before setting the glass back on the bar. "How did you know I liked my martini dirty?" I pass him a sly grin, more than aware of what line's about to follow.

He hovers closer still, the nearness of his lips unhinging me. "I had a feeling you liked things…dirty."

"Wouldn't you like to find out?"

His lips ghost against mine, teasing me, making me desperate for more, regardless of the fact we're in public and anyone can see. Lincoln may have turned in his final grades, but we're still on rocky ground. We will be for a while. Seeing us together like this when I'm still technically a student will certainly raise eyebrows. Hell, seeing us together like this even a few months from now will raise eyebrows.

"You have no idea," he growls, jaw tensing, pupils dilating. I brace myself for the kiss I sense is coming. But it never does. He retreats, the foot or so between us feeling like miles.

"So, I assume you're not from around here." Brushing a lock of hair behind my ear, I bring my glass to my mouth, trying to steady my trembling hand.

"What gave it away?" he jokes slyly.

"All non-New Yorkers have a sign on their foreheads. Only true New Yorkers can see it."

"Is that right?"

"Sure is."

"I see." He looks forward, pretending to pay attention to the Yankees game on TV, but I know the only interest he has in the game is the Yankees losing. Like his father, Lincoln has two favorite baseball teams. The Mets, and anyone playing the Yankees.

"So, where are you from?" I ask after a brief silence, trying to spark conversation.

"Does it matter?" His tone isn't curt. More sensual and amused.

"Excuse me?"

"Does it matter?" he repeats. "I'm not from here. I fly back home tomorrow, so after tonight, you'll never see me again."

"I was just trying to make small talk."

"Is that what you like? *Small* talk?"

After considering his question, I blow out a breath. "I find it dull and ordinary, but it appears most people opt for these kinds of mundane questions."

"And why do you think that is?"

"Because they're too scared to ask what's really on their mind. Scared to voice their deepest desires."

His mouth lifts into a grin, his eyes dancing with amusement. "Take all the rules off the table. Forget about propriety and custom. What would you ask me?"

I curve toward him, bringing my hand to his thigh. His pupils dilate as I inch farther up his leg. "If I were to agree to accompany you upstairs, what did you have in mind?"

"A magician never reveals all his secrets." He winks. "Need to give you a reason to come…if only for curiosity's sake."

"That may be true, but I never buy anything sight

unseen. Or at least without a description of what I can expect."

"A description?" He cocks a brow.

"Yes. A description." I lean back, removing my hand from him in the hopes the lack of touch pushes him to his breaking point, just as it does me. But he's still as composed as ever.

"Very well." He faces forward, brushing the pad of his thumb along his bottom lip. "I'll finish my scotch, thanking you for the enlightening conversation, and slide my keycard your way, leaving the ball in your court, as the saying goes. You'll be unsure at first, wondering if you can do this, if you can really take that key and go up to a stranger's room. But your desperate need to forget your inhibitions for one night will get the better of you." His tone is even and measured, as if discussing an important business deal instead of his plans of seduction.

"You think so?"

"I do. So you'll take that key and use it. You'll walk inside my room, and neither one of us will say a single word. We won't need them. We'll communicate our need with our bodies. You'll be so overcome with an urge to feel me, you'll try to strip off all my clothes, but I won't let you."

"You won't?"

"No." He slowly shakes his head. "Not yet. That's the problem with all these other men you've dated."

"And what's that exactly?" I shoot back, playfully rolling my eyes.

He leans toward me. "They didn't take their time to seduce you. Because they're just boys."

"I've dated older men," I say very matter-of-factly.

"Doesn't matter. They're still boys. A woman should be

savored, like a fine wine, like the delicacy she is. Boys screw. I don't."

"So… What? You'll 'make love' to me," I taunt.

"No. What I plan to do to you is so much more than that."

I swallow hard. "More?"

"Yes." The heat of his breath on my neck causes my lips to part, making me shift as I clench my thighs together to dull the ache. "I will consume you. Hold your desires captive. Possess your every thought from this moment forward. I'll bring you to the brink of utter bliss, only to pull back, drawing out your pleasure as long as possible. You'll beg me to let you come, to make you experience the mind-altering orgasm you'll now be convinced only I can provide for you. But I'll make you wait a little longer. Because you wouldn't have reached your breaking point. Not yet."

His breathing grows heavier, the muscles in his face tightening as the distance between us becomes nearly nonexistent. "I'll feast on your body, memorizing every dip and valley, taking my time to give every inch of you the attention it deserves. When you don't think you can take any more, I'll bring you to the bed. You'll be blindfolded and restrained, completely at my mercy. Your *orgasm* completely at my mercy. Your legs will be spread wide so you can't find any relief that way. You'll *need* me."

"I already need you," I pant, my voice not sounding like my own.

I don't even have to look at his lips to see his smile. "I was hoping you'd say that." He abruptly pulls back and drains his scotch. Then he coolly slides a keycard my way, winking before turning from me, leaving me a bundle of sensations.

I watch as he disappears out of the lounge, exhaling to

calm my overwrought nerves. My legs shaky, I'm careful as I step down from the barstool.

Lost in my thoughts of how Lincoln can affect me like this, considering we spend almost every night together, I jump when a hand grips my arm, my heart ricocheting to my throat. I snap my head to my right, gasping at Lincoln's heated stare. Before I can utter a syllable, he yanks my body against his and kisses me as if it's a regular occurrence for him to do this. It's been so long since he's kissed me in public. Most people wouldn't think it a big deal. Before Lincoln, I never gave it much thought myself. But now I do. And I want nothing more than to keep kissing him.

There's a hint of reluctance as he pulls away, and I search his eyes, unsure if this man kissing me is Lincoln or my mysterious stranger. The sparkle in his gaze as he smiles tells me it's Lincoln.

He runs a soft finger along the contours of my face. "You are fucking incredible, Chloe." He opens his mouth, then stops, as if struggling to find the words. He grips my cheeks, his expression filled with admiration, respect, and something else… Something I've seen for a while now but have been too scared to label. "I…"

"Yes?" I urge when he trails off.

A look of peace washes over him. "I love you."

I blink repeatedly, my mouth falling open, my pulse increasing even more. A fluttering sensation builds in my stomach, making me feel lightheaded, but in the best way possible.

"I know it's not the way most people declare their love," he continues when I don't say anything in response. "The one thing my father's death taught me is to never wait to tell someone how you feel. There may never be a perfect time to say it, especially with us." He cracks a small smile before his expression turns serious once more. "But I love you. You don't have to say it back. I understand this is difficult for you. I just…" He licks his lips. "I just thought you should know."

My head makes a slight motion, like a nod, but I'm not sure what that means. A gesture of acceptance? This is new territory for me. No one's ever told me they loved me. Not like this. Sure, my one boyfriend in college said it, but I didn't hear the meaning behind those words. Not like I do with Lincoln. When he says he loves me, I believe it with every fiber of my being.

"Just give me a few minutes to get ready for you." He places a soft kiss on my nose, then turns from me. I can't take my eyes off him as he walks through the crowded lounge and toward the bank of elevators, my heart fuller than I thought possible from his surprise declaration.

Months ago, I would have run far away if someone told me they loved me. But Lincoln's love doesn't scare me. *Love* doesn't scare me, not like it once did.

Recovering my composure, I grab my purse and offer a nod of thanks to the bartender. Keycard in hand, I turn to make my way up to Lincoln's room when I come to an abrupt stop at the intimidating figure hovering nearby.

You know those scenes in a movie where the main character's worst fears are realized and the camera focuses on them while the background zooms out? That's what this moment feels like. Like my world is giving out from beneath me.

"Hi, Dad."

# Forty

"What the hell are you thinking, Chloe?" Dad hisses, eyes wild, expression frantic. He grabs my arm and yanks me into a quiet corner of the lounge, offering us privacy.

Disoriented, I stare at him with my mouth agape, paralyzed, unable to form a coherent thought. What *do* I say? What does he know? What did he see?

"Are you *trying* to ruin his career?" he continues when I don't respond. "His life? What is it?" He throws up his hands in exasperation. "You couldn't pass the class on your own so you're trying to figure out another way to get a good grade?"

I should be floored my father would even suggest that the only way I'd get a passing grade is by offering my body in exchange, but I'm not. He's never understood me. It's always been easier for him to write me off.

"It's not like that," I argue, my voice trembling.

"No? Then tell me what it's like, because from where I'm standing, I can't think of another reason he'd be here with you, other than that you offered him something he couldn't turn down."

"I care about him. A lot." I should keep my mouth shut, but I'm tired of my father thinking so little of me that I'd stoop to that level. I've put those days behind me. "I want to be with him. And he wants to be with me."

My father looks at me as if I just told him zombies had overtaken the streets or aliens had invaded the country. Then he paces, running his hands through his salt-and-pepper hair. When he stops, he shoves a finger in my face. I stiffen, backing up.

"You can*not* do this. That man has worked his tail off, has made a name for himself in this field. I will not let him throw it all away for someone who will never appreciate it. For someone who will toss him aside when something better, someone with a bigger bank account comes along. His father's legacy deserves better than this. *Lincoln* deserves better than this."

"I won't toss him aside," I argue, but he won't hear it. He has this idea in his head of who I am and nothing I say or do will convince him otherwise. Which is why I don't remind him that it takes two to tango. That we both accepted this risk together.

Even if Lincoln were here trying to accept full responsibility, my father would still find me at fault, insist I've been around my mother too long and learned everything I needed in order to persuade someone to make a decision they normally wouldn't. She was once a powerhouse in politics, after all. She's mastered the art of persuasion. As have I... according to him.

"You go through life thinking people are disposable, just like your mother. You use people, get what you want, then walk away, leaving them to clean up the mess."

I shake my head, my teeth biting into my lower lip, doing everything to reel in my temper, every word he spews like another knife against my flesh. I don't want him to see how much his words hurt. But I've spent too many years pretending his indifference toward me doesn't affect me.

"You flash a smile, bat your lashes just enough to get them into bed. And that's all they are to you, isn't it? Just a bit of fun. That's how it's always been with you. And that's how it will always be. Hell, that's what got you your promotion. Now it can help you get your degree. Is that right?"

With each word, my rage increases until it bubbles over. Fists clenched, blood pressure rising, I bellow, "I love him!" My chest heaves as my voice rings out, everything going still.

His jaw snaps shut, his body paralyzed by my admission. "What did you say?"

Exhaling, I lower my voice, my expression relaxing as a small smile builds on my mouth. "I love him."

"You—"

"I know what you're thinking. I never thought I'd be the type of person to fall in love, either, but I love him. I love how excited he gets when talking about some hard-fought victory at the paper. I love the look that comes over his expression when he's deep in thought, about to figure something out. And I love how he makes me feel more loved than anyone else in my life ever has. I have no way of knowing whether this will work, whether we'll survive. But I want the chance to find out."

Dad rakes a hand over his face, his shoulders falling as he realizes this is more than a passing fling. "You really love him?" He lifts his eyes to mine, searching for any hint of deception. But there isn't any. This is my truth. Lincoln is my truth.

"More than anything."

In a flash, the compassion disappears, the stern, controlling man returning. "Then you'll walk away." He steps back, adjusting his tie.

"Wha—"

"Dean Morrison is in there." He points in the direction of the restaurant just past the lounge. "I'm having dinner with him and a few other colleagues. It's lucky *I* was the one who noticed you two, considering they're all professors at the university."

Nausea bubbles in the pit of my stomach, my pulse increasing at the idea that we very well could have been exposed by someone other than my father, who I hope will keep this to himself.

"Do you want to be the reason Lincoln loses everything he's worked so hard for? The reason he tarnishes his father's legacy?"

I want to say that Lincoln doesn't see it that way, tell him all the times he's reminded me I'm worth the risk. But this brings to the forefront all the internal debates I've had over the past several weeks…hell, months. Can I really ask him to sacrifice nearly twenty years of hard work for me? Will I be able to live with the guilt that will inevitably consume me when I'm forced to watch Lincoln try to find something else he's passionate about? And Lincoln loves his job, loves his career. Am I worth it? Are *we* worth it?

"Listen, Chloe…" Dad licks his lips, lowering his voice. There's a hint of sympathy and compassion about him. "I'll keep this quiet. For now. But it *will* get out. Hell, a few months ago, John Morrison brought up the two of you during a dinner meeting. Asked if I was aware of any other kind of relationship between you. I denied it, said it was ridiculous. At the time, I *thought* it was ridiculous. But it goes to show you that people *are* watching.

"The semester may be ending soon, you may be a few days away from graduating, but that won't matter. You will still be considered his student. And in a profession such as ours where we need to adhere to the highest standard of ethics, this can destroy any chance he has at teaching. Maybe even practicing law. Just..." He blows out a breath, shaking his head. "Think about whether it's worth it." He holds my gaze for another moment, then turns.

I watch as he retreats toward the restaurant. He doesn't need to come right out and say what he really means — whether *I'm* worth it.

This is a man who's always chosen his work over everything else. Over my mother. Over me. Hell, even over his new family. Work has always been his life. His *career* has always been his life, his one true love. When I was little, I often snuck down the hallway toward his office and would listen to him argue certain issues with whomever he was speaking to on the phone. I'd never seen such passion, such fervor, such intensity.

Until I walked into that classroom and observed Lincoln.

He had that same wild, untamed look in his eyes as my father did.

I instantly know the answer, although I fear I've known it all along but didn't want to admit it.

I take a minute to pull myself together, trying to find comfort in the fact my father didn't threaten to out us to the dean. Maybe it would have been better if he had. Then I wouldn't have to be the bad guy. But I knew from the beginning this was how it would end.

Fairy tales *aren't* real.

I've been fooling myself to think I could have my handsome prince and not suffer the dragon's wrath.

On timid steps, I walk through the lounge, the chairs where I'd sat with Lincoln now occupied by another couple who are free to share intimate moments. A brush of a hand. A stolen kiss. A heated stare. But not us. That would never have been us. And I can't ask Lincoln to give up his passion so I can have that.

Instead, I give up *my* passion in order for him to hold onto his. It's not the first time I've had to sacrifice what I want for someone else. And it won't be the last.

# Forty-One

By the time I round the corner onto my street, my feet scream for relief. But I welcome the pain, need it to dull how much it hurt to walk away from Lincoln.

I spent the past several hours roaming the streets of Manhattan, wondering if I did the right thing, if I made the right decision. I couldn't even bring myself to read any of his texts or answer any of his calls, worried I'd crack and allow his assurances to convince me that we *can* have a future.

When my building comes into view, I quicken my steps, wanting to curl up in bed and tune out the world for a minute. But the instant my gaze falls on my front stoop, my heart plummets to my stomach. Lincoln sits on the top step, shoulders slumped, hair disheveled, forearms resting dejectedly on his thighs. It's nearly three in the morning. How long has he been here? I thought by now, it would be safe to come home. I guess I was wrong. What else have I been wrong about tonight?

I consider retreating on the off chance he hasn't noticed me. Then he lifts his weary, tired eyes, as if he has some sixth sense where I'm concerned. I've never seen him so distraught, so uncertain, so...lost.

My lips part. I want nothing more than to apologize,

offer him the comfort he deserves. Maybe if I hadn't been so greedy, been more understanding of our predicament, he wouldn't have felt the need to take me out somewhere we could be spotted.

"Lincoln, I—"

"Was it too soon?" he interrupts.

I furrow my brow. "What do you—"

"It was too soon, wasn't it?" He bites his lower lip, a pained expression on his face as he pinches the bridge of his nose. "I knew it was. That's why I didn't tell you weeks ago. I wanted to tell you the night I found you struggling with your mother. Because I knew back then how I felt. Probably before. I just... There never seemed to be a good time, so I figured fuck it. I'll just tell her. But, apparently, you weren't ready to hear those words."

I blink repeatedly, trying to piece everything together. He thinks I ran out on him because he told me he loved me?

Of course... He has no idea my father saw us.

All night, I'd toiled over what to say to convince him this is the way it needs to be. If he learned my father knew about us, that the dean was suspicious, he'd quit tomorrow. He said himself it'll take a lot more than the risk to his career for him to walk away.

I suppose that's what I need to give him.

Holding my head high, I cross my arms in front of my chest, rebuilding the wall around my heart, brick by brick. "This was never supposed to turn into...this." I gesture between our bodies.

His eyes narrow into slits, anger seeping into his expression. "What are you saying, Chloe?"

I shrug nonchalantly, acting as if my heart isn't bleeding on this very sidewalk, each word I speak another set of feet stomping all over it. "I'm not really a 'fall-in-love' kind of girl." I sidestep him, walking up the stairs so he can't see the truth in my eyes.

"Says who?" He jumps to his feet, his fingers wrapping around my bicep, forcing me to face him. "Your father? Your mother?" The hurt in his words is all-consuming, but I can't let that get to me.

"Me! That's who!" I answer with ice in my voice, giving the performance of a lifetime. "You're a smart guy. You should have figured out by now that I'm incapable of loving anyone."

All I want to do is wrap my arms around him and tell him I don't mean any of this, that I do love him. But love is never enough. I've had a lifetime reminder of that. Love wasn't enough to keep my dad at home. Love wasn't enough to prevent my mom from drinking. And love wasn't enough to keep her clean.

"No, you're not. I see you're not." His voice turns pleading as he loosens his harsh grip on me. "You're just scared. I get that. I'm scared of these feelings I have for you, too. But I'm not enough of a coward to lie about them, to say I don't feel this way about you."

"I'm not a coward." I push out of his hold. "And I'm *not* lying. I feel nothing for you."

"So you say, but your actions these past few months indicate otherwise."

I shrug. "I've just mastered the art of figuring out what men want and giving them that so I can get what I need in return."

His Adam's apple bobs up and down in a hard swallow, his lip twitching. "And what did you need from me?" he asks, although I can sense his reluctance.

"What do you think?" I retort, passing him a demure look. "Do you know how many classes I've had to withdraw from because of my mother? I figured I could use a little insurance that, even if I missed too many classes, I'd still pass. That's all you were. An insurance policy."

"You…" He shakes his head, struggling to form any words.

"And now that you've turned in my final grade, I don't need you anymore." I jut out my chin, shoulders back, neck exposed, doing my best not to show a single hint of weakness, of vulnerability, of the lump growing in my throat, the words difficult to say. But this is the only way. I need him to hate me. Need him to forget about me.

Maybe if I didn't have the past I've had, I'd let him fight for me. But growing up with an alcoholic changes you. Just like growing up with a parent who is constantly disappointed in you. You go through life convinced you'll keep disappointing people, that you're not worth their time or effort. Life becomes a constant decision of "fish or cut bait". And you always cut bait. It's all you know.

It's all *I* know.

"And before?" he asks, his body shaking, lips pinched tight, stare cold and detached, yet filled with so much hurt and betrayal it makes me want to tell him the truth.

"What do you mean?"

"Before you learned I was your professor, what did you hope to get out of me?"

I place my hands on my hips. "I knew who you were in Vegas. I thought you looked familiar, then it hit me. Lincoln Moore, associate attorney for the *Times*. The same Lincoln Moore who would be my First Amendment professor, the last class I needed in order to graduate."

His head continues to shake, every muscle in his body taut.

"So, if you'll excuse me, it's Friday and the gossip mills are turning."

I try to spin from him, but his hand grips my wrist, forcing me back to him. I wince, but he doesn't let go. I watch as his nostrils flare like an untamed bull. I can tell it takes every ounce of self-control not to take his rage out on me further, not to hurt me like I'm destroying him.

"Why don't I believe you?" he growls.

"Well, you should."

"But I don't." He tightens his hold on me, the intensity of his quivering muscles causing my arm to tremble, the pain excruciating. But it's a welcome distraction from the ache in my heart.

With an anguished cry, he releases me, his entire body seeming to deflate. He stares into the distance, searching for an answer he'll never find. Then he floats his eyes back to me, the venom gone, replaced with a compassion I don't deserve.

"What we shared—"

"Was. Not. Real," I hiss through clenched teeth, refusing to soften my resolve. "So leave."

He studies me for what feels like an eternity, meticulously weighing my words against my actions. I wait as I stand judgment in front of him, praying he believes me. Finally, he blows out a breath and retreats down the stairs, defeated. Relief filling me, I turn back around, about to unlock my door when his voice stops me.

"It *was* real, Chloe. I know it was. In here."

I can't bear to turn around, to see the agony covering him as he points to his heart. I don't have to look at him to know that's what he's doing. I know him better than I've ever known anybody else. Which is why this is the only way. He promised he'd fight for me, regardless of the battle. But this is a war we'll never win.

"I don't know what happened to make you feel like you have to push me away—"

I whirl around. "I'm not—"

He holds up his hand, cutting me off. "But I'll go, even though that's not really what you want."

This time, I don't try to convince him otherwise.

"On the outside, you're this strong, enigmatic woman who doesn't take shit from anyone. But on the inside, you're still the same broken girl who convinced herself she doesn't deserve to be loved. Until you convince yourself you do, it won't matter how many times I try to tell you I love you. It won't matter how many times I tell you I'd risk it all for you. You'll never think you deserve it. I can't fight for someone who's not ready to fight for herself." His voice catches as he struggles to finish. "I can't keep loving someone who doesn't love herself."

I swallow hard, wanting to tell him we're at risk of being exposed. That we're no longer protected by that bubble we've survived in. But that would give him hope. And hope is a dangerous thing. These past few months have been proof of that.

"I know how to love myself. It's you I never loved. Now leave, before I report you to the dean." I storm into my apartment, slamming the door behind me.

# Forty-Two

Scattered papers and half-full coffee mugs surround me as I work in the early hours of the morning, firing off story after story of the latest celebrity gossip. Like I've done every other weekend the past several years. I'm actually grateful for the busy news weekend. It helps keep my mind off Lincoln and how difficult the past week has been. How it feels like a huge part of me is missing.

As I put the finishing touches on a column about whether the heiress to a hotel brand is pregnant, based on photos where she's wearing something other than the usual skin-tight dresses, my buzzer sounds. I tear my eyes to my door, a flicker of hope building inside me that Lincoln's here to berate me for being so stubborn. But I know he won't be. I made sure of that.

Lifting myself off the couch, I stretch my legs, then move toward the door, squinting through the peephole to see Izzy, dressed in scrubs, standing on the front stoop. It doesn't surprise me. If my buzzer rings after midnight, it's usually Izzy. She's the only one who works stranger hours than me.

When I open the door, she enters without so much as an invitation. "So you *are* alive." She makes herself at home, plopping onto my couch.

"Umm… Yeah. What would make you think otherwise?" I follow her, sitting beside her, tucking a leg underneath me.

"Oh, I don't know. Evie mentioned you've been distant at work, and Nora said you haven't gone to a single yoga class to taunt her in over a week." She narrows her eyes. "That doesn't sound like the Chloe we all love."

"It's nothing," I lie with a shrug. "Between finishing up this semester, Nora's wedding in just a few weeks, and work, not to mention keeping an eye on my mom, I've been busy."

She tilts her head, lips pursed, eyebrows raised. "And nothing else? There's no other reason you're out of it?"

I meet her eyes, staying strong. "Nope."

She squints, her analytical gaze sweeping over me. I've known this woman since we were little. She's the one who first asked if my mom had a drinking problem before I really understood what alcohol was. She's always had an uncanny ability to pick up on things no one else could.

Leaning toward me, her voice becomes a low whisper, despite the fact no one is around to hear. "Did something happen between you and Lincoln?"

"What?" I exclaim, back straight, eyes wide. "I told you months ago. We cut all ties. Once I learned he was my professor—"

"Yeah, yeah, yeah. You kept things strictly professional," she mocks playfully. "Apart from the time you almost fucked on the desk in his office. I haven't forgotten about that. Evie and Nora may not be able to see through you, but *I* can. You've been secretly seeing him."

Her gaze traces over my face, then to the rest of my body, as if I'm wearing a giant scoreboard with a tally of the number of times we kissed, fucked, and did…other stuff.

"I think you've been seeing him for a while now, despite your insistence that there was nothing going on. But something happened…" She stares into the distance, chewing on her fingernails as she bounces her legs. Then she looks back to me, her tone a mixture of agitation and excitement. "It was around the time you learned your mom never stopped drinking, wasn't it? It makes sense. Traumatic events always seem to bring people back together, make people snap out of…whatever."

"Izzy, life isn't a fucking fairy tale. I am not a damsel in distress. And Lincoln is certainly no Prince Charming." Unless Prince Charming were into kinky role-play and spanking.

"That may be true, but you've never been the Prince Charming type, either. You're more interested in the bad boy who will break a few rules. You can sit here and claim nothing's been going on, but you've been…happy."

"I'm always happy."

"Not like this. Hell, look at your hair! You changed it back to your natural color. Almost like you finally felt you could be yourself and not put on a front."

"I don't know who else to be if I'm not myself."

"You haven't been yourself since you were fourteen," she quips without a moment's hesitation, her words surprising me. And she's right. I haven't been.

That was around the first time I walked into my mother's bathroom and found her passed out, head on the toilet, a mixture of vomit and spilled wine staining the tile. I forget how many times I slipped in it as I attempted to clean the room, then move her to her bed. My mother's no bigger than I am, but that night, she felt like she weighed a ton. It took hours, but I was finally able to get her into bed. The only thing that pushed me forward when I was ready to give up was my fear that my father would learn the truth and petition for custody of me.

"But lately, I've seen a more...carefree Chloe," she continues. She rests a hand on my bicep, and I shift my gaze toward hers, doing my best to keep it together when I've spent the past week on the brink of a complete breakdown. "I can't help but think Lincoln had something to do with that. Am I right?"

I look to the ceiling, chin quivering, eyes welling with tears. I've been through a lot of shit in my life and never cried, never showed emotion. But Izzy's sympathy pushes me over the edge. After what I did, I don't feel like I deserve it.

"Maybe." It's all I can manage to say before the dam bursts.

"Oh, Chloe..." Her arms are around me in an instant, all the tears I've kept at bay rushing forward.

"But Dad saw us," I choke out, soaking her shirt that's covered with SpongeBob SquarePants. "He said I would destroy Lincoln's career if I stayed with him." I pull back, swiping at my cheeks. "And he's right. If people found out about us, it *would* end his career. Any relationship, present or future, would forever be tainted by our past."

She holds me at arm's length, her dark eyes brimming with hope. "I may not know Lincoln that well, or have a full picture of what was going on, but he must have known the risk going in. And he must have been willing to take that risk."

"He was." I swallow hard, shaking my head. "But I couldn't let him do that."

"I'm not sure you have any say in the matter. If he wants to take his chances, isn't that his decision?"

"Not if I made sure he wouldn't make that decision."

Izzy leans back, giving me a sideways glance, almost not wanting to ask. "What did you do?"

"What I had to." I push down the bile rising in my throat

at the memory of that night. The happiness, then the betrayal. The hope, then the despair. The absolute joy of having him declare his love, then the vice squeezing my heart when I used that love against him. "I made him think I was using him all along. That I knew in Vegas he was my professor and the only reason I slept with him was to make sure I passed."

She exhales, closing her eyes, shaking her head. "You didn't."

"I did," I squeak.

"Chloe…"

"It was the only way. Lincoln said himself that he would fight for me. He'd never give up, which would only continue to put his career at risk. Unless I made him hate me."

It's silent for a moment as she processes everything. "And he believed you? That doesn't sound like the Lincoln I know."

"Because I eviscerated that Lincoln. He said he wasn't going to fight for someone who refused to fight for herself." I look back to Izzy. "That he couldn't love a woman who didn't know how to love herself." I grab the box of tissues off the side table and blow my nose, the harsh sound echoing through my tiny apartment. But it doesn't faze Izzy. We've seen each other at our highest of highs and lowest of lows. Nothing is off-limits between us.

"Have you tried to talk to him?"

I snort a laugh at the ridiculousness of her question. "I'm the last person he wants to talk to. The things I said… There's no way he'll ever trust me again. I made him believe I only slept with him so he'd pass me." I shake my head. "There's no fixing this. Our ship has most definitely sailed."

Izzy peers at me thoughtfully. "Maybe Lincoln's right."

I whip my eyes to hers, confused. "What do you mean?"

"Maybe you need to fix yourself first. Then worry about fixing everything else."

My lips part as I consider her words. "I don't even know how to do that."

"Sometimes you need to go back to the beginning before you can get to the end."

"Will you stop talking in code and metaphors, Master Yoda? You've been spending too much time at Nora's meditation studio," I blurt out, exasperated. "We screwed during a blackout in Vegas. That's our beginning."

"No." She shakes her head. "Not your beginning with Lincoln. *Your* beginning as Chloe, as the woman you are. The woman who was born the instant you saw your mother take that first sip of alcohol. You need to come to terms with all of that. Until you do, I don't see you having a future with anyone."

"I've come to terms with it," I try to argue.

"Then why have you still not told Evie and Nora? I've kept my mouth shut because it's not my story to tell. But until you're honest with yourself, I don't see how you can possibly grow and move past this."

She holds my gaze for a moment, then places a kiss on my forehead. "I love you, Chloe." Her steely eyes lock with mine once more. "Think about what keeping this secret has done to you." She offers me an encouraging smile as she makes her way out of my apartment, leaving me alone to consider her statement. I hate to admit it, but there's a hint of truth to her words. But this is all I've known.

I've spent my life covering for my mother, hiding the truth. And where has it gotten me? Maybe I do need to go back to the beginning. Maybe I need to make peace with the girl I was all those years ago. Then I'll have a chance at finally moving forward. Finally realizing I deserve more than I've afforded myself.

With a fresh cup of coffee in hand, I open a blank document on my laptop and do the only thing that's brought me peace most of my life. The only thing that's helped me make sense of everything.

I write.

---

You come from the perfect family and live an idealistic life in an upper middle-class suburb a quick train ride from Manhattan. Both your parents are successful.

Both your parents are happy.

Or so you thought.

Then your father starts spending more time at the office, sometimes not coming home at all on the weekends. You're not sure of the reason. Mom says it's because he just got a huge promotion. You can hear the bitterness in her tone at the idea that his career is blossoming while hers withered up and died after she had you.

Soon, you notice your mother has a glass of wine with dinner when she normally drank club soda. One glass turns into two. Which soon turns into an entire bottle, then two. You wonder if that's normal. You want to ask your dad, but you're worried how he'll react. Because when your mother drinks that wine, she praises you, tells you how proud she is of you. Something your father never says.

So you stay quiet.

And the drinking continues.

Your father works more and more.

You wonder if he ever really wanted to have kids. Or maybe it's you. No matter what you do, no matter how good your grades, no matter how many sports you excel at, it's not enough for him to notice you.

It's not enough for him to take a day off work.

Most nights, you lay awake listening to your parents fight.

Then, seemingly overnight, boobs appear. And boys start to notice you.

You welcome it, considering the people who are supposed to love you don't have the time for you anymore.

The fights at home get worse.

You know the attention from boys at school isn't the type you want, but it's better than the lack of attention you get at home. So when you're only thirteen, you agree to play Seven Minutes in Heaven with a bunch of high school boys.

The fights at home get even worse.

You wear makeup and revealing clothing to make yourself appear older than you are.

The arguments continue.

You lie about your age just for those few seconds of being noticed.

You can't remember what a quiet house feels like.

You lose your virginity before you even understand what a condom is.

Suddenly, the fights stop. You think things are getting better, that you'll finally have a family. Then you walk into the house for dinner, surprised to see both your mom and dad at the table, something you haven't seen in years, their expressions filled with sorrow. They don't even have to say the words. You know.

They're getting a divorce.

You say goodbye to the only friends and family you've ever known and move to a new town with your mother. You're actually looking forward to it. A fresh start. A clean slate.

Then one day, you help your mother take out the garbage and notice one bag is filled with glass bottles. A dozen. Two dozen. Three dozen. All consumed since the last garbage pickup a week earlier. You hoped this habit wouldn't follow her here. But it has, and it's worse, since she doesn't have to hide it from your father.

Sometimes she's too drunk to drive you to your dad's on your scheduled weekends with him. He could come get you, but then he'd learn your mother's been drinking.

You're worried the court will order you to live with your father, something you can't even stomach the thought of because of how inadequate he's always made you feel.

So you lie.

You cover it up.

You tell your dad you're sick.

You need to study.

You have a group project.

Anything to keep your mother's secret.

Thankfully, he's too consumed by his replacement wife, his replacement baby, his replacement family to even question it. He actually sounds relieved when you can't come, which only solidifies your original thought that you've never been anything but a burden.

Somehow you make it through high school. All those hours you lay awake studying to make sure your mother didn't choke on her own vomit means your grades are good enough to get a scholarship to a decent four-year school. You're thrilled to have that fresh start you thought you were getting years ago.

The morning you're scheduled to move into your dorm, you bound into your mother's room, only to see she's still drunk from the night before.

So you have to spend some of the money you saved for books to pay for a last-minute train ticket upstate. But it's worth it. Because you'll finally be able to close this chapter in your life. Finally have a place you feel like you belong.

Until you arrive at freshmen move-in and are surrounded by parents bidding tearful farewells to their children, telling them how proud they are of everything they've accomplished.

Your mother most likely hasn't even noticed you're gone yet. And your father probably has no idea you're even enrolled in college.

You meet your new roommate. At least you were lucky enough to be paired with the jackpot of all roommates. Caring. Compassionate. Sensitive to the fact that there are clearly skeletons in your closet you're not ready to share.

For a while, things seem to get better.

You can focus on excelling and proving to everyone you can be successful.

You can leave behind your somewhat promiscuous adolescence and become who you were always meant to be.

You can fall in love.

Until you learn your mother lost her job because of her drinking. There's no one else she can turn to, so you do the only thing you can in order to save her from losing the house, the only anchor you feel you have in your life.

You ask your father for help.

Except you don't tell him the exact reason. Just that you've decided to leave college.

Of course, he accuses you of never finishing anything you start.

He has a point, but you don't dwell.

You thank him when he says he'll call in a favor to see if he can get you a decent job. Or at least one that will pay a little more than the local Starbucks.

So you go to work as a receptionist at a women's magazine.

You're starstruck the first time a famous actor walks in.

Even more so when he shamelessly flirts with you.

With all the drama at home, you welcome the attention. It helps take your mind off the fact that you're not able to get your mother the help she needs. She promises she's trying to get clean. You have no choice but to take her at her word, the pile of bills preventing you from babysitting her. Your low-paying job isn't enough to afford rehab. You can barely pay the mortgage, but you refuse to let her lose her house. That may only make her drink more.

So you find a second job as a cocktail waitress, as ironic as that is.

The tips are good.

But the stack of bills gets even higher.

You realize you won't be going back to school anytime soon.

You turn on the charm because it increases your tips. One night, a man with a designer suit and a Tag Hauer watch walks in. You make sure you're the one who takes care of him. When he leaves you a one hundred dollar bill for a twenty dollar scotch, you turn on the charm even more to show your appreciation.

He mistakes the appreciation for interest and invites you back to his hotel. You say you can't, that you have to get up early for work in the morning. As it stands, by the time you get home from this job, you'll maybe only get three hours of sleep, but you've trained your body to function on less than that.

Since this man's used to being able to buy anything he wants, he flashes his billfold, promising to make it worth your while.

You're offended at first, wanting to hold on to the small amount of pride you have left. Then you remember the property tax bill that's been taunting you. You'd never seen a bill with so many zeros before. Your mother tries to help. She's been looking for work, but she's being turned down left and right. Jobs she's overqualified for won't hire her because they want someone who won't quit after a few months for something better. Jobs she is qualified for won't go near her because word travels fast in her industry.

So, instead of declining the man's offer, you ask where he's staying. You almost turn back nearly a dozen times. You try to convince yourself you don't need to do this, that you'll find another way. But the fear of losing the house pushes you forward.

When you knock on his room in a hotel you'd never be able to afford, he answers with a smile that sends a chill through you. But you swallow down the bile and walk inside, officially out of options. That night, part of you dies.

When he's done, he leaves a stack of bills on the bed for you. It takes everything inside you not to break down and cry. You dress quickly and leave, not looking back.

You tell yourself you'll never do that again, that there's another way.

Then your mother's house is foreclosed on, despite all your efforts to keep it, and you move into a tiny studio apartment in an area of town where you're scared to fall asleep. But it's all you can afford at the moment.

So you turn on the charm once more. Some men are interested in more of a girlfriend experience, so that's what you give them. Some just want to have fun for a night, so you oblige. They bestow you with cash and gifts—jewels, shoes, purses. All things you can sell to pay your bills and hopefully save enough money to move into a better place, a nicer place…a safer place.

Finally, the clouds seem to part when you come home one day and learn your mother got a job. A good job. You want to burst out in tears at the relief of not having to sell your body anymore.

You go back to school. You quit your waitressing job. You move into your own place. You find out about a promotion at the magazine and put all your effort into that, even if it means doing a few questionable things in order to get it. The pay will be enough that you'll never have to sacrifice your dignity again.

Then you take your mother to her AA meeting and smell alcohol on her breath. So you put your life on hold again, withdrawing from school in an effort to keep a closer eye on her.

You somehow convince yourself it's all your fault. That you deserve everything life's handed you. That maybe you don't deserve to be happy, don't deserve to be loved.

Then a man comes into your life and makes you believe that maybe you are. That maybe you do have worth. Maybe you do have value. Maybe you can be loved.

But you're scared. What if he learns the truth of everything you've done? What if he learns of the lies you told? What if he's able to see past the walls you were forced to build all those years ago and no longer likes what he sees?

Yet, somehow, he does. When you hit your lowest point, he stands by your side and helps lift you up. He doesn't judge when he learns the truth. He doesn't look at you in disgust. Instead, he sees something you never thought anyone would — strength. He doesn't make you feel worthless. He calls you a survivor. Calls you strong. Calls you remarkable.

And those walls around you come crumbling down.

You let this amazing man in. You open up to him.

You fall in love.

Guardedly.

Timidly.

Hesitantly.

But you still do.

Then the bottom drops. Regardless, he tries to fight for you, says he'll go to battle for you.

But you know his love will never win the war. You've lived your entire life on a runaway train, desperately trying to get it back on its tracks. So you do the one thing you can to control this situation.

You lie.

It's not the first time. You've lied to everyone most of your life. About your mother. About where that designer purse you had days ago disappeared to. About the bruise on your arm where one of your new "friends" got a little too rough.

When your parent is an alcoholic, you become a master at deception, so much so that it's hard to remember what's real and what's part of the elaborate façade you built to hide the truth.

You convince yourself you don't need love, that love makes you weak, and you refuse to show even a hint of weakness.

You smile and tell your friends how thrilled you are when they find their own happily ever after that would rival even the cheesiest romantic comedy.

They joke and tell you that you're next. You brush it off, saying you're not interested in all the trappings of love, of finding your happily ever after.

But I did find my happily ever after.

Convincing myself I didn't, convincing him I didn't, is the biggest lie I've ever told.

---

I wipe my tired eyes, stretching my legs out in front of me as I read over what I spent the last several hours writing and rewriting, telling my story, not leaving out a single detail. Izzy was right. It's amazingly cathartic to get it all down on paper. And maybe it will help other people who are just as lost as me, who feel just as worthless as I do.

Content with my work, I sit back, contemplating what to do now that it's out there. But is it?

I'm not sure what comes over me, whether it's lack of sleep or the peaceful glow filtering into my apartment in the predawn hours, but I open up my email and attach the document, then type a message.

To: Evie Fitzgerald
From: Chloe Davenport
Subject: Maybe?


Hey, E. Think Viv would want to run this in next month's issue instead of the piece on the best celebrity Instagram accounts?


C


I hesitate, my finger about to click on the send button. Once I do, my friends will know all my secrets. After these past few hours of soul-searching, it doesn't seem the cataclysmic event I once thought it to be. So I click, listening to the whooshing sound as the email flies into cyberspace. A part of me regrets being so rash.

Until Evie and Nora appear on my doorstep before seven in the morning, tears in their eyes. When they wrap me in their arms without a single ounce of pity or judgment, I'm confident this is the right path. That this is what I need to do to move forward, to turn that page on a new chapter in my life.

Even if Lincoln's name doesn't appear on any of them.

# Forty-Three

A sea of black robes fills the lobby of a state-of-the-art theater, a post-graduation reception underway. Of course, this wasn't the official ceremony, just one the journalism department puts on for its students. A more private affair honoring a few hundred graduates instead of the university graduation, which has several thousand.

I'd been uneasy about the prospect of attending. I'd planned on foregoing walking during my graduation ceremony altogether, not wanting to run into Lincoln. But my friends reminded me of all the obstacles I'd faced in getting to this point. I needed to do this.

That still didn't stop me from nearly turning around and leaving a dozen times as the graduation coordinator had lined us up, unsure whether I could enter the auditorium and face Lincoln. Thankfully, he wasn't among the rows of faculty members on stage.

With the ceremony over, I make my way through the lobby packed with people in the post-graduation celebration, searching for my friends and mother, which proves difficult due to my height. My path obstructed, I place my hand on the shoulder of a tall man in a suit in order to get his attention so I can squeeze through. He turns around, the jovial expression instantly falling from his face when those familiar green eyes lock with mine, cold and distant.

Despite the boisterous voices filling the space, a strained silence, tense and uncertain, echoes in my ears. I've spent the past few weeks doing everything in my power to make peace with my past and move forward. But I can't do that until I finally close this chapter in my life. And that includes apologizing and coming clean with this man.

"Lincoln," I begin, my eyes soft.

He shoots up a hand, cutting me off. His jaw tenses, lip curling. "It's Professor Moore," he states sternly.

"Please, I just wanted to—"

He leans toward me, his harsh voice no more than a whisper. "No. You graduated. You got what you wanted. Now I never want to see you again." He pulls back, straightening his tie. "Best of luck on all your future endeavors, Miss Davenport. But I doubt you'll need it. You'll do whatever it takes to get what you want."

His biting words sting as they linger between us. Then he turns, the crowd seeming to part to allow him passage. I want to call out, tell him I love him, that I did what I did to protect him, but I don't. He wouldn't believe me anyway. Every action has consequences. And these are the consequences of my own actions. Ones I'll have to live with the rest of my life.

Swallowing hard through the lump in my throat, I plaster a smile onto my face, continuing through the lobby, relieved when I see all my friends waiting.

"You did it!" Evie says, hugging me enthusiastically, Nora also getting in on the action before pulling back to allow my mother to embrace me and offer her congratulations.

I gaze upon my friends with a bit of envy as they stand beside the men in their life — Evie with Julian, and Nora with Jeremy. They both look so happy. I try to remind myself I never would have had what they do.

"Come on." Izzy slings her arm over my shoulder. "Let's go celebrate. I hear Camille's been busy back at Julian's making her famous chocolate soufflé."

I peer in his direction. "Is that right?"

"Evie's a sucker for it. And whatever Evie wants, Evie gets."

"Don't I know it." I roll my eyes, following my friends out of the building.

Once we're out of earshot, Izzy leans into me, whispering. "You okay?"

"Never better." I flash a smile, but when she narrows her gaze, I know she can tell I'm not myself. I exhale a long breath. "I just ran into him."

"Oh, Chloe…"

"It's okay. I'm okay." I shrug it off, pretending to be happy so no one else can pick up on my unease.

"No, you're not."

I meet her eyes. "I know. But I have to believe, in time, I will be."

———

After we've all stuffed ourselves with the delicious meal Julian's housekeeper, Camille, prepared, my mother clinks her fork against her glass, then stands from the table. At first, I was hesitant to agree to have any Champagne here, but she insisted she didn't want to ruin any more special moments in my life. I should be able to celebrate my college graduation with a glass of Champagne if I wanted. And to my surprise, she hasn't even looked twice at a glass, drinking club soda instead.

"It's not every day you can stand up in front of your daughter and all her wonderful friends to celebrate everything she did to overcome adversity and graduate college."

I smile, grateful there are no jokes about it taking me ten years, like there would be with my father. But my mom knows the truth now, knows I dropped out to try to keep a roof over her head, keep her from becoming a statistic.

"You are a remarkable young woman, Chloe. And I'm honored to be able to call you my daughter. You may think this isn't a big deal, that it's just a piece of paper, but it's so much more than that. You've proven you'll never give up on your dreams. That you'll fight for them and achieve them, regardless of how long it takes." She lifts her glass, everyone at the table following suit. "Congratulations."

Everyone repeats the word as we all clink glasses.

"On that note…," Nora begins excitedly. "Here…"

She withdraws a t-shirt-sized box from a hiding place under the table and shoves it toward me.

"Guys, I told you no presents."

"You should know by now that we are *horrible* at actually listening to you."

I tilt my head, pinching my lips together.

"Just open it, Chloe," Jeremy says, placing his arm around Nora's shoulders, his broad muscles dwarfing her slender frame. "You know how persistent Nora can be. You won't win with her."

Playfully sighing, I grab the box and tear the wrapping from it. When I open the lid, I'm not sure what I'm looking at. It's a couple pieces of paper. One containing an airline itinerary, the other with information on the hotel in Hawaii where we're all staying for Nora's upcoming wedding. My name is on both reservations, but the dates aren't what I'd originally booked.

"What is this?" I glance around the table, confused.

"I hope you don't mind," Evie begins, grabbing Julian's hand. "But we took a vote, and the consensus is that you need a vacation."

"I'm taking a vacation. For Nora's wedding."

Nora rolls her eyes. "You're flying in Friday and leaving Sunday. The wedding's Saturday. Doesn't give you much of a vacation."

I lower my eyes, not wanting to tell her it's all I can afford.

"So we took it upon ourselves to change your flight and your hotel," Evie explains. "All paid for. And don't worry. The entire staff at the magazine donated some of their paid leave so you won't have to use any of your accumulated time. You even have some extra days now, too. You leave Saturday."

"Saturday?" My eyes widen. "As in seven days from now?"

"Well, since it's Sunday, technically six," Nora interjects. "But who's counting?"

"You," Izzy quips. "If I'm not mistaken, you've been counting down to this wedding since you set the date over a year ago."

"What can I say?" She shrugs, tilting her head to meet Jeremy's dark eyes. "I'm so excited to have one penis for the rest of my life."

I watch as she kisses him. Normally, I would have joked and told them to get a room, but there's something about their love that's so sweet, so pure, so hopeful. It makes me optimistic that I'll find love again.

When Nora reluctantly tears her lips from Jeremy's, she looks at me. "It'll be great. We're flying there Friday. Izzy's flying in on Sunday, right?"

I look to Izzy, who nods.

"And Evie and Julian are arriving on Sunday, too. You were the only one who was flying in, doing the wedding, then leaving the next day. I want some time with my friend."

"You deserve this, sweetie," Mom says. "You've worked your tail off taking care of yourself and me for far too long. Enjoy it."

"I don't know what to say." I shake my head, knowing how much something like this must have cost. The rooms at the hotel alone are close to $400 a night. To pay for me to stay there eight nights? I tell myself it's too much, that I don't deserve it. But I'm trying to learn I deserve better than I've afforded myself.

"Just say you won't miss that plane, because the last thing I want to worry about is rebooking your damn flight. Again," Nora says.

"I'll be there." I reach across the table, grabbing both Nora's and Evie's hands in mine. Izzy covers one of mine and I look at all the incredible women who've supported me through everything, even if they haven't always agreed with some of my decisions. "Thank you."

The celebration continues for a while longer, all of us indulging in the ridiculously rich chocolate soufflé. I don't know how Julian stays in such great shape with Camille's cooking. Based on the way Evie can barely keep her hands off him, I surmise the workout she must give him in the bedroom helps in that department.

"You got a minute?" Evie asks as everyone lounges in the sitting area of Julian's penthouse condo, the breathtaking view of Central Park and Manhattan a stunning backdrop. It's still hard to picture Evie living here, to be in this life with Julian, a man she was just supposed to pretend to date for a summer. I guess we can't control who we fall in love with. The last few months have taught me that.

"Sure." I set my coffee on the marble table in front of me and get up from the couch, following her to a room she's revamped as her office.

A modern, white desk sits in the center, brightly colored chairs on either side of it. The walls are lined with framed photos of various important editions of *Blush*, including the first one that listed her as assistant editor. She's come a long way from being the sex and dating columnist we all read for a quick laugh. I suppose I have, too.

"What's up?" I ask as she walks to the desk and retrieves a large envelope.

She faces me, chewing on her lower lip. "Don't get mad."

I eye her skeptically. "When you start out like that, I have a feeling I might."

"I know. I just…" She blows out a breath. "I really think you need this." She hesitantly extends the envelope toward me.

I stare at her, unsure I want to know what's inside. But intrigue gets the better of me and I open it, pulling out what appears to be a proof of the July issue of *Time*. The cover has the signature red border, the image a single rocks glass filled a quarter of the way with an amber liquid.

"Wha—"

"Viv loved your piece. I mean *really* loved it."

"I know. She was going to make it the feature article in the July issue of *Blush*."

"And she was. Until she found out that *Time* was doing a feature on alcoholism in America. They're running stories from people who dealt with it themselves, as well as family members of alcoholics."

My pulse increases when I see a tab sticking out, marking

a page. I open to it, the air sucked from my lungs when I read the title and byline.

### The Biggest Lie
*By Chloe Davenport, Contributor*

I fling my eyes back to Evie, a dozen questions on the tip of my tongue.

"Viv thought your piece too important to run in *Blush*. So did the editor at *Time*."

I run my finger over my name, still feeling like this can't be real. I often imagined seeing my name in this magazine. I never thought it would happen. Thought all I'd ever do was write about the hottest celebrity gossip. But here it is… My story. In all its tragic, heart-wrenching beauty. Something that never would have been possible if Evie didn't believe in me.

Overwhelmed, I throw my arms around her, squeezing. "Thank you."

"You know I love you, Chloe. Cracks and all."

# Forty-Four

I zip up my suitcase, then check my bathroom and bedroom one last time to make sure I'm not forgetting anything. As long as I remember my bridesmaid dress and shoes, everything else is replaceable.

At first, I was uncertain about spending a week in Hawaii when I could be working, but getting out of Manhattan is exactly what I need. Hopefully it will help clear my mind. And maybe I'll even meet some hot islander to make me forget, even if for a little while.

My buzzer sounds and I check the time, seeing it's not yet 5:30 in the morning. The driver Evie and Julian sent must be early.

I drag my bags into the foyer, then open the door without looking through the peephole, stopping short when my eyes fall on the familiar man standing on my doorstep.

"Dad? What are you—"

He brings his hand from his back, revealing a copy of the edition of *Time* my piece will appear in. It's not supposed to drop until next week, but I'm sure someone in the industry saw my name and sent him a copy, probably to do damage control.

With a sigh, I step back. "Would you like to come in?" I

figure it's best for him to ream me out now instead of having this weigh on my mind during my vacation.

He doesn't say anything. Just nods and walks into my apartment. I follow him, finding it odd to see him here. I don't think he's ever actually been to my place. To be honest, I'm surprised he even knows where I live.

"Can we make this quick? I have a flight to catch." I cross my arms in front of my chest, not even asking why he thought it a good idea to come to my apartment so early on a Saturday. Based on the fact that he's dressed in a suit, his tie loosened, his eyes bloodshot, he's probably been at the office all night working. As always.

He parts his lips, but words don't come right away. I furrow my brow. I can't remember a time my father didn't have an opinion about something. When he held anything back. When he struggled to find the right words.

Then I notice tears forming in the corners of his eyes as he looks at me. I mean, *really* looks at me. Really sees me. There's not so much as a hint of disappointment in his gaze. Only sorrow. And regret.

"Is this true?" His low voice quivers, barely able to get his question out. It's a stark contrast to the man who always seemed so confident, who never cared much for people's feelings. At least not *my* feelings.

I nod slightly.

He slumps onto the couch, burying his head in his hands. I'm not sure what to make of this. Over the years, I've learned to remain guarded around this man, concerned he'd take advantage of any weakness. If I didn't know any better, I'd think this person were an imposter, his demeanor not resembling the man I thought to be my father.

He lifts his weary eyes to mine. He's always had a youthful appearance, and I've often heard some of the other students at the university refer to him as a "silver fox". But now, he looks to have aged immensely.

"You really did all these things just to keep the truth from me?"

I could sugarcoat it to protect his feelings, but he never did that with me. I'm trying to move on, trying to start over. I can't keep lying.

"You already had such a low opinion of me. I figured the truth wouldn't change that. It would probably only make it worse."

He hangs his head again, pinching the bridge of his nose. I don't move, simply observing him, trying to figure out the game he's playing. Then a sob cuts through the stillness of my minuscule apartment.

"God, Chloe..." He briefly looks to the ceiling. "What have I done?"

I remain silent, unsure how to answer that. Unsure I *can* answer that.

"I should have paid more attention to your mother. To you. I was so focused on fighting for a cause I believed in..." His eyes lock on mine. "When I should have been fighting for you. For your mother. For my family. How could I..." He draws in a deep breath. "How could I have been so blind?"

"We're all blind to things we're not equipped to deal with." I lower myself to the couch. I can't remember the last time I sat beside this man. I can't remember the last time we've talked without him belittling me.

"That sounds like something your mother would say." He laughs slightly, swiping at his tears before his expression turns serious. "I don't expect you to forgive me for this. I certainly wouldn't. I've been a horrible dad. When I was growing up, my father was always working, always pushed us to achieve more. Not that it's any excuse for how I treated you, but it's all I knew. And your poor mother…" He trails off as he looks into the distance.

"*I* was the one who begged to have a family with her, even though I knew how much she loved her career. Hell, we met at a rally in support of the Equal Rights Amendment. She was a firecracker back then, even though she was only a college freshman. I should have known she wouldn't be happy at home with kids. But I ignored her, too."

He grabs my hands in his, his grip firm. I peer at them, the feel of my father's skin against mine odd.

"I'm begging you to give me a chance to show you I can be a better person. To make up for…this." Dropping his hold on me, he lifts the magazine that's open to my article. His eyes skate over the words on the page… *My* words. "All of it. You never should have…" His voice catches and he swallows, squeezing his eyes shut. "You never should have had to go through this. To do these things."

Absorbing his heartfelt plea, I look away from him, drawing in a deep breath as I collect my thoughts. I never anticipated my father would show up on my doorstep, let alone apologize. If anything, I figured he'd chew me out for publicizing private matters, as ironic as that sounds for a lawyer who fights to ensure the public has access to important information.

I don't have to forgive him. Don't even have to give him a chance. But one of the things they talk about in the Al-Anon meetings I've made a point to attend is letting go and moving forward. Of accepting the things life has thrown at us and growing from those experiences.

When I look back at him, I respond the only way that makes sense. "I think I did."

His brows furrow. "Wha—"

"I think I did have to go through all of this." I wrap my

fingers around his hand, squeezing reassuringly. "My past has shaped me into the person I am today. For the first time in my life, I like this person. That may have been a different story a few weeks ago, but I'm learning how to accept things and learn from them. If I didn't go through everything I did, I would never have written this." I grab the magazine out of his hands, holding it up. "I may never have seen my name in *Time*. *Time*! That's just... I don't even have the words."

He smiles, then wraps his arm around me, pulling me against him. I thought it would feel awkward, but it doesn't. I inhale, the familiar spicy scent reminding me of my childhood. "I think you would have found your way there eventually, sweetie." He kisses the top of my head.

"Thanks... Dad."

We have a long way to go to bury the past, and some days will be harder than others, just like with my mother. But it's nice to know he finally realizes his approach to parenting has been anything but healthy.

"I just want you to promise me something," I say, pulling out of his embrace.

"Anything."

I pinch my lips together, pausing. "Stop working so much and get to know Midge. She's a really great kid."

A smile covers his mouth, his eyes sparkling. "I can do that."

"And if she doesn't want to ride a horse, or learn archery, or do fencing, or any of the other ridiculously snooty sports you signed me up for, listen to her. Kids should be able to kick a ball up and down a field instead of stab a sword into their opponent."

"You got it. No snooty sports."

"Good."

"Good." It's silent for a moment before he speaks again.

"I'm sorry for what I said to you the last time I saw you. The night—"

"It's okay. Like you said, it never would have worked. He would have always been my professor. He would have had to sacrifice too much to be with me."

He pulls me against him again, holding me like a father who really loves his daughter. Deep down, he probably always has, but just showed it in a...different way.

"If he's smart, he'll sacrifice it all. Just like I should have years ago."

# Forty-Five

I lean my forearms against the railing of my ocean-front room, inhaling the fragrant Hawaiian air, the crash of waves sounding from mere yards away. A breeze picks up, blowing my hair in front of my face, and I relax, exhaling a satisfied sigh.

This is exactly what I needed. Fresh air. Ocean waves. Stunning scenery. I can't remember the last time I've taken a day off to enjoy myself. Now I have ten days to myself, having been ordered by my boss not to pick up my phone or answer an email until I'm back in the office. I'm not sure what to do with all this free time.

A knock on the door interrupts my moment of serenity, and I tear my attention away from a few well-built surfers, their glistening bodies bobbing up and down as they wait to catch a wave. I retreat into my home, leaving the sliding glass doors open to allow the ocean air inside.

When I pull back the door to my room, I'm instantly assaulted by an excited Nora, who practically tackles me to the floor. "You're here! This is really happening, isn't it?"

I hug her back, laughing. When I first landed at the airport less than an hour ago, I wondered if this was a mistake, if I would have been better off staying in New York a little longer. The entire baggage claim area seemed to be filled with couples on their honeymoon, fingers intertwined, a sparkle in their eyes as they struggled to keep their hands off each other.

But seeing Nora, being here for her, spending time with her, is more important than any longing or heartache I feel at the thought of wishing Lincoln were here with me. As I'd reminded myself time and again these past few weeks, he never would have been able to be here with me. Never would have been able to hold my hand in baggage claim. Never would have been able to kiss me as we watched one of the most magnificent sunsets in existence.

This is for the best.

Pulling out of her embrace, I glance from her to Jeremy. They've only been here a day, yet he looks like he's been on the island for a while. He's already acclimated to the tropical attire, wearing a neutral Hawaiian shirt with khaki shorts. His skin is sun-kissed, his sandy hair a little lighter at the ends.

"It is," I answer. "Unless one of you gets cold feet within the next few days."

"Not a chance in hell." Nora wraps her arm around Jeremy's waist, pulling him against her. She meets his eyes. "You're stuck with me."

"Sounds good to me, babe." He kisses her nose. Such a simple gesture, but it has me sighing.

"We'll let you get all settled. We're off to meet with our wedding coordinator anyway, but I wanted to stop by and say hi."

"Do you want me to come and help?" I ask, feeling like I've been a shitty maid of honor lately. Thankfully, Evie picked up the slack, considering she worked as a wedding planning assistant prior to getting the job at the magazine.

"You take it easy this afternoon. Go relax on the beach. Check out the local…flavor." She waggles her brows.

"I already have." I gesture toward the balcony. "This is certainly a room with a view." I force a smile, since that's something pre-Lincoln Chloe would do.

"Good." She grins, but it doesn't reach her eyes. I know she wishes the past several months had a different outcome, too, despite the fact I kept her in the dark until it all fell apart. Then she pulls a piece of cardstock from her purse, handing it to me. "Now, here's our itinerary for the week."

I grimace. "Itinerary?"

"This island is full of fun activities. Sightseeing. Volcanos. Helicopter rides. Snorkeling. Paddle boarding. Surfing."

I scan the sheet of paper. "You left out the waterfall picnic lunch," I jest, reading her plan for Wednesday.

"I know it's not your idea of a fun vacation, but when are we all going to be in Hawaii together again? We should take advantage of it."

I exhale, the idea of having to be somewhere at a certain time making my skin crawl. But if this is what Nora wants, I won't rain on her parade.

"Fine. But only because I love you and want you to have the wedding of your dreams."

"Thank you." She beams, then her expression falls. "On that note…" She pulls her bottom lip between her teeth, nervously shifting her gaze from me to Jeremy, then back again. "We have a favor to ask."

"Okay…," I reply in a drawn-out voice.

"You see… Jeremy's best man has a…" She looks to him, searching for her words. "Reputation."

I shift my eyes up to Jeremy's, hoping for a better explanation.

"He tries to screw anything with a pulse." He smirks.

"Ah."

"And since all our guests are spending a lot of money to be here," Nora continues, "we were hoping you'd—"

"Make sure he keeps his dick in his pants," I finish.

"More or less. You have a low tolerance for bullshit."

I squint, vaguely recalling a conversation I'd overheard recently about Jeremy's supposed best man.

"I thought your best man was no longer able to make the wedding." I place a hand on my hip, studying them. Their expressions exhibit a hint of nervousness. Nora doesn't maintain eye contact, looking anywhere but at me, an overly enthusiastic smile on her face. "That his wife, who's pregnant with twins, was ordered on bed rest so he's staying with her."

Jeremy laughs, sheepishly running a hand through his hair. "That's true."

"I thought you said you were going to go without one."

"He was, but…" She trails off.

"But I changed my mind," Jeremy interjects. "Nora didn't like the idea of things being uneven."

"So you added a completely new best man? Why not ask one of your groomsmen?" My suspicions grow, fearing this is a set-up. Nora's been on my case about meeting someone, thinking it would help me move on. But I have no interest in what I can only imagine is some elaborate scheme to set me up with a guy she thinks is perfect for me. There's only been one perfect.

"His brothers are his groomsmen. He didn't want to pick one over another, so he asked a buddy from college."

I form my lips into a tight line, having trouble believing this story.

"Please, Chloe," Nora begs, clasping her hands in prayer. "It would mean the world to me if you'd just do this." She peers at me with those sad puppy-dog eyes I can never say no to.

"Fine," I huff. "I'll babysit." If nothing else, it will allow me a chance to figure out what game Nora and Jeremy are playing.

"Thank you so much." She wraps her arms around me, squeezing me before releasing her hold. "We have to go. Take it easy. Go soak up some sun. And enjoy the view." She passes me a devilish grin, then grabs Jeremy's hand and tugs him down the hallway. "We'll see you tonight."

"Wait. Tonight?" I call after them. "What's tonight?"

"It's on the itinerary."

I glance down at the paper in my hand. Dinner with Nora, Jeremy, and this mysterious best man.

Great.

# Forty-Six

I check my reflection one last time, smoothing a few strands of blonde hair behind my ear. I wasn't quite sure what to wear tonight. I hadn't exactly packed a dress that screamed emasculation. But since I'm in Hawaii, I figured I may as well attempt to fit in, deciding on a flowing floral sundress.

Content with my appearance, I run a bit more gloss over my lips, then head out, glancing at the blasted itinerary for the location of tonight's "dinner meeting", as Nora referred to it.

It takes me a minute to find my way around the large resort, but I eventually locate the waterfront restaurant. When I enter, I'm immersed in a laidback island vibe, the sound of a local trio entertaining the patrons with Hawaiian-style music filling the air. The entire perimeter of the restaurant is windows, apart from the areas where the sliding glass doors are open, allowing the gentle ocean breeze to fill the place.

I float my eyes around the dining room for any sign of Nora or Jeremy, not seeing them anywhere. Normally *I'm* the one who's late, not Nora.

I walk to the host stand and a woman, who's obviously a local, greets me warmly. She's dressed in a slim-fit floral dress that has an Asian influence, a lone flower pinned in her slick, black hair.

"Aloha, miss. Do you have a reservation?"

"Actually, I'm meeting a few people here. Nora Tremblay and Jeremy Boyd."

She looks at her computer screen. "Yes. I have their reservation right here. They haven't arrived yet, and we don't seat our parties until everyone is present." She gestures to the open-air bar and lounge to my right. "But if you'd like to have a drink while you wait, the view is beautiful."

"Thanks." I consider waiting in the foyer, knowing Nora won't be too long. But the view undoubtedly is stunning. So I head into the lounge, searching for an empty table, since the bar seems to be full.

"A table just opened up right next to the railing," a man wearing all black and carrying a tray of empty glasses instructs. "Grab it before someone else does." He winks, then continues past me.

Shifting my eyes in the direction he indicated, I see a small hightop table and walk toward it. Luckily, I'm able to reach it before anyone else and hoist myself into the chair. A gentle breeze comes off the ocean, and I smooth a few wayward locks behind my ear, listening to the trio play. The sky is an impressive mixture of orange, pink, and red, the hue unlike any I've seen. Couples walk hand-in-hand on the white sand, stealing a few kisses as dusk sets in. I can't help but sigh.

"Maybe one day," I say to myself.

"Here you go, miss," a voice cuts through. I tear my eyes to my right to see a petite woman wearing a crisp white shirt and black pants removing a martini from her tray, placing it in front of me.

I furrow my brow. "I haven't placed my order yet."

The similarities between this and that night in Vegas aren't lost on me. But Lincoln's not here. He's back in New York. Unless my father has him pulling an all-nighter because of some big deadline, he's probably sleeping in his bed.

I swallow past the lump in my throat at the thought that another woman may already be in that bed with him.

"Oh, I'm sorry," the server apologizes. "I'm all mixed up today. Let me go check the ticket, then I'll be back to take your order."

She hurries toward the bar, and I look back to the horizon. For a split second, there was a part of me that *did* think Lincoln was here. But he'd made it more than apparent when I attempted to talk to him at graduation that he wants absolutely nothing to do with me. I can't blame him. No one deserves to be treated the way I treated him.

"Um… Actually, miss…"

I turn to see the same server approaching with the same martini.

"This *is* for you. A gentleman saw you walk in and asked the bartender to send it your way."

"A gentleman?"

I look past her, searching the bar, holding out a twinge of hope that I'd see a familiar silhouette standing there when, in reality, it's probably just some overweight man wearing a gaudy floral shirt who's going through a midlife crisis.

Suddenly, her gaze widens and she backs away, leaving the martini.

"I took a guess at what kind of vodka you'd prefer," a deep rumble sounds.

Paralyzed, every muscle in my body stiffens, my pulse skyrocketing. I blink repeatedly, praying this isn't just a dream, a side effect of sitting by a couple of college students smoking pot during my afternoon on the beach.

"But something made me think you were a Belvedere girl." The heat of his breath closes in on my neck, sending a shiver down my spine. Then a finger runs the length of my arm. "Smooth. Layered. Sophisticated. And so fucking stubborn." He grasps my hand, stepping in front of me.

I stare into Lincoln's brilliant eyes and part my lips, struggling to say something, anything, but no words come. I don't know what to make of this, considering the animosity and pure hatred that covered his face the last time we saw each other. But it's no longer there. In its place is a look of unmatched devotion, complete admiration, and wanton desperation.

"I am so sorry." His voice is choked with emotion, everything about him exuding the same passion and intensity he has since the first time I felt his body against mine.

"Sorry? What are you—"

"That night I took you to dinner." His hands go to my face, gripping my cheeks. "Our first official-unofficial date. Do you remember what I promised you?"

I swallow hard. "That you'd always fight for me."

"No matter the battle. But I broke that promise."

"I didn't give you a choice. You just said it yourself." I laugh slightly. "I'm really stubborn. I'd already decided what I needed to do. No matter what you said, nothing would have made me change my mind. Not after…" I trail off.

"Not after your father saw us together and reminded you of everything I would lose if you didn't break it off with me."

I briefly close my eyes. "He told you."

"Yes, and so did you."

"Me?" I fling my gaze to his.

His lips curve up. "Your father left an early issue of *Time* on my desk this morning, along with a note that said if I didn't get on the first flight to Hawaii, I'm not as smart as he thought and he'd seriously reconsider his decision to hire me."

"Oh." I pull away, unsure how to react to Lincoln reading that article. I knew it was a possibility. I figured he wouldn't care anymore. That my words wouldn't matter. Judging by the anguish in his eyes, they still do.

He lifts his hand to my nape, not allowing me to escape him. "Every man in your life has disappointed you. It kills me that I'm one of them. So I'm here to make it up to you. To promise that I'll do my best to never disappoint you again. I can't promise I won't, but if you just give me a chance, I'll do everything in my power not to deliberately piss you off, like slurp my soup or leave my shoes in the middle of the floor so you trip on them. Hell, I'll even stop stealing your panties."

I playfully slap him. "Don't you dare. My panties will always belong to you."

A peaceful smile crosses his mouth as he closes the distance, his lips so close to mine. "And what about your heart?"

"That will always belong to you, too."

"I was hoping you'd say that." He goes to erase that last bit of space between us, but I put my hand on his chest, preventing him from doing so. He pulls back, an eyebrow raised in question.

"That still doesn't mean this will work. Just because we want to be together doesn't mean we should. It still doesn't fix the fact that I was your student. That you lied for me.

Intentionally kept our relationship a secret so no one would find out you violated the code of conduct. Not even the strongest love will fix this. I'm not sure I'm—"

"You're not sure you're worth it?" His tone is full of fire and zeal as he finishes my thought.

I simply shrug. I've done quite a bit of soul-searching these past few weeks. Have come to terms with my past and know I'm worthy of love. I just don't know if I'm worthy of Lincoln's love. Not with what's at stake.

He shakes his head, looking around, his expression wracked with indecision, as if frantically trying to come up with something...*anything* to make me reconsider. Then a devilish smile tilts his mouth and he leans toward me, kissing my temple.

"Wait right here."

Dropping his hold, he rushes from me, leaving me confused and a bit intrigued, which quickly changes to utterly horrified when he walks up to the stage where the small band has been serenading us. During a break in the music, he talks to the singer, who happily welcomes him up on stage, offering him the microphone.

I meet his eyes, vehemently shaking my head, a heat spreading from behind my ears to my face and chest.

"Aloha, friends." Lincoln's voice comes over the speakers, to which the audience replies with a polite "aloha". "I won't be long, because I'm sure you'd much rather listen to this beautiful island music than me. My name is Lincoln Moore. As you can tell, I'm not from around here." He gestures at his suit, looking incredibly out of place, especially when surrounded by people in casual island attire. Several patrons chuckle, nodding in agreement. "I work as an associate attorney at a little newspaper called *The New York Times*."

My pulse steadily increases as I stare at him, wondering

what he's doing, other than making a complete ass out of himself in front of the crowd, and eventually the entire world once someone decides to upload this to YouTube.

He loosens his tie, sweat forming on his brow, the combination of the June humidity and the lights on the stage beaming down on him. When he shrugs out of his jacket and rolls up the sleeves of his crisp shirt, a few women whistle.

"Thank you very much," he says in his best Elvis impersonation.

I laugh as I'm treated to this side of Lincoln, one I haven't seen in too long now.

"You see, almost five months ago, I met my boss' daughter, although I didn't realize it at the time. And I made the colossal mistake of falling in love with her."

A few *ooh's* sound from the crowd. I have no idea what game Lincoln's playing here, what he hopes to get out of telling our story, but I can't take my eyes off him. Either can anyone else.

"That's not even the worst of it. You see, in addition to being an attorney for the *Times*, I teach First Amendment Law in the journalism program of a local university. And my boss' daughter?"

Gasps echo from the crowd, and he points to the group of women who appear to be celebrating a bachelorette party.

"They guessed it. She walked into my class that first day as a student. Now, I know what you're thinking. How did I not know that not only was she my boss' daughter, but also set to be a student of mine when the semester began?" A devilish glint flashes in his eyes. "Suffice it to say, the early days in our relationship weren't exactly filled with philosophical questions about the meaning of life."

The entire audience erupts in cheers and whistles. It takes a lot to make me blush, but as his gaze catches mine and he winks, causing nearly everyone to turn in my direction, my cheeks heat even more. But it's one of the most fulfilling and satisfying feelings I've ever experienced.

"That's her, ladies and gentlemen." He jumps off the stage, heading toward me. "The woman I am madly in love with. I'd have to be if I'm telling a group of complete strangers about the fact that I've been sleeping with one of my students, which is a very big no-no. The truth is, I loved her before she was one of my students." His voice becomes sincere as he approaches, his eyes trained on mine. He smiles a small smile before addressing the crowd once more.

"But the problem is, she doesn't think this will ever work. In some respects, she's absolutely right. Our love was doomed from the beginning. Like Heathcliff and Catherine. Romeo and Juliet, except for the suicide part."

"Jack and Rose!" an enthusiastic young woman adds.

Lincoln turns around, finding her in the crowd. "We all know there was room on that plank, so that wasn't a doomed relationship. It was murder. Or, at the very least, negligent homicide."

The crowd's roar of laughter echoes against the still night air. When Lincoln turns back to me, his voice grows sincere. "Like Orpheus and Eurydice."

A small breath escapes my mouth.

"Do you remember what Orpheus' problem was?" he asks softly.

I nod, pulling my bottom lip between my teeth to stop my chin from quivering. "He looked back," I barely manage to say.

"He looked back," he repeats. "Something I refuse to do. Not where you're concerned. I only want to look forward. Nothing that happened before this moment matters."

"But—"

"But what? You still don't believe you're worth the risk?" He steps back, spreading an arm and turning in a slow circle. "What do you think I'm trying to prove to you? That you *are* worth the risk. Do you think I care about my job as much as I care about you?"

I wish I could give him the answer he wants to hear, but it's not that easy. Despite this incredible gesture — getting on a plane, flying halfway around the world, making a scene in front of all these people — it's hard for me to trust blindly, to put all my faith in someone's words. Nearly thirty years of experience has taught me otherwise.

He brings a hand to my face, and I melt into his touch. "What do you need me to do to prove it to you? That you're all that matters. That no matter what happens, my life will be full as long as you're by my side." He swipes a tear from my cheek. "I know what life's like without you. And I mean *really* know what it's like. I can survive without my job, without my apartment. Hell, I'd even give up my season tickets to the Mets."

"You can't do that," I sniffle. "You'd probably have to pay someone to take them off your hands instead of the other way around. It's a terrible business decision."

The crowd breaks out in laughter, and I join them, my emotions a wild pendulum. One minute I'm crying. The next I'm laughing through my tears.

"See, Chloe? We're still good together. We still make sense. That hasn't changed. What do I have to do to prove that you deserve that fairy tale? I've already declared my love in a way that would put any cheesy romantic comedy to shame. What more can I do?"

At that instant, the band begins playing the opening chords of "Hawaiian Wedding Song", apparently thinking this moment required background music.

"Please, Chloe," Lincoln murmurs over the opening verse of the classic Elvis song. "If I have to sing to get you to be mine, I will."

My eyes widen, horror crossing my expression. "You wouldn't."

"For you, I certainly would."

Before I can stop him, he takes over the vocals, his hand wrapping around mine. The crowd erupts in applause and cheers that would probably rival if the real Elvis had come back from the dead and were here singing to me. I'm surprised he even knows the lyrics to this song. It's not exactly one you hear on a daily basis, unless you watch *Blue Hawaii* on repeat.

I cover my mouth with my free hand, laughing, crying, then laughing again. This isn't the kind of thing that happens in the real world, is it? At least not in *my* world. I was never the type of girl who necessitated a call from a guy the next day. And here is this amazing, incredible, sophisticated man, singing horribly out of tune in front of dozens of people, passersby on the beach stopping to listen and watch the scene with interest.

"Just kiss him already!" a woman shouts over the melody.

"If you don't, I will," another voice calls out. I shift my eyes, shaking my head at the man toasting me with his mai tai.

Lincoln gives me a questioning look, but when I don't do anything, he only sings louder. While Lincoln Moore has many talents, singing certainly is not one of them. But that doesn't stop him.

As I listen to him sing the lyrics, begging me to promise to be his forever, my heart is on the brink of bursting. All I've ever wanted was to feel like I had value, had worth.

Maybe I do deserve the over-the-top romantic comedy ending.

Jumping off my barstool as he fumbles through the Hawaiian words, I clutch his cheeks, bringing his face toward mine. "Oh, just shut up and kiss me."

His lips kicking up in the corners, he allows the microphone to fall to the table. "With pleasure."

He yanks my body hard and firm against his as his mouth slams against mine. Thunderous applause erupts around us, but that only makes him kiss me deeper. He curves into me, dipping me slightly, his hand running along the contours of my frame as our bodies mold together. His tongue swipes against mine, exploring my mouth like it's the first time. And that's what this is. Our new beginning, one we both deserve.

When he slowly pulls back, I'm met with his breathtaking smile. "Did you kiss me just so I'd stop singing? Or because you want to give us another chance?"

Running my fingers through his hair, I relish in the sensation of his coarse locks, something I've craved so much over these past few weeks. "I never had a chance with you."

"And I never had a chance with you." He brings his lips back to mine.

"And I did want you to stop singing," I add with a smile. "I think I heard a few dogs howl on the other side of the island."

His deep chuckle echoes in the air, filling me with warmth. Before I know what's happening, his arms snake around me and he lifts me into a cradle hold.

"Lincoln!" I playfully swat at him as he makes his way through the lounge, people clapping and cheering as the band transitions into a Hawaiian version of "Over the Rainbow". "Put me down! I'm meeting Nora, Jeremy, and—"

"A best man who can't keep his dick in his pants?" He arches a single brow.

I gasp, putting the pieces together. "That was *you*?"

"What can I say?" He stops walking as his feet hit the sand of the beach, and he slowly lowers me, yet keeps a firm hold on me. "I figured if I was going to give you the cheesy happily ever after you claim you don't deserve, I needed backup. I was worried you wouldn't hear me out if I just showed up, especially with the way I treated you the last time I saw you."

"So you had my friend lie to me?" I give him a playful look of disapproval.

"It was Izzy's idea. Anyway, I'd like to consider it more like an alternate version of the truth." He circles his hips. "I do have trouble keeping my dick in my pants. At least when *you're* around."

I lift myself onto my toes, feathering my lips against his. "You lawyers. Always getting off on a technicality," I murmur.

"I haven't heard you complain." With a wink, he pulls back. "Now, let's go. I have plans for you." He grips my hand and tugs me along the beach.

"And what plans are those?"

A mischievous smile builds on his mouth as his eyes darken. "To finish what we started a few weeks ago before you stood me up. Don't think you can get off that easily."

I come to a stop, forcing him to face me. Then I hook my arms around his neck and touch my lips to his. "With you, it's all easy."

He breathes into the kiss, then meets my eyes. "I love you, Chloe Davenport."

"And I love you, Lincoln Moore."

"Say it again."

My lips curve as peace washes over me. "I love you."

"God, it's even better than I imagined it would be."

Then he kisses me…fully, completely, madly.

The best kiss in the history of kisses. Because finally, after everything, I know I'm worth this man's love. And there's no better feeling in the world.

# Forty-Seven

"It's strange, isn't it?" Izzy asks, scanning my apartment, the last of my items officially boxed up. This place has been home for years now, has served as a meeting spot for our little circle of friends. It'll be a bit of a readjustment to not come home to this every day, but I now have a new place to call home.

"We've had some great memories in this shithole," I agree.

Izzy laughs, squeezing my arm. "We sure have. But now you'll make new memories. Happier memories. In an even better shithole, although I'm not so sure I'd consider Lincoln's apartment a shithole. I've seen that place. It's incredible."

I beam, considering the road ahead. For the longest time, I never thought much about the future. Now I look forward to every day I spend with Lincoln. So much so that when the lease on my apartment was up for renewal, I didn't hesitate when he suggested I move in with him, considering I spend every night at his place anyway.

"Well..." Izzy pulls away, her voice brightening. "I should get going."

"Do you want to order Chinese and eat on the floor like we did when I first moved in? One last memory?"

"I wish I could, but I have plans."

"Plans?" I tilt my head. "What kind of plans? You never have plans that don't involve us or work."

"I do have a life, Chloe," she retorts, avoiding my eyes.

"No, you don't. You've admitted you don't on a regular basis." I narrow my eyes, leaning into her. "Do you have a date?"

"Most certainly not," she answers quickly. Too quickly, which only serves to increase my suspicions.

"Who's the lucky guy?" I waggle my brows. "How did you meet? Is he a doctor at the hospital? Better yet, a patient whose life you saved who wants to…repay the favor? Or is it one of the guys I saw flirting with you at Evie and Julian's wedding?"

"Chloe!" She playfully punches me. "None of the above. First of all, I don't hook up at weddings. Second, most of the doctors I work with are married. Third, and most disturbing, I work in *pediatric* oncology. All my patients are minors."

"Then you'd better tell me who you're going out with or I'll keep making up ridiculous scenarios. You can't drop a bomb like that and expect me to leave it alone." I place my hand on my hip, tapping my foot in mock irritation. "You know how I can be. Soon, Evie will call you to ask why you've been dating a crowned prince and never told her."

She stares at me, then huffs out a breath. "Fine." Her expression turns severe as she shoves a finger in my face. "But you cannot mention this to anyone. I swear to god. Not one…fucking…soul. Not even Nora or Evie."

"Fine. You got it." I pretend to zip my lips and throw away the key. "Sealed tighter than Fort Knox."

She assesses me for a moment, then nods. "Okay." She

draws in a deep breath. "Jessie York is in town and asked to see me." She cringes, stealing a glance at me to gauge my reaction.

"And you told him to go fuck himself, correct?" I place my hands on my hips, annoyed.

"Chloe…" Her tone is a cross between a warning and a plea.

"So… What? He calls and you drop everything? Need I remind you that the prick cheated on you? While you were engaged, no less."

"Thanks for the reminder, but I was there, remember? And I'm not dropping everything for him. He said he needed to speak to me."

I lower my voice. "Do you think he found out about Asher?"

Biting her lower lip, she slowly shakes her head. "I don't know how. I didn't tell him, and I doubt Asher would have said anything. Not to mention, with the way his music's been taking off, he probably doesn't have time to think about that night. Not with all the groupies hanging all over him." She averts her eyes, crossing her arms in front of her chest.

When I learned Lincoln was my professor and we could no longer be together, I struggled with the constant reminders of what I could never have. I can't imagine how it must be for Izzy to have a front row seat to Asher's rise to fame over these past few months. Once it was announced he was the musical genius behind Fallen Grace's new album, he was bombarded with offers. Within months, he'd signed with a label, released a solo album of his own, and is now opening for one of the top rock bands. It's only a matter of time until he's headlining and selling out stadiums, too.

But despite the longing I spy in her eyes whenever Asher's voice comes on the radio, Izzy insists it doesn't bother her, that nothing could ever come of their one night together. Not when he's her ex-fiancé's older brother.

"Izzy," I begin, about to voice my concerns.

"He said it was important."

"And you believe him?"

"It sounds crazy, but yeah." She shrugs. "I do. There was something in his voice that made me think he wouldn't reach out to me after all this time unless it were."

"I don't like this. I don't like *him*."

"I know you don't." She runs her hands up and down my arms, reassuring me. "He could be full of shit, but if I don't find out what's going on, I'll never be able to forgive myself. Especially if it has something to do with his family."

As much as I don't like the idea of her seeing that prick again, I know how she is. Izzy is one of the kindest, most sympathetic people I've ever met. And she *was* close to Jessie's entire family, until he broke her heart. Not only did she lose him, she also lost his family.

"Want me to be your out? What time are you meeting him? I can call you after fifteen minutes to give you an excuse to leave."

She smiles at the memory of our old ways whenever either one of us had a date. "Thanks, but I'll be okay." She wraps her arms around me, hugging me tightly. "I'm so happy for you, Chloe."

"Thanks, Iz."

"You bet." We hug each other a moment longer before she drops her hold on me, then walks out of my apartment.

Once I'm alone, I turn in a slow circle, taking one last look at the place I've called home for the past several years. These walls have seen a lot of laughter, tears, and everything in between. It's time I finally leave all that behind and start fresh.

"You ready?" Lincoln's deep voice cuts through, and I spin around to see him standing in the foyer.

"Are *you* ready?"

"You've been practically living at my place these past six months anyway." He smirks as he approaches.

"True. But now *all* my shoes will be at your place. You'll—"

He covers my mouth with his, interrupting me with a kiss. "*Our* place, Pixie." He holds my face in his hands, his eyes intense. "It's *our* place."

"I like the sound of that."

"Me, too."

I whisper my lips against his. "So why don't you take me back to *our* place so we can christen it. Then we can spend all weekend snuggled in bed and watch the snow fall." I pull back. "Unless you have work to do."

He slowly shakes his head. "I'm taking the weekend off. In fact, I'm taking the entire week off."

"You *are*?" I cock a brow, unable to mask my surprise.

Ever since my father retired back in September and tapped Lincoln to take his place as chief general counsel, Lincoln's been working his tail off. It doesn't bother me, since he still makes a point to spend time together. My new position as the current affairs editor at *Blush* has had me working a lot, too. At least now I no longer feel like I have to work myself to the bone to get the inside scoop on celebrity gossip before anyone else. And I get to write stories with substance.

"Yup. I didn't bring home a single file. And I spoke with Evie. She says you can take the week off, too." A devilish glint flashes in his eyes.

"We can have a lot of fun with that much time to ourselves," I say, recalling our time together in Hawaii.

"We sure can," he murmurs, his lips inching even closer.

"So why don't we go so we can get started."

"Always so eager, Miss Davenport," he croons in a sly voice.

"Always, Professor Moore. So take me back to your...*our* place."

"I'd love to." He abruptly pulls back. "But I have a better idea."

I grin deviously, knowing all too well where this is heading. At least once a month, Lincoln has sent a box of panties to the office, along with a card dictating a place and time for me to meet him, usually a swanky hotel bar. It doesn't matter that our relationship is now out in the open. We still go back to our roots, if for no other reason than to remember how far we've come.

"Role-play? What'll it be tonight? I can be a sweet Midwest girl who's never been to the big city, and you can be a mysterious stranger who will open her mind to her darkest desires."

"Tempting, but why don't we try something...different."

"Different? What did you have in mind? Something kinkier? I can do that. I love the kink."

"I know you do. But I was thinking of maybe getting away with you instead." He licks his lips, a nervous twitch in his eye.

"Getting away?"

He smiles, pulling my body against his. "Yeah. Vegas. After all, in just a few days, we'll be celebrating the one-year anniversary of that blackout. I thought maybe we can recreate our own little blackout."

When his lips meet mine, I moan, the idea of getting out of Manhattan and into a warmer climate exactly what I need, even if it is to Vegas, a city I once despised. But now, I don't mind it as much. In fact, I actually like the notion of revisiting the proverbial scene of the crime with Lincoln.

"And since I stole something of yours last time I was there, maybe I can convince you to come home with something of mine. A souvenir of sorts."

"A souvenir? What kind of souvenir? If it's panties, you're only going to steal them anyway."

"No, not panties." He leans in for another kiss. "I want to give you my last name."

My breath hitching, I stiffen, pressing my hand against his chest. "What did you say?"

A look of serenity washes over him. "I want to give you my last name, Chloe. I want to spend the rest of my life with you." He reaches toward my ear and, with a magician's flourish, reveals a stunning round-cut solitaire, the band inlaid with diamonds. "I want to marry you."

"How did you do that?" I breathe.

His lips curve playfully. "A magician never reveals his secrets." He winks, then his expression turns serious, his green eyes peaceful and steady. "So, what do you say? Will you marry me? Let me show you how incredible you are every day for the rest of your life?"

"In Vegas?"

"If you'd rather something else, we can do that," he says quickly. "Whatever you want, it's yours. If you want a huge, elaborate wedding in the Hamptons, like Evie and Julian, we can. If you want to get married on a white sand beach in Hawaii, like Nora and Jeremy, I'll give you that, too." He gets down on one knee, taking my hand in his and bringing the ring up to my finger. "You deserve the fairy tale. So if your fairy tale ends in walking up the aisle while wearing a train that would rival any royal wedding, that's what you shall have."

I stare at him, words escaping me as I wrap my head around the fact that this man is kneeling before me, begging me marry him. I was never one of those girls who envisioned her own wedding, not like Evie, Nora, and even Izzy, although she'll never admit it. Until I met Lincoln, I didn't think I *wanted* to get married. Didn't think I *deserved* to find love. But he's taught me I do deserve that happily ever after.

In one swift move, I drop to my knees. He stares at me, worry evident in his gaze. Then I smile. "*You're* my fairy tale. And I can't think of a better place to start my life with you."

He exhales, his muscles relaxing as he slides the ring into place. The perfect fit.

"I know Vegas is a bit…unconventional, but—"

I curve into him, pressing my lips to his. The first kiss of the rest of our lives.

"It may be unconventional, but when have we ever played by the rules… *Professor?*"

Thank you for reading WICKED GAMES! I hope you enjoyed Chloe and Lincoln's story. Wondering what happened between Izzy and Asher during the blackout in Vegas? Find out today! Scan the code to the right or  enter the below web address into your browser to grab your copy!

https://www.tkleighauthor.com/t-k-s-books/mind-games

I appreciate your help in spreading the word about my books. Please leave a review on your favorite book site.

# Mind Games

**Eight years ago, I agreed to marry the man of my dreams.**
**Eight years ago, I realized I'd also given a piece of my heart to his brother.**
**Eight years ago, I made the decision to walk away from both men.**

What choice did I have?
I couldn't stay with Jessie knowing the flame I carried for Asher burned just as bright.

Maybe even brighter.

So I did the only thing I could. I walked away with no intention of seeing either man again.

Until I step into a bar in Vegas and see a much more mature, much sexier version of Asher York, a guitar strapped to him, his soulful voice reminding me of everything I've tried to forget.

But there's no forgetting Asher York. And when he looks at

me with the same raw hunger, there's no denying the fire between us still burns.

Can I look past the reason I left all those years ago for one night with him?

There's only one way to find out.

**Let the games begin.**

# Playlist

*Wicked Love* - Sara Bareilles
*Hit and Run* - LOLO
*No Roots* - Alice Merton
*In My Head* - Maisie Peters
*Power Over Me* - Dermot Kennedy
*Anxiety* - Julia Michaels
*Natural* - Maygen Lacey
*Light as the Breeze* - Billy Joel
*Let You Love Me* - Rita Ora
*Be Scared with Me* - Canyon City
*If This is Love* - Ruth B.
*Devils Don't Fly* - Natalia Kills
*All This Love* - JP Cooper
*Symphony* - Thomas Daniel
*You & Me* - James TW
*Terrible Love* - Birdy
*Don't Wanna Think* - Julia Michaels
*Birthday* - Maisie Peters
*Bitter Pill* - Gavin James

*Let it all Go* - Birdy
*Rush* - Lewis Capaldi feat. Jessie Reyez
*Move Together* - James Bay
*Orpheus* - Sara Bareilles
*Human* - Christina Perri
*Marina del Rey* - Lola Rhodes
*Heaven* - Julia Michaels
*Bad guy* - Billie Eilish
*Ain't Gonna Lose You* - Brett Dennen
*Speechless* - Dan + Shay
*More Like Love* - Ben Rector
*The Greatest Bastard* - Damien Rice
*Break My Heart Right* - James Bay
*Our Story* - Graham Colton
*You and I* - Jon McLaughlin
*Hawaiian Wedding Song* - Elvis Presley
*Connection* - OneRepublic
*Passport Home* - JP Cooper

# Acknowledgments

Book twenty. Wow. I probably say the same thing every time I sit down to write these acknowledgments, but I'm still blown away to think that I'm still doing this, that I'm still writing stories for you all to enjoy. I never thought it would turn into this, but I'm so glad it has.

I couldn't do any of this without the support of my number one fan, my husband, Stan. He's supported me from the very beginning, not even batting an eye when I told him I'd written a book. And I'm so grateful to have him by my side.

And of course, a big thank you to Harper Leigh, for always being a source of inspiration. (And to Karissa and Bree, my two nannies who help watch Harper so I can find the time to write.)

There's only one woman I trust with my babies, and that's Kim Young. Thank you for your advice and expertise (and flexibility when I keep moving my release dates around.) I couldn't do this without you.

Another huge thanks to my PA, Melissa Crump. You

came in when I was at my breaking point, so thanks for stepping in and doing this job with little direction. It took me years to finally break down and hire a PA, and I'm so glad you're here to pick up the slack... And there's a lot of slack on my end.

On that same note, thanks to my admins who help me maintain my reader group and author page — Vicky, Lin, Lea and Joelle. Thanks for taking the time to help out whenever you can.

A huge thanks to my beta readers for reading this and giving me your opinion, even when I constantly change my mind about how many books this will be. (Yay for getting it down to just one book! Even if it is a loooooong book). Stacy, Melissa, Vicky, Lin, and Sylvia - thanks for everything.

Another big thanks to Emily and the team at Social Butterfly PR for handling this release (and adjusting when I changed my release plan a month beforehand. Never a dull moment with me as a client!)

Thank you to my wonderful reader group on Facebook. I absolutely love having a special place where I can hang out and interact with all my amazing readers, even if it is just drooling over some eye candy.

And last but not least, thank you to YOU! Thanks for picking up this book and taking a chance on me. Whether this is your first T.K. Leigh book or your twentieth, I'm grateful you made it this far. I hope you enjoyed the ride. Just wait... Izzy and Asher are up next.

Here's to another twenty books!

Peace and love,
  ~ T.K.

# About the Author

T.K. Leigh is a *USA Today* Bestselling author of romance ranging from fun and flirty to sexy and suspenseful.

Originally from New England, she now resides just outside of Raleigh with her husband, beautiful daughter, rescued special needs dog, and three cats. When she's not writing, she can be found training for her next marathon or chasing her daughter around the house.

f   facebook.com/tkleighauthor

○   instagram.com/tkleigh

♪   tiktok.com/@tkleigh

BB  bookbub.com/authors/t-k-leigh

℗   pinterest.com/tkleighauthor